PRIMEVAL WATERS

A NOVEL BY WILLIAM BURKE

Claudia,

Congratulations on
winning! Watch out for
The piranhas, sharks
and snakes!

William Burke

SEVERED PRESS
HOBART TASMANIA

PRIMEVAL WATERS

Copyright © 2021 by William Burke
Copyright © 2021 by Severed Press

WWW.SEVEREDPRESS.COM

ISBN: 978-1-922551-99-3

CRITICAL PRAISE FOR WILLIAM BURKE'S

SCORPIUS REX

"If you want an exciting adventure, giant monsters, lots of shooting, and non-stop action, this is the book for you! Highly recommended!" — *THE COLUMBIA REVIEW OF BOOKS AND FILM*

"A non-stop roller coaster ride… As over the top and satisfying as a widescreen Hollywood blockbuster. A thoroughly terrifying, creepy, and spellbinding techno-thriller." — *THE PRAIRIES BOOK REVIEW*

"Great character development with a fast and heart pounding plot. This is a wonderful horror, action/adventure military-esque novel." — *THE INDIE EXPRESS*

"Lots of blood, guts and close saves. Reads like a Syfy action movie put to page, and that's a very good thing."— *SCI-FI & SCARY. COM*

"Burke writes economically, compellingly and well. More than enough thrills, chills and snickers for readers to enjoy. Recommended." – *THE US REVIEW OF BOOKS*

"This was an amazing read from the start! Dark and creepy in the best way. Military, horror, scorpions… what more do you need?" — *TEXAS BOOK NOOK*

"This book was an exciting, thrilling and captivating fast read… I loved every minute of it."
— *ON A READING BENDER.COM*

AVAILABLE FROM

SEVERED PRESS

Dedicated to Giorgio A. Tsoukalos, who's ideas helped inspire this novel.
Merriam-Webster's Dictionary offers two definitions of panache.
#1—Dash or flamboyance in style and action.
#2—An ornamental tuft, especially on a helmet.
Mr. Tsoukalos is blessed with both.

CHAPTER ONE

Mouth of the Amazon Tributary, *Rio Pandora*— Brazil

Dr. Ian Stewart trudged up a steep bank running alongside the newly completed earthen dam. The pain in his arthritic knees was a constant reminder that his days in Her Majesty's Royal Engineers were long behind him. Back then, he'd been a young officer, building pontoon bridges and disarming mines in the Falklands; now he was a fifty-eight-year-old academic, better suited to lecture halls than mosquito-infested jungles. But he'd retained much of his youthful knowledge, if not its vigor. Under his supervision, a crew of barely literate laborers had erected a thirty-five-yard dam from nothing but downed trees and mud. Even more impressively, he'd done it all in an unmapped rainforest, hundreds of miles from civilization.

Ian stopped to catch his breath, thinking, *Not bad work, for a prisoner*, before continuing the long climb. Passing groups of laborers offered their boss a respectful nod, while AK-47-toting sentries just eyed him suspiciously.

Ian thought, *The workers think I'm the boss, but the guards all know I'm just a prisoner.*

He reached the dam's crest and turned away from the workers, pretending to polish his glasses. In truth, he just didn't want to be seen struggling to catch his breath. The expedition's thirty-eight laborers were all river trash, who spent their off hours engaging in drunken knife fights; not the sort you wanted to show frailty around. After a few seconds, Ian felt his wind and dignity returning enough to supervise the next, critical phase.

The dam's crest offered him a panoramic view of the site. On its upstream side, the now dammed Rio Pandora tributary had swollen into a vast floodplain. The two-hundred-foot cargo barge *Opala* was moored there, its generators powering the work site.

On the dam's downstream side lay a circular lake, roughly two miles in diameter, surrounded by a thirty-foot earthen rim—a textbook example of a meteorite impact crater. The dam had reduced the lake's depth to barely seven feet, exposing the most important scientific discovery since Copernicus. A brilliant full moon shone on the partially submerged object resting in the lake's center—a sixty foot in diameter sphere Ian had christened "The Anomaly."

The Anomaly was, by definition, a meteorite. But in his decades of experience as a planetary geologist, Ian had never seen anything like it—nobody had. It had been buried beneath the lakebed for thousands, perhaps millions of years, until a recent earthquake forced it to the surface. The Anomaly's ancient descent through the earth's atmosphere had left large sections scorched black, but other areas gleamed in the moonlight like a gigantic jewel. That resemblance wasn't merely cosmetic; the Anomaly was, for lack of a better term, a gigantic diamond. Ian had analyzed shards of ejecta discovered around the lake and concluded that they all possessed the brilliance and clarity of the finest gemstones. Meteorites often contained flecks of diamond, created by heat and intense pressure, but this defied all logic.

Ian stared down at it, muttering the same question he'd pondered for weeks. "What the hell are you?"

A team of laborers had just finished constructing a sixty-foot-long log causeway connecting the shore and the Anomaly. Its completion marked the beginning of the next phase—drilling into the Anomaly and, hopefully, discovering its secrets.

Ian's thoughts were interrupted by a barrage of Portuguese profanities coming from the other side of the dam. He turned around to investigate, thinking, *Christ, not another knife fight.*

He traced the shouting to the dam's base, where eight bickering laborers were unloading the geotechnical drill rig from a motorboat. One of the men lost his grip on the rig, almost dropping it into the water.

Ian shouted, "Be careful," but couldn't be heard over the *Opala*'s generator. He fumbled for the bullhorn slung over his shoulder, his panic rising. The drill's tip was forged graphene, the hardest substance on Earth. It was the only tool, short of a laser, that could cut through diamond. Losing it would bring the entire operation to a screeching halt.

Ian was about to shout into the bullhorn when his foreman, Ursa, slapped him on the back.

Ursa said, "Relax, *chefe*. You got to know how to talk to these *idiotas*." He bellowed a torrent of physical threats at the men below then turned back to Ian. "Don't worry; we'll have that drill up and running quick as hell, *chefe*." With a yellow-toothed grin he added, "Then maybe Mr. Batista will let you and your wife go home, safe and sound," while stretching his arms to ensure Ian saw the .357 strapped to his hip. He ambled down to the drill rig.

Watching him walk away, Ian muttered, "Bastard." Ursa's last comment had been a cutting reminder that Ian was indeed a prisoner, and Ursa was his jailer.

A month earlier, Ian had been invited to speak at a planetary geology symposium in Rio de Janeiro. But the invitation had been a ruse, engineered by a sociopathic mineral dealer named Hector Batista. He'd abducted Ian and his wife. Now Margaret was a hostage on his yacht, hundreds of miles away. Earning her freedom meant ensuring that Batista's expedition was a success. Thankfully, Ian was on the verge of achieving just that.

Under Ursa's abusive supervision the drill rig was mounted onto its tracked platform. It began rumbling up the incline on its six wheels. With its hydraulic drilling arm folded down the rig resembled a miniature Mars Rover. Its geotechnical drill would reveal just how thick the Anomaly's diamond layer was. If it was merely a shell, surrounding a ball of iron ore, it would still yield more quality diamonds than De Beers could mine in a year. Gem quality diamonds, cut from a one-of-a-kind meteorite, would become the ultimate status symbol, earning Batista billions.

Enough to buy Margaret's freedom, Ian hoped. The irony of the situation wasn't lost on him. *The greatest scientific discovery in history and Batista is forcing me to chip it into bits to sell off for jewelry. That's why he'd resorted to kidnapping—no legitimate scientist would willingly participate in this atrocity.*

Ursa's voice boomed through a bullhorn. "We're ready down here!"

Ian raised his binoculars, surprised to discover that the drilling crew was already in position, waiting for permission to begin.

Christ, how long have I been standing here brooding?

He switched on his bullhorn, and, after a second of feedback, shouted, "Commence drilling!"

The operator raised the hydraulic arm, pressing its drill tip against the Anomaly's diamond surface. The drill roared to life, clanging like a giant bell. Ian watched anxiously, reminding himself that the operator had been recruited from one of Batista's emerald mines. The man handled a drill like a surgeon wielded a scalpel.

Taking a few calming breaths, Ian gazed up at the stars, contemplating the Anomaly's mysterious origins and its myriad of contradictions. *How could a solid meteorite this size be pushed to the surface? And why is the crater lake so small? The impact of a solid object this size should have created a crater three times larger. But if the Anomaly is hollow that would indicate some intelligent—*

His concentration was shattered by a brilliant flash of lightning shooting across the starry sky. A second, equally intense bolt followed. Black clouds rolled across the night sky, blocking out the full moon.

A bolt of lightning shot down, striking the water near the *Opala.* Ian spun around, his hair tingling from the static electricity. Men scrambled across the *Opala*'s deck, checking the electrical connections.

Ian felt the dam rumbling beneath him and muttered, "Another aftershock?" But that made no sense. The earthquake had occurred weeks earlier, meaning any aftershocks should have long subsided. Yet the ground trembled again.

Turning back to the lake he watched the drill operator boring into the Anomaly, blue sparks of static electricity dancing around the drill tip. A blinding flash of light erupted from the Anomaly's surface. The drill and operator were momentarily engulfed in what appeared to be ball lightning. A second later, the electrical discharge vanished, and all that remained of the drill and its operator was a heap of smoldering ashes. The surviving drilling crew scrambled along the causeway toward shore.

Ian stared in amazement, asking himself, "Did the Anomaly just generate power?"

The earth rocked again, throwing Ian to the ground. He heard screams echoing from the floodplain side and turned around.

The *Opala* was rocking violently as if in a storm, yet the water around it was dead calm.

The work lights on the lakeside flickered then died, plunging the area into darkness.

Ian muttered, "Bloody hell," certain the power lines from the generator had been jarred loose.

He knelt atop the dam, trying to see in the darkness. Another bolt of lightning shot down, striking the water twenty yards from the boat. Then, in one horrifying moment, the two-hundred-foot *Opala* listed sharply to port. Screaming men spilled off the deck. A moment later, the boat capsized, crushing the men in the water.

Ian gaped in disbelief. Nothing had struck the boat, and the water had been perfectly calm. It was as if some giant hand had risen from beneath, tipping it over.

Lightning crackled across the sky, offering fleeting moments of illumination. Ian glimpsed a dark, serpentine shape rippling across the water. Then all went dark, until a series of lightning bolts flashed across the sky in succession, like a giant strobe light.

The shape raised its head from the water, a screaming man dangling from its mouth. The glistening nightmare was at least seventy feet long and thick as a redwood tree, its gray body dotted with brown saddle-shaped markings.

It was an impossibly huge snake.

The serpent spat out the man then slithered across the overturned boat's keel. Its flat, arrow-shaped head rose up, reflective green eyes fixing on new prey. The head snapped down like a piston, plucking another man from the water. Despite its enormous size the snake moved like greased lightning. Screaming men tried to swim away, only to be crushed beneath its weight or snapped up in its jaws.

Then there was darkness.

Ian crouched down, heart pounding, awaiting the next flash of lightning. It came.

Now the snake was slithering across the floodplain water, heading straight for the dam.

Then darkness again.

Ian realized the men on the lakeside had no idea what was coming. He fumbled with the bullhorn, desperate to warn them.

The next flash of lightning revealed something huge hurtling through the air, coming straight for Ian. Without thinking, he dove off the dam's edge, bouncing down the steep slope. He felt his shoulder crack and heard himself scream before splashing down into the lake. A twenty-foot motor boat crashed down into the water mere yards away.

The snake crested the dam, slithering down to the lakeside. Lightning reflected off its green eyes—they were locked on Ian.

Pockets of light suddenly appeared along the dark lakeshore. The laborers had lit up emergency flares and were holding them aloft.

The snake veered away from Ian, making a beeline for the flares. Despite its size, it shot through the water like a torpedo, covering the three hundred yards in the blink of an eye.

Ian heard the crack of Ursa's pistol, followed by volleys of rifle fire. The snake launched up from the water, its jaws latching on to a man clutching a flare. With a snap of its head, it tossed the man straight up. His burning flare spiraled across the horizon like a skyrocket. Terrified men tried to scramble up the crater lake's rim. The snake continued its onslaught, plucking five men off the incline. Others waded into the lake, only to be crushed by the snake's whipping tail.

Ian's first instinct was to dash into the rainforest to escape, but then he realized he couldn't. *If I leave here empty-handed, Margaret will die.* In the dim light he could barely make out his lakeside tent some thirty yards away. Inside it were the meteorite shards they'd gathered. They were evidence of what he'd discovered—enough to at least buy his wife a stay of execution.

Ian waded to shore then crept along the lake's edge, ignoring the distant screams. He prayed that the snake was too busy gorging itself to care about a lone man. After two minutes of stumbling through the darkness he reached the tent.

Yanking the flap aside he spotted the satchel of fragments resting on the camp table. With trembling hands, he slung it over his shoulder. One sample fell to the ground, so he scooped it up and stuffed it into his pocket.

He muttered, "Think, think, you have to survive out there," then grabbed a flashlight, bottled water, and a pair of emergency flares, stuffing them in the satchel. He turned to leave.

Something struck the tent like a cannonball, trapping him under a blanket of collapsed nylon. Ian clawed his way out and saw what had crushed the tent. Ursa was sprawled across the fabric. His body was twisted grotesquely, and one leg was severed at the knee, but he was alive. Ursa reached out, grabbing Ian's ankle, pleading with his eyes.

Ian pulled away.

Ursa screamed, "Don't leave me here, you bastard!"

Ian saw the snake slithering along the shoreline, heading straight for the tent. There was no way he could outrun it.

Ursa screamed again.

Ian whispered, "Quiet, you idiot."

Then an idea struck him. He lit one of the flares, tossed it on the ground next to Ursa and ran like hell.

Enraged, Ursa shouted, "Come back here, you son of a bitch!"

Drawn to the light and screaming, the giant serpent descended on Ursa.

Ian made an adrenaline-fueled charge up the earthen dam. In the distance he heard Ursa scream twice before being crushed in the serpent's jaws.

Reaching the crest, Ian glanced back at the lake. The snake was still on the rampage, snapping up men trying to hide in the brush. There was no hope for them. Ian slid down the other side, rocks and branches tearing at his legs until he splashed down into the floodplain. He surfaced, spitting out water while taking in the carnage around him. The *Opala* was on its side, half submerged, mangled bodies drifting around it.

The shoreline was littered with floating bodies. He spotted one forgotten motorboat moored to a post. He climbed aboard, reaching for the outboard motor, then stopped.

Too much noise. Better to gain some distance.

Using a floating log, he slowly paddled out until he passed the capsized

Opala. After two pulls on the cord the outboard roared to life, drowning out the echoing screams behind him.

Glancing at the motor he saw that the gas gauge read below half. The boat wouldn't get him far, but that didn't matter—somehow he'd reach civilization and save his wife, even if he had to crawl.

CHAPTER TWO

Bela Adormecida Mountains, *Amazonas*, Brazil - 15 days later

Dr. Micah Clark stood at the peak of the Sleeping Beauty Mountains, gazing down at the fog-shrouded rainforest and winding Amazon tributaries stretching farther than the eye could see. It was the kind of photographic backdrop money couldn't buy, which was good because he didn't have any.

His camera person, Catalina Abril, shouted, "Camera's ready, boss!"

Micah said, "Okay, give me a minute," and gave himself a final once over.

Close-cropped blonde hair mussed to just the right degree—check. Logo on his signature Rolex Explorer watch facing camera—check. He smoothed out his meticulously wrinkled tan linen shirt and made sure his cargo pants were impeccably dirty. Getting it all right was critical because every thread of clothing, from his Ray-Ban sunglasses right down to his perspiration-wicking socks, was some form of product placement. Thanks to a dwindling budget, his complimentary wardrobe wasn't just a C-list celebrity perk anymore—these days he just needed the free socks.

For two seasons, his reality adventure series *Meteor Micah* had been the Outdoor Exploration Network's top show. Its combination of exotic locales, survival skills, and scientific expertise combined with wild speculation about ancient aliens had made him into a real-life Indiana Jones. Network executives had christened him a modern day "Marlboro Man"—a ruggedly handsome intellectual who appealed to everyday viewers, especially ones who wore tin foil hats.

But all idols, especially the basic cable variety, eventually topple, and this season his ratings had plummeted like a meteorite. Looking out at the majestic view he pondered the eternal question, *Where did it all go wrong?*

After a thirty-second pity party, he asked Catalina, "Do I look okay?"

Catalina said, "Give me a second," and went back to gossiping with the local farmers who'd just sold him some meteorite fragments.

Micah took the delay in stride. Catalina usually seemed more interested in chatting up his vendors than doing her myriad of jobs. But since she was technically an intern, he couldn't complain. Last season, he'd traveled with a documentary cameraman, a sound recordist, and even a makeup artist. But now, thanks to declining ratings, his entire staff consisted of a single grad student acting as camera person, research assistant and general fixer. On the plus side, Catalina was competent with a camera, along with being fluent in Portuguese and Spanish—pretty much all you could ask for from an intern getting a two-hundred-dollar-a-week stipend, plus meals.

Micah used the time to study the meteorite sample he'd just paid twenty dollars for. His truncated shooting schedule didn't allow any time for actual exploration or discoveries, so now he just bought whatever local farmers plowed up in their fields. At least this sample was interesting. Noting the gleaming slivers embedded in it, he mentally rehearsed his spiel. *Notice the minute traces of diamond in this piece. Could this be a fragment of some intelligently engineered probe, utilizing diamonds, one of the universe's hardest substances, as a protective shell? Blah, blah, wild speculation, yada, yada.*

Catalina was politely shooing away the farmers, who seemed intent on hanging around. Micah couldn't blame them. His intern was a striking woman of what he guesstimated as mixed Brazilian and African heritage—hitting a genetic home run on both sides. She was tall, clearly athletic, but perhaps her most attractive feature was an unwavering confidence, landing just short of arrogance. In a man it might be called swagger. She was definitely the kind of woman he was drawn to, but making advances on an intern would be the final leap into becoming a full-on television sleaze.

Catalina had just gotten rid of the farmers when something caught her eye. She yelled, "Oh shit, Faye! Micah, get over here!"

Snapping out of his inner monologue, Micah rushed over. "What's wrong?"

His nine-year-old daughter, Faye, was perched on a camp stool. With her flowing blonde hair and sweet face she could have modeled for an American Girl doll, except those dolls didn't have a Goliath beetle the size of a grapefruit clamped to their forearm.

Catalina said, "Uh, honey, I don't think you should be playing with that."

Faye giggled and said, "Why? Goliaths don't bite," then went back to petting the insect like a puppy.

Catalina asked Micah, "So you're cool with this?"

"Uh, only sort of." Micah knelt down next to his daughter and explained, "Faye, you still have to be careful, 'cause those mandibles can crush a walnut."

Faye said, "I know, they're really strong," then held her arm up to Catalina, proudly displaying the beetle. "Did you know they can lift eight hundred times their own weight?"

Catalina said, "Pretty cool. Maybe I can get her to lug this equipment."

"This one's a boy, you can tell by its horns."

Micah smiled, amazed at his daughter's encyclopedic knowledge of Amazon wildlife. Thanks to a bitter divorce he only got to spend two months a year with her, and he liked to think she'd learned it all to impress him.

He came up with a diplomatic solution. "Tell you what, honey, why don't we use him in the shot?" He looked to Catalina. "It'll be free production value."

"Our favorite kind."

Micah glanced over at Santos, their new bodyguard and driver. The six-and-a-half-foot Brazilian was slouched against the nearby Range Rover, watching disinterestedly.

Micah said, "Hey Santos, if you see her grabbing any more insects could you kinda give me a shout?"

"Not a babysitter," was his monotone response.

Despite his arctic demeanor, Santos was all you could want in a bodyguard—namely, a giant with a body that looked like it was made out of rebar. He was equally intimidating above the neck, with a soup bowl haircut framing a face like one of those Easter Island stone heads, except less expressive.

Micah coaxed the beetle from Faye's arm onto his then placed the meteorite sample on the ground and rested the beetle on top of it.

"Okay, let's get this done and head back to the lodge."

Catalina framed up a shot and said, "Rolling."

Micah knelt down, making a point of lifting the beetle toward camera, and said, "After days of hiking through these mountains, following accounts from local tribes, we've uncovered the meteorite site. But I suspect this celestial object broke up before impact, spreading fragments like this across the mountainside." He set the beetle aside and lifted the sample. "One can clearly see the traces of diamond in this fragment, indicating a possible intelligent construction. Could this be a fragment of an intelligently engineered probe, using diamonds, one of the universe's hardest substances, as protective armor? In the ancient past could these alien engineers have visited our world? These, my friends, are the eternal questions we're seeking the answers to." Micah looked into the lens with his best scholarly contemplative look then drew his hand across his throat. "Cut. I think we've got everything."

Catalina lowered the camera and asked, "What about the 'days of hiking through the mountains'? Don't we have to shoot that stuff?"

"There's a bunch of footage of me hiking through mountains from last season that didn't get used, so we'll just cut that in. I'm even wearing the same shirt."

"Whatever you say, boss. But it kinda feels like we're phoning this episode in."

Micah shrugged. "They might not even air it anyway."

"Really? Are you officially canceled?"

"Cancelation would be too merciful. OEN still has a year on my contract, so they'll just keep slashing the budget until I can't breathe. They've already given my time slot to a guy who lets bullet ants and scorpions sting him. I mean, how do you compete with a weekly suicide attempt?"

"Sorry to hear that, boss." Picking up a camera case, she added, "Look on the bright side, maybe a murder hornet will kill the new guy and you'll get your time slot back."

"I love your optimism." Micah saw Faye picking up the beetle again. "Honey, why don't you just leave him be?"

With a deep sigh, Faye asked, "Can't we take him with us?"

"Do you think he really wants to live in a cage?"

Faye begrudgingly said, "No," and set him down with all the faux drama a nine-year-old girl could muster.

"Good girl."

Catalina said, "Maybe you should put her in the show, she's a natural."

In a gruff tone, Micah replied, "The network keeps saying the same thing, but there's no way I'm dragging her into child star oblivion. In a couple years she'd wind up robbing a liquor store with Honey Boo-Boo."

Catalina was taken aback, and he realized his answer had been sharper than intended.

"Sorry about that, Catalina, it's kind of a sore point."

His three-year television whirlwind had already cost him time with Faye; priceless years he'd never get back. There was no way he was going to place his daughter on the sacrificial altar of ratings.

Putting his arm around Faye, Micah said, "How about we head back to the lodge and have dinner? If I get any hungrier I might just eat your new pet."

"Yuck."

"Yuck? Your grandpa taught me how to roast 'em up. Their shell's like a built-in bowl. Tastes like chicken."

"That's super gross."

"Well, when you grow up in the jungle like I did, you learn to eat what's around."

Faye said, "I'd rather become a vegetarian," and trotted over to the Range Rover.

Santos watched Catalina lug the cases over, making no effort to help.

"Don't trouble yourself, big guy," Catalina said, shoving the case into the rear compartment. "I've got it."

Santos just grunted.

Micah gazed out at the rainforest again, wondering where it all went so wrong. Once he'd been a rising star in the field of planetary geology, until his theories about ancient aliens reduced him to a laughing stock among the scientific community. But thanks to some talk show appearances and his photogenic looks he'd been wooed into reality television. For three years he'd traveled the globe on OEN's dime, certain that he'd uncover evidence to prove his discredited theories. But he'd found nothing, and his media meal ticket was slipping away. He'd officially run out of rope.

He muttered, "Maybe if I start drinking now, I can get on one of those celebrity rehab shows."

"Sorry, I didn't catch that, boss."

Micah had been too lost in thought to notice Catalina standing behind him. "Uh, nothing. Let's head back to the lodge."

#

The Range Rover bounced down an unpaved road threading through the pitch-black rainforest. Santos was at the wheel, his soulless eyes locked on the road. Catalina slouched in the passenger seat trying to nod off, but her efforts were thwarted by the crater-sized potholes. Micah and Faye huddled in the backseat with a flashlight, studying the meteorite samples he'd bought.

Faye asked, "Did you and Grandpa really eat bugs when you were a kid?"

Micah said, "Once in a while, mostly so I'd know how to survive in the jungle. But sometimes we just ate them to be polite. In Vietnam, scorpions were the local delicacy, so if we wanted the locals to help us find all the rare plants and rocks we had to partake. You getting hungry yet?"

Faye giggled. "Yeah, but not for scorpions."

"I don't think the lodge is serving those." That reminded Micah of something. "Hey Catalina, I need you to get some shots of the eco lodge before we leave tomorrow. Make sure you shoot the sign."

"More product placement?"

"It's the backbone of poverty row television." He went back to studying the fragments. "These are actually pretty interesting."

Peering over his shoulder, Faye asked, "Can I look?"

"Sure." Micah handed her the magnifying glass. "If you look close you can see the flecks of diamond."

Straining to see, Faye asked, "Does that make it valuable?"

"Only to science. Some people think the diamonds are caused by carbon being super compressed during impact."

"I bet that's not what you think."

"Right as usual. I think they're fragments of something larger that came here with the diamonds already part of it."

"Came from where?"

"Well, that's kind of the mystery."

"Are there spacemen? Mom says you believe in spacemen."

"Yeah, I'll bet she says a lot of things." Micah's ex-wife was a university professor and staunch academic who called Micah's theories, "The worst kind of pseudo-science." She'd even brought it up during their custody hearing.

Faye said, "Now that you're done shooting can we go look for the pink river dolphins?"

"We can try, but they're really rare."

"Please?"

The elusive pink river dolphins, technically known as botos, had become Faye's latest obsession, running a close second to monkeys.

"Okay, I promise we'll find some." Micah noticed headlights trailing behind them. "That's weird, an unpaved road's not usually where you run into other people."

Catalina said, "We've got taillights in front too." She turned to Santos. "Should we be worried?"

Santos shook his head then pulled a folded sheet of paper from under his vest. He passed it back to Micah and said, "I need you to read this."

Micah asked, "What is it?"

"Read it."

He did and felt his blood run cold.

The neatly typed note read, "Dr. Clark, you are being abducted. I recommend you come along quietly to avoid upsetting your daughter. If you resist we will take you by force, potentially endangering the little girl. Please pass this note to your associate and advise her to comply. I assure you that nobody will be harmed."

Micah's fingers tightened around the paper.

Faye asked, "What's wrong, Dad?"

Pasting a smile on his face, Micah said, "Nothing, honey." Then he leaned forward, passing the note to Catalina and whispering, "Read this, but don't react."

She read it, and Micah was relieved to see how calmly she took being kidnapped.

Catalina handed the paper back to Santos, asking, "Is this your doing?"

Santos replied, "No," without taking his eyes off the unpaved road.

Micah put his arm around Faye, cheerfully informing her, "Honey, we're not going to the hotel."

"Why?"

"Well, we're going on a little trip."

"Where?"

"It's going to be a surprise."

Catalina muttered, "No shit."

#

They drove in silence for the next forty minutes. Luckily, Faye's backpack contained an Android tablet loaded with episodes of *Awesome Animals*. The show kept her from picking up on the tension.

Micah leaned forward, whispering to Catalina, "Don't worry; I've been kidnapped twice and made it out safe and sound both times. Hell, it turned out to be the season two cliffhanger."

She asked, "But were you really kidnapped or was it all BS?"

"Nope, it was genuine. Once in Sudan and another time in Indonesia."

Santos said, "Stop whispering," his voice still monotone.

Catalina noticed how Santos's English had miraculously improved, with barely a trace of an accent. The kind of English that was only taught at professional language schools or in the military—she was betting on the latter.

Santos slipped a satellite phone out of his vest and pressed a pre-programmed number. In Portuguese he said, "Ten minutes out," and hung up.

Catalina said, "Wow, Santa brought somebody a fancy phone."

"No talking."

The three vehicles turned down a steep, muddy incline, putting their four-wheel drives to the test.

Catalina watched Santos expertly use a combination of downshifting and clutch, keeping the vehicle glued to the muddy path.

Definitely military, she thought.

The path ended at the bank of a wide tributary—one of a thousand smaller offshoots of the mighty Amazon.

Micah said, "I think this is *Rio Curicuriari*."

Santos said, "No talking."

The moment they stopped, work lights came on, revealing a dilapidated boat house connected to a sagging log dock. A gleaming De Havilland Beaver, single-engine floatplane, was moored at the end of the pier.

Santos said, "You two in the backseat, out."

Micah slipped Faye's headphones off and told her, "It's time to go, honey."

Faye put her tablet away, asking, "Are we there?"

"Not yet. I think we're taking a plane ride first … aren't we?"

Santos nodded.

Micah grabbed Faye's backpack and helped her out. He was swept away for a moment by the intoxicating sensory medley of the Amazon. The smell of decaying vegetation mixed with the chorus of insects and frogs always took him back to his childhood, accompanying his parents on their geological and botanical expeditions.

Once they were out, Santos told Catalina, "Get out and walk directly to the plane."

She said, "You would have made a marvelous tour guide."

Santos's hand shot out, clamping onto her wrist like a vice. "Remember something, I was hired to fetch him and the little girl. You're optional, so don't get smart."

Trying to pull away, Catalina said, "You're hurting me."

Santos released her wrist. "When I want to hurt you, you'll know it."

Rubbing her arm, she said, "Why Mr. Santos, your English has certainly improved," and hopped out before he could react.

Men spilled out of the lead and follow vehicles, forming a loose cordon around the trio, herding them towards the plane. Santos walked several paces behind.

Micah caught a glimpse of the handguns stuffed in the waists of the men's pants. Tapping Faye's shoulder, he pointed to the plane. "Pretty cool plane, right?" It diverted her attention from the armed men.

Santos knelt down to Faye and, with an out of character smile, asked, "Faye, remember when you told me you liked *Pepperidge Farm* cookies?"

"Uh huh."

"Well, I made sure they have some on the plane for you."

The little girl's face lit up. "Really?"

"Yup, they're waiting for you."

"Come on, Dad, there are cookies," Faye yelled, almost dragging him down the pier.

As Catalina walked past Santos, she asked, "Do I get cookies too?"

"Watch it, *cadela*, people disappear out here all the time."

They climbed into the six-passenger plane. Once they were seated, Santos doled out bottled water along with the promised cookies. He sat down across from them, his shoulders taking up two seats.

Micah asked him, "Not to be difficult, but is there any chance we'll see our luggage again? It's all at the hotel."

"It's already been loaded into the cargo compartment. You checked out of the eco lodge this morning, leaving a generous tip. So don't expect them to call in a missing persons report. You even posted a Yelp review."

"Five stars I hope."

Faye offered one of the cookies to Catalina.

Micah watched her sniff it then lick the edge before biting into it. He thought, *She seems pretty savvy for someone on her first kidnapping.*

Micah encouraged Faye to put on her headphones, allowing the adults to speak freely.

Swallowing a mouthful of Mint Milano, Catalina asked Santos, "How'd you guys find these out here in the boonies? Is there a Costco in the rainforest?"

Santos glared at her.

Micah said, "It's their way of showing they've done their homework on us. These gentlemen are pros; I mean right out of our vehicle, straight onto a floatplane. That takes experience. Hell, when I was kidnapped in Sudan we had to walk for two days because their truck broke down. They used me as a pack mule."

Santos said, "Thank you," without a trace of emotion.

Catalina asked Micah, "Your bosses are gonna pay the ransom to get you back, right?"

Micah laughed. "They wouldn't pay ten cents to get me back."

"Great thing to say in front of our kidnappers."

Looking directly at Santos, Micah said, "These guys already know that. They want something, but it ain't money."

Santos stared back like an Easter Island tourism poster.

The engine roared to life, and the plane bobbed forward across the water.

Buckling Faye's seatbelt, Micah asked Santos, "How far are we going?"

Santos didn't respond.

Catalina whispered, "These De Havilland Beavers are only good for about five hundred miles, so it must be someplace here in Amazona."

Micah looked at her, surprised by her expertise.

With a shrug, she said, "I dated a rich guy once."

"I see."

Santos cut in with, "No whispering."

Thirty seconds later, they were airborne.

CHAPTER THREE

Doctor Ian Stewart drifted in and out of consciousness, unable to speak or even move. He was aware that he was on Batista's yacht, where he'd lain for days, living off an IV of saline and morphine. Gradually the pain had given way to a bone-weary fatigue that there was no awakening from. He could sense his wife Margaret seated next to him, felt the grip of her hand, yet he couldn't communicate. Then, gradually, he felt himself drifting off, knowing that, this time, it wasn't sleep.

#

Hans Maier stood in the infirmary doorway, an impassive observer to the inevitable. Dr. Stewart's wife was seated at her husband's bedside, as she had been for days, holding his hand and whispering words of hope. Hans couldn't help but admire her reserved British dignity—the kind of woman who'd calmly brew tea while the Blitz raged just outside her window.

After taking a moment to collect herself, she turned to Hans and said, "He's so cold."

In a soft voice, Hans asked, "Margaret, may I examine him?" and stepped into the cabin.

It only took a few seconds for Hans to confirm that Ian Stewart was dead. His demise came as no shock, considering the scorpion stings he'd suffered and waterborne diseases he'd contracted while navigating the rainforest.

Kneeling down to Margaret, he said, "I'm sorry, there was nothing we could do. The rainforest is a savage environment. He might have survived the dehydration, scorpion stings or the Chagas Disease, but not all three."

Wiping the tears from her eyes, she said, "You should have taken him to a hospital."

"That would be hundreds of miles from here, and I fear the journey would have killed him. We had all the needed antibiotics and antivenins on board. A younger person might have survived. I'm very sorry, he was a brilliant man."

She took her husband's hand, and, in an almost inaudible voice, asked, "Mr. Maier, may I have some time?"

Hans said, "Of course, take all the time you wish," and left the stateroom. He stood in the passageway for a moment, listening to her sobbing. Dr. Stewart had been a brilliant planetary geologist, and his death was a blow to the project. Fortunately, Mr. Batista had already taken steps to replace him.

As for what would become of Dr. Stewart's widow… That would be Mr. Batista's decision.

#

The flight lasted nearly four hours. Faye lay with her head in Micah's lap, sleeping soundly. Santos neither dozed off nor moved from his seat for the flight's duration. Micah doubted he even blinked.

Micah gazed out the window into blackness and said, "Night landing one of these floatplanes can be pretty tricky."

Sounding bored, Santos replied, "He does it all the time."

The floatplane banked sharply, and Micah saw a cluster of lights off in the distance. Seconds later, a trio of aerial flares launched into the night sky. The flares' parachutes popped open at nine hundred feet, bathing the area in a flickering orange light. The floatplane began its descent.

Micah pressed his face to the small window, seeing a hive of activity on the water below. Small, open hull, tender boats laden with cargo zipped out from shore, servicing an impressive assortment of larger craft.

The biggest of those was a two-story, three-hundred-foot-long cargo ferry. Such ferries were omnipresent along the Amazon. Their remarkably low drafts made them ideal for moving cargo and passengers along the main river and its shallow tributaries.

The boat moored alongside the ferry wasn't so ordinary. Micah pegged it as a sixty-foot Multi Cat utility boat—a top of the line maritime workhorse. The flat barge sported a deck-mounted hydraulic crane at its bow, along with a tall central pilothouse. The pilothouse's paint looked factory fresh.

But the real oddity was a gleaming white, eighty-foot yacht, floating like a swan among the ugly duckling working boats.

Micah asked, "Is this some kind of port?"

Santos mumbled, "Something like that."

Micah was ready to badger him further when the plane bounced onto the water. Micah clung on to Faye as the aircraft skipped across the surface.

Loosening his grip, he asked, "You okay, sweetie?"

Faye was grinning. "That was cool."

Turning to Santos, Micah said, "I gotta admit your pilot's pretty damn—"

But Santos was already on his feet, yanking life jackets from a compartment and tossing them at Micah. He said, "Put those on," and strode up the aisle.

Looking at the life jacket with disdain, Faye said, "But I'm a good swimmer."

Micah said, "So am I, but I'm still wearing one." Tickling her side he added, "It'll give the piranhas something to nibble on first."

Faye giggled and, with Catalina's help, donned the orange vest.

Tightening the last strap, Catalina muttered, "Like they say, any landing you can walk away from."

#

The trio climbed out of the plane, balancing on the float. A large inflatable Zodiac pulled alongside, expertly making fast to the float's strut. A crewman hopped out and began transferring their luggage.

The first of the aerial flares drifted down on its parachute, splashing into the river. Micah struggled to take in their surroundings before the others were extinguished. He counted at least fifteen small craft. A cacophony of megaphone-amplified voices and distorted Brazilian music echoed across the water.

Micah said, "This isn't a port, it's a damn flotilla."

An assortment of twenty and thirty-foot aluminum-hulled tenders shuttled supplies and fuel drums from shore. All sported planing hulls and larger than normal outboard motors, meaning they were high speed capable. Their crews were a racially mixed bag, with one thing in common—they were all armed.

Catalina leaned closer, asking, "What'd you think they're up to?"

"I don't know. Maybe it's a cartel."

"Doubtful. Drug cartels are all about speed, so they wouldn't get bogged down by barge boats and cargo ferries."

Micah gave her a perplexed look.

Catalina added, "What? I listen to a lot of true crime podcasts."

"Uh huh."

Micah got a better look at the cargo ferry. It was nearly three hundred feet long, sixty of those being its uncovered, coal shovel-shaped front deck. The name *Valentina* was stenciled across its pitted hull. It was the oldest craft of the bunch and the only one that looked at home.

The spanking new Multi Cat barge moored alongside it was set up as a floating repair shop and gas station. Wrench-toting grease monkeys scrambled around its deck, strapping down fuel drums.

Micah thought, *They're getting ready for a long trip.*

The next oddball was a thirty-five-foot Duckworth Landing Craft, resembling a D-Day style beachhead boat with a rear pilothouse. Its deck was packed tight with weatherproofed crates of industrial equipment.

Once the bags were loaded, Santos bellowed, "Get aboard!"

Micah reached down to help Faye into the Zodiac, but she was already climbing in, shouting, "Come on, Dad!"

Micah muttered, "She's actually enjoying this."

Catalina said, "Beats the alternative," and climbed aboard.

The Zodiac was bouncing across the water before she even sat down. A fifty-foot fast trawler zipped past them, buffeting the small inflatable.

Fighting to be heard over the roaring outboard, Catalina shouted, "Look at th,at!" and pointed to an oncoming boat.

A thirty-footer roared past, rocking the Zodiac. The boat's pilothouse was located amidship with circular turrets fore and aft. The hull was olive drab, but the bow was emblazoned with a freshly painted set of Flying Tigers style shark teeth, complete with narrow, predatory eyes.

Micah saw pairs of belt-fed machine guns mounted in the turrets. "Christ, is that a gunboat?"

"Yup, and it's got friends!" She pointed to a pair of identical craft circling the flotilla like sheepdogs.

Faye clamped down on Micah's arm, shrieking, "Oh no! They're drowning!" while pointing at a slow-moving tender.

The thirty-foot tender boat was stacked high with crates of live chickens. A pair of what looked like horses were tied behind the launch, their legs thrashing in the brown water to keep up.

Micah shouted to Santos, "You're bringing horses?"

Santos shook his head, replying, "Donkeys."

Tussling Faye's hair, Micah said, "It's okay, pumpkin, donkeys have huge lungs that make them float, so they're really good swimmers."

The tender and its swimming donkeys steered towards the *Valentina*.

Micah kissed Faye on the head, whispering, "They won't drown, honey."

"Promise?"

"Cross my heart—"

Catalina leaned closer to Micah, saying, "Please don't finish that phrase. So, why're they bringing live chickens?"

"They must be establishing an outpost. The best way to preserve meat out here is to keep it alive till you need to eat it."

Micah contemplated what he'd seen. *Whoever's in charge is an expert in planning and logistics. And they've got money, lots of money.*

The Zodiac approached the rear of the yacht, gleaming pearl white against the brown river. Micah pegged it for an eighty-foot, flybridge style Blohm & Voss. Costing at least four million dollars it was the alpha and omega of pleasure craft.

Its hydraulic rear tender deck began to lower, revealing the name *Esmerelda* emblazoned across its stern. There should have been bikini-clad euro models lounging on that tender deck, but instead there were a pair of men holding AK-47s.

Catalina said, "Looks like we're about to meet the boss."

#

A dilapidated motor boat laden with bananas and mangos weaved among the other craft, its aged outboard motor belching black smoke. The occupant was a tall, dark-skinned woman wearing a stained T-shirt and battered shorts. Her only companion was a capuchin monkey perched atop a mound of bananas.

She tooled past the various boats, holding up fruit, shouting, "Fresh bananas, fresh mangos, all cheap, cheap!"

Most of the boat crews dismissed her as just another peddler working the river, while others grabbed their crotches, shouting obscene suggestions.

The peddler just smiled and waved, while thinking, *Two men with AK-47s on each tender boat, all new weapons, very nice.* She pressed on, mentally tallying the men and armaments on each boat. A Zodiac zipped past her. Among its passengers was a white man and a child—both looked very out of place.

She muttered, "Curious," adding them to her scorecard while falling in behind the Zodiac, hoping for a closer look at the shiny yacht. As soon as she drew near, a gunboat cut across her path, its siren blaring. The startled monkey leapt up onto the woman's shoulder, clinging to her neck.

She petted the monkey and in a sing-song voice, said, "Oh, did the bad men scare you, little one?"

The gunboat pulled alongside; a crackling voice on its PA system shouted, "You're not authorized to be here! Get lost!"

She grinned, holding up a bunch of bananas, shouting, "But I got all fresh stuff, real cheap!"

The front turret rotated, bringing its twin machine guns to bear on her.

She smiled at the gunner, making a mental note. *Russian PK machine guns and 82 mm mortars ... very nice.*

The gunner stood up, yelling, "Hey *vaca*, do you work this stretch of the river all the time?"

The woman smiled. "Yes, every day, selling the best fruit, so cheap!" She seemingly ignored the fact that he'd just called her a cow.

Holding up a coin, the gunner asked, "Have you seen any activity downriver? Like pirates?"

Her eyes widened. "Pirates? You mean like ... Queen Caveira?"

The gunner tensed at hearing the pirate's name. He asked, "Have you seen her?" while hugging his machine gun a bit tighter.

Emphatically shaking her head, the woman replied, "Oh no, but people say she's like a rabid dog, murdering everyone she sees."

"Yup, she's one psycho bitch. Anyone else on the river? Thieves? Navy?"

She shook her head while holding up a bunch of bananas, shouting, "Good, cheap!"

The gunner tossed the coin to her, saying, "Thanks for the info, now get lost. Nobody wants to buy your rotten fruit."

The woman held up the coin, grinning like a child on Christmas morning, while thinking, *Five centavos? You cheap piece of shit.* Spinning the boat around, she sped off, leaving a cloud of black smoke in her wake.

Choking on the exhaust, the gunner shouted, "Goddamn river trash!" then gestured for the gunboat's captain to move on.

As soon as she was out of sight, the woman began tossing her cargo of rotting fruit overboard. Tucked beneath the fruit was a loaded AK-47 along with three hand grenades. The monkey hopped off her shoulder, snatching up a final banana before they went over the side. The curious monkey paused, poking at one of the grenades.

The woman playfully shooed it away, saying, "Don't touch them, little one, they're reserved for Mr. Batista."

The fruit peddler steered into a small channel. A fleet of river pirates was moored a few miles down, awaiting her return.

Queen Caveira smiled, knowing she should have sent one of her pirates to spy on the flotilla. It would have been the prudent move, considering the bounty on her head.

But, she thought, *where's the fun in that?*

CHAPTER FOUR

Micah, Catalina and Faye were escorted onto the deck, where the thugs were replaced by two neatly dressed porters. The decks were polished, almost pristine. Santos led them through a sliding glass door, where they were struck by a blast of cool air.

Taking a look around, Catalina said, "Pretty sweet."

Micah replied, "That's an understatement."

The walls were teak, polished to a brilliant luster. The rich, inlaid floors were covered with oriental rugs. Micah studied the abstract paintings lining the walls, recognizing an original Burle Marx that any museum would have died for. The contemporary art was incongruously mixed with glass cases of antiques. Micah was drawn to a case containing a steel helmet. A plaque next to it read, "Helmet of Conquistador Lope de Aguirre, 1510–1561. Conqueror of the Amazon."

Micah was familiar with Aguirre and wondered how anyone could revere a genocidal monster with delusions of godhood.

Santos waved them over to a white leather sofa. A steward entered pushing a beverage cart laden with bottled water, soda and sandwiches.

Faye eagerly grabbed a can of soda.

Micah said, "Honey, drink some water first. You need to get hydrated."

Faye said, "Okay," and set the can down on the marble coffee table.

Micah noticed a pool ball-sized stone resting next to the can. "Jesus, look at that. It's incredible!"

Catalina asked, "What, the coffee table?"

"No." Micah scooped the stone off the table. The dirt and lack of polish couldn't hide the green facets shining through. He grabbed a conveniently placed magnifying glass. "Incredible."

"If you say so."

"What community college did you flunk geology in? This is a perfect emerald. It's uncut and unpolished but exquisite."

A booming voice said, "Excellent eye, Dr. Clark. You live up to your reputation."

A tall, dark-complexioned man stood in the entryway, his shoulders almost filling the doorway. He wore a white, raw silk shirt, custom tailored to his barrel-chested physique. His English was flawless, with the barest trace of a Brazilian accent.

The man strode across the saloon, extending his hand to Micah. "My name is Hector Batista, allow me to welcome you to the very edge of civilization." He took Catalina's hand. "Ms. Abril, a pleasure."

Catalina noticed that, while Batista's clothes were elegant, his hands were calloused, with the swollen knuckles of a prize fighter.

Batista said, "You're holding one of my finest specimens. I keep it unpolished to test if potential geologists recognize its value."

Micah studied the emerald through the magnifying glass. "The diaphaneity is near perfect, with almost no irregularities, but I couldn't even begin to assess its value."

With pride, Batista said, "Given its size and perfect structure it will easily fetch half a million US dollars from a well-funded museum, even more from some obscenely wealthy cretin."

"Incredible."

"It's yours."

"What?"

"Dr. Clark, I have a mission for you. Complete it and that emerald is yours, along with a substantial paycheck." Batista leaned down to Faye, asking, "Did the young lady enjoy the cookies? They're very difficult to get out here you know."

Faye politely replied, "Yes sir, thank you."

"You're very welcome." He turned to Catalina, his tone less congenial. "I'm puzzled that your assistant didn't react to the emerald. Any qualified geologist would recognize it as a treasure. Perhaps she isn't really a professional. More of an … attractive traveling companion?"

Catalina said, "Well, I know enough geology to recognize the president of Consolidated Minerals, South America's largest emerald mining company. I read your op ed in *Mineral Journal* about the market shift from gems to rare earth elements. It was …prophetic. I heard you've expanded into mining iridium."

He smiled, his ego responding to her stroking. "Correct. As much as I love emeralds, rare earth elements are my new passion."

Forcing a smile, Catalina said, "Sorry I didn't recognize your emerald, it's my first kidnapping."

Cocking his head towards Faye, Micah whispered, "Let's avoid using the 'K' word."

Batista said, "She is correct though. It was, how we say in Brazil, a *seqüestro*, and completing the mission will be your ransom, with a generous payday to boot."

Micah said, "But you don't need me to help you mine emeralds."

"This isn't about emeralds." He shouted, "Hans, bring in the sample!"

A thin, nervous looking man entered, sweating despite the air-conditioned room.

Batista said, "Allow me to introduce my senior mining engineer, Hans Maier. You'll find his expertise extends to many things."

Hans said, "Unfortunately planetary geology isn't one of them." He popped open a steel box and placed a finger length piece of twisted, blackened mineral on the table. "The surface carbonizing is from external sources that fused with it. The piece itself is pristine."

Batista asked, "Does it look familiar?"

Micah studied the sample, transfixed. "Yes."

"Similar to the shard you discovered in Peru eight years ago?"

"Yes, but this one is pristine."

"Give him your report, Hans."

With a slight Austrian accent, Hans said, "It appears to be a naturally occurring mineral, with the properties of a diamond, if a diamond were to be melted down and molded."

Still staring at the sample, Micah said, "Which would mean the diamond was artificial."

"That was my initial suspicion, so I performed a high-voltage chemical deposition test to look for traces of Boron in the lattice." Hans turned to his boss, silently asking permission to continue.

Batista said, "Go on, we haven't got time for secrets."

Hans continued, "It did not conduct electricity."

Micah said, "So no free electrons, meaning it's an organic diamond."

"Instead, the sample produced energy, at least ten orders of magnitude greater than what was being applied."

Batista interjected, "A burst of energy that could have powered San Paulo."

Micah just stared at them, dumbstruck.

Hans added, "Yet the sample did not suffer at all and would have continued producing energy as long as power was applied."

Batista smiled. "Unfortunately, the burst of energy destroyed the machinery … and the building it was in. It was a magnificent sight. The sky glowed for hours."

Hans said, "Yet the energy release produced no radiation or harmful emissions and barely a trace of heat. Just pure clean energy."

Micah said, "It sounds like you're talking about cold fusion."

"That's not a term I'd use in educated company, but its capability dwarfs any fuel, even helium three."

Setting the sample down, Micah said, "But there's nothing like this on Earth—"

Batista clapped his hands and grinned. "And that's why I need a planetary geologist! This is a fragment of a meteorite, a huge one if the information I got was correct. I believe the sliver you discovered in Peru was a bit of airborne ejecta, released before the impact. But I've found the source. Intact. Something we're calling the Anomaly."

Micah looked incredulous. "Why me?"

"You sound surprised. I realize most people in the geological community don't respect you."

"Well, I wouldn't—"

"Oh please, they call you a strutting pretty boy, spouting nonsense about ancient aliens to an ignorant fanbase."

"I don't know if they say that."

Hans nodded. "Oh, they do."

Batista stepped closer, putting his hand on Micah's shoulder. "But I've read your old papers and believe you possess the knowledge and vision I require. This is what you've been hunting for these past years."

"But how'd you find it?"

"I have to share credit with Mother Nature. She unleashed a .8 earthquake, opening the ground at the base of an unexplored tributary. I routinely send teams to survey such natural events. One never knows what treasures a quake might push to the surface. They returned with aerial photos that were … intriguing. Recalling your research, I financed an expedition to the site. Forty men, machinery, all supervised by a *Vetlesen Prize* winning geologist."

Columbia University's *Vetlesen Prize* was the highest award a geologist could receive. Micah's father had been awarded it, often waving it around to punctuate his disappointment with his son.

Batista continued. "They radioed about finding a massive deposit. I originally intended to harvest it for the gemstone market, until Hans ran his test. We believe the deposit is large enough to power the world indefinitely."

Micah said, "Possessing that would make you the most powerful man on Earth."

"Only if I can get it. Sadly we've lost all contact with the outpost. My geologist made it back with that sample, claiming everyone else was dead. But he was delirious from malaria and insect venom, so most of what he said were probably ravings."

"Can I speak to him?"

Hans said, "I'm afraid he's—" He paused for a moment then, in deference to Faye, said, "Permanently unavailable."

Batista looked surprised. "When did this happen?"

"A short while ago. I was about to inform you."

Micah said, "I'm very sorry."

Batista looked nonplussed. "It was to be expected. Frankly I'm shocked that he hung on this long." He turned to Santos. "I need you to make the final arrangements. Oh, and please be … respectful."

Santos nodded and left.

Faye picked up the fragment, eying it curiously.

Catalina said, "Don't play with that, honey, it might—"

Batista said, "No, let her. It has no radiation or harmful properties." He watched Faye for a moment. "How interesting that she ignores a priceless jewel yet is fascinated by a burnt piece of gemstone. She's definitely, how do you say, Daddy's little girl."

Something about Batista's tone chilled Micah.

#

Santos slid open the infirmary door. The widow still sat at her husband's bedside, clutching his hand, sobbing softly. After maintaining a respectful silence, Santos coughed softly to get her attention.

He said, "I'm sorry to intrude at such a difficult time."

The widow quickly collected herself, assuming a dignified posture.

Santos stepped into the cabin. "With your permission, I'd like to remove the IV needle so we can move the body."

"Of course."

Santos leaned down over the dead man.

The widow watched him work, gradually building up the courage to say, "When I was brought here, Mr. Batista promised that, as long as my husband did what he asked, I'd be released."

"Yes, that's what he said."

"So, can I go home now, and may I take Ian with me?"

Santos slid the three-inch needle out of the cadaver's arm, replying, "A promise is a promise."

Without warning, his left hand shot out, grabbing the widow by her hair. He yanked her onto her feet while shoving her face against his chest, muffling her screams. With his right hand, he drove the IV needle forward, sending three inches of steel straight into her ear canal. The needle tore through her eardrum before piercing her brain, instantly shutting down all higher functions. Santos felt her body stiffen and her breath coming in short, ragged pants. By twisting the needle clockwise, he shut down her brain's basic functions. As soon as she went limp, he turned her body around, clamping his right hand over her mouth and nose for three solid minutes. Confident that she was dead, he removed the needle.

Placing his mouth to her ear, he whispered, "You'll leave tonight, together," and flopped her down on the bed next to her late husband.

A stream of saline solution dribbled out of her ear, but there wasn't a drop of blood. Her death had been painless and instantaneous.

Or, as Batista had phrased it—"Respectful."

#

Batista continued his pitch. "This expedition is the culmination of all your research. I've already assembled everything required."

Micah said, "Including your own private navy?"

"Ah, you saw my gunboats. Amazing craft. You know, I had to outbid the Peruvian Navy to get them. Hopefully they won't be necessary, but the Amazon is full of pirates. Most of them just rob tourists and drug smugglers, but if it was pirates or angry *bugre* that attacked my outpost, we'll need to eliminate them."

Bugre was a Brazilian racial slur for indigenous river tribes.

Faye put down the sample and leaned against Micah, yawning. Micah stroked her hair as she dozed off.

Batista asked, "Is something still nagging at you, Doctor?"

Micah said, "This sample would have enticed any planetary geologist to come along willingly, with bells on. So why go to the trouble of kidnapping me?"

"Because time is short. My geologist is dead, but the expedition is ready. Postponing would be expensive and dangerous to my interests. But you're ideal for another reason."

"How so?"

"You're a brilliant man who's been forced to shill television rubbish to a dwindling audience of morons. Very soon, you'll be broke, with zero respect from your peers and equal job prospects. But, if you do what I ask, I'll provide you and your daughter with financial security."

Micah pondered that and asked, "Just how much financial security are we talking here?"

"Three million dollars, plus that emerald." Turning to Catalina, he added, "I hadn't anticipated your assistant's involvement, but I can add another million US dollars for her participation."

Micah asked, "And if I say no?"

"I think you've lived long enough to know that desperation and opportunity are rivers that rarely cross."

Micah looked down at his sleeping daughter, knowing that he was right.

Batista said, "Shall we drink to our new partnership?" He waved to a waiting steward who wheeled in a chilled bottle of champagne and filled three glasses. "A toast, to a new world of clean energy for all."

They took a sip.

Setting his glass down, Micah gently stroked Faye's hair. "I'll need to send my daughter back to New York before we leave."

Batista shook his head. "Given our time constraints that's quite impossible. I'm afraid she'll have to accompany us."

"What? This is a dangerous expedition. You can't expect me to let her—" Micah tried to stand, but his knees felt weak.

Catalina dropped her glass and muttered, "Aw shit," before slouching over on the couch.

Micah shouted, "You drugged the champagne!"

Batista took a sip, saying, "And waste Dom Perignon? I coated your glasses. Sleep well, we have a great deal of work ahead of us."

Micah tried to protest but couldn't form words. His vision blurred. All he could do was sit, listening to the echoing voices around him.

Batista turned to Hans, asking, "How long?"

"The drug should last six hours, but I'll inject them with a second dose to keep them under until we reach the tributary."

"Yes, well past the point of no return."

Micah slumped over, unconscious.

Santos entered the saloon, barely acknowledging the three unconscious people, and said, "It's done, sir."

"Good. Wait until we're in caiman country before you dump the bodies. Now move these three over to the *Valentina*."

Santos said, "You know, I could have just drugged them at the hotel and delivered them downriver."

Eyeing Micah's inert form, Batista said, "No. I needed to meet him in person to judge his expertise. Now I've confirmed he's brilliant, desperate, and will do anything to protect his daughter. An ideal combination."

Santos asked, "And what do we do with them when we're finished?"

Draining his glass, Batista said, "The caimans will still be hungry on our return trip."

CHAPTER FIVE

Micah's eyes snapped open, but his thoughts felt like they were being filtered through mud. Gradually, he pieced together that he was lying on a cot, still wearing the same sweat-soaked clothes. He tried to sit up fast, but it felt like someone was hammering a nail into his forehead. A second, gradual attempt was more successful. After a few more seconds he pieced together that he was on a boat. His suitcase was lying on the floor nearby, unopened. Faye's open bag was next to it. The cabin was large and reasonably clean with one wall-mounted cot and several hammocks stowed against the bulkhead. It was a first-class billet on Batista's cargo barge, the *Valentina*.

The memories all came flooding back to him—the flotilla, the yacht, and his meeting with Batista.

A man sat at a folding table playing solitaire. He paused his game, eyeing Micah suspiciously.

Micah yelled, "Where's my daughter? What've you done with her?"

Without a word the man went to the cabin door and leaned out, shouting something in Portuguese. Without glancing at Micah he returned to his card game.

Micah was about to yell again then noticed the man's shoulder holster and elected to stay silent.

Moments later, Santos appeared in the doorway, gesturing for Micah to follow him.

Micah asked, "Where's my—"

Santos cut him off. "The kid's safe with your lady friend." He turned to the guard, shouting in Portuguese.

Through his mental fog Micah caught something about informing Batista he was awake.

The man scrambled out the door.

Santos said, "Let's go."

Micah groped around until he found his boots. He turned them over and shook them—standard procedure in an environment full of scorpions and centipedes. Something tumbled out and rolled across the floor. It was the large, uncut emerald Batista had offered him.

Okay, he thought, *at least Batista's holding up his side of the deal, if you consider kidnapping to be a deal.*

Santos yelled, "Move it!"

Micah stuffed the emerald in his pocket and pulled on his boots.

They exited onto a side deck, the humidity and heat smothering Micah like a wet blanket. He gazed out at the river, searching for any landmarks. All he saw was churning brown water and an endless canopy of fog-shrouded rainforest. The waterway was too narrow to be the Amazon proper, meaning they were cruising down a wide tributary. That narrowed it down to a few hundred possibilities. Batista's yacht cruised along behind them, flanked by gunboats. The other vessels were scattered in a loose formation. He didn't see any trace of local river traffic, meaning they'd passed even the remotest settlements.

Santos shoved him forward, pointing to a gangway leading down.

From there, Micah was herded through the ship's lower level deck—an open space with floor-to-ceiling screened windows. The deck was crammed with supplies and fuel drums. Deckhands sat on crates, arguing over card games, while the night crew snored above them in suspended hammocks. Despite the large screened-in windows the area still reeked of diesel fuel and sweat.

After navigating the maze of supplies and humanity, they exited onto the sixty-foot-long front deck. It was like stepping into an open market place. Suspended wicker baskets of fruits and vegetables hung just beyond the reach of six pigs, straining against rope leashes. Crates of live chickens were stacked on either side, while a few luckier birds patrolled the deck, pecking at insects. A pair of braying donkeys was tied to the railing. At the far end of the deck, long barbecue grills roasted slabs of pork and chicken slathered in *dende* oil. The roasting meat shrouded the deck in a thick haze of citrus-fused smoke. A tape deck blared distorted *Sertanejo* music, forcing the men to shout over it in Portuguese, Spanish and a few dialects Micah couldn't place. It was exactly the kind of sensory overload you didn't want while nursing a Rohypnol hangover. But then a shrill voice rang out over the cacophony, and his pain was forgotten.

"Daddy!"

Micah saw Faye at the far end of the deck, waving excitedly with one hand while holding Catalina's with the other. Both wore clean clothes and looked unharmed.

He pushed through the crowd, sweeping up the little girl in his arms. "Oh baby, I was so worried." He hugged her tight. "Are you okay, princess?"

"My head hurt, but it's getting better now."

Micah looked over at Catalina and asked, "How're you doing?"

Catalina said, "Considering I got roofied and shanghaied, I'm doin' okay." She cocked her head towards Santos. "Tall, dark and ugly's been giving us the evil eye, but so far nobody's tried to hurt us. Hell, they even laid out our clothes for us."

"How long were we out?"

"I woke up about two hours ago, so you've been out for at least twelve. Screwy thing is that I didn't swallow any of that champagne, 'cause Mama taught me never to accept drinks from kidnappers. Faye didn't drink any either."

"Batista coated the glasses and dosed those cookies with something."

"Well, the combo was enough to put me down hard." She held up her arm, revealing a tiny needle mark inside her elbow. "After that, somebody must have topped us off. Faye woke up around the same time I did, so I figured we should get some air and clear the spider webs out of our brains."

Micah set Faye down.

Tugging his sleeve, she pointed to a cluster of wooden crates, saying, "Look Dad, they've got monkeys!"

Six shrieking capuchin monkeys were locked in the crates. To Micah, their cries were like nails on a chalkboard.

Catalina handed Micah a plastic cup. "One of the boys squeezed us some fresh juice, it'll help numb that power drill in your forehead hangover."

Faye was already leaning close to the monkeys, offering them chunks of banana. "Dad look, there're so many of them!"

"Don't get too close to 'em, monkey girl, 'cause they bite." Micah didn't want to break the news to her that the monkeys were probably destined to be lab animals or bush meat. He emptied his cup, feeling renewed by the combination of juice and Faye's laughter. After all they'd been through, his daughter should have been traumatized, yet there she was, giggling, engrossed in the monkeys.

Raising his cup to Catalina, he said, "Thanks for this, and for, well, everything."

"No sweat. She's a pretty resilient kid."

Micah crushed the plastic cup, saying, "I can't believe those bastards drugged a child."

A familiar Austrian-tinged voice said, "I assure you the drug was medically approved for use on children and I personally monitored the dosage."

Micah turned and saw Hans emerge from the throng and shouted, "I'll give you a fucking dose!" as he lunged towards him.

Santos latched on to Micah's forearm with a bone-crushing grip, effortlessly holding him back. Pulling Micah close, he said, "Batista needs your brain, not your hands. Next time you try something, I start breaking fingers." Then he released his grip.

Fumbling with a cigarette, Hans said, "I can understand your anger, but try to remember we're on the brink of changing the world."

Batista stepped out onto the deck, resplendent in an ivory-white linen suit. The crowd parted, clearing his path. He approached Micah, saying, "Hans is correct, we'll be reshaping mankind's future while proving your theories in the process. Not a bad compromise."

A shrill siren cut through the din, silencing the workers. A tender boat came alongside, blasting its police style siren.

The speedboat's pilot held up a bullhorn, shouting, "We've got red flags behind us!"

Batista muttered, "*Merda*!"

Without a word, Santos rushed to the edge of the deck and vaulted over the railing, landing in the boat. It roared off, churning up a brown wake behind it.

Micah asked, "Problem?"

Batista replied, "Perhaps," then strode off toward a ladder leading to the upper deck. He turned back to Micah. "You and Ms. Abril should come along. This could be entertaining. Don't worry; Hans will keep an eye on your little one."

Hans just nodded, clearly annoyed at being reduced to a babysitter.

Catalina whispered, "I say we tag along, maybe we'll learn something."

They followed Batista up the ladder. A gangway led them to the rear observation deck, where a crewman waited with two pairs of binoculars.

Peering through the binoculars, Batista said, "There it is, the small boat at three o'clock. It's a scout for the Red Flag Fleet."

Through the binoculars, Micah sighted a dilapidated speed boat displaying a red flag. It was clearly shadowing the flotilla. "Who are they?"

"The Red Flag Fleet are river pirates, though calling it a fleet is generous. More like a floating junkyard of stolen boats with a crew of half-starved *bugre* trash."

Catalina asked, "So they're not dangerous?"

Batista shook his head. "Very dangerous. They're led by a psychopath calling herself Queen Caveira."

Catalina told Micah, "That's Queen of Skulls in English."

Micah muttered, "Of course it is."

The two gunboats made a beeline for the red-flagged boat. Santos's speedboat was right behind them.

Micah said, "Is she a real queen?"

Batista said, "Only to her crew. Those wretches worship her, and she has a personal grudge against me."

"Why?"

Batista shrugged. "The have-nots always hate their betters."

He graciously handed his binoculars to Catalina who watched the battle.

The red flag boat turned sharply in retreat, black smoke belching from its exhaust. The first gunboat opened fire, sending up plumes of water around the escaping boat.

Ignoring the hail of bullets, one of the pirates stood up, firing an assault rifle. The pirate's gunfire was accurate but merely ricocheted off the gunboat's armored turret. The fleeing boat cut hard right—an evasive maneuver that put them squarely in the second gunboat's crosshairs. The second gunboat's initial burst cut down the armed man. A second destroyed the boat's outboard motor. The pirate's boat lost speed until it was drifting in a cloud of black smoke. One of the pirates returned fire while a second launched a skyrocket into the air. The gunboat fired again, cutting both men down.

Batista said, "He's using that skyrocket to signal another scout further down, telling him he won't be coming home."

Micah lowered the binoculars, struggling to process what he'd just witnessed. He'd experienced plenty of danger in his life, but he'd never been exposed to this kind of savage violence.

Seeing the blank expression on Micah's face, Catalina turned to Batista, asking, "Do you think they'll attack us?"

"No. She's probed our defenses and knows she's outgunned. Now she'll hang back, waiting for any boats that fall behind. God help any who do. If you ever meet Queen Caveira there's only one thing you can do."

"What's that?"

"Dive into the river and let the black caimans get you. They'll only take minutes to kill you, but the queen will torture you for days. Inflicting pain is like a hobby to her." Batista let that sink in for a moment then added, "But as long as we keep our formation tight, we'll be safe."

Micah recovered his composure enough to ask, "Why are we using boats at all? Couldn't we just go in by floatplane or helicopter? It'd be a lot faster and safer."

"We already tried that. The first plane simply disappeared. The second time we sent a helicopter. It got out a radio message then vanished."

"Saying?"

"It was a distress call declaring they'd lost all power near the outpost, as if something fused the electrical system. Even if they survived the crash, the natives probably got them. They're an un-contacted tribe who eat strangers."

Micah said, "Cannibals?"

"So the story goes. That's why we're going in by water. Armed men and gunboats are the most effective way to deal with … indigenous peoples."

Batista's tone gave "indigenous" a sinister edge.

Micah asked, "How long till we reach your outpost?"

"It's another ten hours to our refueling depot then two days to the outpost. That's two days on a caiman-infested river, crossing into the territory of a cannibal tribe while being shadowed by river pirates. Things you should remember if escaping crosses your mind." Batista stared at him silently, letting the grim reality of the situation settle in.

Micah knew he was right—the boat was a perfect prison without bars.

Batista grinned, saying, "Ah, look who's joined us."

Micah turned around and saw Hans leading Faye over.

Pasting on a smile, Micah asked, "Did you feed all the monkeys?"

"Yup. And the donkeys too."

Hans said, "And with that out of the way perhaps we can get to work. I recommend you grab some food and come with me. I've set up a workspace in your cabin, and you'll be happy to know it's air-conditioned."

Taking Micah's hand, Faye said, "Dad."

"What, baby?"

"You stink worse than the monkeys."

Micah pulled at the soiled clothes he'd been wearing for two days and said, "You're right. I better take a shower and change."

Catalina said, "Someone's probably laid out your ensemble by now," then raised the binoculars for a final look.

Micah said, "Real five-star accommodations."

Catalina watched Santos's craft pull alongside the pirate boat. Santos hopped aboard, dragging a wounded pirate up onto his feet. After shouting a few questions, he drew a pistol and casually executed his prisoner.

Catalina tossed the binoculars back to the deckhand, muttering, "Yeah, all the comforts of home."

#

Micah and Catalina spent the next four hours ensconced in their cabin, which Hans had repurposed into an office. The overtaxed air conditioner barely took the edge off the sweltering heat. The table was covered in aerial photographs and paperwork. Among the mess, Micah noticed a nautical chart, half buried beneath a stack of aerial photos.

Hans asked, "Any thoughts on what you've seen?"

Micah picked up a photo of a circular lake surrounded by a rim of ejected earth. A small, glittering dome was visible in the lake's center. "This lake is definitely an ancient impact crater, like Lake Pingualuit in Québec. But the meteor should be buried hundreds of feet below the lakebed."

Hans shook his head. "It isn't. The earthquake must have pushed the Anomaly to the surface. Our first expedition began damming the river that feeds the lake, but we haven't gotten any photos since then."

Staring at the photo, Micah said, "The thing is that meteorites are mostly composed of iron ore, meaning they're heavy as hell. An earthquake should have sunk it deeper, not pushed it to the surface."

In truth, Micah's eyes were focused on the chart the photo had been covering. His father had been an amateur cartographer, creating detailed charts of the remote locations they'd explored. From childhood, Micah had displayed a gift for reading and memorizing maps. This nautical chart showed where they were headed and he quickly committed every contour and bend in the river to memory.

Hans said, "Perhaps it has a hollow core."

"There's no such thing as a hollow meteorite, it just can't happen naturally."

"It's a genuine mystery, which is why we brought you along." Shifting his gaze to Catalina, Hans asked, "Any observations?"

"I concur," was all she said.

Her lack of meaningful input wasn't going unnoticed by Micah or Hans.

Micah thought, *So she says she's a grad student but clearly knows jack shit about geology, and she just witnessed men being killed but showed less emotion than someone watching a football game.*

Micah glanced over at Faye, who was stretched out on the cot reading some novel about a vampire high school and asked, "You doing okay?"

"Yup."

Batista had provided a stack of age appropriate YA novels to help occupy the nine-year-old. The man had thought of everything.

Faye set the book aside and asked, "Dad, can monkeys swim?"

"Yeah. They don't like to, but they can."

"Why don't they like it?"

"Because they'd rather swing around in the trees where they're safe from crocodiles and jaguars."

"Crocodiles are nasty."

"No they're not, they're just crocodiles."

Micah relished these childish conversations, but to Hans they were exasperating. He dug into his pack of cigarettes.

Catalina said, "Uh, I know this is a hostage situation and all, but could you not smoke in a closed room with a kid?"

Hans got up, saying, "Fine, but when I come back we'll analyze the remaining aerial photos in detail." Glancing over at Faye, he added, "Uninterrupted," and stalked out.

Faye muttered, "He's meaner than the crocodiles," and went back to her book.

Micah leaned closer to Catalina and whispered, "Did you really just say 'I concur'? We're not on an episode of *Gray's Anatomy* here."

"What're you saying?"

"Okay, to be blunt, do you know anything about geology?"

"Huh?"

"Hans has been asking basic questions for the past two hours, and I can tell you don't have a clue what he's talking about. We're playing for our lives here and keeping safe means staying useful."

Catalina scribbled something on her pad and tapped the pen against it.

It read, "This room is probably bugged."

Micah whispered, "True, but that has nothing to do with why you didn't know an emerald from a cinder block."

She scribbled again, this time writing, "Not a grad student."

Glancing at the page, Micah muttered, "No shock there."

After a frustrated breath, Catalina wrote again, this time in very small letters.

Micah stared at the paper, speechless. Catalina tore the piece off, balled it up and swallowed it.

Hans returned, renewed by the nicotine. Taking his seat, he asked, "Can we please get some work done now?"

Micah stood up and said, "Sure, but we need to grab some more juice."

"Now?"

"Yes now. Next time you drug somebody for twelve hours you should feed 'em first. We're hungover and in desperate need of some vitamin C. It'll only take a few minutes. Come on, Faye."

The little girl's face lit up. "Monkeys?"

"Sure, you can visit the monkeys, but just for a few minutes. Let's go."

The trio left. Hans went back to analyzing the aerial photos, muttering Teutonic obscenities.

Micah walked along the deck holding Faye's hand while struggling to process the three words Catalina had scrawled.

"*I'M CIA, DUMMY!*"

#

Once they reached the front deck, Catalina yanked a banana from an overhead basket and tossed it to Faye. "Go feed your monkeys, honey."

The nine-year-old scampered off.

Catalina grabbed Micah's wrist, guiding him over near the blaring tape deck.

He blurted out, "Are you saying the goddamn CIA's watching me?"

"There's a lot of international trafficking in rare earth elements. Langley figured if I was attached to you, I'd have access to some of the shady folks you buy meteorite chunks from. We didn't know they were all just farmers."

"So I was a... What is it you call them?"

"The term's useful idiot. But don't be insulted, there are some really smart useful idiots. They also needed to make sure you weren't masterminding any illicit deals."

"And?"

"I informed them you couldn't mastermind anything."

"Cute."

"I meant you were an honest guy. And before you start acting all wounded, remember that you're the one who forced grad students to do all your legwork, plus shoot your damn show for a whopping two-hundred dollar-a-week stipend."

"Plus meals!" Micah took a breath and said, "Sorry, I know we need to focus on the situation."

"Which is a lot worse than you think. I may know squat about geology, but I know all about Batista. He's been all over Langley's radar."

"Why?"

"Because he's a goddamn monster, a former cartel boss who seized control of the emerald trade by eliminating competitors and labor organizers; hell, he's wiped out whole indigenous tribes around his mines, which are all pretty much slave labor camps. And he's sure as shit going to eliminate us as soon as we're done. That way nobody'll know about his find."

"What about Faye?"

"Do you think everyone in those tribes were grown-ups? On the plus side, he probably won't do anything until he knows his treasure's secured."

Micah thought for a moment and said, "What about Hans? He's intelligent. Any chance he'd take our side?"

"Forget it. Hans has been Batista's right-hand man through all his evil shit. He drank the Kool Aid a long time ago."

"So what do we do?"

Catalina shrugged. "I don't know. If we see a chance, we might have to cut and run."

"With a nine-year-old girl, in the rainforest?"

"It's bad, I get that. This is all a work in progress. But I need to know one thing. If we have to run, are you really any good at that living in the jungle stuff you talk about on your show?"

"I'm a little rusty, but yeah. Being a survival expert is the only part of my TV image that's not complete horse shit. I grew up traveling with my mom and dad. Jungles, mountains, you name it."

"Good, 'cause we may need that."

Micah watched Faye feeding the monkeys. Her complete innocence was heartbreaking.

Catalina squeezed his hand. "Just know this; I'm not going to let anything happen to your little girl on my watch, no matter what it takes."

"Thanks."

"Oh, and you're still a really smart planetary geologist, even if it took you three weeks to figure out I was a fraud."

"Well, you were pretty good with a camera, plus Faye liked you."

A klaxon sounded, followed by a distorted PA voice announcing, "We are one hour from arrival at the fuel depot, prepare to dock."

Catalina said, "Maybe this is our chance."

Santos shoved his way through the crowd, pointed at them and announced, "You two are going ashore with the fueling detail."

Micah couldn't believe their luck but kept a poker face. "Okay, I'll just grab Faye and get her ready."

Santos grinned, shaking his head. "Uh-uh. The brat stays here."

"Are you crazy?"

"No, not crazy, or stupid. Anytime we stop, I'm separating you. It's just my way of making sure you don't get any wild ideas."

CHAPTER SIX

"But Dad, why can't I come with you?"

Micah looked down at his daughter, pasted on a smile and said, "We're going someplace that's a little too dangerous for you, but I swear we'll be right back." He bent down, kissing Faye's forehead.

The little girl didn't look convinced, so Catalina added, "Don't worry, honey, I'll take good care of your dad."

"Can I go visit the monkeys?"

Micah said, "I need you to stay in the cabin. But when I get back, we'll visit all your poop-flinging pals."

Catalina knelt down. "And maybe we can give them all names. Wouldn't that be fun?"

Faye grinned and said, "Yeah."

Growing impatient, Santos snapped, "Family time's over, we don't have all night."

Micah tussled Faye's hair and shooed her into the cabin.

Santos pointed to a thirty-foot tender boat moored alongside the *Valentina*. "Let's go."

Hans was leaning against the deck rail, waiting for them.

Micah asked, "Why do you need us to tag along on a refueling stop? Are you making us pump gas too?"

Hans said, "No. Our original geologist only managed to get this far on his own. He was half dead by then, so a floatplane evacuated him to Mr. Batista's yacht."

"So?"

"He told us he'd been carrying a satchel with additional samples, but in the confusion, our men didn't send it along with him. It was a happy accident that he had the one sample in his pocket. We haven't been able to contact anyone at the depot, so we need you to locate the missing bag and bring it back, along with any other relevant materials. I won't be coming along."

Off in the distance Micah saw Batista standing on the deck of his yacht. "I take it the big boss isn't coming either?"

Hans said, "Why should he? It's a simple refueling stop."

Micah thought, *At a remote site you've lost all contact with.*

Leaning closer than necessary, Santos said, "Get in the boat."

Before Micah could reply, Catalina gently grabbed his arm and steered him to the tender, whispering, "Not the best time for a confrontation."

The tender boat made its way towards the depot, allowing time for Micah to mull over what he'd been told. *Why did they lose contact, and what the hell are we wandering into?*

Santos sat a few feet away, blank faced.

No surprise, Micah thought, *the guy could probably take a nap in a tiger's cage.*

From a distance, the fuel depot looked like any one of hundreds of fishing villages along the Amazon. There was a roughly hewn floating dock lit by strings of yellow bulbs. A dozen stilt houses dotted the riverbank. As they drew closer Micah could see larger structures set further back from the riverbank—likely fishermen's bunkhouses and mess halls.

He asked Santos, "Is this a fishing village?"

"It was. Mr. Batista took it over as a fuel depot 'cause we'll be moving a lot of boats through here."

Micah could only imagine what "took it over" really meant. He noticed a network of steel towers clustered around the buildings with reflective plates mounted on them. "Are those solar arrays?"

Santos nodded. "It's cheaper than running the generators all night. Once we establish the outpost, those solar arrays will get transported there. Mr. Batista thinks of everything."

The tender boat pulled alongside the dock. Santos was already shouting orders before it was even tied off. The men climbed out, making straight for rows of fifty-five-gallon drums.

Minutes later, the Multi Cat barge pulled alongside the dock. Men shouted back and forth as hoses were spooled out from the barge's large fuel storage cubes.

Micah asked, "Problem?"

Santos said, "The pumps aren't working. The main generator must be down." He strode off into the compound. Glancing back, he shouted, "Come on!"

Micah and Catalina jogged to catch up.

Looking around, she asked, "Aren't there supposed to be people here?"

Santos spat on the ground, muttering, "The assholes are probably all drunk."

At the far end of the compound, they found an industrial generator surrounded by jerry cans of gasoline.

Micah aimed his flashlight at the fuel gauge and said, "It's bone dry."

Santos kicked the generator, shouting, "*Ramerrão*," then grabbed a jerry can. Without looking up, he shouted, "That green building's the infirmary, so start looking in there. Get to work!"

Catalina said, "You heard the man," while steering Micah towards the green building. She whispered, "I don't want to spend an extra thirty seconds around that Franken-psycho. Plus, who knows, we might find something lying around that'll help us."

Santos shouted something. Seconds later, one of the deckhands jogged over to join Micah and Catalina.

Tapping the AK-47 slung over his shoulder, he said, "Santos told me to keep an eye on you."

Catalina muttered, "Fucker doesn't miss a trick."

The gentle breeze picked up, blowing leaves and dust along the dirt laneway.

Catalina said, "At least there's a breeze."

Micah said, "That means there's a storm coming in. That's why Santos is in such a rush to get out of here."

Lightning flashed across the sky, brilliantly illuminating the surrounding rainforest.

Micah counted the seconds before they heard the low rumble of thunder. "It's about an hour out."

Sniffing the air, Catalina asked, "You smell that?"

Micah caught a whiff of something that stung his nostrils. "Whew, smells like blue cheese and Drano, but it's not coming from anything here."

Pointing at the rainforest, Catalina said, "No, it's blowing in from the trees."

Micah sniffed again. He couldn't place the caustic odor, but there was something familiar about it.

The strands of yellow lights strung along the laneway flickered, growing dimmer by the moment.

Micah said, "The solar batteries must be running low."

"So the crew's drunk, the generator's empty and the batteries are dying. Our man Batista runs one tight operation."

The deckhand either didn't understand her, or didn't care.

Micah heard a metallic squeak and rhythmic knocking coming from their left. Panning his flashlight, he said, "This must be it."

A wooden sign swinging in the breeze read *Enfermaria*. The dirt walkway led to a green clapboard stilt house.

In Portuguese, the deckhand said, "Go ahead, I gotta piss," and jogged off towards the trees.

Catalina watched the infirmary's open screen door blowing back and forth on squealing hinges and said, "Looks inviting."

#

Faye sat on the cot, trying to read her book, but couldn't stop worrying about her father. Being alone was scary, but it was still better than having that weirdo Hans hanging around. He reminded her of the creepy principal in *Vampire High School*.

Lightning flashed outside the porthole and she instinctively counted the seconds before the thunder rolled.

It's just lightning, she told herself, *nothing to be scared of*, but her vampire book suddenly lost its appeal. She sat on her cot, knees to chest, hugging her pillow, wishing she was brave like Catalina. The thunder rolled in. *Five seconds, still miles away.*

The cabin was silent. Then she heard a soft tapping sound coming from somewhere in the room.

Faye yelled, "If you're a mouse, go away!"

The tapping started again. Growing curious, she got up, following the sound to the big work table. The black-and-silver mineral fragment lay there, shaking like a cell phone on vibrate. There was another flash of lightning outside. Faye ignored it, leaning in closer, watching the sliver dance in place.

She whispered, "Are you alive?"

The vibration stopped and the fragment went still.

"Why'd you stop? Are you scared of the lightning?"

Thunder boomed and Faye nearly jumped out of her skin. She retreated back to the cot, hugging her pillow while keeping an eye on the fragment.

#

Micah took a few tentative steps into the infirmary and heard something crunch beneath his boots. Panning his flashlight down, he saw that the floor was littered with broken glass. Catalina flicked a light switch, but the ceiling fluorescents barely flickered. It was just enough light to see that the place was a shambles. Tables were overturned, and the beds had been pushed against another door. The mattresses looked like they'd been fed into a tree shredder, and the weird chemical odor permeated the room.

Catalina whispered, "Everything about this place is wrong." She bent down and plucked a scalpel off the floor, tucking it into her boot.

Micah whispered, "No shit. Let's get out of here," and headed for the door.

As soon as he stepped off the porch, he stopped and whispered, "Listen."

"I don't hear anything."

"Yeah, no crickets, no birds … nothing."

"Maybe it's the storm."

"No, the night critters don't shut up till the rain's right on top of them." Micah walked closer to the tree line, the black mud sucking at his boots. He played his flashlight along the trees, but all he saw were branches swaying in the rising wind.

There was a sharp bang, followed by a low rumble. Micah jumped then realized it was only the generator lurching to life. The dim strands of yellow bulbs sprang to life, illuminating the area. The noxious jungle odor grew stronger.

Sniffing the air, Micah said, "I've smelled that before, but I just can't place it." He looked out at the trees again.

Pointing her flashlight at the ground, Catalina shouted, "Holy shit!"

The dark mud was littered with gleaming white bones. She focused the beam on a pair of human skulls.

Micah knelt down closer and said, "They're perfectly clean, like the meat was boiled off. Looks like they went down fighting too." He pointed the flashlight at some pistols still clenched in the skeletal hands. "I wonder if it could've been those cannibals."

Catalina said, "Well, they were pretty damn hungry," and pointed at the ground ahead.

There were more bones, all picked clean. At least five human skulls were littered among the remains. It was a killing field spanning from their position out to the rainforest.

Micah said, "We need to get out—"

Then something burst out of the trees, barreling towards them. Micah snatched up a leg bone to use as a club.

The charging shape let out a shrill scream. A flash of lightning revealed it to be the deckhand, his body drenched in blood. He ran toward them, stumbled and collapsed at their feet.

Micah bent down to help then jumped back. The deckhand's body was covered in huge red insects—each at least seven inches long. Two of them were latched on to his face, peeling the flesh away as he screamed. Another was burrowing into his throat.

Something flashed in Micah's mind—the smell. He looked out at the trees blowing in the wind. In a flash of lightning the rainforest floor came alive. A writhing carpet of red insects was bearing down on them.

Micah grabbed Catalina's arm, shouting, "Driver ants!"

He spun around, ready to run for the dock. Another wave of ants emerged from the rainforest behind them, cutting off their escape.

Pointing to a cluster of buildings, he yelled, "This way!" and ran. After a few seconds he glanced back. Catalina wasn't with him. He raced back to find her picking through the bones—the writhing mass of insects closing in.

He ran over, grabbing her arm. "What're you doing?"

She stood up, holding an arm bone. "I needed to do something!"

"What, die?"

He tried to pull her away when the screaming deckhand reached out, clamping his hand around her ankle. A stream of the monstrous ants crawled along his outstretched arm, making a beeline for her leg. Micah slammed his foot down onto the man's wrist, breaking it, along with his grip. An ant leapt off his arm, latching on to Catalina's pants leg. Micah kicked it free before it could get a grip. It rolled off onto its back, legs thrashing furiously.

Micah stared at it in amazement. It was clearly an ant—but unlike anything he'd seen before. The insect was easily seven inches long with vertical serrated pincers.

Staring in disbelief, Catalina asked, "Are there really ants the size of rats?"

Grabbing her arm, Micah shouted, "Sure looks that way. Move!"

They ran, with the wave of ants only yards behind them. Micah weaved through the cluster of buildings, hunting for a clear path to the river.

Screams echoed in the distance.

Catalina said, "They're already at the docks."

"So much for that plan." Micah saw a faded yellow building with the word *Refeitorio* stenciled on it. Grabbing her arm, he yelled, "There!" and charged up the stilt building's stairs, kicking his way through the front door.

Without slowing down, Catalina shouted, "Why here?"

"Trust me!"

Micah ran through what appeared to be a mess hall, straight into the kitchen. A dozen ants swarmed through the open doorway and stopped. An instant later, their ranks swelled to twenty, then a hundred. Then, almost as one, they marched towards the kitchen door, ignoring the bounty of food around them.

Micah slammed the kitchen door closed and scanned the room—a long, narrow space with a stainless steel island running down its center.

Catalina said, "Can we hide in the refrigerator?"

"They'll chew their way in, or we'll suffocate." Then he saw a large pantry and ducked inside.

Catalina asked, "What can I do?"

Micah emerged carrying a ten-pound paper sack labeled *Pimento-de-caiena.* "Grab more of these!"

The bottom of the door buckled inward as the first wave of ants crawled under the doorjamb. Micah tore the top of the bag open and shook it out, covering the base of the doorway in black pepper. His eyes burned as if he'd been riot sprayed.

The first ants stopped, writhing in place.

Micah yelled, "Ants can't handle pepper, even these monsters."

Catalina ran out with more bags.

Micah shouted, "Cover the floor!"

She tore one open, scattering the contents, then backed up against the stove, waiting for instructions. She heard a clanging sound behind her and jumped away. A cluster of ants tumbled out of the ceiling vent onto the stove. Catalina hit the ventilator switch, turning the exhaust fan on. The blades ground up the oncoming ants, momentarily halting their advance. Thinking fast, she twisted the rows of burners to "On." Ants squirmed, roasting on the flaming burners. She tore open a bag of pepper and released it in the air under the exhaust vent. The black dust was sucked up the exhaust pipe.

"Huff on that."

Micah threw two more bags down, blanketing the floor in black pepper, grateful that the locals used so damn much of it. Ants crawled onto the barrier, only to curl up in agony. But their success was short-lived. While the pepper paralyzed the first wave, the second wave just used their bodies as a walkway.

Catalina asked, "Where to now?"

Micah heard mandibles tearing at the wooden walls and saw splinters already falling away. He glanced around and announced, "We're going up, but first…" He grabbed an industrial-sized jug of vinegar, pouring it over her body then drenching himself. "They hate vinegar, it screws with their sensory stuff."

Micah looked up at the vaulted ceiling and its network of horizontal and vertical rafters. "There!" He pointed up at a trap door leading to the roof. Catalina grabbed a chair, placing it on top of the kitchen island. They climbed up. The chair raised Micah high enough to grab the overhead beam and pull himself up.

A chunk of wall near the stove caved in, unleashing a squirming torrent of ants.

Micah leaned down and grabbed Catalina's arm, hauling her up. Ants were already swarming up the steel kitchen island.

They climbed up the rafters to the ceiling hatch. Micah slammed his shoulder against it three times until it popped open.

They crawled out onto the roof, which offered a view of the dock. Micah couldn't make out what was happening there, but the screams echoing in the night told the tale. The ground beneath them was now covered in ants, some of which were already scaling the building.

Micah said, "Any ideas are good at this point."

Catalina shouted, "Look!" She pointed to the electrical lines running a few feet above the building. They were connected to a junction box atop a wooden pole. From there, the wire ran on a downward slope to another building closer to the docks. "We jump out onto that post, climb it, then go hand over hand down the cable to the next building."

They jogged to the edge of the roof. Up close the post was further out than she'd thought.

She asked, "Do you think you can jump to it?"

Micah saw a wave of ants erupting from the roof hatch. "I can now."

Catalina took a few steps back, ran and leapt off the roof. She barely caught the pole. Using the nodes as handholds, she scrambled up.

Micah backed up enough to get a running start and charged forward. Just as he reached the edge the roof buckled, almost tripping him. He launched himself forward, latching on to a climbing hold with one arm, swinging back and forth until he got a grip with his other hand. The roof behind him was already blanketed in ants. Climbing up, hand over hand, he reached Catalina. Then he felt something tugging at his boot. An ant was latched on to it, dangling by its mandibles.

He shouted, "There's one on my boot," while kicking at an ant the size of his hand. It hung on like a pit bull.

Catalina locked her leg around a climbing strut, freeing her hands, then yanked the scalpel from her boot. She slashed at the ant three times, but the blade barely scratched its thick exoskeleton. The enraged ant latched its front legs around Micah's boot, dislodging its pincers to snap at her.

She yelled, "Kick it!"

Micah did. The ant tumbled into the darkness, leaving the side of his boot shredded and bloody.

Catalina asked, "Did it bite you?"

"Just enough to hurt like hell."

Micah looked down. The bottom half of the pole was covered in a rising mass of ants. He shimmied up further, reaching the top junction box. It took him a few hard pulls to yank the cover off. With the flashlight in his mouth, he examined the connections.

He muttered, "Shit!" The line wasn't connected to the solar panels—it was the direct feed from the generator, carrying enough voltage to kill them both.

Catalina reached for the line.

Micah yelled, "Don't! There's still current running through it." Grabbing the line would electrocute him, but he noticed that the dangling junction box cover was lined with rubber. After a few hard tugs the ancient glue gave way, allowing him to rip out the rubber liner.

Wrapping it around his hand, he grabbed the electrical line and yanked hard. It tore loose, creating a momentary Tesla coil of electricity. The disconnected wire swung in the air, spraying sparks.

Micah said, "We're good now, but that wire's not strong so we'll go one at a time. Get moving."

Catalina went hand over hand down the descending wire. Micah watched her progress while glancing down at the oncoming ants. They were already two thirds of the way up the wooden pole and climbing fast.

He muttered, "Come on, come on," but even if he started climbing down immediately, the ants would be on the wire within seconds.

Catalina reached the other building and jumped down onto the roof.

Micah grabbed the wire and swung off the pole just as the first ants reached his level. Hanging by one arm he reached back, grabbing the sparking power cable and pressing it against the wooden pole. A blast of sparks singed his hand, but he managed to hang on to the cable. The high voltage coursed through the rain-soaked wood, jolting the ants loose. The highest ones fell by the dozen, knocking the lower ones loose like dominos.

Micah released the live power cable and began descending, hand over hand, his upper back muscles screaming. Once he was level with the other building he swung off, landing flat on the roof. The impact tore the aged shingles loose. He slid down, scrabbling for something to grab. Catalina latched on to his wrist, digging her heels into the mushy tar roof.

Micah saw ants already traveling single file along the cable and yelled, "The scalpel!"

Catalina tossed it to him. Micah sawed at the cable while watching the approaching ants moving along it like tightrope walkers. After some frantic cutting he severed the line. It fell away, taking the ants with it.

Looking around, Catalina said, "There are no ants up here."

"That's 'cause there weren't any people to chow down on. Give 'em time."

Micah looked out at the river, so near yet so far away. One of the gunboats launched a series of aerial flares into the night sky. The brilliant red flares slowly drifted down on parachutes, illuminating the hell scape awaiting them.

Looking down at the hordes of ants on the ground, Catalina said, "Those bastards must be starving."

"No. There's plenty to eat here. There were even bags of sugar in the kitchen. They're not here to eat."

"What then?"

"They're here to kill. Oh, and that nasty smell was formic acid. Colony odor. I should have recognized it and run like hell."

"Nobody's perfect."

Micah had hoped there'd be a second line from this building that they could shimmy down, but there was just an electrical conduit pipe running to the ground. "We're trapped," he said.

Roof shingles behind them began to tremble, until one crumbled inward.

Catalina said, "Here they come."

CHAPTER SEVEN

Santos finished pouring enough gas into the generator to get the job done. Then he jogged back to the pier, thinking, *Let these drunken assholes fill it up when we're gone.*

The fuel pumps were already running when he arrived. Drums of fuel were being loaded onto the Multi Cat's deck, while its internal storage tanks were being filled. The men were working hard, but Santos tossed in some verbal abuse for motivation.

He stood on the Multi Cat's deck, observing the operation while avoiding any physical work.

That's when he heard the first screams.

Two men had been rolling drums over towards the pier when they released the drums and started screaming. Both dashed towards the water until one fell to the ground.

Santos panned the Multi Cat's searchlight onto the men. The running man was covered in some kind of reddish mud. A second later, Santos realized that mud was alive.

A man on the dock fell to the ground, screaming. His body was covered in huge red insects—at least a dozen of them. The man managed to stand and charge up the ramp onto the Multi Cat. As soon as Santos saw the insects he raised his AK-47, slamming the butt into his chest. The screaming man tumbled into the water.

One of the insects fell onto the deck. Santos saw the huge ant and brought his rifle butt down on it hard, but it kept squirming. It took two more hits to crush its thick exoskeleton.

The pier had descended into chaos. At least three men were under attack, while others were scrambling to get to the tender boat.

Santos turned to the Multi Cat's crew, yelling, "Turn on the drafting pumps, and unhook those fuel hoses, now!"

The drafting pumps kicked in, sucking river water into the boat's fire suppression system.

Santos unspooled the thick black fire hose from its gurney, feeling the pressure rumbling inside. He opened the nozzle, unleashing a three-hundred-PSI stream of water. The high pressure line washed back the first wave of ants coming up the gangway while also knocking down the men trying to escape.

Despite the spraying hose, two men managed to crawl onto the deck, where they lay screaming.

Santos threw down the fire hose, drew his knife and slashed the mooring ropes, shouting, "Pull out, pull out!"

One of the crew disconnected the fuel lines running from the pier. The Multi Cat pulled away, leaving the hoses pumping gasoline into the river.

Santos looked back from the departing Multi Cat. The men on the dock would probably die, but at least he'd managed to get the storage tanks half full.

Batista would approve.

#

Micah stood on the roof, searching for a way to escape. The drifting aerial flares illuminated what lay between them and the water—a hundred-yard gauntlet crawling with ants. The entire run would only take twenty seconds, but the ants would be on them before they'd gotten halfway.

Catalina shook the conduit pipe leading to the ground and said, "What if we just shimmy down and run like hell?"

"Trust me; that's a bad idea." He slapped his forehead, muttering, "Come on, dumb shit, think."

Catalina glanced over the side of the building and said, "Hey, why's the ground right under us clear?"

Micah heard the generator rumbling below. "They must not like that little patch 'cause the ground's saturated with fuel."

One of the aerial flares drifted to the ground, landing about forty yards in front of them, its magnesium core still burning brightly.

Micah's mind flashed back to the rows of gas cans around the generator. He wondered, *How many did Santos use?* He turned to Catalina and said, "Okay, we shimmy down."

"But—"

"But we don't run till I say. I'm going first."

Micah grabbed the conduit pipe, half shimmying, half falling. He hit the ground hard, already scrambling for the generator.

Catalina landed, shouting, "You're going the wrong way!" But she followed anyway.

Micah kicked the line of eight jerry cans. The first four were empty, but the rest were full. He unscrewed the cap, picked up another full can, and said, "Grab one more!"

He kicked furiously at the generator's fuel tank until the feeder hose ruptured. Gasoline gushed out onto the ground.

He ran back the way they'd come, pouring gas onto the ground as he went. Using his running start, he lobbed the open gas can. It landed, bouncing across the ground, spraying gasoline in every direction. But it stopped, falling yards short of the burning flare, alerting the ants to their presence. Now they were approaching from both directions.

Catalina hurled her can. It landed halfway between them and the first can.

Micah muttered, "Way short!"

Catalina said, "No it wasn't," then reached under her shirt, drawing a handgun.

Micah said, "Where the hell—"

She fired twice, hitting Micah's jerry can. Unlike in the movies, the bullets didn't ignite the gasoline but the impact launched the half empty can over to the dwindling flare. It burst into flames. A trail of fire rolled across the ground, heading towards them. The running flames enveloped the jerry can Catalina had thrown.

She grabbed his arm, shouting, "Take cover!"

Both huddled beside the building as the jerry can detonated in a mini fireball. The trail of flame continued across the ground, running past them, straight for the leaking generator.

Micah noticed a tall rain barrel and knocked it over, dousing them both in water.

He watched the ants in front of them inching back from the flame and yelled, "Fire-walking time!"

They ran full tilt, staying perilously close to the burning line of fire—so close that steam billowed from Micah's wet pants leg. Burning ants rolled across the ground in front of them, while others shrank back from the flames.

Glancing back, Micah saw a regiment of ants swarming past the generator, heading straight for them. The blazing trail of fire reached the generator, igniting the fuel gushing from the tank.

Without slowing down, Micah opened the last jerry can and threw it ahead of them. It was already burning by the time it left his hand. The cartwheeling ball of fire extended their flaming path to the pier.

The generator's gas tank superheated, exploding in a ball of fire. A blanket of flames swept across the ground, engulfing the pursuing ants.

Micah kept running full tilt for the rough-hewn pier, yelling, "Don't even stop; just dive into the water!" Then he realized Catalina had passed him.

Both of them bolted across the burning pier, launching themselves over the edge. Micah sank under the pitch-black water, surfacing a moment later. Catalina came up a few feet away.

Micah saw the tender boat drifting to their right. A lone sailor stood inside, waving his arms frantically. They swam towards it.

One of the distant gunboats launched another aerial flare, lighting up the area.

Micah realized the frantic sailor was covered in ants. The screaming man leapt into the water and never surfaced.

Micah turned to Catalina, shouting, "That boat's an ant farm," then looked back at the burning dock. Most of the ants had been consumed by the fire, but the next ranks were crawling across their smoldering bodies and tumbling into the water. And they weren't sinking—they were swimming.

Micah said, "I forgot, ants can swim."

Catalina yelled, "So can you! Get moving!"

They both swam towards the distant flotilla. The descending aerial flare lit up the water's surface in a glittering rainbow, meaning the water was coated in a layer of fuel.

Micah glanced back at the burning dock thinking, *If it's diesel we're fine, but if it's gas…*

The burning pier collapsed into the river. The surface of the water ignited into a rolling sheet of flame.

… we're fucked.

Micah yelled, "Dive!"

Catalina dove straight down. Micah followed. Rolling onto his back he saw the surface above them burst into flames. He kicked hard. Catalina swam a few feet to his right. The fire raged above them, spreading faster than they could swim.

Micah kept moving, the mantra, *Got to get back to Faye*, repeating in his mind.

Catalina tugged his arm, pointing up. The water above them was dark, showing no sign of fire. Three hard kicks got him to the surface, gasping for air.

Two sailors who'd somehow escaped the carnage bobbed in the water ahead of them.

Micah took a final look back at the depot. The water was a sheet of flames, but at least that fire had killed the pursuing ants. The depot itself was an inferno. Turning towards the flotilla, he was relieved to see the two sailors being hauled into a rescue boat. Catalina treaded water while waving her arms and shouting to the boat.

Micah swam over to her. After coughing up a mouthful of water, he asked, "Where'd you get that gun?"

"I picked it off those skeletons. They weren't using it. But let's keep it to ourselves till we can put it to good use."

After a few minutes of treading water, they were hauled into the boat. The two shell-shocked sailors were huddled inside, glazed eyes locked on the burning depot.

Catalina asked, "How many got away?"

Staring into the distant flames, one said, "Santos took off on the fuel barge with two wounded guys. Those things killed everybody else." He turned to Catalina, his face a mask of terror. In a near whisper he said, "I've been on this river all my life and there's nothing like that… They are *o diabos*."

Catalina recognized the Portuguese word for demons.

Micah tallied the numbers in his head. Batista had lost at least eight men, his reserve fuel and at least one boat.

Catalina whispered, "Maybe Batista will stop and regroup or just turn the hell around."

The tender boat passed Batista's yacht, now moored near the *Valentina*. Micah saw the big man himself, standing on its deck, watching the inferno while holding a glass of wine. Not the posture of someone planning to turn back.

The shell-shocked sailor just sat, staring into the distant flames, muttering, "*O diabos,*" again and again.

Micah watched Batista take a sip of wine and muttered, "You got that right, brother."

#

The moment the boat came alongside the *Valentina*, Micah was off and running for the cabin, Catalina only seconds behind him.

As soon as the door opened, Faye raced over to Micah, shouting, "Daddy!"

Micah held her tight, relief washing over him. "I told you we'd be back, honey. Are you okay?"

"Yeah."

Catalina stood in the doorway watching them.

Micah asked, "Can you stay with her? I need some answers."

Catalina nodded, and Micah was out the door. He heard screams coming from the deck below and followed the sound.

After pushing past a cluster of deckhands he barged into a large cabin. Hans leaned over a shrieking deckhand laid out on a wooden table. A squirming seven-inch ant was clamped onto the man's forearm. Hans alternated between studying the insect and flipping through an iPad.

In Portuguese, the man screamed, "It burns, somebody kill that little bastard!"

Another man wielding pliers was poised to dislodge the ant.

Micah yelled, "Stop! If you kill it with the pincers embedded the bite will go gangrenous. Somebody run to the mess and grab some vinegar. Now!"

A deckhand scrambled for the galley.

Micah noticed Santos seated at the far end of the table, shirtless, looking bored.

The wounded man shrieked, "It burns!"

Hans leaned over to Micah, asking, "What's causing the burning?"

"Ants inject formic acid. We're just lucky these aren't giant bullet ants." He leaned in closer, studying the monstrous insect. "This ain't my first rodeo in the Amazon, and I've seen some crazy shit out here but never ants the size of my shoe."

Hans scrolled through an iPad encyclopedia. "You're correct. The Amazon giant ant is the largest, but that's an eighth of this one's size. I think we're looking at a Titan ant."

"Never heard of it."

"That's because they only exist in fossils."

"What's that supposed to mean?"

"Paleontology is kind of a hobby of mine. Here, look for yourself." He handed the iPad to Micah.

Onscreen was a photo of a fossilized ant, placed next to a ruler for scale—it was roughly six inches.

Hans continued, "A million or so years ago, there were ants like this, back when everything in the Amazon was bigger. These must be an aberration, some kind of holdover."

Micah tossed the iPad back to him, shouting, "Where's that vinegar?"

The deckhand pushed through the crowd blocking the doorway, holding up a bottle of vinegar.

Micah grabbed the bottle and said, "Be ready to grab it with those pliers."

He poured vinegar over the ant, sending it into spasms. After a few seconds it released its grip and lay wriggling on the table. The deckhand clamped the pliers around its head and held it up high. The deckhands crowding the doorway muttered in amazement.

Hans found an empty mason jar and they dropped the ant inside, clamping the lid tight.

Micah examined the injured man's wound and said, "Flush the bite with clean water till the burning stops; then get some antiseptic on it."

He turned to Hans. "Here's what doesn't make sense to me. Those things killed everybody in that fuel depot, stripped 'em to the bone, then went back into the jungle to wait. If they were on the march they should have eaten everything, even the bark off the trees. That mess hall was jammed with food, but they didn't even touch it. I want to know where they came from and why they have such a sweet tooth for people."

Hans stared at the ant, furiously throwing itself against the glass jar, and said, "I have no explanation. It can only be an aberration that we've never seen before, perhaps something forced out of the deep rainforest by deforestation."

The PA system crackled with feedback then Batista's voice rang out. "Now hear this. We've suffered an unfortunate setback, but be assured we have enough fuel to reach our destination, where additional supplies and boats are waiting. So we will press on. That is all." After a burst of static, the PA system went quiet.

Micah thought, *That's it. Not a moment of silence or even a mention of the men who died.*

He glanced over at Santos, sitting placidly at the table, and said, "Hey Santos, thanks for all your help back there."

Santos glared at Micah then stood up, revealing a torso drenched in blood. Two writhing Titan ants were locked on to his upper abdomen. Micah could only imagine the pain.

Stifling a yawn, Santos asked, "You mind pouring some vinegar on them?"

#

It was another hour before Micah got back to the cabin. Catalina shushed him as he stepped inside then pointed to Faye, sleeping soundly.

"What'd you find out?" she whispered.

Micah sat down next to Faye, watching her sleep, and said, "Exactly nothing, except that they lost eight guys and one boat. Plus Santos must be related to *Robocop* or something, 'cause he's a freak of nature."

"What about your foot?"

"A lot of blood, but it was a minor cut. I put some super glue on it."

"I heard Batista's announcement, so I guess we're pressing on."

"Yeah, Batista didn't even bother making an appearance. Oh, did you stash that you know what?"

"Yup, and I got you one too." Catalina slid her hands under the cot's mattress, producing a pair of pistols. One was a compact Glock, the other a stubby .32 revolver, colloquially known as a Saturday Night Special. Handing him the revolver, she said, "It ain't much, but at least it's something. But we need to wait for the right moment."

Eyeing the feeble weapon, Micah asked, "How come I get the little one?"

"You may know what you're doing in the jungle, but I'm the one who can drop a moving target at fifty feet."

"Fair enough." Micah slipped the tiny handgun in his pocket next to the emerald and zipped it tight.

Lightning flashed through the porthole, instantaneously followed by thunder loud as a gunshot.

Micah said, "The storm's here."

A deluge of rain came down, pounding the hull like drumsticks.

Micah peeled off his shirt and started removing his pants.

Catalina asked, "What are you doing?"

"A warm Amazon downpour is the best shower you'll ever have. Do you wanna go first? All you do is step out the door, spin around awhile and let nature do its thing."

"I don't think taking a shower with this crew watching is the safest move."

"They're all huddled down below. Plus, from what I've seen, most of the crew hasn't had a bath since baptism." He turned his back to her and said, "Don't worry; I won't peek."

After a moment's deliberation, Catalina said, "Sure, I'm pretty rank." She quickly undressed and stepped out onto the deck.

But Micah did peek, a little. He wasn't being a voyeur, it was just that, after all the horror, it was healing to gaze on something beautiful.

CHAPTER EIGHT

After his shower, Micah hung up his hammock and stretched out. He heard Catalina snoring peacefully a few feet away, amazed at how quickly fear and adrenaline gave way to physical exhaustion. Faye was fast asleep on the cot to his right. Micah pushed the evening's terrors out of his mind, focusing instead on the rain rhythmically pounding at the deck and the engines rumbling beneath him. He quickly drifted off.

Something bumped against the hull, jarring him awake. He sat up, unsure how long he'd been out. The rain had slackened, though lightning was still flashing through the porthole. He was about to roll over when another flash of lightning lit up the cabin.

The cot beside him was empty.

Micah jumped out of the hammock, scanning the cabin, shouting, "Faye!"

Catalina bolted awake, asking, "What's wrong?"

"Faye's gone."

"Gone? Where would she go?"

Something slammed against the hull, jostling the boat.

Micah's mind reeled until he recalled one of Faye's incessant questions. *"Dad, can monkeys swim?"*

Grabbing his boots, he shouted, "Come on!" and scrambled out the door to the exterior passageway.

Catalina yelled, "Where're we going?"

"The front deck."

One of the gunboats roared past the *Valentina* followed by a second, their searchlight beams trained on the water.

Catalina said, "Something's up."

Micah rounded the corner, almost slipping on the rain-soaked gangway leading down. Once at the bottom he dashed toward the front deck. Something wet and furry hit him in the face, almost sending him over the railing. He pried a squealing monkey off his head, tossed it aside, and kept running. The passageway opened onto the fifty-foot-long, uncovered front deck.

Faye was already releasing her second crate of monkeys, shouting, "Go, swim away!"

But the monkeys were content to scramble around the deck, snatching fruit from the hanging baskets.

In frustration, Faye shouted, "You're not listening, run away!"

Something slammed hard against the *Valentina*. The boat listed right sharply, a wave splashing across the deck.

After catching her balance, Catalina looked over the side. In a flash of lightning, she saw what looked like a whale swim past the boat—but it was thinner and longer.

One of the gunboats let loose a burst of automatic weapons fire, followed by a second. A moment later, Catalina watched flares rocketing up from one of the gunboats.

Micah ran towards Faye, only to be rammed by a frantic donkey. He tumbled onto the deck, muttering, "You had to let him loose too?"

The flares reached their apex then popped open, releasing parachutes. The river lit up in the flickering red light of the aerial flares.

The loose monkeys all froze in place then leapt into the water—like rats abandoning a ship.

Micah muttered, "That can't be good," then got back on his feet, shouting, "Faye! Get over here! Now!"

The little girl froze, knowing she was busted.

The boat listed again and something rose from the water on the port side—a huge serpentine shape, towering twenty feet over the deck. Gray skin and brownish spots glistened in the flickering light. The head was arrow shaped, with emerald-green eyes reflecting the burning flares. A huge, forked tongue darted out, tasting the air.

Micah was staring up at an impossibly huge snake. It stared right back at him.

A gunboat came alongside, its machine guns firing erratically. A few bullets must have struck the target. The snake twisted in the water, slamming its body against the *Valentina*. The entire boat listed starboard, sending crates and animals over the side.

Micah ran towards Faye, only to be struck by a crate full of chickens. He watched in horror as his daughter slid across the deck.

Faye screamed, "Daddy!" then vanished over the side.

Micah bellowed, "No!" and without hesitation, he dove overboard.

#

The snake twisted around, hammering its head down onto the gunboat like a club. The impact sent two men over the side. The machine gunner swiveled his turret, trying to draw a bead. The snake snatched him up in its jaws, biting him in half then spitting the upper portion into the river. The gunboat listed sharply, water flooding into the pilot's cabin, until it was on its side, half submerged.

The snake vanished beneath the water.

Catalina ran to the edge of the deck, scanning the churning river. She spotted Faye about forty feet out, barely staying afloat. She could also see Micah splashing around, desperate to locate her.

Catalina yelled, "Three o'clock," while training her flashlight on Faye.

Thankfully, Micah heard her and swam toward his daughter.

The *Valentina* lurched again, sending two more men overboard. A braying donkey kicked aside some loose crates then leapt over the side. Catalina clung on to the deck rail, desperate to help rescue Faye. A sailor rolled across the deck, flailing at the air. Catalina grabbed his arm just before he went over the side. The desperate man's other arm latched on to the deck rail, hanging on for dear life.

The snake's head rose from the water, looming over Catalina, its open mouth a midnight-black void. Its head slammed down, jaws locking around the cowering sailor and the railing he clung to. It rose, the railing and man dangling from its jaws. It shook its head three times then spat both out.

Catalina rolled for cover, barely avoiding the steel rail crashing onto the deck. The sailor's pulverized body was entwined in the metal. She crawled to the port side, hoping to gain some distance.

Another aerial flare shot upward, illuminating a new horror—clusters of black caimans swimming in from the riverbank. The lead caiman clamped down on a drowning sailor, dragging him under.

Catalina shouted, "Shit!" knowing that Faye and Micah were doomed unless she did something. She saw the gunboat, partially submerged and sinking fast. But its front-mounted machine guns were still above the waterline. The *Valentina* was passing the crippled gunboat, so it was now or never.

Yelling, "Screw it!" Catalina took ten steps back and charged. She leapt across the gap, splashing down a few feet short of the foundering gunboat. Swimming frantically, she managed to grab the partially submerged railing and haul herself up. A caiman lurched from the water behind her, its snapping jaws barely missing her leg. After failing to get a foothold it slid back into the water to search for easier prey.

The close call barely even registered with Catalina, now totally focused on reaching the machine guns. By gripping the mooring tie-downs she managed to climb the tilted deck. She was able to grab the edge of the gun turret, pull herself up, and peer inside.

The good news was there were a pair of belt-fed machine guns mounted to a dual tripod. The bad news—the snake had bitten the gunner in half, leaving his lower body wedged in the turret. His entrails were wound around the guns. Catalina ignored the sickening tableau.

The twin guns were Russian made belt-fed machine guns. Catalina stared at them for a moment, cursing under her breath. Then she realized that, like many Russian designs, they were knockoffs of American models.

"I can do this!"

They were copies of M240 Bravo medium machine guns—a weapon she'd trained on during her army hitch. The barrel of one gun was hopelessly twisted, but its sister weapon looked intact. The problem was that the turret was hopelessly locked, and, given the listing boat, she could only shoot straight up.

She muttered, "No choice," while reaching under the gun's mount, fishing through the human entrails wound around it. After a few seconds of blind groping, she found the cotter pin and yanked. The functional machine gun came free of the mount, allowing her to hold it and fire—Rambo style.

#

Micah saw Faye struggling to stay afloat and swam toward her. A black shape slid past him, bearing down on the little girl.

Recognizing the caiman, Micah yelled, "Faye! Stop kicking, just float. You hear me? Float!"

Amazingly, she followed his instructions. But a nearby deckhand failed to heed the warning, splashing frantically. The caiman changed course, making for the drowning man. He only screamed once before vanishing beneath the water. Micah knew the caiman would hold him under until he drowned.

A twenty-foot tender boat zipped across the water, making a beeline for a cluster of drowning men. Its presence offered Micah a ray of hope.

The monstrous snake rose directly into the boat's path. The tender tried to veer off, but the snake's head hammered down. The impact capsized the boat, sending its crew into the river. The snake snapped one man up in its jaws, spat him out, then went for the other.

Micah swam harder, desperate to reach Faye. Glancing left, he saw a pair of caimans coming straight for him. There was no way he was outfighting the Amazon's apex predator. He heard the chatter of an automatic weapon, and a line of bullets stitched the water. One of the caimans lurched, twisting wildly. A second burst of machine gun fire tore into the other caiman.

#

Catalina shouted, "Yeah!" and loosed another burst.

By now she was ankle deep in water with expended shells floating around her. Within minutes she'd sink enough to be caiman bait, but all that mattered was saving Faye. Aiming was a challenge, but, thankfully, the 7.62 ammo belt was interspersed with tracer rounds. The tracers acted like a laser pointer, guiding her aim.

She saw a cluster of caimans approaching Faye and fired another burst, careful to keep the little girl out of the line of fire. It appeared that Faye and Micah were in the clear, at least for the moment.

Catalina saw a pair of sailors bobbing in the water about fifty feet away. A group of caimans had seen them too. A few carefully aimed bursts killed two of the beasts. Their bleeding bodies sent the others into a cannibalistic frenzy. The men paddled towards an approaching tender boat while waving gratefully to Catalina.

The giant snake's tail burst from the water, lashing out like a whip, capsizing the boat. The snake's head broke the water, snatching up one of the men.

Catalina felt helpless, unable to fire at the snake without killing the men around it. Then she saw the snake's tail whipping through the water.

Shouting, "Your ass is mine!" she opened fire on the tail.

Some rounds struck home, forcing the snake to retreat beneath the surface. The grateful sailors crawled onto the overturned tender.

#

Micah swam hard until he grabbed on to Faye, yelling, "I got ya!"

The little girl latched on to him, almost dragging him under.

He yelled, "I got you, but remember what they taught you in swim class."

After a few seconds of panic, Faye relaxed, cradled under his arm, allowing him to backstroke.

He thought, *But where can we go?*

The sheer number of caimans meant that the riverbank was suicide. He could see the lights of the *Valentina* slipping off into the distance, so that was out. Their best option was the gunboat, and thankfully a brilliant stream of red tracer rounds made it easy to locate.

Micah started swimming, saying, "If you want to kick a bit, honey, that'd sure help."

She did, adding some speed. With each kick, the gunboat grew closer until he could see Catalina standing on the deck holding a huge machine gun.

He muttered, "I'll be damned," and, inspired by the sight, kicked even harder.

The only problem was that the closer he got, the less boat there was above the water.

#

The rising water forced Catalina to retreat up onto the coxswain's flat—the boat's center-mounted pilot cabin. The climb was a Herculean effort given the combination of water, the machine gun and the extra ammo belt. She reached the top knowing that, within minutes, it too would be underwater. In the distance she saw Micah swimming towards her, Faye in tow.

Looking around, she muttered, "Where the hell are those other gunboats?"

Then she caught sight of them orbiting around Batista's yacht, which was well outside of the fray. She muttered, "Bastard," then fired at a pair of approaching caimans, killing one and discouraging the other. The machine gun clicked empty. "Great."

The fast trawler roared past, creating a wave that only washed Micah out further.

He swam harder, pushing through the trawler's wave. Catalina knew he was fighting a losing battle. She set the machine gun aside and reached out, but they were too far away. Then she remembered the extra ammo belt and cast it out like a rope. After two tries Micah was able to grab the end.

Gripping it tightly, he said, "Faye, grab this and let Catalina haul you in."

The frightened little girl said, "But—"

"Do as I say!"

She grabbed on to the string of bullets. Catalina hauled her closer until she was able to grab the child's hand. She yanked Faye up onto the coxswain's flat then prepared to cast out to Micah.

Faye pointed, shouting, "Look!"

Catalina saw the terrifyingly familiar shape surging through the water—coming straight for them. Suddenly the ammo belt was needed for its original purpose.

She shouted to Micah, "Hold on!" while coiling the ammo belt.

Faye screamed, "It's coming!"

Catalina said, "I know, I know!" while staring at the machine gun. Firing the weapon was one thing, but reloading it was a trickier affair. Taking a deep breath, she struggled to recall her gunnery sergeant's shouted instructions, hoping they translated to this Russian knockoff. Eyes locked on the weapon, she muttered, "Perform the following in proper order. Open feed tray cover, load rounds into the feeding block, pull charging handle to rear, lock bolt in place, charging handle placed in forward position… Now kill something!"

The bolt snapped into position.

She yelled, "Yeah!" while raising the weapon. The snake's head emerged from the water—so close she was staring directly into its eyes. Its mouth opened wide, poised to strike.

Catalina fired a long, unbroken burst straight down its open maw. The sheer impact stopped the snake from striking. She kept hammering rounds down its throat. The snake twisted wildly, its tail thrashing against the water. Catalina kept firing, the tracer rounds illuminating the snake's open mouth. Something warm sprayed across her face. It was snake blood … gallons of it.

#

Micah tried to swim out of the snake's path but couldn't escape its thrashing tail. The sheer force pushed him underwater while washing him further from the sinking gunboat. He tried to surface, but the snake's whipping tail struck a glancing blow against his head. Despite the adrenaline surging through him, his thoughts became cloudy until he barely registered that he was sinking.

#

The thrashing snake turned profile, allowing Catalina to unleash a final burst into its emerald-green eye, reducing it to a black-and-crimson void.

The machine gun clicked empty as the last link in the disintegrating belt flew off.

Someone launched another aerial flare, illuminating the snake's twisting death throes. Its obscenely long body slammed down into the river, sinking beneath brown water that quickly bloomed red.

Catalina threw down the now useless machine gun and embraced Faye.

The crying child tried to pull away, scanning the water, pleading, "Where's Daddy?"

Catalina looked out at the water but saw nothing. She wanted to comfort Faye, but there was a more urgent problem. The water was up to her waist, and rising fast, and the river was still crawling with caimans drawn by the snake's blood.

Someone with a bullhorn shouted, "Hang on!"

A thirty-foot tender boat came alongside, its deckhands reaching out to rescue them. Catalina hauled Faye up into their waiting arms then climbed aboard. She sank down inside the boat; ten half-drowned men huddled around her. At least four were badly wounded, including one whose arm had been severed by a caiman. Those who weren't wounded started shouting excitedly.

Anticipating some new terror, Catalina muttered, "What now?" Then she realized they were shouting at her.

It was a chorus of, "*Mangusto! Mangusto! Serpente assassina!*" followed by cheering and applause.

It took her a moment to translate that to "mongoose," and "lady snake killer." Catalina was officially a hero.

But Micah was nowhere to be found.

CHAPTER NINE

Feeling his consciousness slipping away, Micah struggled to focus. He heard one of his father's survival credos echoing through his skull. *When your thoughts turn blurry, focus on one thing—finding the surface.*

Someone must have launched an aerial flare, illuminating the murky water above him.

He thought, *Now I know which way is up.*

He started kicking. Thanks to the flare's flickering light he spotted a rope dangling down into the water above him. After a few more kicks he was able to grab it and felt himself being pulled along. With a combination of kicking and climbing he got close enough to the surface to make out something with four legs thrashing furiously through the water above—the rope was attached to an animal.

Micah kicked and pulled until his head finally broke the surface. Spitting out water, he took one glorious breath. After a few more gasps of air, he was coherent enough to identify his savior.

It was the donkey Faye had freed.

The burro must have jumped overboard and was paddling for the riverbank. Micah hung on to the rope as the donkey towed him to shore, braying in annoyance at the added ballast. Feeling guilty, Micah kicked along with his hoofed rescuer. The minor exertion nearly made him pass out.

#

Catalina ignored the embraces and back claps from her grateful boat mates and scanned the water for any sign of Micah. In the distance she made out what looked like a horse swimming towards shore.

Faye pointed to it and said, "It's the donkey."

Catalina said, "Yup," and kept studying the water. Nothing.

Faye's eyes lit up and she shouted, "Daddy!"

"Where?"

Faye pointed, but all Catalina saw was the swimming donkey. A moment later, the aerial flare splashed down into the river, plunging them into darkness.

Catalina put her arm around Faye and said, "Sorry, I didn't see him, baby."

Faye's eyes lit up. "It was him! He's okay."

But Catalina was almost certain the little girl was letting hope cloud her vision. She turned to the boat's pilot and said, "One of our people might be over there! Can we take a look?"

The pilot shook his head, pointing to the bleeding men around her. Catalina understood his priorities.

The tender pressed on, its outboard motor struggling to catch up to the distant *Valentina*.

Faye said, "I saw him, I really, really did."

Feeling the little girl trembling, Catalina held her tight, whispering, "I know you did, honey, I know you did. We're going to be alright."

A distant gunboat launched another aerial flare, casting a hellish light on the floating wreckage and bodies, reminding Catalina just how miraculous their survival had been.

#

As soon as the donkey's hooves touched the riverbed it stopped, braying loudly to announce the free ride was over. Releasing the rope, Micah waded the final twenty feet to the riverbank. It felt like miles. He knelt down on the bank, watching Batista's flotilla slip away into the night, praying that Faye and Catalina were safe.

"Gotta get up, keep moving."

But when he tried to stand, it felt like a nail was being driven into his head. Dropping back down to his knees he probed the sore spot. His fingers came back bloody.

Another aerial flare popped open, casting a flickering light on the jungle around him. The donkey stood behind him, peacefully sampling the local vegetation until it found some agreeable leaves.

Micah's stomach twisted into a knot—a sharp reminder that he'd sucked down enough river water to ensure a case of leptospirosis. Even the initial symptoms of that waterborne disease would incapacitate him. Out here that would be a death sentence.

Muttering, "Better get this over with," he jammed two fingers down his throat, vomiting up a quart of river water along with his last meal.

After a few gut-wrenching dry heaves, he sat up, glanced at the bushes in front of him and froze in terror. A pair of luminous green eyes stared back at him.

Slowly, he reached into his pocket, withdrawing the mud-encrusted revolver.

The glowing eyes grew closer until the flare cast a light on the animal's orange-and-black fur. It was the Amazon's other apex predator—a jaguar. Micah had seen the big cats in action and knew that he was no match for two hundred pounds of coiled muscle.

He tried to pull back the revolver's hammer, but it was hopelessly jammed.

As if sensing his helplessness, the jaguar leaned back on its haunches and pounced.

#

The tender boat pulled alongside the now anchored *Valentina*. Batista's yacht was moored alongside it. Catalina boosted Faye up into the arms of a waiting deckhand then climbed aboard. Six crewmen rushed over to unload the wounded. Catalina weaved through the broken crates and other wreckage strewn across the front deck. The livestock were gone, save for a pair of chickens pecking at insects. She noticed three dead bodies wrapped in plastic lying to one side and steered Faye away from them.

Members of the crew eyed her as she passed, whispering to each other. A throng of grateful men hovered around her.

Batista stood at the far end of the deck, engaged in a heated conversation with Santos. Catalina overheard snatches, mostly relating to the condition of the boats. Batista caught sight of Catalina and marched towards her.

Catalina muttered, "Aw great."

Faye tugged hard at her sleeve, imploring, "Catalina, come on, we have to go look for my dad."

"Okay, I'll see if someone'll take us out there."

One of the deckhands draped a blanket over Catalina's shoulders and said, "If you want, me and the boys can take a boat out and look."

"Thanks."

"It's the least we can do after you saved our asses."

Upon hearing this, Batista snapped, "Belay that, I'm not wasting time on a search party. You all know that if he fell in the river, the caimans have gotten him."

Faye pulled away from Catalina, slapping at Batista's chest, shouting, "That's a lie! He's alive, I saw him!"

Catalina pulled Faye back and wrapped the blanket around the sobbing child. She glared at Batista and said, "Thanks a lot."

Brushing Faye's muddy handprints off his ivory jacket, Batista asked, "Santos, do we really need this woman? She clearly lacks Dr. Clark's expertise."

Santos loomed behind his boss, savoring Catalina's discomfort. "I got no use for her."

One of the deckhands stepped forward, draping his arm around Catalina, saying, "No use for her? Did you see her take down that snake? If it wasn't for her, we'd all be dead!"

This earned Catalina a hearty round of cheers and backslaps from the crew.

The deckhand eyed Santos, asking, "Hey, where were you during all that shit?"

The crew glared at Santos, their cheering giving way to angry muttering. Catalina sensed the rising tension.

Locking his eyes on the crewman, Santos said, "Watch it, *babaca*."

Catalina said, "Don't worry; I can pull my weight."

Sensing that his crew was hovering on mutiny, Batista chose not to press the issue. With a curt, "See that you do," he walked away.

Catalina watched him board his yacht, and she let out a long sigh of relief, thinking, *Bullet dodged. But for how long*?

A crewman handed her a hot cup of tea while another man added a generous helping of rotgut to the mug. Catalina took a long swallow, relishing the warmth coursing through her. She thought, *It's so strange, most of these guys would cut someone's throat for a dollar, but they just saved both our lives.*

Handing the empty mug to one of the men, Catalina said, "Thanks boys, but I think it's time I put her to bed."

There was another chorus of gratitude as Catalina led Faye towards their cabin.

In a near whisper, the little girl said, "He's alive. I saw him."

Squeezing her hand, Catalina said, "I know, baby," desperately wanting to believe her.

#

Micah hit the ground feeling a rush of air as the jaguar leapt over him.

The big cat was opting for different prey.

The jaguar landed squarely on the donkey's back. The burro instantly snapped into action, kicking its rear legs high, catapulting the jaguar off. The big cat hit the ground rolling then sprang back onto its feet. The donkey pivoted, rearing up onto its hind legs as the jaguar pounced. Its front hooves struck the jaguar in midair. The cat slammed down on top of Micah, its jaw shattered. The donkey galloped forward, rearing onto its hind legs, launching another attack. Micah rolled onto his side, narrowly escaping as the hooves pummeled the cat's ribs. The jaguar feebly lashed out with its paws, roaring in agony. The donkey hammered down three more rib-shattering blows then stood, almost motionless.

The big cat lay there, its fluid-choked breath rising and falling against shattered ribs. The donkey sniffed at it then placidly turned away.

Micah muttered, "All hail the donkey king," then felt blood stinging his eyes. That meant the gash in his forehead was bleeding like a faucet. But this time, wiping the blood out of his eyes didn't clear his blurred vision. The rainforest around him rolled in and out of focus, beating time with the throbbing in his skull.

His vision came into focus again, and he was shocked to find a man standing over him. The dark-skinned man wore only a loin cloth. His painfully thin body was crisscrossed with red ceremonial paint. He was old, to the point of being ancient. There were two fresh wounds on his chest, circular, bleeding holes that Micah guessed were bullets. But the injuries didn't seem to bother the old man in the least. He leaned down over Micah, so close he could make out strange red rings around his irises. The old man grinned. It was the warmest smile Micah had ever seen.

"Hello," was all Micah could muster before his vision blurred again. He shut his eyes tightly, trying to focus, then opened them.

The old man was gone.

Micah muttered, "Got to keep moving," and forced himself back up onto his knees—a big mistake. He teetered, head reeling, muttering, "Aw shit," before flopping face first into the mud. Summoning his last ounce of strength, he rolled onto his side to keep from drowning in the muck. He lay there, spooning with the dying jaguar. Then, whispering Faye's name, he sank into unconsciousness.

#

Catalina tucked Faye into bed, wishing she'd been able to offer her a bath, pajamas, or a teddy bear—any of the comforts of home.

She wondered, *Do nine-year-olds still have teddy bears?*

Catalina wished she had some child nurturing experience to draw on, but a

60

career in intelligence had left her better suited to the role of cool aunt who shows up with an Xbox at Christmas. Up till now she'd been, more or less, okay with that.

Thankfully, sheer physical exhaustion put Faye's body to sleep, but it failed to quiet her mind. She constantly kicked at the sheets, like a dog dreaming of rabbits, while murmuring unintelligibly.

Catalina stroked her forehead, asking herself, *How much terror, loss, and physical punishment can a little girl endure?*

Catalina's childhood in Equatorial Guinea had proven the emotional resilience of a child—but at what cost? She'd only been seven when a failed coup d'état left the nation's dictator thirsting for vengeance against revolutionaries and intellectuals. Her school teacher father had fallen into the latter category, forcing them to join the fleeing bands of refugees. The passage of time had left Catalina's memories of their nightmarish exodus hazy, but certain images were tattooed onto her soul. The forced marches, near starvation, cowering in the night from soldiers, and the roadside ditches piled high with fly-covered bodies. But through all that darkness, one memory shone brightly—her parents' selfless devotion, always protecting their baby girl from the grim realities and never allowing her to lose hope. Their compassion and courage had been the key to her physical, and emotional, survival.

Faye squirmed, mumbling softly. But one word chimed through with crystal clarity.

"Daddy."

Catalina curled up next to her, thinking, *If believing your dad's still alive helps you get through this, then you just go ahead and believe.* In a near whisper, she sang a Portuguese lullaby, promising sweet dreams and a better tomorrow. It was the same melody her mother had sung to keep Catalina's childhood nightmares at bay as they'd huddled in the darkness.

After a few verses they both fell sound asleep.

#

Micah was hauled up onto his feet, feeling dizzy and nauseous, with no clue how much time had passed. Someone poured water over his head. Glancing up at the sky, he made out faint traces of blue in the rainforest canopy—dawn.

A shirtless man armed with an AK-47 held him upright while a second, smaller man removed his Rolex watch then tugged at his wedding ring.

A female voice bellowed something in Portuguese and both men froze. The big man released Micah, who flopped back down onto the dead jaguar.

A tall figure stepped out of the jungle. From the ground, all Micah could see were combat boots and bare, clearly feminine legs.

The taller man shined his flashlight on the ground in front of the woman, lighting her path. The smaller man trotted over, surrendering the watch and wedding ring. After pocketing both she took a few steps towards Micah.

The woman wore an open, ankle length, duster style raincoat and khaki shorts. A sheen of sweat gleamed indigo against her dark skin. Micah couldn't make out her face, but her piercing eyes shone in the flashlight's beam. A pristine, white, navy captain's hat was perched incongruously on her head.

The taller man held up Micah's mud-caked revolver. The tiny pistol earned a hearty round of laughter. Then he popped open the cylinder and held up six unfired bullets. The laughter died.

The woman looked down at the dead jaguar and in a throaty voice said, "He must have killed it with his bare hands."

Two more men emerged from the jungle, laden with boots, rifles and goods scavenged from the carnage. One of the boots still had an ankle poking out of it.

She yanked the severed foot from the boot and flung it into the jungle, declaring, "Those damn caimans don't leave anything worth stealing." Staring down at Micah, she said, "Give me a better look at him."

Micah was doused with another bucket of water, washing away a layer of mud.

The shorter man leaned forward, grabbing his hair and, with a note of surprise, shouted, "*Loiro!*"

Through the echoing in his skull, Micah caught the Portuguese word for blonde. He was yanked onto his feet. The woman leaned forward, inches from his face. Up close she was even more striking, with a pointed chin and knife sharp cheekbones framing wide, almond-shaped, brown eyes.

In English, she asked, "You're one of the Americans Batista kidnapped?"

Micah nodded. "How'd you know?"

"Nothing happens on this river without me knowing." She kicked the big cat's carcass. "Did you kill it?"

Micah nodded, shamelessly taking credit for the donkey's handiwork.

After an appraising look up and down, she said, "You must be some kind of man to kill a jaguar with your bare hands. You're just lucky the caimans were too busy stuffing themselves on Batista's sailors to test your strength any further. So, *mista sortudo*, tell me what happened, and don't bother lying."

Micah's new nickname, "Lucky Man," earned a hearty round of laughter.

Seeing no advantage in lying, Micah rattled off his tale of the giant snake.

For a few seconds the woman just glared at him, then she laughed. "That story is such nonsense it must be true, or maybe you're just *louco* from the river."

"I'm not crazy, but I know there's no snake that big on Earth."

She reached out, gently stroking his neck, whispering, "That snake is not part of your Earth," then abruptly yanked her hand away.

Micah felt a stinging pain in his neck.

She held up a bloated leech she'd plucked from his neck, grinned, and asked, "So what's your name, Lucky Man?"

"Micah, Micah Clark."

She flicked the leech into the darkness then leaned closer, as if coming in for a kiss, whispering, "They call me Queen Caveira."

Micah instantly remembered Batista's warning. Queen Caveira—the Queen of Skulls. He muttered, "Oh shit," and blacked out.

CHAPTER TEN

Micah hovered between unconsciousness and vivid hallucinations. At some point he heard inaudible voices echoing around him and, in his darkest moments, an anguished voice screaming in the distance. Images flashed through his mind—pulling Faye onto the boat, the donkey, the jaguar, the mysterious old man, and, finally, the face of the pirate woman who butchered people for pleasure—that's when he snapped back into reality.

He awakened, staring into the saucer eyes and barred fangs of a capuchin monkey.

He thought, *Did they just leave me in the jungle to die? But, if that's the case, why's the monkey wearing a sailor's suit and a tiny hat?*

Slowly he pieced together that he was lying on a cot, on a boat, in a below deck saloon, being accosted by someone's overdressed pet monkey.

A muscular, pockmarked man eyed him from across the room.

Micah politely asked, "Hey. Could you please get this monkey off me?"

Without a word the man stood and clamored up the gangway to the upper deck.

Micah muttered, "Thanks," then cautiously shooed the monkey back until he could sit up. He probed his forehead. The wound had been closed, probably with super glue, and he caught a whiff of disinfectant. Rendering first aid was a good sign that they wanted him alive. Massaging his temples, he muttered, "I gotta stop waking up on strange boats."

He surveyed the cabin. It was spartan, consisting of only a few mismatched chairs and a folding table with a large nautical chart tacked to the wall above it. Another table in the far corner was draped in red cloth and decorated with small statues, a few cigars and a bottle of rum. From past experience he knew it was a Macumba altar with figures of spirits and sacrificial offerings. Its centerpiece was a ceramic snake coiled atop a mound of skulls.

"Cheerful."

He heard footsteps coming down the gangway. The big man returned, followed by Queen Caveira. The pirate queen had changed into a bright red Victorian-era naval jacket sporting enough gold trim and adornments to make Michael Jackson blush. The ensemble was set off by a thick leather gun belt sporting two revolvers. It should have looked ridiculous, but she somehow pulled it off. She yanked off her captain's hat, shaking her hair out into a mountainous afro.

Shrieking with excitement, the monkey leapt off the cot onto her shoulder.

Queen Caveira scratched the monkey's chin, and in a sing-song voice asked, "Hello, little *Ladra*, have you come to steal something?"

Taking its cue, the monkey rooted through her breast pocket until it found some fruit slices. It perched on her gold shoulder epaulet, gorging itself.

Turning her attention to Micah, she said, "Well, look who's alive." She snapped her fingers and the pockmarked man handed her some loose Brazilian *reais.* "Poor Umberto lost our bet. If you died, he would have gotten your watch."

Seeing the disappointment in Umberto's eyes, Micah said, "Better luck next time."

Another man came down the gangway and handed a steaming mug to Micah. The concoction smelled like a boiled diaper.

Queen Caveira pinched her nose and said, "Just do that and swallow it all. You sucked down a lot of river water, but those herbs will keep you from shitting yourself to death."

Micah held his nose and swallowed the entire mug. Its taste matched its smell, and he struggled to keep the vile brew down.

Looking mildly impressed, she asked, "Are you curious why the evil pirate, Queen Caveira, hasn't tortured or killed you?"

"Yeah, kind of."

"When a man is kidnapped by Batista and escapes, then manages to survive caimans and kill a jaguar with his bare hands, I think to myself this is one lucky *gajo.* Not someone to kill … maybe better to keep close and let some of that luck rub off."

"Okay."

She pulled a long cigar from her jacket and took her time lighting it. "Now, Lucky Man, tell me your story again."

Micah did, going into greater detail about the monstrous snake.

The queen's face lit up. "You should feel blessed to have witnessed such a miracle."

"The only miracle was not getting eaten."

She went to the altar, reverently stroking the snake statue. Umberto lowered his eyes, mumbling some kind of blessing.

Queen Caveira said, "That snake you saw was Boiúna, the serpent spirit of the river. He has risen to protect his domain. That piece of shit Batista has invaded its sacred territory so it seeks vengeance. But Boiúna would never attack my boats."

"It didn't seem too picky."

'Hmm, maybe you're just an ignorant white man after all. Probably content to worship your peace-preaching carpenter god."

It took Micah a few seconds to figure out that she was referring to Christianity.

The queen asked, "Do you know what Quimbanda is?"

"Yes I do." Micah was familiar with the distinctly Brazilian branch of the Macumba faith—and it was bad news. While Macumba was a recognized religion preaching charity and good works, Quimbanda was based in demonology, embracing black magic and blood sacrifice.

Queen Caveira said, "I am not only the queen of the river pirates but also a Quimbanda priestess, blessed in the eyes of Boiúna."

Micah said, "Okay, cool."

"Now, on to business."

Queen Caveira dangled something shiny in front of the monkey, just out of its reach. It was Micah's watch. The Rolex Explorer had been a gift from Micah's network bosses—back when high ratings made him their fair-haired boy.

Micah said, "You can keep the watch."

"Was that ever in doubt?" She read the watch's inscription aloud. "'To our brightest star, from your friends at the Outdoor Adventure Network.' This inscription tells me you're an American television celebrity, so your bosses will pay good money to get you back alive."

Micah thought, *You're a season too late. They'd probably consider kidnapping an easy way out of their contract.*

Strapping the watch onto her wrist, she said, "I kidnapped a guy from National Geographic last year. I demanded twenty thousand dollars, but they only gave me ten to get him back. I accepted their pathetic offer but chopped off his hands first, to teach them a lesson. Let's hope your bosses aren't so cheap."

Micah felt the herbal concoction rising in his throat but managed to choke it down.

She asked, "Do you know the other television people... Netflix?"

"Uh, yeah. They're all good friends of mine." Micah would say anything at this point to keep his hands attached.

"Good, they will want a show about a beautiful pirate queen and her adventures. America would rather watch me than some fat piece of *merde* who wrestles tigers, yes?"

"Uh, absolutely. Fantastic idea!"

"Then you will help me, how do you say, 'throw this' to them, so the whole world will know and revere Queen Caveira."

Micah thought, *Oh my God, this insane black magic priestess and pirate is pitching me a TV show while also threatening to cut my hands off.* But he said, "I'd love to help you set that up, but right now Batista has my daughter."

Queen Caveira shrugged. "Then he'll kill her, unless the pig has some other use for her. Now, let's talk about my *televisão* show. Do you know Beyonce? She would be very good as me."

Desperately trying to stay on track, Micah said, "I don't think he'll kill her just yet, and there's a woman who might be able to keep her safe, maybe even help them escape."

Queen Caveira shook her head and sighed. "At this point I think escaping would be worse than Batista."

"Why?"

"This section of the river is deadly. I only traveled down here because Batista built a fuel depot to support some secret operation. But some idiot set the place on fire before I could rob it. I'd love to find that stupid bastard!"

His stomach lurching, Micah asked, "What's that have to do with my daughter?"

Queen Caveira stroked the monkey on her shoulder, cooing, "Lucky Man is so impatient."

Having finished its snack, the monkey climbed off her shoulder. It scurried over to Micah, pawing at his pants leg.

Queen Caveira walked over to a nautical chart, identical to the one Micah had seen in Batista's cabin. Pointing to a section of river, she explained, "By now Batista has reached this area. It's the territory of an un-contacted tribe. Their name is impossible to pronounce, so we call them *Morte Tinto*."

"The Red Death. I've heard about them."

The monkey climbed up Micah's leg. Rather than offend his clearly insane pirate hostess, Micah just let it continue.

Queen Caveira watched her monkey with amusement. "Don't bother fighting my little friend, he won't give up until he steals something. A habit he picked up from me. If your daughter escapes in their territory, they'll capture her."

"And?"

"They're cannibals."

The monkey nimbly unzipped Micah's pants pocket and fished around until he found something. It scurried into a corner, clutching its prize.

Micah implored, "If you can just get me close to Batista's boats—"

"Sorry, Lucky Man, I've tested Batista's firepower firsthand and I don't want it all pointed at me."

In a Hail Mary attempt to entice her, Micah blurted out, "His secret project is a mining operation."

Sounding unimpressed, she said, "Good. If he ever digs up something I'll rob his boats, one at a time."

The monkey tried to bite into its prize, but when it proved inedible, he threw it away. It rolled across the floor, landing at Queen Caveira's feet.

She picked up the pool ball-sized emerald. Mentally connecting the dots, she shouted, "Umberto, get out!"

The frightened man scrambled up the gangway.

Once he was out of earshot, she held up the emerald. "Is this what they're mining?"

Seeing the greed in her eyes made Micah even more brazen. "That's the smallest of what was brought back on the first trip. They've already dug up a huge supply, and it's all sitting at the mine, ripe for the plucking. But if Batista gets there, he'll dig in with his army and it'll be impossible to steal."

She stared into the emerald, pondering a potential fortune, then shook her head. "If I attack Batista, his gunboats might cut us to pieces. Even if I beat him, I still don't know where his mine is." She ran her finger across the chart. "There are dozens of tributaries and lakes, and if I go exploring in that territory, the *Morte Tinto* will pick us off one by one."

Micah grinned and said, "What if I could lead you right to the mine?"

"How?"

"I saw it marked on his charts."

Queen Caveira tapped the chart. "You won't be able to remember the exact spot."

"I was studying charts before I could read. I remember exactly where it is. If you hit Batista while he's still on the water and vulnerable, all those emeralds plus the mine will be yours."

"Being rich is no fun if you're dead."

"But if you attack him, won't that snake god ... Bonnie..."

"Boiúna."

"Yeah, Boiúna will come to your aid. Killing Batista will elevate you in the eyes of a god."

Nodding slowly, she said, "Perhaps it is destiny."

"And you know who else would love it... Netflix!"

She clapped her hands excitedly. "Ah, yes, the season finale! With my brilliance and Boiúna's aid we'll slaughter that bastard. Now, show me where this mine is."

"Only if you help me get my daughter back. All I need is a small boat so I can sneak over and grab her before you attack."

The pirate took the cigar out of her mouth and blew on the red-hot tip. "You've got some balls, Lucky Man. Maybe big enough to put my cigar out on."

Micah gulped, realizing he'd set himself up for torture.

Then her mood swung a hundred and eighty degrees. She smiled and tucked the emerald into her breast pocket, tapping it softly. "But I am a kind soul and your daughter's plight has touched my heart, so I will help you. You can keep your secret for now, but you must at least tell me the area so I can plan my attack."

Micah put his finger on a maze of tributaries and small lakes, careful not to touch the precise location.

The queen cursed under her breath and said, "That region is sacred to the *Morte Tinto*. Only their high priest goes there." She bellowed in Portuguese, and Umberto raced back down the gangway. "Take Lucky Man to the guest quarters and make sure he's comfortable."

Umberto grinned and shoved Micah toward the gangway.

She added, "But remember this; if you cross Queen Caveira, you won't be a lucky man anymore."

With that, Micah was half led, half dragged up the gangway.

#

Micah was pushed onto the main deck. He tried to get his bearings until Umberto shoved him towards a ladder. It led to a flat platform resting over the pilothouse—the boat's highest point.

Micah asked, "Why're we going up top?"

Umberto answered with another shove that sent Micah crashing onto the deck at the base of a ladder. He felt a sharp pain in his back. Twisting around he saw a piece of rusted metal sticking out of the hull.

"Great, now I've got tetanus too."

Umberto shouted, "Climb!"

"I'm going, I'm going!"

Once up top, Micah stepped onto a steel platform slick with algae and bird droppings. Out of nowhere, Umberto kicked him squarely in the butt. Micah slipped, landing flat on his elbows next to a set of chains secured to the platform—manacles.

"What the fuck?"

Umberto knelt on Micah's back, pinning him down, while slapping manacles onto his left wrist. Once secured, he flipped Micah onto his back.

Micah shouted, "Shit man, is this about the watch? I'll buy you one!"

Umberto shouted, "Quiet!" while manacling Micah's other wrist.

"Come on, we're on the same team here, remember? I'm the queen's Netflix guy!"

"And that's why she's given you her finest guest cabin." He pointed above Micah. "Or would you rather be like your shipmate?"

Umberto shined his flashlight onto a bamboo cage dangling above the platform. A naked man was slumped inside, his face beaten to a pulp, his body a roadmap of shallow knife wounds—precision cuts designed to inflict pain, without killing. The man looked down at Micah, who suddenly recognized what was left of his face. He was one of Batista's deck cooks. The poor bastard must have survived the snake attack only to be scooped up by the pirates.

"Your friend also talked about a giant snake, but even after hours of cutting he couldn't tell me anything else."

That brutal interrogation must have been the screaming Micah heard during his delirium.

Umberto leaned close, breath reeking of dende oil and garlic. "In the morning, you can watch the birds peck out his eyes."

"Why are you doing this?"

"Because the queen isn't stupid. Right now you'd say anything to save your miserable hide. But after a few days in the hot sun, you'll be more honest ... or dead. And all you have to do is look up at your old shipmate to remember what happens if you lie to our queen. Sweet dreams... Lucky Man."

He slipped down the ladder, leaving Micah and the dying man to their own devices.

Micah shouted, "You can forget about getting an associate producer credit, buddy!" Then he squirmed around. After some contorting, he was able to sit up and assess his sorry situation. The high platform reeked of decay and bird droppings, but at least it offered a crow's nest view of Queen Caveira's pirate fleet.

He was chained to the top of what appeared to be a sixty-foot motor yacht serving as the queen's flagship, likely hijacked from some unlucky tourists. Its luxurious trappings had long been stripped away, replaced by military functionality. Every inch of deck space was covered in supplies. A series of tattered bullet proof vests bearing Brazilian coast guard emblems were lashed to its deck railings, creating a wall of improvised armor. On its bow, a split, fifty-gallon drum had been repurposed into a gun turret. A guard sat there, manning an aged belt-fed machine gun.

A forty-foot trawler cruised along the port side, her brown painted hull nearly invisible against the muddy water.

Orbiting the two large boats was an armada of smaller, sharp-bowed dhow style go-fast boats—the same type favored by Somali pirates. All sported oversized, or dual, engines that could easily overtake fishing boats or even drug smugglers. The rear of each boat was fitted with a shelter draped in rope and barrels, so, at a distance, it could pass as a fishing boat. By the time anyone realized their error, it would be too late. Men with assault rifles sat at the bows. The compact fleet was ideal for piracy or smuggling but didn't compare to Batista's armada. But Queen Caveira had the advantage of being a genuine psychopath, with a crew who worshipped her.

Micah also got a look at her minions who were working the deck—a mix of brown and black faces with some Asian and indigenous natives thrown into the mix.

Well, he thought, *at least the queen's an equal opportunity tyrant.*

The only common traits were hard features and sinewy muscles, along with similar scars criss-crossing their backs—healed over lash marks from long ago.

He was certain of one thing— the pirate queen was crazy as an outhouse rat and willing to kill anything in her path, including Faye and Catalina. His only hope was to appease the mad queen and somehow escape before the attack, free the ladies, and make a break. Then all they had to do was avoid the angry pirates, cannibal natives and monster snakes. It seemed impossible, but there was no alternative.

Micah spotted a ray of hope lashed to the flagship's stern—a three-man, fully inflated dinghy with an outboard engine. He assumed it was the queen's escape craft, meaning it would be kept fueled and ready. It wasn't much, but at least it was something.

Micah lay back on the slimy platform, determined not to let himself slip into despair.

"Hey," he muttered to himself, "it could be worse. It could be raining!"

A few minutes later, the rain started.

CHAPTER ELEVEN

Hans sat rifling through research documents in what doubled as a workplace and Catalina and Faye's sleeping quarters.

Holding up one of the aerial photographs, he asked Catalina, "What observations have you made regarding the crater?"

Catalina tensed. The past two days had been an ongoing struggle to pass herself off as a geologist, while constantly looking for an opportunity to escape. Her CIA trainers had given her a crash course in geology, with added focus on meteorites, but it was barely enough to bluff her way through an academic dinner party.

She replied, "Before I make any assumptions, can you explain how you intend to cut up the Anomaly without it reacting?" Shifting her response to another question was a standard intelligence bluff.

With a smile, Hans said, "It was simply a matter of careful analysis."

Catalina relaxed a bit. Like many intelligent but lonely individuals, Hans was always eager to trumpet his achievements. His OCD level attention to detail ensured them at least twenty minutes of safety.

Hans went on. "I immersed the fragment in liquid helium. At minus four hundred and fifty degrees it simulated the temperature of deep space. Once that was done, I used a ten kilowatt ytterbium fiber laser cutting torch with a parallel refracting beam to cut into it. Due to the extreme cold the fragment did not react. I've brought a larger version of the laser and will apply the same logic."

Catalina gave him an enthralled look that virtually screamed tell me more. And he went on. She thought, *Another bullet dodged.* Micah had been much easier to fool, primarily because she'd maneuvered herself into becoming Faye's babysitter and BFF. But Hans was a scientific polyglot, with knowledge of engineering, geology and even zoology.

One of the cooks entered carrying trays. He set one down in front of Catalina and said, "For the *serpente assassina,*" uncovering an aromatic blend of fish and vegetables. "A grilled *Patarashca* with chilies and onions, and a bowl of shrimp *Tacacá.*"

Catalina inhaled deeply. "It smells amazing."

The cook said, "Anything for you," and quietly set down an identical tray for Faye who was napping.

He set the final tray down in front of Hans and left.

Hans uncovered his tray. It was just sliced Spam on some white bread. Catalina avoided eye contact with the Austrian. While she appreciated the crew's admiration, it made dealing with Hans more awkward.

Santos barged into the cabin unannounced. Without a word he rifled through her luggage. It was a classic intimidation tactic, designed to keep her on edge. But Catalina knew he wasn't really looking for anything in her bags—in truth, he was studying her reactions, hoping to see a flash of guilt in her eyes. He'd been suspicious of her since the gunboat incident, looking for any excuse to throw her and Faye overboard without inciting a mutiny. Thanks to her CIA training, his tactics hadn't borne fruit.

Dealing with Hans was challenging, but Santos was the genuine threat. The massive thug had the same flat, emotionless eyes she'd seen in CIA wet boys— as if someone had surgically removed every trace of poetry from their soul. Catalina pegged him as an ex ABIN operative; Brazil's ruthless version of the CIA. She knew that any successful escape meant killing him first.

Santos stepped over to the fold down cot where Faye was napping and contemplated waking the child up.

Catalina said, "I just got her to sleep. It really helps us to focus on our work."

He stared at her with those dead eyes then left the cabin, grunting what passed for a goodbye.

In a near whisper, Hans said, "Such a distasteful man," before continuing his dissertation on laser-cutting torches.

Catalina nodded, thankful he'd left without trashing the cot. The Glock remained safely tucked beneath the mattress.

#

Micah spent the next twenty-four hours manacled to the platform, roasting in the tropical sun with only the occasional short bursts of rain preventing sunstroke. Umberto only made two appearances, bringing him just enough food and water to stay alive.

Micah heard a pitiful moan from the cage dangling above him and yelled, "Hang in there, *amigo*, we'll get out of this somehow," amazed that the poor wretch had hung on this long.

With a loud caw, a pair of brightly plumed tropical crows settled onto the cage. They roosted there, contemplating the helpless man's eyeballs. Micah rolled onto his back, kicking at the cage, scaring off the birds. But crows were smart, and he wondered how many times this tactic would work.

Umberto climbed up onto the platform carrying a gourd. He pulled Micah upright, saying, "I've got something for you. Now drink!"

Holding Micah's head, he poured some of the contents down his throat. Micah, who'd been anticipating water, choked on the caustic liquid.

Umberto slapped him, shouting, "Drink it!" and forced him to take another long swallow.

Micah did as ordered, recognizing the drink as cachaca, a sweetened Brazilian rum, mixed with another ingredient he couldn't place. Then his tongue went numb and he felt a tingling in his spine. The secret ingredient must have been coca leaves—the plant used to produce cocaine.

With a yellow-toothed grin, Umberto said, "Drink it down, Lucky Man, you'll need the energy."

After forcing a few more swallows, Umberto unlatched the manacles. Micah stood up, massaging his wrists, while mentally debating whether to dive overboard. But Umberto shoved him towards the ladder, pointing down.

Once on deck Micah, was herded towards the captain's cabin. The crew stood around idly, smiling and muttering to one another as he passed.

Micah asked, "What's going on?"

"Shut up," was all he got.

Umberto led him through the pilothouse to the main cabin. He banged on the door once, slid it open and shoved Micah inside.

The cabin was pitch black, the humid air thick with cigar smoke. Micah closed his eyes for a few seconds, adjusting to the darkness. Even then, all he could make out were a few candles and someone sprawled across an oversized bed.

Queen Caveira said, "Well, Lucky Man, I see you survived the night."

The queen reclined on the bed, the monkey perched on her chest. She lit a match and slowly sucked at a fresh cigar. And that's when Micah realized she was completely naked.

She said, "Boiúna came to me in a dream last night and said that earning his aid will require two sacrifices. You may choose which you provide. One is blood."

Gulping, Micah asked, "The other option?"

"Seed." She lay back, stretching out her long legs. "Which do you choose?"

"Is this a trick question?"

She put down the cigar, her tone growing sharper. "Boiúna requires strong seed, so I've chosen the man who killed a jaguar with his bare hands."

Micah thought, *I never should've taken credit for that donkey's work.*

She added, "Plus most of my crew has syphilis."

Micah was stunned. The same madwoman who'd threatened to cut off his hands and then manacled him to the crow's nest was now trying to seduce him.

She slapped the mattress, commanding, "Come here and do your duty. How can you expect to save your daughter without Boiúna's aid?"

"Uh, can we leave her out of this?"

"What's wrong? Are you a *boiola*?"

"No, no, I'm straight."

"Then give me your seed like a man or I can give you to the crew for their amusement! Choose!"

The prospect of being beaten or buggered by her syphilitic crew held zero appeal. Micah took a deep breath, muttered, "Screw it," and peeled off his shirt.

Queen Caveira swatted the monkey aside and lay back, her arms outstretched. "That's it, now come to me, Lucky Man."

And Micah did. Maybe it was desperation or just the fear of witnessing her next psychopathic mood swing. Being tanked up on cachaca and coca leaves didn't hurt either. Seconds later, he was on the bed, her muscular legs clamped around him while he struggled to get his pants off. What followed wasn't so much foreplay as unarmed combat. She wrenched his spine, gnawed his ear, and clawed at his buttocks while shouting obscene instructions. Then the monkey leapt back on the bed, jealously yanking his hair as they rutted away. Thankfully Micah's body responded in a sort of carnal fight-or-flight instinct.

The pirate queen seemed to enjoy their entanglement, moaning loudly and repeatedly screaming Boiúna's name. That's when Micah realized the sounds weren't physical pleasure but rather some kind of religious ecstasy. It was the most bizarre sexual experience he'd ever had—and he'd worked in reality television.

After a few minutes of fevered thrashing, it was over. Micah rolled onto his back panting; Queen Caveira's body wound around his.

She whispered, "Did you give me your seed?"

All Micah could muster was, "Uh huh," followed by a stretch of awkward postcoital silence.

Stretching like a cat, she proclaimed, "Now, with Boiúna's blessing, I shall put Batista in the bamboo cage, take out my knives and have my revenge."

"So you two have … a history?"

After a moment of quiet reflection, she said, "I was a little girl when my parents sold me to one of Batista's emerald mines as a slave. You soft Americans can't imagine the things they did to children like me. After nine years of torture, I staged a revolt. My crew were all part of that escape."

This moment of emotional sharing seemed to make Queen Caveira uncomfortable. She climbed out of bed and began lighting candles on a statue-laden altar. The flickering light revealed the lines etched across her bare back—lash marks from her childhood of slavery. The same kind of marks Micah had seen on the crew, explaining their utter devotion. The sight of her standing there, naked, her physical and emotional scars laid bare, made him feel a twinge of sympathy. A childhood like hers would have driven anyone mad.

Muttering a prayer, she touched the snake spirit's statue. Micah couldn't shake the sensation that it had been watching them.

Eager to break the silence, he said, "I'm sorry your parents sold you to those horrible people."

The queen turned to him, grinned and said, "Not as sorry as them."

The glowing altar candles revealed the cabin's full splendor. Micah glanced at the far wall and shuddered, as if someone had thrown ice water on him. It was stacked floor to ceiling with rows of human skulls. There were at least fifty, the bottom rows yellowed with age, the upper still gleaming white.

Micah thought, *She really is the Queen of Skulls.*

Pointing to her wall, the queen said, "Mother and Father were the first to decorate my wall. Do you like my trophies?"

Micah said, "Oh yeah, impressive collection," though inside he was screaming.

The queen slipped on a poncho, saying, "I'll be back in a moment," and padded out the door.

Micah stared at the wall of skulls, fighting the impulse to dive overboard—monster snakes and hungry caimans be damned. But if there was the faintest chance of saving Faye and Catalina, he had to stick out this nightmare. He heard a commotion from up on deck, followed by chanting male voices and, finally, a chorus of cheers.

Feeling horribly naked, Micah groped around for his pants, muttering, "What the hell are they doing now?"

But before he could find them, Queen Caveira returned, clutching something to her chest. She carefully placed it on the altar, proclaiming, "The second part of the sacrifice is now complete."

Micah stared at the altar in horror. Resting among the statues and candles was the severed head of Batista's cook.

Queen Caveira slithered into bed next to him, running her bloody fingers through his hair, whispering, "*Boiúna* be praised my Lucky, Lucky Man." Wrapping her arms around him, she asked, "So, how will you convince Beyonce to play me?"

CHAPTER TWELVE

Batista's flotilla continued downriver. The tributary gradually narrowed, becoming roughly one hundred and fifty feet wide.

Catalina and Faye were ensconced in the workroom. The little girl was sprawled on her cot, reading one of her YA novels, but Catalina could tell she'd picked up on the tension growing between her and Hans. It was Catalina's fourth day of trying to impersonate a geologist—a facade that was unravelling more every hour.

After another of her attempts to deflect a question, Hans slapped his papers onto the table. "Do you know anything about geology?"

Catalina said, "Yes, though I certainly lack your level of scientific expertise." But one look told her flattery wasn't cutting it.

"I'm an engineer, with only a working knowledge of geology, yet I clearly know more than you!"

Catalina said, "Please, you're scaring Faye."

Hans stood up. "I must inform Mister Batista of your incompetence. He'll decide what to do with you… stowaways."

Catalina tensed, knowing exactly what Batista would do with them. Her fingers inched across the table to a stapler, hoping it was heavy enough to cold-cock the Austrian before he got to the door.

Just then they heard an ear-splitting crack, followed by a thunderous roar. The boat shuddered. Faye leapt off the couch, locking her arms around Catalina.

Hans shouted, "What the hell?" and rushed out the door.

Catalina heard shouting and pounding feet on the deck below. Gripping Faye's hand, she said, "Why don't we go out and see what happened?"

The little girl asked, "Out there?"

"We're safer if we know what's going on. But I want you to stick to me like glue, and if I say run, you run. Okay?"

The child nodded, fear in her eyes.

Catalina asked, "Are you a good swimmer?"

"Yeah. I got a medal at school."

"That's good to know, just in case." Catalina reached under the cot and slipped the Glock into her waistband. "I'm going to peek outside for a second, just wait here." And she slipped out the door.

Faye sat, listening to the commotion outside. Then another sound caught her attention—a soft rattling. She glanced around, unable to place the source. She heard it again. It was coming from the fragment on the table.

Leaning over it, she whispered, "You're back."

The finger-sized sliver continued vibrating.

Faye picked it up. It felt warm as it quivered in the palm of her hand. She asked, "Are you alive?"

The vibrating stopped. Faye remembered what a huge deal this tiny fragment was. Hans kept saying it would prove all her dad's theories—the same ones everyone said were crazy. If that happened, he wouldn't have to run around the jungle and be so far away all the time.

Catalina leaned into the cabin and said, "Let's go."

Faye slipped the fragment into her pants pocket, zipped it shut, and scurried over to Catalina.

They reached the front deck just in time to hear another deafening crack echoing from the port side.

Faye pointed to the riverbank, shouting, "Look!"

A huge tree pitched forward. Five men clad in loincloths were perched on its trunk, riding it down. It crashed into the water ahead, blocking the boat's path. The moment it splashed down the men raced along its trunk toward the riverbank.

Santos muscled past Catalina, pistol drawn. She pulled Faye aside, shielding her body. Santos fired six shots at the fleeing men, hitting none. One of the men actually stopped to wave his arms in what Catalina assumed was an obscene gesture then ran off. Santos holstered his sidearm, cursing at the natives.

The *Valentina* shuddered to a stop, barely fifty feet from the fallen tree. A shorter tree had already fallen from the opposite bank of the tributary, forming a blockade.

Catalina was impressed. Canadian lumberjacks couldn't have done a better job.

Batista's yacht pulled alongside the *Valentina*. Batista climbed off, shoving sailors aside, bellowing, "God damn bastards! Somebody get me a radio!" One of his men raced over with a walkie talkie. Batista shouted into it, "I want gunboats along the shoreline, and get my divers up here, now!"

Hans cautiously approached Batista, asking, "Do you have a moment, sir?"

Catalina's hand inched closer to the hidden Glock.

Batista shouted, "Do I look like I have a moment? Leave me the hell alone!"

The terrified Austrian retreated to his cabin. Catalina relaxed, knowing Hans's timidness had bought them some time.

She whispered to Faye, "Let's go over and talk to the big creep."

Faye made a face.

Catalina laughed. "Trust me; I don't like it either."

Holding Faye's hand, Catalina strolled over to Batista. She'd made it a point to stay close to him, knowing the bastard would be well protected if creatures or natives attacked. Being a certified narcissist, Batista interpreted this as attraction.

She asked, "What happened?"

Upon seeing her, Batista assumed a calm facade. "It's those savages, the *Morte Tinto*. They're dropping trees in our path to block us. Those Stone Age bastards think they own this part of the river."

"How'd they manage to chop down those trees? I mean, they're huge."

"Never mistake primitive for stupid. They're industrious shits who probably stole axes from my own outpost."

One of the gunboats roared along the riverbank, churning up a wake of brown water. Once in position it opened fire, its machine guns shredding the tree line.

Batista handed Catalina a pair of binoculars and said, "Take a look, the *Morte Tinto* are squatting out in the bush laughing, but we're going to put the fear of God in them."

A barrage of arrows flew from the river's edge, bouncing off the gunboat's armored hull. The boat let loose with another salvo.

Batista said, "They'll shoot arrows at us then slink back into the jungle."

Catalina said, "Arrows ain't much against machine guns."

"Don't let those tiny arrows fool you. They're soaked in dart frog venom. Just being nicked by one will kill a man in ten minutes. We need to keep them back while the divers work."

A second gunboat slid alongside the first, cutting its engines. It drifted silently for a minute, arrows pinging off its armored hull. The silence was broken by a dull thud, followed by a puff of smoke on its deck. A second later, an explosion tore the jungle apart, showering the riverbank in mud and debris. The gunboat fired three more mortar rounds in rapid succession.

Catalina instinctively pulled Faye closer, but the little girl kept squirming, trying to see.

Batista slammed his fist on the guardrail, shouting, "How do you like that, you Neanderthal shits?" He turned to Catalina. "They're not so brave once they get a taste of mortar fire."

Catalina had known about the machine guns, but the mortars were a surprise addition. If she and Faye tried to make for the riverbank, they'd be blown to bits.

Batista radioed to the boat, "Cease mortar fire. Machine gunner, lay down intermittent suppressive fire." He lowered the walkie talkie and said, "We should be safe for now."

Faye jumped up and down, trying to see over the railing. Catalina lifted her up for a better look and asked Batista, "What do you mean, 'for now'?"

"We need to be moving again before sundown because those primates own the night." His frustration mounting, Batista shouted, "Where are those divers and is someone bringing that case from my yacht?"

A pair of crewmen raced over carrying red plastic cases. Batista popped them open, unveiling a bounty of plastic explosives.

Catalina was stunned. Then she sensed someone looming behind her. It was Santos.

Having seen the expression on her face, he asked, "So you recognize explosives?"

Catalina recovered quickly. "I'm a geologist, it kinda comes with the job."

Batista chimed in. "Same here. When you own mines, you never travel without Semtex. My divers will use it to dislodge those trees."

Faye knelt down, looking at the coiled detonator cord and Semtex, exclaiming, "Cool!"

Catalina gently pulled her back. "Not cool, dangerous," while making a mental note of the explosives stored on Batista's yacht.

Batista shouted, "Where the hell are my divers?" He saw two men hauling scuba gear over from the passenger area and yelled, "You two go to the bow."

The divers scrambled towards the front deck. Batista fell in behind them carrying the cases of Semtex while telling Catalina, "Tag along, this should be entertaining. Once we're moving again, perhaps you'll come over to my yacht for drinks. I'm sure Hans can look after the little one for a few hours."

The offer made Catalina's flesh crawl and she stammered for a reply.

Faye squeezed her hand tightly, pleading, "Please don't leave me alone," tears in her eyes. "I'm scared. If you're gone the monsters will come."

In a soothing tone, Catalina said, "It's okay, I'll just bring you with me."

Annoyed at the prospect of babysitting, Batista said, "Perhaps another evening then, after we reach the outpost."

Catalina nodded, holding Faye close. "Maybe I should take her back to the cabin."

Batista waved them off, barely hiding his annoyance.

Once they were out of earshot, Faye whispered, "Is he gone?"

"Yeah."

Faye sniffled one more time then smiled. "Good, 'cause he's gross. I think he wants to get in your pants."

Catalina couldn't help but laugh. "Where'd you learn that?"

"Mom has HBO."

"Maybe you should stick with the Disney Channel for a while. That was some pretty good acting."

Faye giggled, but Catalina felt her small hand tremble. She knelt down, looking into the little girl's eyes.

"Honey, I know you're trying to act brave, but it's okay to be scared."

The little girl hugged Catalina with all her might. Now the tears were genuine.

Catalina stroked her hair, whispering, "It's okay, I'm not going to let anything hurt you." But she knew her words were hopeful at best.

Faye wiped her nose and said, "Don't worry, my dad's coming back."

"I know, honey, I know."

With pride, Faye said, "He's still alive because he grew up in jungles and mountains and knows everything." Then she gazed out at the river. "Catalina, did you ever see pink dolphins?"

"No, but they sound pretty cool."

"They're really called botos and they're super rare, but dad promised we would find some. After he rescues us, we'll all go and find pink dolphins." She gazed out at the river and, in a near whisper added, "He'd never break a promise."

Catalina wished she could believe that too.

#

Micah lay on his back, baking in the sun, wrists manacled to the high platform. He'd hoped his new role as the queen's captive stud would have improved the accommodations and therefore his chance of escape. But the only perk had been an extra ration of food and water to keep his strength up.

Glancing back at the stern he saw the dinghy lashed to the railing—so close yet so far. He was rarely let loose from the manacles, and when he was, Umberto was never more than a few feet away. Even during his thrice daily romps with the queen, Umberto lurked outside the cabin door, jealously listening in.

Micah heard an approaching engine and sat up for a better look. One of the queen's go-fast boats roared in from the opposite direction, pulling up along the port side. An excited crewman shouted until the queen emerged from her cabin to hear his report. Micah only made out brief snatches—something about Batista's armada being stalled around the next bend.

The queen bellowed orders then slipped into the engine room. The boat transformed into a hive of activity, with men being issued weapons and assuming their posts.

The flagship lurched forward, increasing speed until the surrounding boats could barely keep pace.

Minutes later, Umberto climbed up top and unclamped Micah's manacles. After the traditional verbal and physical abuse, he shoved Micah toward the ladder. Climbing down, Micah made it a point to look weak and disoriented.

Umberto mockingly shouted, "What's wrong? Not man enough for the queen?" to the amusement of nearby men.

Once on deck, Umberto produced a length of rope and tied Micah's hands behind his back. A go-fast boat came alongside and the crew shouted something to Umberto. They spent the next two minutes yelling back and forth.

Seizing the opportunity, Micah leaned back against the hull, groping with his bound hands until he found the jagged piece of metal. While Umberto argued, he sawed away at the ropes.

One of the men on the boat tossed a cloth sack up to Umberto then sped off.

Digging into the bag, Umberto declared, "Now we'll show those bastards who rules this river." He proudly showed Micah a round metal object. It was a hand grenade.

Micah didn't know much about grenades, but he was pretty sure they weren't supposed to have peeling paint, a coating of rust and a white chalky substance seeping from their seams. The grenade was probably older than the man holding it.

Umberto stuffed his treasure back into the sack and shoved Micah towards the bow, yelling, "She wants to see you."

Micah carefully made his way along the narrow deck, muttering, "Christ, we must be doing thirty knots."

Umberto proudly declared, "The queen is a mechanical genius. Her boats can outrun anything on the river." And he continued on, the grenades in his sack clanking together as he walked.

Queen Caveira stood at the bow, bellowing orders to passing boats like Lord Nelson at Trafalgar. Micah and Umberto obediently waited for an audience with Her Highness. Rifle-toting crew members scrambled around the deck, preparing for battle. Micah noticed that most, like Umberto, had sacks of grenades slung over their shoulders.

When the queen finally deigned to turn and address them, Micah's blood froze. She'd painted her face into a white Macumba skull mask with an intricate network of religious symbols drawn onto her forehead. Her untamed hair blew in the wind, framing the skeletal visage. Deep black circles painted around her eyes only amplified their madness.

With an evangelical fervor, she announced, "Batista is up ahead, and his boats are blocked by fallen trees." After a long swig of coca-infused liquor, she added, "Now I'll make that bastard pay!"

Micah pleaded, "But what about my daughter? You said—"

"You won't need her anymore."

"Come again?"

"Last night, Boiúna came to me in a dream and proclaimed that I would bear a child from you. So you will not need your clearly inferior daughter."

Micah shouted, "That's insane!" earning a cuff across the ear from Umberto that knocked him onto the deck.

The queen looked puzzled. "But it is Boiúna's will. You should be honored."

Micah got back up onto his knees, pleading, "Please, just give me a boat and a few minutes, maybe I can get to her!"

"And warn Batista? No. Umberto, chain him up again so he can watch my victory. And don't despair, Lucky Man; after I triumph, Boiúna will demand another sacrifice." The queen raised her fist in the air shouting, "*Mate todos! Mate todos!*"

Micah was dragged off as the crew took up her war cry of, "Kill them all!"

Micah walked along the deck, twisting his hands, straining at the frayed rope. It refused to break.

Umberto mumbled, "What a waste of time. By now, all the best guns are taken," and shoved Micah toward the ladder.

Feigning losing his balance, Micah dropped to his knees. Leaning back against the hull, he found the jagged piece of metal and whittled at the rope.

Umberto shouted, "Get up there," and kicked him in the stomach.

Micah slumped down, groaning, buying himself a few more seconds of cutting time. Umberto grabbed his shirt and hauled him back onto his feet.

Micah felt the rope snap. It was now or never.

He lashed out with a perfect right cross to Umberto's jaw. Umberto staggered, more surprised than hurt. Micah hit him again, followed by a kick to Umberto's shin. The big man stumbled on the slick deck, slamming his head against the hull, and collapsed.

Micah raced for the stern where the dinghy was lashed. He grabbed the damp rope, fumbling with the knot, trying to pry it apart, cursing himself for not grabbing Umberto's knife. The knot finally came loose.

"There we go—"

Something hit him from behind like a pile driver—Umberto was back. The body slam threw Micah forward, into the inflatable boat. He bounced off, like a wrestler hitting the ropes, and pivoted around. His unexpected move threw Umberto off balance. The big man staggered back a few steps. That's when Micah saw the knife in his hand. Using the inertia, Micah launched a headbutt down onto the bridge of Umberto's nose. There was a sharp snap of cartilage, but the big man's knife arm was already swinging. Micah caught Umberto's wrist, holding the knife at bay. But his strength was ebbing. With each breath the blade inched closer to his face.

The flagship's speed suddenly dropped by half. The lurch sent both of them sprawling into the inflatable boat. The untethered dinghy flipped upward, over the railing and into the river.

The two men went with it.

CHAPTER THIRTEEN

Six of Batista's men, each toting a machete, climbed onto the downed tree trunk. The underwater explosives would blast the fallen trees from the riverbed. But to ensure success they needed to hack down the jungle of tree branches showing above the water line, to prevent a logjam when the current carried it off.

Batista and his divers, Zé and Rafa, squatted at the edge of the *Valentina*'s front deck, their collection of explosives neatly laid out. Crewmen and cooks hustled around them, pushing back the long barbecue grills and moving the remaining livestock to make room.

Batista said, "We only need to dislodge the larger tree. We can steer around the other one." He cut eight-foot lengths of detonator cable, connecting a series of blasting caps to the precut cord, explaining, "The cord's cut long enough for two wraps around the tree trunk." He then broke a ten-pound block of Semtex into butter stick-sized chunks. "This should be more than enough explosive for each wrap. If the branch looks really thick just use two sticks. This isn't about precision."

Zé, the lead diver, nodded and said, "Okay, sir. You really know your way around Semtex."

Batista pressed the blasting caps into the Semtex, saying, "Explosives are one of my passions. They can solve virtually any problem. Are you ready?"

Both divers nodded. Batista walked away, leaving them to their work.

Zé zipped his explosives inside a sack and slung it over his shoulder then asked Rafa, "Is it just me, or does the boss get a hard-on when he plays with explosives?"

Rafa replied, "You got that right," and finished prepping the last blasting cap, adding, "Man, I don't like this pre-wiring shit."

"Me neither, but it's safer than doing it down there where you can see fuck all. Relax, nothing's going to blow without the detonator."

He pointed over at the detonator—a mini fridge-sized electronic plug box. A curious chicken was pecking at its connections.

Zé kicked the chicken, shouting, "Can somebody please keep these goddamn birds away from us?"

Cooks ran over, shooing the birds away.

Zé said, "Alright, switch on your beacon." Red flashing lights mounted to their air tanks flicked on. "Now put on your tank and let's get this over with."

#

Catalina stood back with Faye, watching the preparations. She'd intended to bring the child back to the cabin but then decided against it. Faye was bright, and curious beyond her years, so keeping her mind occupied distracted her from being terrified. The absurdity of their situation wasn't lost on Catalina. To their right, men raked the shoreline with machine guns, while here on deck the divers had enough Semtex to blast the *Valentina* into splinters. Despite all those dangers, being up on deck was still safer than being in the cabin—at least on deck they had room to run.

Faye said, "Look, the divers are getting ready. Did you ever do that?"

"Yeah, I went scuba diving a bunch of times with an old boyfriend."

"What are those flashing red lights on the tanks for?"

"The water down there's really muddy, so those lights help them find each other. Plus they have those really bright headlamps to help see what they're doing."

"How long will they stay underwater?"

Hearing another round of machine gun fire raking the shoreline, Catalina said, "They can't finish soon enough for me."

#

Zé spat into his mask then gave final instructions to Rafa. "You go right, find the anchor points, plant your wraps and run out the cable. I'll do the same on the left." He grabbed a long spool of electric "zip cord" affixed with a flashing red beacon. "I'll sink the spool down close to the boat, so we can both run the det-cord over to it for hookup. Once we're both back on deck I'll plug the zip cord to the detonator and we'll blow 'em all."

Rafa gave him an unenthusiastic thumbs up.

Zé picked up the zip cord, slung the sack of explosives over his tank and slipped off the deck. Rafa followed a few seconds later.

Once underwater they split up, heading for their predetermined zones. Zé watched his partner's beacon vanish into the distance then kicked hard until he reached the bottom. With all the sediment he could barely see six feet in front of him, but he counted three thick branches embedded in the muddy riverbed.

At the first, he wedged a chunk of Semtex and wrapped the detonator cable around it. The blasting cap was already connected.

Zé was about to move on when something shot past him. All he could make out was that it was four feet long and brown.

Maybe a river otter, he thought. From experience he knew the otters were curious but not dangerous.

A second one swam by, bumping him as it passed.

Fucker.

It swam thirty feet then spun a hundred and eighty degrees, heading right back at him—the light from his headlamp reflected off a mouthful of razor-sharp teeth. Zé swam back, trying to find cover in the branches. But the fish latched on to his outstretched arm like a vice, crushing the bones. It thrashed in place, trying to drag him out. Zé latched on to a branch with his good arm, fighting to hang on. The fish bit down harder, tearing through flesh, muscle and bone until it severed his arm. A cloud of blood billowed in the brown water. He clung to the branch even harder, terror and adrenaline cancelling out the pain.

Zé felt a tremor ripple through the water—a low shockwave coming from beneath the riverbed. The tremor was strong enough to shake the downed tree.

Another fish shot out of the darkness, targeting his outstretched leg. He pulled it back in the nick of time. The fish missed, chomping down on a thick branch instead. It thrashed frantically, its teeth embedded in the wood.

Its struggle gave Zé his first clear look at his attacker. It was a piranha but ten times the size of any normal fish.

#

Catalina felt the deck beneath her vibrating and grabbed Faye's arm. The felled tree in front of the *Valentina* trembled, as if shaken by some giant hand. The men working on the tree trunk threw down their axes, grabbing for branches. Three of them tumbled into the water. A second, more intense rumble sent two more into the river.

Shouting, "Man overboard," Catalina grabbed a life preserver and tossed it down to the closest man. She glanced around the deck, yelling, "*Homem ao mar!*" and saw Santos idly leaning against the railing. "You maybe want to help us out here?"

Shamed into actually doing something, Santos trotted toward her.

The nearest man latched on to the life preserver. He looked at Catalina, giving a grateful thumbs up.

Then his eyes widened and he screamed, "*Agudo!*" An instant later, he was pulled beneath the surface.

It took Catalina a second to translate what he'd screamed—it was "biting." Another man screamed and vanished.

Then she saw blood in the water.

#

Rafa watched the huge piranhas swarming around the felled tree. Killing his headlamp, he slunk back into the thick branches. The fish still hovered around him, biting at the tree limbs.

Shit, he thought, *they can see the goddamn beacon*. The flashing red light was like wearing a target on his back.

He groped behind his back, trying to turn it off, but couldn't reach the switch. Shutting off the beacon meant unstrapping the tank.

He felt a tremor surge through the downed tree. The trembling ground kicked up a cloud of silt, further muddying the water.

A man splashed down into the water a few yards away. A heartbeat later, the piranhas swarmed the drowning man from all sides, latching on to his thrashing limbs. They all pulled in opposite directions, until he was drawn and quartered.

Rafa saw something else darting among the piranhas. It was at least twelve feet long and rippling through the water. It zeroed in on a nearby piranha carrying a severed arm in its mouth. But it didn't attack—instead it merely brushed past. The piranha spasmed violently, releasing its prize, and sank to the bottom. The attacking creature snapped up the severed arm and moved on.

Rafa thought, *It's a goddamn monster electric eel.*

Another man splashed down, thrashing in the water, only to be set upon by piranhas.

It's now or never, Rafa thought, *go while the fish are busy stuffing themselves*. After unlocking the chest clamp, he slipped the tank off his shoulders. Without his headlamp it was nearly impossible to find the beacon's off switch.

He fumbled in the darkness, thinking, *Shit, shit, shit*, too distracted to see what was coming.

A piranha punched through a gap in the branches, locking on to his leg. It clamped down with the bite force of a great white shark, crushing his femur. Grappling with the attacker, he lost his grip on the tank. The aqualung sank, yanking the air mask off his face. He watched in horror as the flashing beacon receded to the bottom. The piranha on his leg clamped down harder, tearing through sinew and muscle like paper. The fish dragged him out of the sheltering branches, where he saw another piranha coming straight for him. Its impossibly wide mouth clamped down around his head. Rafa let out one final, silent scream before his skull collapsed in a swirl of crimson bubbles.

#

Adrenaline surged through Zé's body as he fought to keep himself from hyperventilating. After some fumbling, he managed to loop a length of detonator cord around his arm stump and pulled it taut, reducing the billowing crimson cloud to a light mist. Hunkered down in the branches of the fallen tree he watched men thrashing in the water around him—all becoming easy meat for the piranhas.

But maybe their misfortune could be his salvation. In an effort to control his breathing, he told himself, *Stay on the bottom, move slowly and make for the boat. It can't be more than thirty yards away.*

Zé tried to ditch the bag of explosives, but the straps had become hopelessly entwined with his air tank's harness.

Hugging the riverbed, he crawled for the *Valentina*, intentionally kicking up a cloud of sediment to conceal his presence. A pair of piranhas bore down on him then veered off to attack another drowning man.

It's taking too long, he thought, the blood loss making him groggy.

Once the piranha had gone, he kicked with every ounce of strength until the *Valentina*'s underside loomed above him. He pushed off the river bottom, beginning his ascent. Something zipped past, undulating through the water like a ribbon. Through the murk he made out a serpentine body and leopard spots. It was an eel at least twelve feet long and thick as a tree trunk. A second later, it vanished into the muddy gloom. Zé kicked frantically until he was able to touch the metal hull.

Almost home.

An instant later, the eel was back, rippling through the water at ten miles an hour. It slammed headlong into his chest, delivering nine hundred volts of current. The shock sent his body into violent spasms.

For the Semtex and detonator cord strapped to his body, the nine hundred volts was a call to action—a biological detonator. Twenty-five pounds of

Semtex and detonator cord exploded as one, vaporizing Zé and the eel. The shockwave tore open the *Valentina*'s thin hull, while Zé's ruptured steel air tank punched through the deck like a torpedo.

CHAPTER FOURTEEN

The lip of the *Valentina*'s deck exploded. Catalina threw herself on top of Faye, chunks of steel and deck plank rocketing past. Catalina looked around, but there was only black smoke.

The bow of the ship lurched violently, sinking ten degrees. Catalina clung to a tie-down to keep from being swept forward. She heard men screaming and glanced toward the stern. The explosion had overturned the cooking grills, leaving the deck awash in fire. A screaming man tumbled overboard, his body wrapped in flames. The sheet of fire spread to nearby cans of cooking fuel, setting off a daisy chain of smaller detonations. Wounded men dove over the side.

The giant piranhas were waiting.

With a scream of twisting metal, the bow sank another ten degrees. A quarter of the front deck was now underwater. The downward slope sent flaming debris rolling straight at Catalina and Faye.

A tender boat pulled alongside the sinking *Valentina*, its pilot yelling for men to get aboard. Santos calmly walked to the edge of the deck and hopped off into the boat.

Catalina grabbed Faye, scrambling for the boat, shouting, "Wait for us!"

Santos shoved the boat's pilot aside, grabbed the tiller and sped off.

Catalina screamed, "Asshole!"

Santos looked back at her and waved—it was the first time she'd seen him smile. Then the bow lurched, sinking another ten degrees.

Faye pointed aft, screaming, "Look!"

The wall of fire was closing in on them.

Putting her mouth to Faye's ear, Catalina said, "Take the deepest breath you ever took and hold it." Then, clutching the child to her chest, she jumped overboard. An instant later, the deck became an inferno.

They sank halfway to the bottom. Catalina's first instinct was to kick for the surface, until she saw the swarm of huge fish tearing at the drowning men above. Swimming into that charnel house was certain death.

Faye tugged at Catalina's sleeve then pointed to the river bottom. All Catalina could see was cloudy muck, until a dim red light flashed.

Catalina thought, *It's the diver's beacon.* A plan flashed in her mind—it was crazy, but it sure beat being fish food.

Holding Faye to her chest she kicked down until she could grab a submerged tree branch. Hand under hand, lungs burning, she pulled them down to the bottom. A scuba tank lay half buried in the mud, the bag of demolition charges still tangled around it.

Catalina grabbed the face mask, pulled the regulator free and jammed it in her mouth. She made sure Faye saw what she was doing then pressed it to the little girl's lips. After an initial bout of panic, Faye began to breathe. They passed the regulator back and forth twice, establishing a rhythm.

A huge piranha swam past them. Catalina slunk back into the thick branches. She turned around and found herself face-to-face with the diver—or at least his head. Covering Faye's eyes, she swatted the head away. It drifted out beyond the branches where a piranha snapped it up.

Catalina and Faye huddled among the branches, passing the air hose back and forth.

A low, audible thump echoed through the water. A torrent of air bubbles and oil burst from the *Valentina*'s ruptured hull. The bow pitched forward, sinking deeper. Catalina didn't know what happened if you were too close to a sinking ship, but she wasn't sticking around to find out. After getting Faye's attention she pointed up and mimed climbing. The little girl nodded and they began their underwater ascent, using the tangled branches as cover.

A sudden tremor shook the tree, followed by a burst of air bubbles rising from the riverbed.

Catalina thought, *Seriously? An earthquake, now?* and clung on tight.

The rumbling ceased and they continued climbing. To Catalina it felt like scaling a mountain, with a cinder block strapped to her back, while hauling an eighty-pound sack. After what seemed like hours they broke the surface, crawling onto the half-submerged tree trunk. It was as big around as a tractor trailer tire, allowing them enough space to lie back and savor the air, amazed to be alive.

Faye gripped Catalina's hand, saying, "You saved us."

Tussling her sodden hair, Catalina said, "I told ya I wouldn't let anything happen to you."

The tree trunk was a foot above the water's surface, offering a panoramic view of hell. The front half of the *Valentina* was now underwater. The rear was pointed into the sky, enveloped in black smoke and flames. Batista's tender boats buzzed around the sinking ship, scooping up a few fortunate men. The unlucky ones were dragged below the surface, never to be seen again.

Catalina muttered, "What a complete and utter pig fuck." Then she noticed Batista's yacht, safely moored beyond the danger zone. She slipped off the aqualung and untangled it from the waterproof sack. She was delighted to discover the sack was full of Semtex. "Oh, we're definitely hanging on to this." She didn't have any way to detonate the explosives, but she sure as hell wasn't throwing them away.

Faye stood up, stretching to get a better view.

Catalina said, "Stay close to me, honey, it's not—"

A piranha burst out of the water, landing inches from Faye's leg. The child tumbled backward, nearly falling into the river. The wriggling fish inched closer, gnashing at the air with razor-sharp teeth.

Catalina grabbed the air tank and swung it down hard onto the piranha's skull. Undaunted, it kept inching closer to Faye. Catalina brought the tank down twice more. On the final swing the enraged fish clamped its jaws around the tank's shoulder strap. Catalina flung the aqualung with all her might, sending it, and the fish, into the river.

"Chew on that for a while!"

Faye crawled over, wrapping her arms around Catalina.

"It's okay, baby, it's gone. We're safe." But she knew that wasn't true. Staying on the tree was suicide, and being rescued by Batista's men was also a death sentence. Their only option was to use the fallen tree as a causeway to the riverbank and hope the local cannibals weren't hungry. "Come on, honey, it's time to walk the plank."

And they did. It was barely a hundred feet to the riverbank, but getting there meant clawing through a horizontal jungle of branches and vines. The trek was further complicated by a troupe of acrobatic capuchin monkeys exploring the downed tree.

Faye yelled, "Look, monkeys!"

Catalina muttered, "That's bordering on an obsession, sweetie."

One of the monkeys effortlessly zipped by Catalina, who momentarily lost her footing. She shouted, "Goddamn showoffs!" and pressed on.

The monkey troupe suddenly froze in place, letting out a chorus of howls, and then fled en masse back to the riverbank.

Sensing trouble, Catalina grabbed Faye's belt and shouted, "Stop!"

She felt the tree vibrating beneath her hand until it grew into violent shaking—worse than they'd felt underwater. Catalina flattened out on the tree trunk, one hand clamped to Faye's belt. "Just hang on, honey."

The water beneath them churned. A torrent of air bubbles burst to the surface till the river looked like a boiling cauldron. Then it stopped.

Catalina muttered, "What the fuck was that?"

Faye said, "I don't fucking know," and actually giggled.

Catalina thought, *This kid's as bad as her dad; laughing at danger must be genetic.*

They were over three quarters of the way across when Catalina saw a small boat approaching. She said, "Keep moving, honey, maybe they'll ignore us."

That's when she saw Santos standing in the boat. A second later, he opened fire.

#

Micah hit the river, sinking like a rock, his lungs filling with water. A few hard kicks got him to the surface, but it was pitch black. After a moment's panic, he realized he was beneath the overturned dinghy. Grabbing the edge, he swam out from under.

Umberto was waiting.

The big man grabbed his hair, pushing him under the water. Micah flailed, hands groping, till he latched on to something—Umberto's crotch. He clamped down on the fistful of testicles. With a shrill scream, Umberto released him and sank beneath the brown water.

Micah bobbed to the surface, crawling onto the overturned dinghy. He grabbed the oarlock and leaned back, flipping the boat. Once it was righted, he gripped a tie-down and heaved himself inside.

Something flashed in the corner of his eye. Micah pitched sideways as the knife blade zipped past his face.

Micah yelled, "Son of a bitch!" while groping for some kind of weapon.

Umberto hauled himself halfway into the Zodiac, the knife now clenched in his teeth. Micah latched on to an oar velcroed to the hull. Tearing it loose, he swung blindly, striking Umberto squarely in the face. Umberto spat out the knife, along with a few teeth, and flopped back into the water. But a second later he was back, grabbing at the oarlock.

Micah held up the oar, ready to strike. Umberto swung the cloth sack he'd been carrying like a club, striking his shin. Wincing in pain, Micah dropped to his knees, wrenching the sack out of Umberto's hand. Umberto lost his grip, treading water alongside the dinghy.

Micah rose up, gripping the oar like a baseball bat, shouting, "Just stay down, you fucking maniac!"

Umberto suddenly vanished beneath the water, as if sucked straight down. The water erupted in a crimson geyser and Umberto shot back to the surface, letting out a banshee wail. He kicked frantically, trying to swim with one leg— the other was reduced to a bloody stump below the knee.

At first Micah thought the attacker was a bull shark, until he saw a flash of copper-colored scales break the water. A split second later, the huge fish clamped on to Umberto's outstretched arm.

Micah recognized the fish ... sort of. It had the body and head of a piranha but was at least four feet long.

With one bite the fish severed Umberto's arm and submerged clutching its prize. A second fish broke the surface, clamping its jaws around Umberto's throat. An instant later, the man was yanked beneath the water, a bloody stain spreading around the dinghy.

Micah shouted, "Shit!" and grabbed the engine's pull start. He yanked once, twice, but the engine just sputtered. "Think, dumbass, think!" Then, remembering his youth on the river, he found the engine's manual choke and pulled it out. He yanked the pull start again—this time it caught, roaring to life. "Yes!" He saw a huge fish bearing down on the stern. Grabbing the tiller, he pushed it straight down while flattening himself to the deck.

The roaring engine prop cleared the water just as the fish leapt at the boat. The whirring prop tore into its belly, gutting it in a fountain of blood. The giant fish tumbled into the water. A split second later, another giant piranha latched on to it, dragging it below.

Micah lowered the engine into the water. The dinghy lurched forward, gaining speed.

Another giant piranha was coming at the dinghy head-on. Micah gunned the engine, closing the gap, rolling right over the fish. The dinghy went airborne for a moment, splashed down and continued on. The fish didn't give chase.

The dinghy shot past the queen's flagship. Glancing back, Micah saw Queen Caveira standing at the bow. She must have seen him too. Her stream of curses momentarily drowned out the roaring outboard motor.

The queen's go-fast boats were up ahead, advancing in loose formation. Micah raced past them, shocked that they didn't open fire. Instead, three of the boats accelerated, mistakenly assuming that Micah was leading the charge.

Micah came to the bend in the river and gunned the engine, gambling that Faye and Catalina were still on the *Valentina*. He had to get to them before the queen turned the river into a shooting gallery.

But as soon as he rounded the bend, all the hope within him died.

The *Valentina* was sinking, its rear half engulfed in flames.

#

Santos's boat bore down on Catalina and Faye. He knelt at the prow rapid firing an AK-47.

Catalina grabbed Faye and hunkered down behind a thick branch, bullets shredding the wood around them.

She fumbled for the pistol, shouting, "That son of a bitch really hates me!"

More bullets slapped at the tree trunk, all going wide of the mark. Catalina was thankful that Santos was firing from a moving boat—it was the only thing saving them. He may have had her outgunned, but at least she'd be firing from a stable platform.

There was a momentary lapse in the fire. Gambling that he was reloading, Catalina poked her head up, aimed and snapped off four rounds. Santos had smartly hit the deck while reloading, so she opted for the man piloting the boat. His being close to the engine meant even a missed shot might do some damage. She dropped down, just as Santos resumed fire, showering them in shredded leaves and branches.

Catalina knelt down beside Faye, asking, "You okay?"

The wide-eyed little girl just nodded. Catalina peered over the tree trunk, hoping she'd hit the other man.

The attacking boat veered wildly. Santos stepped back from his firing position, kicked the wounded pilot overboard and took control.

Knowing she only had a few bullets and no spare ammo, Catalina prayed he wouldn't make a second attack. Taking a chance, she stood up for a better look.

Santos was seated at the tiller, turning the boat away. She watched him roar off, fighting the impulse to give him the finger. Something jarred the tree, almost knocking her into the river.

She grabbed on to a branch, shouting, "Hang on tight, honey."

The fallen tree trembled, nearly shaking them off. They were no more than fifty feet from the shore, but there was no way they could move safely.

The water around them churned and bubbled.

Looking up to the sky, Catalina yelled, "Really? What do you got for us now, a volcano?"

A moment later, her theory was proven wrong.

A blackish coil, thick as the tree trunk, rippled along the water and sank back down.

Catalina muttered, "The goddamn snake's back," and grabbed Faye. "We need to run for shore!"

CHAPTER FIFTEEN

Micah steered the dinghy towards the sinking *Valentina*, praying that he'd find Faye and Catalina. There was no sign of life on the burning ship or in the water around it—just crimson stains on the brown water, marking the piranhas' feeding frenzy.

One of Batista's gunboats pulled alongside him but roared off without incident. Apparently a lone man in a dinghy wasn't deemed a threat.

Micah steered towards a huge kapok tree blocking the tributary, hoping the girls might have used it to escape. As he drew close, the water around him began churning, buffeting the inflatable boat. Massive air bubbles burst onto the surface.

Struggling to stay afloat, he yelled, "What the—?"

The hundred-and-fifty-foot tree trunk rose up from the water, like a drawbridge spanning a canal. Micah saw a serpentine coil break the surface, pushing the fallen tree upward. A moment later a reptilian head the size of a refrigerator burst from the water directly in front of him.

"Holy shit."

The massive snake's emerald-colored eyes locked on to him, its tongue flitting back and forth. Then it vanished beneath the water.

Micah jammed the tiller hard, cutting right just as the tree slammed back down into the water. The impact wave almost capsized him.

A flash of movement on the tree trunk caught his eye—someone clinging on to the branches as it bobbed in the current. At first Micah thought it was a sailor. Then he realized it was a woman.

Micah shouted, "Catalina!" knowing she couldn't hear him.

The snake's head rose from the water again, this time mere feet from Catalina.

#

Catalina saw the snake looming over them and pulled Faye under the thickest branch. Most of the snake's body was underwater, coiled around the tree. Its every move set off shockwaves that rippled through the trunk. The snake's head shot downward, locking its jaws around the thick branch, mere inches from Catalina and Faye. It pulled away, taking the branch with it.

Catalina's first instinct was to shoot, but doing that meant letting go of Faye. Releasing the child for even a second could be disastrous. All they could do was cower behind the remaining branches.

She looked around, desperate for some way to escape. Then she saw an orange dinghy bearing down on them. The maniac inside it was screaming at the top of his lungs, trying to get the monster's attention. When she finally saw the lunatic's face, her spirits rose.

Micah was alive.

#

Gunning the engine, Micah made for the downed tree, screaming at the top of his lungs, "Come on, you son of a bitch! Come after me!"

But the creature ignored him. Micah fumbled around inside the dinghy, searching for something to distract the snake. The first thing he saw was Umberto's satchel of grenades, but that was too dangerous. He yanked open the boat's emergency kit. Packets of water, food bars and some first aid gear tumbled out. Among the pile were three pull-cord style emergency flares— small, inaccurate, almost feeble, but at least it was something.

The snake pressed its weight onto the tree, poised to attack. Micah throttled down the engine till he was almost drifting. He raised the flare, aiming it at the snake's neck, and yanked the cord.

The flare zipped through the air, striking just below the snake's head. The impact didn't penetrate its skin, but the burning flare fell, landing in the snake's coil. The bright red flare seared at the snake's hide.

Micah stood up waving his arms, getting the snake's full attention. He fired a second flare. This one shot harmlessly past the snake's head, but now the creature had clearly identified the source of its pain. It vanished beneath the water, but Micah saw its body rippling just below the surface, heading for him.

Gunning the engine, he headed straight for Batista's flotilla, muttering, "You're gonna have plenty of folks to munch on."

Once the snake became Batista's problem he'd go back for the ladies.

#

Catalina saw the snake recoil from the flare and turned to Faye.

"When I say run, we run! Got it?"

Faye just nodded.

The snake writhed in pain, pushing the tree trunk upward, forcing Catalina to hang on for dear life. Then it submerged, passing underneath the fallen tree in pursuit of Micah. Its massive tail struck the underwater branches, uprooting the tree trunk from the muddy riverbed that had held it in place. The current caught the now freed trunk, sweeping it downriver, spinning it like a giant drill bit.

For a moment Catalina was submerged, desperately clinging to Faye. After what seemed an eternity, the tree trunk righted itself. It continued downriver, leafy branches catching the current like oars, driving it faster. Catalina realized they were on a hundred-and-fifty-foot log ride with no brakes.

The tree trunk rocked back and forth then pitched over again.

Catalina shouted, "Hold your breath!" as they were spun underwater. She thought, *Okay, we can just let go and swim for shore.*

Then a brown shape zipped past her, followed by a second.

The piranhas were back.

#

Micah's dinghy skipped across the water, pummeling his kidneys with every bounce. He didn't bother looking back, certain the snake was right behind him.

A tender boat pulled alongside, coming recklessly close. Micah glanced over and saw Santos extending an AK-47 in one hand. Micah cut right hard, bullets zipping past his head.

Then Santos must have seen the oncoming snake and changed his target. The snake rose up then slammed the front half of its body down onto the water, nearly crushing Santos's boat.

One of the gunboats roared into the fray, its dual front machine guns spraying lead across the water. A twenty-foot tender boat came in from Micah's left. Two men kneeling at its bow opened fire with assault rifles.

Plumes of water sprayed in every direction, but the snake kept coming.

Ducking low, Micah shouted, "How can you assholes miss a seventy-foot snake?!"

He was trapped in a hornet's nest, with Batista's men blazing away with the accuracy of *Star Wars* stormtroopers—a bad place for an inflatable boat. But at least they'd pissed off the monster. Seeing no other option, Micah continued forward, hoping to clear the shooting gallery then make a wide turn to double back for the girls.

Keeping his head down, he barreled towards the bend in the river. After a white knuckle minute, he felt confident that he'd cleared the line of fire. Then he saw red-flagged go-fast boats coming straight at him.

"Aw shit!"

The queen's flotilla was bearing down on him. He could even see Her Highness's flagship straight ahead.

"Okay, they ignored you before, so maybe—"

Muzzles flashed on the queen's flagship, tracer rounds zipping over his head. Two of the go-fast boats opened fire on him, adding to the chaos.

Micah cut sharply, turning right back into the first firefight.

#

Queen Caveira stood at the bow of her flagship, arms held high, howling with religious ecstasy.

"Boiúna has risen!"

The glorious serpent god had come to her aid, just as she'd prophesied. All her life she'd dreamed of seeing the river spirit, but no dream could compare to the sheer majesty of its physical form. Men around her shouted in excitement, firing their weapons in the air.

The queen yelled, "Stop firing! You'll need those bullets." Then she raised her binoculars for a better view of her god—but what she saw instantly dampened her evangelical fervor.

Her stolen orange dinghy was bouncing across the water, headed straight for them. Perched in it was the American who'd betrayed her.

"After all I did for you!"

She yanked the gunner out of the makeshift turret and fired off two long bursts, sending bright red tracer rounds at the American. Other armed men ran to the bow. By following the tracers, they were able to identify her target. They fired as one, sending a hundred rounds downriver.

#

Batista's mind struggled to process the last few minutes' parade of disasters. The *Valentina* was burning in the water while multiple boats were locked in a firefight with some unknown opponent. Only moments ago there'd been roaring gunfire. Now it had gone quiet.

Clutching his walkie talkie, he shouted, "Santos, situation report!"

Panicked cross talk from multiple boats reduced all communication to gibberish. Black smoke from the burning *Valentina* choked the air, rendering his binoculars equally useless. Batista turned to a frightened crewman behind him, shouting, "Idiots, goddamn idiots!"

The crewman gulped and said, "Look," pointing to a tender boat coming alongside.

Batista leaned over the rail, demanding, "What's the situation?"

The tender boat's gunner replied, "It's another snake, sir, bigger than the first!" Then he just stared slack jawed at Batista.

"Well then, get out there and help them kill it!"

Batista watched the tender speed off, muttering, "Idiots, nothing but—"

The water in front of the tender erupted. Suddenly there was thirty foot of writhing snake looming in its path. The tender boat banked sharply. The panicked gunner fired volleys that hit nothing. The snake's head hammered down, plucking the gunner out of the boat. The snake crushed the man in its jaws, and, with a shake of its head, spat him out. The tender slewed wildly, trapped in the snake's wake.

The snake slammed straight down, using the front half of its body like an axe, crushing the boat. Both serpent and boat vanished beneath the water. A moment later, the snake resurfaced, a man clenched in its jaws. It turned to focus on its next prey—the yacht.

Batista stared into its emerald-green eyes, his heartbeat pounding in his ears.

That silence was shattered by machine gun fire. One of the gunboats came in fast, front machine guns blazing. Unfortunately, Batista's yacht was also in the line of fire.

Batista hit the deck while keying his walkie talkie, shouting, "You idiots are shooting at us!"

The snake spat out the dead man and slipped beneath the surface.

The gunboat ceased fire, throttling back its water jets. It performed a slow circle of the area, guns trained on the water for any sign of the snake.

Batista came out of hiding and scanned the water. There was nothing, not even a bubble. "Come on, you bastard, where are—"

The gunboat's bow shot straight up in a geyser of water. The snake had struck from below, like a vertical battering ram. The impact shattered the gunboat's fiberglass hull, catapulting men over the side. The gunboat splashed down into the river, its fractured bow already taking on water. The snake surfaced again, stretching its body across the foundering gunboat's hull—capsizing it.

The snake vanished beneath the surface once again.

Screaming men paddled around the capsized boat, desperate to crawl onto the overturned hull. One managed to latch on, only to be dragged back under, screaming. Giant piranhas descended on the drowning men, pulling them under in a feeding frenzy.

Batista grabbed a deckhand by the arm, shouting, "Go below and bring me the two gray cases marked *Bazalt*, now!"

The deckhand scrambled below.

A second gunboat came alongside the yacht, barely slowing down.

Its crew chief shouted over the PA, "Incoming boats. They're coming around the river bend!"

Raising his binoculars, Batista saw a fleet of boats coming around the bend—all bearing the Red Flag Fleet's insignia.

Batista muttered, "That bitch."

Queen Caveira was coming, and she was out for blood.

CHAPTER SIXTEEN

Batista charged into the yacht's pilothouse, barking orders into his radio. "Break off from the snake. Focus all machine guns and mortar rounds on those pirates."

A panicked radio voice came back asking, "What about that thing?"

From the pilothouse, Batista could see the snake tearing apart one of his tender boats.

Batista said, "Leave it to me. I want everything but the Multi Cat and the landing barge hitting the pirates! Santos, take command of the attack!"

Batista set down the radio.

Hans ran in, wide-eyed, stammering, "Sir, what happens if that thing comes after us?"

Fighting the impulse to slap him, Batista said, "If it decides to follow our boats into the attack it'll be as much of a menace to the pirates as us. If it stays back here it'll likely attack the slow Multi Cat, which is expendable."

"Yes, yes, I see," Hans said, nodding like an imbecile. "What can I do?"

Disgusted with him, Batista said, "Go down into the cargo hold and make sure our equipment isn't damaged," and waved him off.

The two crewmen returned, lugging a pair of gray fiberglass cases with *Bazalt* stenciled across them.

Batista yelled, "Bring them up top, quickly!" and climbed the ladder to the fly bridge.

He had ensured that the yacht's highest platform was armored with reinforced steel, while still offering a three-hundred-and-sixty-degree view.

Santos's voice crackled over the radio. "May I commence the attack?"

Keying his radio, Batista said, "Yes, keep those bastards away from me."

"Copy that."

#

Micah turned fast enough to escape the oncoming pirate armada, only to run straight into Batista's oncoming flotilla.

At least they ain't shooting at me.

He barreled through them without incident.

But he had a bigger problem—the snake had broken off from pursuing Batista's boats, turning back on a course for Faye and Catalina's position.

In frustration, he shouted, "Goddamn monster's got OCD!"

Micah made a beeline for the snake, knowing the only thing between it and the ladies was Batista's yacht, the Multi Cat and the landing barge.

Micah caught up to the snake, running alongside it, screaming at the top of his lungs. But the damn thing wouldn't even look at him. In desperation he reached down for Umberto's bag. He fished out a grenade while keeping one hand on the tiller.

Staring at the rust-coated grenade, he thought, *Okay, just like in the movies.*

Squeeze the handle doodad in and pull the pin.

He squeezed the grenade's spoon while clamping his teeth around the pin and yanked. His front tooth chipped, but the grenade's rusted pin didn't budge.

So much for movies. Got to use two hands.

He wedged the tiller between his legs and winced as the bouncing handle delivered rabbit punches to his groin. Squeezing the aged grenade's spoon in, he gripped the pin with his other hand and yanked. This time the pin came out—but the rusted spoon broke off in his hand.

He stared at the smoking grenade for one precious second, yelling, "Rusted out piece a shit!" and lobbed it hard in the snake's direction while turning sharply from the blast.

The grenade came within twenty feet of the snake, detonating midair. The hailstorm of shrapnel peppered the snake. Enraged, it twisted in the water, hunting for the source of its pain.

Micah yanked the cord on the last aerial flare and let it fly. It zipped harmlessly past the snake, getting the beast's attention.

Now it was coming at Micah. He veered off, making for the lumbering Multi Cat. The snake was right on his tail, like some monstrous water skier.

Two men on the Multi Cat's deck saw what was coming and opened fire with AK-47s.

Micah heard bullets zipping past him and cut left sharply.

The snake submerged, and the water became calm. The men on the Multi Cat scanned the water, rifles at the ready.

The snake erupted from beneath the Multi Cat, sending it listing starboard. The two armed men rolled off the deck into the river, where the piranhas were waiting.

The snake's body slammed back down across the deck, crushing the pilothouse. Its upper body thrashed left and right, knocking over fuel drums like bowling pins. Ruptured fuel drums sprayed gas and diesel across the decks. The snake snapped up another man in its jaws and spat him into the river. The barge's hydraulic hoist collapsed onto the snake's back. The beast squirmed and writhed, attempting to dislodge itself.

Micah saw the stacks of fuel drums and remembered that the Multi Cat also had internal tanks. It gave him one Hail Mary opportunity to ensure the monster didn't go after Faye and Catalina.

Turning the dinghy around, he lined it up to pass alongside the Multi Cat. He knelt down, the tiller wedged between his knees, and grabbed the sack of grenades. Three remained. Keeping one hand outside the bag, he squeezed the spoon of the top grenade. With his other hand he reached into the sack, found the corresponding pin and pulled it free. This time the spoon didn't break off. He kept his hand clamped around the outside of the bag and grabbed the tiller again.

He muttered, "Do it right, do it right."

The dinghy scraped against the side of the Multi Cat, almost capsizing. As soon as it made contact, Micah lobbed the sack hard while gunning the outboard motor.

The snake wrenched itself free of the collapsed hoist, slithering across the barge.

The sack of grenades clattered across the deck. All three grenades exploded in a series, igniting the fuel-soaked deck, detonating the fuel drums, and rupturing the internal fuel tanks—the whole daisy chain took under a second. A mushroom cloud of fire and black smoke shot into the sky, raining steel and snake meat in every direction.

Micah felt a blast of heat and saw chunks of steel and burning fifty-five-gallon drums splashing into the water around him. Thankfully, nothing hit the fragile dinghy.

Raising one hand in the air, he screamed, "Yeah!" Then he spun the dinghy around, making for the downed tree.

But when he arrived, the tree wasn't there anymore.

#

Queen Caveira stood at the bow of her flagship, binoculars pressed to her eyes, staring in disbelief. One moment Boiúna had been tearing apart Batista's fuel barge—a truly glorious sight. Then that American bastard threw something, and she saw her god consumed in a blazing inferno. The sight of Boiúna's flaming, severed head splashing down into the river was like a dagger piercing her soul. She sank to her knees screaming, "No!" and slamming her fists against the deck.

The pirate next to her said, "Queen, they're coming straight at us!"

Queen Caveira spun around, glaring at him, her flowing tears smearing the skull makeup. The rage burning inside her suddenly transformed into ice.

In a terrifyingly calm voice, she ordered, "Let them come close, then use the grenades."

"Yes, Queen."

Grabbing the rifle lying at her feet, she added, "We have to kill them all!"

She watched the orange dinghy vanishing into the cloud of thick black smoke.

In a near whisper, she said, "Boiúna, I swear you will live again. And I will be the instrument of your revenge."

#

Micah closed in on the fast-moving tree, desperately trying to get Catalina's attention. He saw a piranha launch itself from the water. Catalina batted it aside before it could latch on.

That's when he saw Faye cowering behind her.

Heart pounding, Micah drew closer, pushing the dinghy's outboard motor to the breaking point.

The current battered the tree, rocking it back and forth until it rolled over, submerging the two women.

Micah screamed, "No!"

Seconds later, the tree righted itself. The women still clung on, but now piranhas were lodged in the branches around them—one mere inches from Faye.

Catalina grabbed the branch, bent it back, and let go. The fish catapulted past Micah into the river. Keeping one hand on the tiller, he waved maniacally, finally catching her attention.

She shouted, "Micah!"

The tree hit an eddy, the altered current spiraling the back end around clockwise. Micah cut right as the tree spun a hundred and eighty degrees. Then it cleared the eddy, maintaining a straight path long enough for him to draw alongside. Catalina squirmed closer to the dinghy, one arm locked around Faye's waist.

Micah reached out with his free hand, grabbing a branch. The dinghy bounced up and down, his extended arm tethering it to the tree. He clung on, every muscle throbbing, yelling, "Now!"

With no other option, Catalina lobbed Faye like a basketball, dropping her into the dinghy.

The terrified little girl yelled, "Daddy," and crawled over, throwing her arms around him.

The embrace nearly made him lose his grip. "Not now, honey!"

The boat rocked violently, nearly yanking his arm from the socket. Now it felt like they were dragging an anchor. Glancing back, he saw a piranha clamped on to the back of the inflatable, its teeth shredding the rear baffle. One third of the dinghy was deflated, its buoyancy decreasing every second. The fish hung on with pit bull tenacity.

Micah shouted, "Now! Now!"

Catalina leapt off the tree, her upper body landing in the partially deflated boat. The impact almost sank them. Micah released the branch and grabbed her arm while steering away from the tree.

Catalina crawled into the dinghy, snatched up an oar and hammered at the fish. It refused to let go, gnawing its way toward the next intact baffle.

She yelled, "Fuck it," drew the pistol and shot it through the eye. The fish jumped in a spastic aerial ballet before landing next to Micah. He jammed his knee onto its gills, pinning it down.

Micah shouted, "Bail, bail!"

"With what?"

The tree floated past them. Micah steered the partially submerged dinghy toward the riverbank, keeping an eye peeled for any caiman lurking there. With cupped hands, Catalina and Faye bailed the rising water. The outboard motor sputtered under the strain of what was becoming more bathtub than boat.

"Come on, come on," Micah muttered, eyeing the piranha swimming past them.

The dinghy struck the mud bank just as the waterlogged outboard motor sputtered and died.

Micah yelled, "Out, out! Check for caimans!"

Catalina was already moving, pulling Faye to shore with one hand, clutching the Glock in the other.

Micah hopped out and dragged the deflated dinghy up the riverbank. Once there he sank down to the muddy ground, physically and emotionally spent.

Faye ran over, throwing her arms around his neck. This time he didn't let her go.

She kissed him, tears in her eyes. "Daddy, you came back!"

"You bet I did. Did ya miss me?" Faye just buried her face in his chest. "I'll take that as a yes." He lay back, holding her tight.

Catalina knelt down next to them, her body caked in mud, and said, "She never lost faith in you, not even for a second."

"What about you?"

Catalina laughed and said, "Eh, I figured you'd pop up eventually," then sank down beside them, laughing.

The three lay there, reveling in the sheer joy of being alive.

CHAPTER SEVENTEEN

Santos took command of the attack from his tender boat, radioing orders to the other boats. The queen's armada was coming at them fast, but their assault lacked cohesion. It was more of a race than an attack. A pair of twenty-foot go-fast boats were in the lead, hellbent on grabbing the brass ring—Batista's yacht.

Santos radioed, "Remember, these are pirates. They're used to attacking fishing boats and tourists. So follow orders and maintain discipline."

Coming up behind the lead go-fasts was the queen's forty-foot trawler, flanked by small boats. Their undisciplined attack was a blessing.

Santos radioed his vessels. "Get three tender boats up front now. Focus all their fire on the lead go-fast. I want our remaining gunboat to hold back with the fast trawler and catch the second one."

Three tender boats descended on the pirates' lead go-fast, unleashing the concentrated firepower of six AK-47s. The attacking tender boats shredded the lead go-fast, killing the pilot. The go-fast boat slewed sideways, losing speed. A second wave of gunfire struck the engines, leaving it belching fire and black smoke.

The other pirate go-fast should have held its position, supporting its comrade. But instead, it just raced on, eager for glory.

Santos ordered, "Tender boats break off, you killed them, so don't waste another shot. We've got a trawler and more go-fasts inbound. Focus everything on the left go-fast; then circle around for the trawler." He knew the pirates would eventually wise up but was determined to inflict as much damage as possible in the meantime.

The queen's lead go-fast ran straight into the gunboat's twin front machine guns. A hail of bullets shredded its hull below the waterline, leaving it bobbing in the current. The gunboat pressed forward, its rear turret pummeling the go-fast with machine gun fire as it passed. The go-fast's engine exploded, throwing men into the river. The gunboat kept moving, heading for the oncoming trawler.

Santos shouted, "Where are my other tender boats?"

"We're coming up behind you."

Santos saw a skyrocket launch from the queen's flagship. It burst in a halo of yellow sparks. The queen's boats saw the signal and instantly slowed down, forming into a group.

Santos muttered, "They finally wised up."

#

Despite all the terrors and hardships she'd endured, Faye still managed to give Micah a nine-year-old's breathless recounting of their exploits, including their scuba escape.

Micah looked over at Catalina and said, "Nice work. Thank you doesn't even begin to—"

She waved him off. "No sweat, it's all in a day's work for your friendly neighborhood CIA." She pointed at the fish lying in the dinghy. "A whole army of those douche-nozzles attacked the boat."

Micah grabbed a stick and prodded the fish until he was satisfied it was dead.

He said, "It's a piranha but ten times the size of a normal one."

Peering down at it, Faye said, "Megapiranha."

"What?'

"I saw it on Animal Planet. They're giant piranhas that lived like a couple million years ago."

Catalina said, "That was just a scary movie, honey," before remembering their reality was more terrifying than any film.

Micah poked at the fish. "But what she's saying makes sense. The ants, the snake, now these. It's like the ancient world is coming back for the sole purpose of killing us. You said the piranhas attacked people en masse?"

"Yeah, it was a bloodbath."

"Despite what you see in movies, piranhas only do that if they're starving. But there's plenty enough to eat around here, even for these monsters." He rooted through the dinghy's survival kit. "Perfect. The queen really knew how to pack."

In addition to the usual emergency items there were small binoculars, a folding knife and even a pint bottle of infused cachaca. He tossed two pouches of survival water and some nutrition bars to Catalina, who doled some out to Faye. He stuffed the liquor into his pocket.

A deafening roar echoed through the trees above them. Catalina drew the pistol and dropped down into a combat stance, shouting, "What the fuck was that?"

A second roar followed. It sounded like a cross between a lion and a belching giant.

Scanning the trees, Micah said, "Relax. Faye, can you tell us what that was?"

Faye listened to another roar and said, "It's howler monkeys, right?"

"Good ear. There are some up in the trees, warning the troupe that we're trespassing."

Faye stared up at the trees and pointed to a male howler monkey the size of a German shepherd squatting above them. "There he is. He's a male, warning the rest of the troupe."

The monkey eyed her and let out another roar.

Putting the pistol away, Catalina said, "Thank you, midget Jane Goodall."

Faye said, "She studied chimps, not monkeys," and then waved to the big male.

Micah said, "Don't go near them, honey. Howlers are ornery and carry yellow fever."

Machine gun fire chattered in the distance, followed by muffled explosions.

Micah grabbed the binoculars and gestured to the riverbank. "What say we grab a seat and catch the last half of the battle?"

They all sat on the riverbank, feasting on nutrition bars. The current had carried them at least a kilometer downriver, but they could still see the battle raging in the distance. Micah watched for a minute then passed the binoculars to Catalina.

Small boats bore down on each other, machine guns blazing like World War Two fighter planes. Several vessels were burning.

Catalina said, "I know this sounds bad, but I hope whoever that is kills Batista." Then she passed the binoculars back to Micah.

Watching the chaos, he said, "I'm hoping for a total massacre on both sides. Trust me; they're all something out of a nightmare."

#

Santos watched the queen's armada break off their ragged attack, converging into a rough formation.

He muttered, "This just got harder," then keyed his radio. "Enemy approaching in formation. I want our gunboat and fast trawler to hold at the center, all tender boats break left and right and slash them from both sides."

A chorus of radio voices copied his transmission.

Santos knew exactly what had to be done, but he didn't need to be in the middle of it. He turned his boat, making for the rear as his tender boats advanced.

The queen's armada came at them in rough v-formation, the trawler in front, protecting her flagship. The armada was moving at a steady eighteen knots—a rapid approach but slow enough to maintain formation.

Santos's boats cut left and right, while the gunboat's machine guns focused on the center. The tactic forced the pirates to protect themselves on every side, while Santos's boats focused their firepower on the passing targets.

To the left, a line of tender boats came at the pirates in a straight line, unleashing a barrage of AK-47 fire into the passing vessels. By the time his third tender boat struck, two of the queen's go-fasts were burning. Two pirates on a go-fast started hurling grenades at the third tender boat. The tender boat's gunner cut both men down, but not before one grenade struck home. The tender boat exploded on the water.

In the center, Batista's gunboat and the fast trawler reduced their engines until they were treading water. They were letting the enemy come to them.

Santos's attack plan was being duplicated on the right, but this time the pirates were ready. The first tender boats passed the queen's trawler, their guns blazing. Pirates stood up on the trawler's deck lobbing hand grenades, destroying one passing tender boat.

One of the pirates pulled the pin on his grenade, only to have the rusted spoon break off. An instant later, the antique grenade exploded in his hand, killing him and three other men. A second loose grenade rolled across the deck and exploded. A ruptured fuel can burst into flames, engulfing the deck in fire. The burning trawler pressed on, absorbing gunfire intended for the queen's flagship running behind it.

A grenade landed on another tender boat, sending it veering wildly. It struck one of the pirate's go-fast boats head-on, capsizing both. Men from both sides spilled into the water, drew knives and continued the fight—until the piranha struck. The fish tore into the survivors. Only one man managed to make it onto the hull of the overturned go-fast.

The gunboat's twin front machine guns let loose with a steady barrage of fire into the queen's oncoming trawler. The rear gunners used the opportunity to fire mortar rounds. It was a long shot that any round would hit a target but worth trying. The first round landed in the river just in front of the queen's flagship and sank without detonating. Four more followed with equally dismal results. A fifth mortar round missed the queen's flagship but struck a go-fast boat just starboard. The round detonated, reducing the twenty-five-foot go-fast boat to timber. Flying debris struck a second boat, capsizing it. Men floundered in the water, quickly becoming chum for the Megapiranhas.

The queen's burning trawler kept coming until it suddenly exploded in a spectacular ball of fire. A go-fast running alongside it was showered in burning debris, killing all aboard.

The queen's flagship cut around the sinking trawler, powering straight into one of Santos's tender boats, capsizing it. There were at least six pirates crouched on the flagship's bow, firing at the gunboat.

To the left, one of Batista's tender boats was circling a go-fast in a furious close quarters firefight.

Santos knew he'd suffered huge losses but was pleased that the queen's flagship was heading straight for the gunboat. It didn't stand a chance against the gunboat's armored turrets and dual machine guns.

The gunboat continued firing at the queen's oncoming flagship—then suddenly their machine guns fell silent.

Santos muttered, "Idiots," knowing they'd overheated the belt-fed machine guns, fouling the barrels.

The queen's flagship roared past the impotent gunboat. Without slowing, it came alongside Batista's fast trawler, almost scraping the side. Pirates on the flagship hurled at least a dozen grenades onto the trawler's deck, reducing it to a flaming wreck. The flagship sped on.

The gunboat spun around to pursue, but with its front machine guns out of commission it was nearly useless.

Santos cursed to himself. Now nothing stood between the queen's flagship and Batista's yacht. The naval battle had turned into a duel.

CHAPTER EIGHTEEN

Batista listened to Santos's voice crackling over the walkie talkie. "We couldn't get 'em all. Her flagship's coming straight for you."

Batista peered out from the fly bridge, bullets pinging off its armor plating, and replied, "I figured that out already." Then he switched to the yacht's intercom, announcing, "Cut engines, and hold position. If she wants me, she can come and get me." He turned to the two crewmen behind him.

One was huddled on the deck, staring up at Batista with terror in his eyes. The other lay sprawled across the deck next to him, most of his skull shot away.

Batista shouted, "If you don't want to join him, open up those cases!"

The terrified crewman flipped open the first case, unveiling a new Russian-made *Bazalt* RPG-32 reusable grenade launcher; a model vastly superior to the crude RPGs the Russians pawned off on third-world countries. The second case contained a pair of rocket grenades, each color coded to indicate its purpose.

Grabbing the grenade launcher, Batista said, "Hand me the white-striped round."

The crewman obeyed, gently cradling the RPG round.

Batista shouted, "Quickly! It's a Russian grenade, not a Fabergé egg!"

After loading the round, Batista peered through the RPG's digital sights. The queen's flagship was seven hundred yards out, coming straight for them, guns blazing.

He muttered, "Perfect."

The RPG-32 had an advanced digital rangefinder but lacked automated target acquisition, meaning it was only as accurate as the man firing it, and Batista was very good. But he knew that hitting a moving vessel from another boat was damn near impossible and only an amateur would waste munitions trying—he had a different tactic in mind.

Batista said, "Stand by with that red-striped round, I'll need to reload fast." He took aim, counting down the rangefinder's readings, his finger hovering over the trigger. "Seven hundred yards... Six fifty, six twenty-five. Six ten."

Batista fired. The rocket propelled round soared out, veering slightly to the target's port side. It was well within effective range.

By design, RPG rounds self-detonate upon reaching their maximum range of seven hundred yards; a safety feature easily altered by trimming the fuse. This thermobaric, anti-combatant round was set to self-detonate at six hundred yards.

The crewman held the red-striped round at the ready, until a stray bullet tore into his skull.

Batista shouted, "Second round now," then noticed the partially decapitated crewman at his feet. "I'll get it myself."

#

The queen stood at the bow, rifle at her shoulder, emptying a magazine at

Batista's yacht. Slapping in a fresh magazine, she screamed, "Faster! I want that bastard to suffer!"

All her hatred for Batista came boiling to the surface—flooding her mind with memories of the whippings, the beatings, and other acts so dark she refused to acknowledge them. The only tragedy was that she wouldn't have time to torture Batista—finding the American and avenging Boiúna had to take priority. Batista would die quickly, but the American's suffering would linger.

She saw a flash on Batista's yacht, followed by a rocket contrail and the roar of an RPG round. But the rocket missed the yacht—going high and to port.

She said, "That fat bastard couldn't hit—"

The RPG round detonated thirty feet overhead, showering the deck with hundreds of steel balls and incendiary pellets. The queen felt a ball brush harmlessly through her hair; it continued on, sheering the head off the man behind her. The explosive impact swept another crewman off the deck, leaving behind a wide crimson smear. Incendiary pellets seared through the wooden deck, igniting anything flammable.

But what really angered Queen Caveira was that her boat was losing speed. She knelt down over a bleeding man, shoved her rifle into his lap and yelled, "Keep firing!"

Remarkably, he found the strength to do it.

Stepping over more wounded men, she stormed into the pilothouse, yelling, "Why are you—" before nearly slipping on the blood-soaked floor. The cabin walls were peppered with shrapnel. Her screaming helmsman lay in a fetal position, fingerless hands clutching at the remains of his face.

The queen yelled, "Get out of my way, you lazy shit," and kicked him aside. Grabbing the controls, she gunned the engine, bearing down on Batista. She'd ram the pig if that's what it took.

#

Batista loaded his last RPG round. The red stripe indicated it was set to detonate at four hundred yards—dangerously close. The queen's flagship was now on a collision course, gaining speed. Batista locked the round in and fired.

The RPG round detonated at twenty feet over the deck, just to starboard. This time, the engine of the queen's flagship belched black smoke, followed by flames.

#

The queen saw another flash on Batista's upper deck. The second rocket contrail soared over her flagship, detonating in midair, twenty yards off the stern. The explosion was followed by a chorus of screams.

The boat lurched, engine sputtering, until it was dead in the water.

The queen screamed, "No!" slamming her hands against the wheel.

A haze of black smoke filled the cabin. Despite the cacophony of grinding metal and agonized screams, a soft, familiar sound caught her attention. Cursing under her breath, she slid open the door to her private cabin. The whimpering monkey leapt onto her shoulder, hugging her neck.

The queen stroked its fur, whispering, "It's okay, little one."

Grabbing a fire extinguisher, she strode out onto the blood-slicked main deck. Picking her way through the dying men, she followed the drifting black smoke to the engine compartment. The hatch cover had been blasted off, the deck around it scored by shrapnel. She emptied the fire extinguisher down into the hatch. The dissipating smoke revealed an engine damaged beyond repair.

She heaved the extinguisher over the side and stared down at the bloodstained deck. Her volcanic rage ignited her brain's network of chemically imbalanced, misfiring synapses, leading her to one conclusion—it was all the American's fault. His destruction of Boiúna had cursed the operation. His sacrifice must also have been insincere, delivering poison seed that weakened the snake god. To resurrect Boiúna, she must sacrifice that which the American held dearest—his child.

She stroked the monkey perched on her shoulder, whispering, "We still have work to do."

#

Santos radioed Batista, asking, "Sir, her engine's burning. Should we finish 'em off?"

Keying his walkie talkie, Batista said, "She's a wounded animal, and that makes her even more dangerous. We can't afford any more losses, so just get us out of here." He trained his binoculars on the river, assessing his situation.

His fast trawler was burning on the water. Most of the tender boats were capsized or burning, and another of his precious gunboats had been destroyed by the snake. The monstrous snake was dead, but any men who'd fallen into the river had become fodder for the huge piranhas. No point crying over them.

On the plus side he still had one intact gunboat, his landing vessel and its cargo, along with a thirty-foot tender. Aside from some small arms damage, his own yacht was intact.

Hans climbed up to the fly deck, a blood-soaked rag pressed to his forehead.

Batista glanced over at him, asking, "The equipment?"

"The laser torch and other gear came through undamaged."

Batista said, "Good, then we're still in business," and went back to scanning the battle scene.

Hans wanted to say, *It's just a cut, I'll be fine. Thanks for asking.* But he settled for, "I'll be below."

Batista chuckled, his eyes still pressed to the binoculars.

Hans paused, asking, "Something amusing?"

Batista laughed again, declaring, "Cheer up, Hans, the battle is won."

Batista ran a quick tally of the opposing side's wreckage. The queen's infamous Red Flag Fleet had been reduced to just her crippled flagship and two go-fast boats.

Batista said, "So much for the Queen of Skulls. She'll be lucky if her own men don't skin her alive." He keyed his walkie talkie, ordering, "All boats rally to me. The barrier is clear and we've got work to do. Good work, Santos, we shut that bitch down for good."

Santos came on the radio. "Sir, the American woman and the kid got away. I think that bastard we kidnapped grabbed them. You want me to hunt 'em down?"

"No, let the *Morte Tinto* have them. They'll be some cannibal's dinner within a day. Gather up all survivors and get ready to move on."

But Batista secretly wondered if that was true. He'd certainly underestimated the planetary geologist, dismissing him as some television pretty boy with an advanced degree. Maybe there was more to the man.

Then he shrugged those thoughts off, muttering, "Nothing could survive out there."

#

Queen Caveira stood at the bow of her flagship, eyes riveted to the horizon. The remains of Batista's flotilla were moving downriver again, slowly vanishing into the haze of black smoke left by burning vessels. She robotically stroked the monkey perched on her shoulder, soothing her nerves.

A pirate stood ten paces back, silently awaiting an audience. He coughed once, trying to get her attention. The monkey turned to him, baring its canines.

Without looking back, the queen asked, "What is it?"

"Queen, we only have ten able-bodied men, twelve wounded and two operating boats, but one of them is only a four-man."

She nodded in acknowledgment. Hours earlier, her Red Flag Fleet had been fifty pirates strong, feared by all who traveled the river. Now her crew was reduced to less than half of that, and most of them were wounded who'd die within a day.

After a lingering silence, the pirate asked, "Your orders?"

She turned to him, her face a smeared mass of ceremonial makeup, blood and soot. "Have the larger go-fast tow us to the riverbank. Then load the wounded aboard it and send it to the nearest dock with a doctor. Any man who can still fight stays. Send the smaller boat up ahead to scout for that American bastard and report to me." She went back to studying the river, but by that point, Batista's boats were long gone.

The pirate backed away slowly, leaving the queen alone with her private thoughts and beloved monkey.

#

Micah was pulling supplies from the deflated dinghy when something caught his eye. He called out to Catalina, "Hey, check this out!"

Catalina and Faye came over. Micah gestured for them to stay hidden and pointed to the river.

Batista's yacht, a gunboat, the cargo carrier and a tender were passing by.

Catalina said, "Jesus, after all that he's still pressing on?"

"Yup, he's just like his idol, Aguirre."

"A who?"

"Aguirre was the conquistador who navigated the Amazon back in the fifteen hundreds."

"That's kind of impressive."

"Except he was a murdering psychopath, obsessed with finding El Dorado. We're talking a textbook narcissist who slaughtered entire tribes and even christened himself the *King of Tierra Firme*."

"How'd that work out for him?"

"The King of Spain had him cut in half and thrown in the river."

"Ouch!"

"That meteorite is Batista's El Dorado, and he'll find it, no matter how many people die along the way."

Catalina shook her head. "A rich man who only dreams of getting richer. Kind of pathetic."

"Batista doesn't care about being rich. He wants to be a king and make the world kneel before him."

Catalina smiled down at Faye and said, "Well, we're a couple of simple gals who'd settle for a hot shower and something to eat."

Reaching into the dinghy, Micah said, "I can provide exactly one of those," while deftly slicing the Megapiranha's head off.

Faye asked, "Yuck, are we going to eat that?"

"They were gonna eat us, so fair's fair. Besides, piranhas are delicious."

Catalina asked, "Is it wise to eat the monster prehistoric fish that shouldn't even exist?"

Micah gutted the fish and said, "If you'd prefer, I can dig up some grub worms to fry."

"Fish it is."

Micah dug through the raft's emergency kit and found a bottle of salt tablets. Using a rock he ground the tablets down to powdered salt, smeared it on the piranha and set the fish aside. "That'll keep it from turning for an hour or so. You know, one perk of the Amazon is that food's usually within reach." He walked about twenty feet into the brush and returned with an armload of red fruit, covered in spiky green leaves. "It's pitahaya, better known as dragon fruit."

Eyeing the weird fruit, Catalina said, "I think I saw those once in a scary downtown grocery store."

"It's good stuff, tastes kind of like a mango." He tore one open, handing out slices. "The juice is the closest thing to safe drinking water we're gonna find for a while."

Catalina bit into it, suddenly realizing how dehydrated she was. "I bet piranha with a side of dragon fruit would cost a fortune in some swanky restaurant." After swallowing another piece of fruit, she asked, "So, what're we doing after dinner?"

"Dinner's to go. We need to move away from the river, stay out of sight, and find shelter before sundown to recharge our batteries. After that, well, I haven't figured that part out yet." Micah grabbed some downed branches and pointed to some nearby brush. "Grab some more branches, anything big and leafy will work." Then he dragged the shredded dinghy up the bank and began covering it.

Dragging some branches over, Catalina asked, "If Batista's gone, who are we hiding this from?"

"The pirates."

"You mean like yo-ho-ho pirates?"

"Yup. Believe it or not she was the pirate queen."

"Look at you, hanging out with royalty. Did you have tea?"

"No, she's more of an 'off with their heads' kinda queen."

Catalina said, "You're just full of surprises." Then she added her branches to the camouflage.

"Yeah, and they've joined the growing list of stuff that wants to kill us."

"Fantastic." Catalina dragged a final pile of branches over to the dinghy. "Did you have to grab the fluorescent orange one?"

"There weren't a lot of color options." Stepping back, he said, "That oughta do it. Those pirates just got their ass handed to them, so maybe they'll be too busy licking their wounds to care about us anymore."

The male howler monkey crouching in the trees let out another deafening shriek.

Catalina looked up, shouting, "Would you shut the fuck up!"

The monkey just howled again, which Faye found hilarious.

Catalina smiled, relieved to hear the little girl laughing again. She thought for a moment and said, "Oh, there's also a tribe in this area that ain't exactly friendly."

Micah nodded. "Yeah, the Red Death. I got the lowdown from my pirate pals."

"Do you think they're also on that 'wants to kill us' list?"

Micah glanced over at Faye, intently prying open another dragon fruit, and gestured for Catalina to follow him. He led her a few feet into the rainforest where two posts had been jammed into the mud—each topped with a red-painted human skull.

Micah said, "I think we better avoid the locals. Let's move out."

Gathering what supplies they had, the trio marched into the rainforest.

As soon as they departed, the emboldened monkeys climbed down from the trees. Howler monkeys are among the few animals able to see in full color. The combination of trichromatic vision and their insatiable curiosity drew them to the bright orange dinghy like a magnet. The carefully laid out camouflage was quickly scattered across the ground and the shredded boat dragged close to the riverbank.

Within minutes, Queen Caveira's scout spotted the dinghy.

CHAPTER NINETEEN

One of the queen's go-fast boats towed her flagship to a muddy bank where it was tied off. The other remaining go-fast headed out in search of the Americans.

Rooting through the still smoking engine compartment, Queen Caveira concluded that the motor wasn't salvageable and the boat was taking on water. In a few hours her beloved flagship would be a sunken wreck.

She climbed up onto the deck, wiping her greasy hands on her tattered jacket. The monkey hopped onto her shoulder and rooted through her pocket.

She whispered, "Sorry, little one, there's nothing left to steal."

Looking down, she surveyed her remaining crew. All were hollow eyed, their clothes caked with blood.

"Listen to me!"

Even the wounded stopped moaning out of respect.

"I want half of you loading the wounded into the go-fast. The rest root through my ship to pull anything salvageable."

The pirates set to work loading the wounded men. Queen Caveira knew most would succumb to their injuries before reaching a doctor, but they were her crew, her family.

The sound of an approaching engine sent the men scrambling for their weapons.

Queen Caveira shouted, "It's just our scout, get back to work!"

The go-fast boat pulled alongside the flagship.

The pilot said, "I saw your inflatable washed up on shore about a klick downriver. It was all torn up."

"Anyone with it?"

The pirates all clustered around her, listening intently.

"No, but I found three sets of footprints leading into the jungle. A man, another, smaller set, so probably a woman and a kid."

Queen Caveira thought, *The bastard's still alive*, and bellowed, "Umberto!"

A pirate named Javier announced, "He's dead."

The queen nodded solemnly. "A good man, and a fine executive officer. He'll be missed. Javier, you're now my executive officer."

Javier snapped to attention, shouting, "Yes, Queen!"

"Take three men to where he found my boat and follow the Americans' trail from there. They have a child with them, so they can't be moving very fast."

Javier asked, "And if we find them?"

"I want the American and the child alive."

"And the woman?"

"Kill her, but do it quickly."

Javier nodded, looking disappointed. The queen's rules against rape had always been a sore point for him.

Queen Caveira continued, "Leave a trail so we can follow you. Once the wounded are away, we'll join the hunt. Now get moving. The rest of you, back to work!"

Javier and three other men piled into the overloaded boat and set out.

Queen Caveira slipped a hand into her pocket, massaging the pool ball-sized emerald. The jewel would fetch her enough to retire from raiding fishing boats and stealing pigs. Yet, for a fleeting moment, she pondered tossing it in the river. Personal greed had been the sin that wooed her into letting the American live. A mistake that led to Boiúna's downfall. Now all that mattered was setting things right.

For Boiúna to be resurrected the American and his child must die.

#

Micah, Catalina and Faye trudged through the thick brush. Despite gnawing on the dragon fruit, the inside of Micah's mouth still felt like a cotton field. He could only imagine how exhausted Faye must be.

He spotted a rough trail ahead and declared, "Perfect."

Catalina looked down at the hoof prints in the mud, asking, "What're we looking at?"

"It's a tapir trail."

"Is that like a deer or something?"

Faye jumped in, stating, "Tapirs are giant wild pigs."

Mussing her hair, Micah said, "Smart girl. Now tell me why that's good?"

After pondering it for a moment, Faye said, "Because tapirs will lead to water."

"And?"

Faye grew excited. "Because Jaguars are afraid of tapirs, so they'll stay away from the trail!"

"Bingo."

Catalina asked, "What about the Red Death?"

"Even people out here don't like running into tapirs. If you ever meet one, you'll find out why."

Faye added, "They're mean and weigh like six hundred pounds."

Catalina asked, "Aren't there any cute, fluffy bunnies out here?"

Micah bent down to Faye and said, "Honey, grab some of those dry sticks over there, we're gonna need 'em."

Faye said, "I get it, kindling!" and began scooping up dry twigs.

Once she was clear, Catalina whispered, "I know she's putting on a good show, but I don't think she'll be able to go on much longer."

"I know, I know. I just want to get an hour between us and the river. After that we'll fry up the fish and rest for a—" Micah stopped mid-sentence, his eyes locked on the trail ahead.

The mysterious old man stood about fifty feet away, staring back at him.

Micah pointed and whispered, "Do you see him?"

Catalina squinted hard. "See who?"

The old man smiled, gesturing for Micah to follow, then slipped into the brush. Micah chased after him.

Catalina yelled, "Where're you going?" Then she crouched down, taking Faye's hand, while gripping the pistol in the other.

Micah stumbled through the brush, looking in every direction, but there was no trace of the old man. Finally, he bent over, hands pressed to his knees, catching his breath. Something on the ground caught his eye.

Catalina shouted, "Hey Micah, you're being weird and scaring us."

Micah knelt down, studying the ground and yelled, "Everything's okay, but you really need to see this."

Catalina led Faye over. "What've you got?" Then she saw a crude arrow etched into the muddy ground.

"I saw the old man."

"Are we doing this again?"

"I know you don't believe me, but he's real and I think he's leading us somewhere."

"Like to our deaths? The Red Devils could have just carved that as bait."

"It's the Red Death, and they've been hunting out here for centuries, so if they really wanted to kill us we'd already be dead. I say we follow the arrow for a while then take a break."

With a frustrated sigh, Catalina said, "You're the boss."

#

Batista stood in the yacht's pilothouse, poring over his charts while monitoring boat-to-boat radio chatter. He was confident they were closing in on their destination, but the atmosphere had grown tense. His remaining gunboat chugged directly ahead of the yacht, machine gunners at the ready—perhaps too ready.

It had been four hours since they'd left the wide tributary. Now they were traveling a series of narrow channels. The hundred-foot canopy of trees on either side plunged the area into permanent midnight. Navigating the dark waterway meant slowing to barely three knots. The glacial pace was agonizing, worsened by the *Morte Tinto*'s ongoing war of nerves.

Within the first hour the gunboat had been pelted with arrows. There were no casualties, but it had put the already shaken men on edge. The following hours brought more hit and run arrow attacks. Each time, the machine gunners had torn the riverbank apart, but they were shooting at phantoms.

An hour ago, two of Batista's men had stolen an inflatable life raft, paddling back the way they'd come. Their escape had put bad ideas in the other men's heads.

Batista peered out the window, muttering, "The bastards are squatting out there, waiting."

Hans commented, "Ho Chi Minh would be proud of them."

"What?"

The Austrian sat at the chart table, dissecting one of the massive piranhas that had jumped onto the deck. Without looking up, he said, "Their tactics are very much in accord with Ho Chi Minh's book, *On Revolution*."

"I don't think they're big readers." Sniffing the air, Batista asked, "Do you have to do that in here?"

"There aren't many other places left."

Batista couldn't tell if Hans was being insolent or just his usual Asperger's self.

The gunboat's machine gunners suddenly opened fire, sending hundreds of rounds at the riverbank. Hans ducked under the table.

After three more long bursts, Batista grabbed his walkie talkie, shouting, "Cease fire, cease fire! Santos, what are they shooting at?"

After a long silence, Santos came back with, "Nothing. Not a goddamn thing."

A minute later, Santos walked in. He slung his AK-47 over his shoulder and lit a cigarette.

Batista asked, "What happened?"

"Our boys just blew away a family of river otters, so we can add that to the armadillos they shot an hour ago."

Batista shook his head. "If they keep this up Greenpeace will be coming after us. Did you do a headcount?"

"Yeah. You've got twenty-six men in total, counting me."

Hans crawled out from beneath the table, looking paler than normal, and said, "My God, that means we've lost almost fifty men."

After a drag on his cigarette, Santos said, "Give or take."

Batista said, "More than I'd anticipated, but we'll manage."

Santos added, "But most of them are hired-on shitheads that I can't vouch for. There's already been some rumbling."

Batista nodded. "There always is."

They heard approaching footsteps on the deck above.

Batista said, "Speak of the devil," while slipping his hand into a drawer near the control panel.

Six crew members crowded into the pilothouse doorway, their faces roadmaps of cuts and insect bites. The men in back made a point of displaying their rifles, while those in front merely gawked at the pilothouse's rich wood, fine furniture and inset lighting.

Santos flicked his cigarette out of the porthole and tightened his grip on the rifle. Batista gave him a subtle "stand down" gesture while keeping his other hand behind his back.

He addressed the crew. "Why aren't you men at your posts?"

The crew's designated spokesman stepped forward, saying, "We took a vote and want to get paid what we're owed and go home."

In his best diplomatic tone, Batista replied, "Gentlemen, I'm afraid that's impossible. We don't have enough fuel to make it back. But we do have enough to reach the outpost, where there'll be plenty of fuel and fresh boats waiting."

The spokesman grew more confident. "We figured that if we transfer all the fuel to this yacht and abandon the other two boats we could make it back."

"Interesting plan. But I'm quite fond of this yacht and don't intend to give it up." Batista moved his hand from behind his back, revealing a block of Semtex plastic explosive wired to a blasting cap. "But you're welcome to try."

The men took a nervous step back. Hans saw the explosives and dropped his scalpel to the floor. The room fell dead quiet as Batista faced the men. It was a Mexican standoff.

The silence was shattered by the gunboat's wailing siren. Its blinding searchlights snapped on, illuminating the riverbank.

Batista peered out of the window. His stolen inflatable lifeboat lay shredded on the riverbank. The two missing crewmen were directly behind it. At first Batista thought the men were sitting on some kind of high poles until he saw the sharpened stake points protruding from their mouths. He realized they'd been impaled in the most savage way imaginable.

Batista waved the crew's spokesman over. "You should see this."

The nervous man looked out and audibly gasped.

After taking a look, Santos leaned close to the spokesman, whispering, "Damn. Asshole to esophagus, that ain't no way to die."

Batista waved the other men over. "Gentlemen, come take a look, but try not to track mud on the carpet."

The men stood silently, eyes riveted on the ghastly spectacle.

Batista seized the moment, asking, "Shall we review your options? If you try to take this yacht I'll blow us all to bits. If you try to take the gunboat or the tender boat my machine gunners will cut you in half. And if you jump ship … well, you can see what happens."

The men looked at each other, muttering anxiously.

Bouncing the block of plastic explosive in his hand, Batista said, "I'll offer you an alternate proposition. Come with me and I'll pay each of you five times the contracted fee. Just a few days of work and you'll earn enough to stay drunk for a year."

The spokesman asked, "Do you think anyone at your outpost is still alive?"

"Even if they're dead the fuel's still there waiting. Those savages have no use for it, and our mortars and machine guns can stop any attack. Or, time permitting, we can just wipe out those filthy Neanderthals for good."

The concept of extra money and a bonus massacre earned a round of positive murmuring and head nods.

The spokesman said, "Okay, we'll stick with you."

"Your loyalty is inspiring. Now get back to your duties!"

The men filed out. Santos relaxed the grip on his rifle.

Batista said, "Eliminate that mouthy one first chance you get."

With a nod, Santos replied, "He's chum."

With trembling hands, Hans picked up his scalpel and said, "That was tense."

Batista laughed. "It was nothing." Then he tossed Hans the chunk of Semtex.

The Austrian fumbled with the explosive, almost dropping it. When he saw Batista's amused expression, he asked, "So, you were bluffing about the explosive?"

Batista pulled a wireless detonator from his pocket. "I've made it a point in life never to bluff. Now, let's get back to business. How problematic is the loss of our planetary geologists?"

Hans said, "The woman was a useless moron."

Santos mumbled, "And a pain in the ass."

Batista said, "And a nice ass it was. And what about our television star?"

"His knowledge and expertise would have proved invaluable. There are tests we should run before cutting into the Anomaly, the type only he's qualified to perform."

"The hell with tests. I'm tired of scientists slowing things down. Plus, they always want to share their discoveries with the world. They'll all say it's for the good of mankind, but it's really just about their egos. I need this kept a secret until we've extracted every gram of that rock. That whole area is part of a federal protectorate to keep that tribe of primates from being contaminated by civilization. The government can swoop in and take control the second they smell money."

Hans replied, "I'll do the best I can," and went back to studying the dead fish, while mumbling to himself in German.

Batista asked, "Is there some problem with your new pet?"

"Yes there is… It's perfect."

"Perfect is a problem?"

Polishing his glasses, Hans explained, "I'm not a zoologist, but I've done my share of research. Piranha are carnivorous and competitive. They fight each other and, like all carnivores, have food borne parasites."

"So?"

"This fish is perfect. No scars, broken teeth or fin damage. All the things you'd call natural wear and tear. And, as far as I can tell, it has no internal parasites. It's as if it was just born but fully grown."

"Your point?"

"Have you considered the possibility that something, some force we don't understand, is trying to prevent us from reaching the site? The ants, the snakes and these piranha are all freaks of nature that should be extinct. And they've all tried to kill us, which isn't how animals naturally behave."

"So, now you want to turn tail and run home?"

Hans shook his head. "No, I want to find out the truth." He went back to probing the fish, adding, "Even if it kills me."

#

Micah, Faye and Catalina continued trudging through the rainforest until he spotted another arrow carved in the trail.

Micah said, "That's a good sign."

Catalina nodded then cocked her head toward Faye. Micah could see the faraway look in his daughter's eyes—like a soldier's thousand yard stare.

He knelt down and said, "Come on, honey, I'll give you a boost."

The fiercely independent little girl didn't protest; a sure sign she was exhausted.

Micah hoisted her up onto his shoulders, whispering, "Only a little longer," and kept trudging up the steep incline, his leg muscles burning.

At the summit they looked down onto a flat, marshy area fed by a fast-moving stream that would qualify as a river anywhere else.

Catalina gazed down at it and said, "This looks like a good spot to make camp." Then she hiked down the incline.

The trio stood at the edge of the marsh. A group of tapirs on the far side studied them, snorted in annoyance and ambled off. Catalina gazed out at the marsh. Almost every inch of its surface was covered in circular floating plants, some easily ten feet around.

Pointing to them, she asked, "What are those giant pancake looking things?"

Micah said, "They're Queen Victoria lilies."

"Do they eat people or spit poison?"

"Nope, they just float around. After dark, their flowers bloom. It's really pretty."

Catalina turned and walked to the edge of the stream, dipping her hand in.

Micah shouted, "Don't drink that!"

"Seriously? It's clear running water."

He scanned the area. "Give me a minute and I'll find something safe." After a few minutes of searching the area, he shouted, "Over here!"

Faye and Catalina rushed over. Micah stood at the edge of a smaller waterway branching off the marsh. The stream bed was black and the water the color of tea.

Micah scooped up a palm full of water and tasted it. "This'll work."

Eyeing the brackish water suspiciously, Catalina said, "It looks nasty."

"Welcome to the rainforest where up is down and dirty is clean. It's a blackwater creek, but the black is just sediment deposits, decaying plants create tannins that seep in—"

Catalina cut him off. "Yes or no. Can we drink it?"

"Yeah, the tannins leave it almost sterile. Next best thing to rainwater."

"You're the expert, now step aside."

The ladies took turns drinking and splashing each other.

Micah sniffed the dead piranha, and, satisfied it hadn't turned, began slicing off strips. "When you two finish your water fight, how about getting a fire started?"

Looking embarrassed, Faye confessed, "I lost most of the kindling. Sorry."

After a deep breath, Micah said, "That's okay, we'll find something." But he knew that every twig around the marsh would be sodden. In the rainforest, something as simple as dry firewood could be the difference between survival and starvation.

Catalina dug into the satchel she'd been toting. "I think I've got something that'll do the trick," and produced a butter stick-sized chunk of Semtex.

Faye's eyes widened and she asked, "Isn't that the exploding stuff?"

"Yup, one hundred percent pure Compound Four explosive."

Micah just stared at her.

Catalina peeled the waxed paper off, explaining, "Relax, plastic explosive only goes off with blasting caps or detonators. You can't set it off with a match or by dropping it or even shooting it with a gun. It's safe as milk and makes a great campfire. And, since it didn't come with any detonators, that's about all it's good for."

With a shrug, Micah said, "You're the expert."

#

Javier knelt down, studying some footprints at the base of a sharp incline. The three Americans must be close. Tracking them had been easy, almost to the point of embarrassing.

He muttered, "Amateurs," and tied a strip of cloth to a tree branch, marking the trail for the queen.

The American bastard had killed Umberto, the queen's first executive officer and his best friend. Now it was his turn to inflict some pain. He waved his three men forward. They trotted over, rucksacks clanking.

Javier whispered, "You idiots sound like a fucking samba band."

The men all mumbled apologies.

"Shut up! Remember, the man and the kid have to be taken alive. The woman's mine, at least until I'm done with her."

"But the queen said—"

"Who's the executive officer here?"

The trio nodded then silently moved up the incline.

Javier reached the summit first. Down below he could make out a marsh connected to a stream, all surrounded by hundred foot kapok trees. He heard something and raised his fist. The men halted. At first the sound was faint; then he distinctly heard laughter.

Using a stick, Javier drew a diagram in the mud, explaining, "They're down there. I want one man left, another right. Once you're in position sit tight and don't move until I do. Juan, you come down the center with me."

The men obeyed. Javier crawled forward until he saw the Americans nestled under the trees near a marsh. They were cooking food over a fire, and the smell wafting up reminded him how hungry he was. After allowing enough time for his men to get in position, he crept forward, keeping to the trees, thinking, *It'll be hours before the queen gets here. Plenty of time to get payback for Umberto and have some fun to boot.*

CHAPTER TWENTY

Micah bit into a piece of roasted Megapiranha. The burning Semtex lent the fish a chemical odor, and the blackwater stream water tasted as bitter as three-day-old coffee. It was the best meal he'd ever eaten.

He asked, "Do you guys realize we're the first human beings to ever eat a Megapiranha?"

Catalina spat out a bone and said, "Maybe you can do a cooking show next."

"My TV career's as extinct as this fish is supposed to be."

After swallowing another hunk, Catalina lay back on the ground, listening to the chorus of frogs coming from the marsh. "Those frogs make this place sound almost serene."

Faye said, "You have to be really careful of the frogs out here."

"Yeah, I heard. The poison dart frogs are really bad."

"But there's also the cane toads that spray poison."

Micah said, "And don't forget about the smooth-sided toads; touch one of those bad boys and you're really in trouble."

Not to be outdone, Faye added, "And there's the Amazon milk frog. They're super-duper dangerous!"

Catalina playfully tossed a chunk of piranha at Faye and said, "Okay you two, I get it. In the Amazon even Kermit the Frog's a killing machine."

Her joke earned a round of laughter, but to Micah it felt forced—like whistling in a graveyard.

The ambient light dimmed, as if a giant shadow was passing over them. Catalina looked up but could barely see the sky through the canopy of trees.

She asked, "Is it nighttime already?"

After swallowing another hunk, Micah said, "Nope, not for another three hours. The trees are so thick it's always twilight down here."

A flash of lightning lit up the treetops. Faye jumped a little and slid closer to Micah.

Catalina asked, "Rain coming?"

"It doesn't feel like rain. Maybe it's just heat lightning." Another flash lit up the canopy of trees.

Faye fidgeted for a second, feeling something warm in her pocket. Then she felt the vibration and remembered the fragment she'd grabbed. She muttered, "Uh oh, it's talking again."

Micah asked, "What's talking, honey?"

"It's the—"

A gruff voiced shouted, "Get up!" in Portuguese.

A man wielding an assault rifle emerged from the brush. Micah pulled Faye close, shielding her. The man walked forward, his rifle trained on Micah. Two more armed men stormed out of the brush to their left and right.

Catalina's hand slid toward the pistol. Then she felt a machete blade pressed against her throat from behind.

Javier shouted, "Get up real slow and don't try anything."

Holding Faye close, Micah said, "It's okay, we're not armed."

"I know that, I've been watching you *ramerrãos* for ten minutes."

Faye pressed so close to Micah that he could feel her trembling.

Then Micah recognized the armed man. Forcing a smile, he said, "Hey, I remember you. You're Umberto's buddy, right?"

"And you're the bastard that killed him!"

"That's not true ... technically."

"Did you think you could betray the queen and live?"

"I didn't betray anybody. I just had to get to my daughter."

Shoving the gun barrel against his chest, Javier shouted, "You killed Boiúna!"

"That was an accident. But he's a god, so he'll pop up again. You know, gods love that death and resurrection stuff."

"Oh, he'll return, once the queen sacrifices you and that brat!"

Catalina stood up slowly, the machete blade pressed under her chin. The man holding it reached around, cupping one of her breasts. She tensed but didn't protest. She was pretty sure she could take her handsy attacker down but elected to play along for now. Being groped was degrading, but it kept him from frisking her properly and finding the pistol in her pocket.

Javier saw what his man was doing and shouted, "Hey, cut that shit out. I told you she's mine!"

Lightning flashed again, this time with a sharp crack. Micah caught a whiff of ozone and the hair on his arms bristled from the static electricity. Glancing upward he saw the violet glow of St. Elmo's fire dancing among the tree branches.

The chorus of frogs suddenly fell silent.

Micah thought, *That ain't normal.*

Leering at Catalina, Javier said, "You've got a pretty lady, Lucky Man. I'm going to enjoy her," while grabbing his crotch for emphasis.

Catalina said, "Unzip those pants and you'll leave here shy a few parts."

Javier was about to make an obscene comment when something landed behind him with a loud thud. He spun around, rifle at the ready. There was nothing there.

Micah saw something dark drop from the trees behind them. A long, brown shape scuttled across the ground at blinding speed—heading straight for Javier's leg.

Javier jumped into the air, kicking, as it scrambled up his leg and onto his back. With a scream he spun around. A huge centipede was locked on to his back, its pincers embedded in his rucksack.

Micah had seen plenty of centipedes but nothing like this. The thing was at least four feet long and thick as a man's forearm. Its brown-and-black mottled exoskeleton gleamed like armor, surrounded by dozens of tan, spike-tipped legs. A vicious set of red pincers sprouted from beneath its head.

Javier dropped his rifle, grabbing the centipede with both hands. Luckily it had only bitten into his rucksack. He pulled it away and threw it.

Micah saw another land a few yards away. The creature was coiled up into a basketball-sized sphere. It rolled a few feet on impact then sprang open, already on the move.

Micah yelled, "They're dropping from the trees!"

Catalina saw two more, racing straight for her. The man with the machete was staring up at the trees, paralyzed with fear. She jabbed her elbow back hard while slamming her foot down on his, knocking him off balance. Twisting her body, she shoved him forward, right on top of the approaching centipede. He screamed, his body spasming as if from electric shock, then rolled onto his back. The centipede was locked around his throat, its massive pincers already burrowing into his flesh.

Thrown off balance, Catalina fell to the ground while drawing the pistol. The second centipede was only inches away when she fired, blowing it in half. She saw at least a dozen more centipedes, all converging on their group.

One of Javier's men opened fire on full auto, blindly tearing the ground apart.

Micah dropped down on top of Faye, shielding her body. He rolled left as bullets shredded the earth around him. Thankfully one of the panicked shots killed an attacking centipede.

The terrified man kept firing until his rifle clicked empty. As he fumbled for a magazine, a centipede attacked from behind. It raced up his calf, its head disappearing into the leg of his baggy shorts. With an ear-piercing squeal he toppled onto his back. Another centipede dropped from the trees overhead, landing next to him. It reared up, latching its pincers on to the screaming man's tongue.

Micah scooped up the fallen machete. Faye screamed as a centipede slithered up her leg.

Micah pushed her onto the ground, yelling, "Don't move!" then pressed the blade flat against her chest. The centipede scrambled up her torso. As it crossed the blade, Micah jerked up hard, launching the creature into the air.

Another of Javier's men went into panic mode, firing at the ground just inches from Catalina. She rolled left while snapping off a single shot into the man's kneecap. He dropped, howling in pain, clawing at his bleeding leg. The blood and noise were like a magnet to the centipedes. Micah saw five scrambling up the man's chest. Two latched on to his face with their front pincers, their spiked legs coiled around his head. Grabbing one with each hand the screaming man yanked them off. But their pincers and legs held fast, peeling off his face like a rubber mask. His skeletal visage kept screaming.

Another one tried to run up Micah's leg. He swung the machete, severing its antenna. The blinded centipede reared up, latching its pincers around the machete blade. Micah held it up high then flicked his wrist hard, launching the centipede into the fire. Its body crackled as it writhed in the flames. Micah was trying to grab Faye when needles of pain shot up his spine—moving spiked legs.

Faye shouted, "It's on your back!"

The centipede burning in the fire gave Catalina an idea. She grabbed the stick she'd been roasting piranha on, jamming it into the fire and spearing the hunk of burning plastic explosive.

Shouting, "Hold still!" she jabbed it like a branding iron against the centipede on Micah's back. The centipede twisted wildly then dropped off, flaming globules of plastic explosive clinging to its back like napalm.

Micah grabbed his own stick but discovered there wasn't any more explosive in the fire. Catalina kicked the satchel by her feet. A thick chunk of plastic explosive landed near Micah. He speared it and stuck it into the fire's burning embers. It ignited like a Roman candle.

Faye pointed to the ground, shouting, "Look out!"

Micah swung the flaming torch onto an oncoming centipede then pulled the stick away quickly. Dripping plastic explosive clung to the centipede's exoskeleton, roasting it alive. Micah swept the torch low over the ground, brushing it over another centipede. It squirmed, a sheen of burning liquefied plastic explosive painted onto its shell.

Micah heard more dropping from the trees—it was literally raining death.

Javier was back on his feet and running full tilt for the marsh.

Micah saw him and yelled, "He's got the right idea, go for the water!"

Catalina shouted, "Form up in a circle, Micah on point!"

Micah saw a bright flash of light to his right. Faye had speared another chunk of Semtex and lit it up.

"Good girl!"

Catalina snatched up the half empty satchel of explosives and heaved it into the fire. A second later it ignited into a brilliant, six-foot pillar of flame.

Her gambit worked. Centipedes, being nearly blind, were attracted to the sudden heat and light. The bulk of the dropping centipedes zeroed in on the dancing column of fire.

The trio shuffled toward the marsh, Micah in the lead, their outstretched torches sweeping the ground in front and behind. Micah cautiously steered them away from the overhanging trees. The dripping plastic explosive left a trail of tiny fires behind them. Progress was painfully slow, complicated by centipedes charging them in kamikaze attacks.

Walking backwards gave Catalina a glimpse of what was coming, and it wasn't good. The ground around the campfire was now a writhing mass of four-foot centipedes. But the creatures had figured out that there was no potential prey at the campfire. The swarm was turning to pursue them, propelled on a million legs.

Micah shouted, "We're there!" and stepped into the marsh water.

Javier was already wading deeper into the marsh, noisily splashing through the maze of Queen Victoria lilies covering the surface.

The oncoming mass of centipedes were only twenty feet from Micah when they suddenly swerved, making a beeline for Javier.

Micah said, "It's okay, they can't swim."

Catalina watched the swarm for a moment and said, "They don't have to."

She was right. The centipedes leapt onto the closest Queen Victoria lily and, using it as a bridge, moved to the next. A procession of at least thirty scrambled towards Javier, who was using a lily to stay afloat.

Seeing the inevitable, Micah said, "We need to make for the stream!"

Catalina saw that the stream was only forty yards away, but getting there meant running a gauntlet of low-hanging branches crowded with writhing centipedes. She said, "We'd get nailed by those paratroopers before we got halfway."

Her stick finally burnt through. The flaming mass of plastic explosive plopped to the ground. Faye grabbed a bamboo stalk and tossed it over. Catalina managed to spear the burning mass and jammed it into the face of a charging centipede.

The centipedes reached Javier, forming a circle on the lilies around him. The desperate man dove under, trying to swim beneath the enormous water lilies. But the lilies weren't floating freely—they were connected to the marsh bed by a web of stalks. Finding himself entangled he shot to the surface. The centipedes were waiting. In the brief instant he was above water, three of them bit down, injecting toxic venom that coursed through his body like acid.

Micah muttered, "Think, stupid, think," until an idea struck him. He handed his burning torch to Catalina and waded into the marsh, machete in hand.

Catalina yelled, "What're you—"

Micah dove underwater before she could finish.

The nearest Queen Victoria lily shook on the water then rose straight up—Micah was standing underneath, holding it over his head. He waded to shore, flipping it onto the ground. The normally underwater side was honeycombed with curved, needle-sharp spikes.

Grasping the smooth side, Micah hoisted it over his head again, shouting, "Get underneath! Catalina, you work the ground in front!"

As soon as they were under he started jogging towards the stream. Catalina ran her torch along the grass, burning any centipedes in their path.

They could hear the steady thump of centipedes landing on top of the pad.

Catalina yelled, "They'll crawl under!"

Breathing heavily from his burden, Micah replied, "They can't. Those curved spikes will bind up their legs or tear them off." He bent his knees then jerked the pad up sharply. Three centipedes fell to the ground behind them—one missing most of its legs. Micah kept soldiering on.

Hearing his labored breathing, Catalina yelled, "Hang in there, the stream's only a couple yards away. Coming up in fifteen seconds, fourteen, ten—"

There was a steady drumbeat of landing scorpions as she counted.

Micah finally felt the cool water on his ankles. He kept going until he was waist high in fast moving water then started walking against the current. Faye pressed herself tightly against his back, her head barely above the waterline.

Catalina threw away her torch and reached up to take on half the load. She was amazed at how heavy the ten-foot lily was.

"How the hell did you haul this alone?"

"Strong motivation."

They heard more centipedes dropping from the overhanging branches above them.

After a deep breath, Micah said, "When I say bounce, bounce the lily up and back. Three, two, bounce!"

Together they jostled the lily sharply up and back. Centipedes tumbled into the water behind them, only to be swept away by the current.

Catalina asked, "What if some drop down up ahead and swim back at us?"

Micah said, "Hey Faye, tell us what has a hundred legs but can't swim?"

The little girl yelled, "Centipedes! Plus they don't have lungs. They breathe through pores under their legs, so they drown super-fast. See!"

A lifeless four-foot centipede floated past them.

They kept moving, their legs straining against the current.

Catalina asked, "How far should we go?"

Micah said, "Till we don't hear the patter of a million tiny feet," and pressed on.

CHAPTER TWENTY-ONE

After twenty minutes of marching against the current the sound of falling centipedes gave way to the patter of raindrops.

Micah said, "We've got to stop, I'm dead."

Between heaving breaths, Catalina said, "Me too."

To their right he saw a break in the trees. "Over there." He steered them to the stream's edge. "On three we toss it—one, two, three!"

They flipped the Queen Victoria lily onto the water, spike side down, ensuring any trapped centipedes would drown.

Micah dropped down onto the muddy bank, panting like a dog. Faye huddled next to him.

Catalina sprawled out a few feet away and said, "If any more monsters come just let 'em eat me, 'cause I'm too beat to fight."

They lay there, too exhausted to move or even speak. The rain came down harder. Catalina let it wash over her. Micah stretched his throbbing arm muscles and felt something odd. He tapped at the ground next to him, muttering, "That's funny."

Catalina asked, "Funny ha ha or funny gonna eat us?"

"Just weird. I'm lying next to a slab of cement."

"That's impossible, unless the Red Menace have figured out how to make Redi Mix concrete."

"They're the Red Death."

"Whatever."

Micah dug the flashlight out of his pocket, relieved to find it still working. He played it across the ground and said, "Yup, I'm right, it's old and overgrown, but it's cement. It looks like there's more of it. Like an old sidewalk."

"Should we follow it?"

"Yeah, but I want to check something out first."

Micah waded into the stream and flipped the floating lily over. Two drowned centipedes were tangled in the network of curved thorns. With a Herculean effort he pried one loose. He tossed the four-foot creature's body onto the ground and bent down closer.

Faye looked at it, fear in her eyes.

Micah said, "Relax, honey, it's dead." Inspecting it closer, he muttered, "This thing's incredible."

Catalina and Faye peered over his shoulder.

Catalina asked, "So this isn't an everyday critter out here where even the frogs want to kill you?"

"No, the biggest centipede on Earth is maybe ten inches long."

Faye said, "I bet it's prehistoric. Way, way back, the world had more

126

oxygen, so everything grew super big."

Poking at it, Micah said, "That makes sense. It's just like the Megapiranhas and the Titan ants."

Catalina laughed. "Please, nothing we've seen makes sense, even the stuff that's true."

"The thing is that centipedes are pretty solitary, so a swarm like this doesn't fit their behavior."

"Okay, before you start getting all Nutty Professor again, I've got an idea."

"What's that?"

Catalina picked up the dead centipede. "I say we ditch this hundred-legged turd and follow that cement trail to wherever it goes." She lobbed it into the stream. "Who knows, maybe there's a 7-11. I could do with a big gulp right now."

Faye added, "And a burrito!"

Micah watched the centipede being carried off by the stream and said, "I bet you city folks will want me to find a Starbucks after that."

With a grin, Catalina said, "Would you? A latte would be super refreshing."

And they set out.

The light rain escalated into a downpour, dark clouds blocking the meager late afternoon sun. Occasional flashes of lightning shot across the sky, but otherwise it was black as night.

Micah studied the ground as they walked, saying, "There are definitely slabs of cement, like an old walkway. Most of it's sunk, but it's there."

Something caught Catalina's eye. "Hey, Micah. Look straight ahead at roughly three o'clock."

"I can't see anything."

"Wait for the lightning."

They stood patiently until a flash of lightning cut across the sky.

Micah stared ahead, muttering, "What the heck?"

Up ahead of them, hidden among the trees, stood a five-story steel tower.

Catalina said, "Shall we?"

After five minutes of walking they came to a complex of decaying buildings. Broken concrete foundations dotted the area. The wooden buildings they'd supported had long been reclaimed by nature. In the center stood a three-story, warehouse-sized building of brick and steel. To its right was a five-story steel lattice radio tower. The tower's peak had collapsed, but the rest had survived, becoming a giant garden trellis for hundreds of vines.

Despite the vines, they could still make out four-foot-high, steel letters welded to the tower. The lightning flashing across the orange sky lent the complex a gothic tone. In that brief flash of lightning, they were able to read the letters.

They spelled out—HELL.

Catalina read it and said, "Well, I guess we've officially arrived."

\#

Queen Caveira and her remaining pirates followed Javier's cloth markers through the rainforest. The trail ended at the top of a rise. Standing at the peak, she signaled the men to stop then studied the marsh below. She could hear the stream babbling but no frogs croaking or birds singing—just an unearthly silence.

She gestured one of the pirates forward. "Paulo, come with me. The rest of you wait here."

Keeping to the brush, she crept down the incline, Paulo at her heels. The thick canopy of trees blocked out the sun, turning late afternoon to night. Up ahead she recognized the white plumage of a king vulture. It was perched atop a partially eaten human body. The cadaver was mutilated beyond recognition, but the weapon lying beside it was from her arsenal.

Paulo took aim at the vulture.

The queen pushed the gun barrel down, whispering, "Never shoot a vulture. He'll take his revenge by feasting on you in the afterlife." She pointed a few yards away. "Look there."

To their right, a chestnut-colored jaguarundi gnawed at another, equally mangled corpse. Her three kittens trailed behind her, playfully batting around brass bullet shells.

The vulture raised its bald head, a chunk of meat dangling from its orange beak. It croaked once before lethargically spreading its six-foot wings and soaring off.

The startled jaguarundi family slipped into the brush.

Queen Caveira knelt over the first body, noting the spent bullet casings on the ground. "They went down fighting."

The area was littered with long brown shapes she initially mistook for logs. Using the barrel of her rifle, she lifted one up. It was a dead centipede, five times larger than anything she'd seen before.

Paulo stared at it, stammering out, "What the hell is that?"

The queen tossed it aside, calmly stating, "It's exactly what it looks like." But despite her calm demeanor, the discovery had rattled her.

Paulo asked, "But what happened?"

Ignoring him, the queen walked on until she spotted something in the marsh water. A shredded cadaver lay sprawled atop a floating Queen Victoria lily, dead centipedes drifting around it. The body was mutilated, but she recognized Javier's clothes.

Turning to Paulo, Queen Caveira said, "Javier is dead, so you're my new executive officer," then continued walking.

The newly promoted Paulo tagged along, silently pondering the fate of her last two executive officers.

The queen spotted three sets of human footprints, all grouped together. One of them had been walking backwards. She followed the prints to the stream and abruptly stopped, transfixed by what she saw. Mounds of dead centipedes bobbed in the water. She estimated at least fifty, all clumped together in some lemming-like mass suicide.

Using his rifle barrel, Paulo prodded one of the dead creatures, asking, "What killed 'em?"

"The water. Centipedes can't swim."

"Then why'd they jump in?"

"They were spirit entities, manifested for one purpose. They died trying to fulfill it."

"What purpose?"

"To kill the American of course."

"Did they get him?"

The queen scooped up a dead centipede and hurled it at Paulo, shouting, "Do you see his body or the body of the child?"

Paulo stepped back, electing to keep his mouth shut.

Queen Caveira gradually pieced the evidence together. The American had escaped into the stream and the dutiful centipedes had waded in after him. When their first wave drowned, the second crawled over them, meeting the same fate, until all were dead.

Using a stick, she carved a Quimbanda symbol in the mud while whispering incantations. Then, in an almost maternal tone, she explained, "The American is a trickster, touched by the *Exus*."

The *Exus* were the spirits of the Quimbanda faith. Most were benevolent, but she was devoted to the demonic ones.

Hoping to redeem himself, Paulo blurted out, "He can't be as powerful as you."

"Of course not. But he stole energy from me during *fodor*. When I was taking his seed, he was siphoning magic from my *cona*. The *buceta* of a Quimbanda priestess holds enormous spiritual power. Letting him *chupar* my *cona* gave him the power to kill Boiúna."

The hardened pirate lowered his eyes in embarrassment at the queen's pornographic description.

She let out an ear-piercing whistle, summoning the other pirates. They clamored down the rise, eager for a fight, but that fervor died at the water's edge. The pirates stared down at the floating centipedes, whispering to each other.

Queen Caveira shouted, "Quiet!" silencing the men. "Soon it will be too dark to follow, so we'll stay here. I want you to gather up all the dead centipedes. Boiúna wills that we cremate these noble creatures."

A soft rain began to fall. The queen looked up into the sky then pointed to Paulo, saying, "I need you to follow the stream until you find their trail."

"Me? Shouldn't we all—"

She cut him off. "The rain will wash away their trail. So follow it until dark then wait for us. Now go!"

Picking his way through the dead centipedes, Paulo reluctantly waded into the stream, trudging against the current.

Watching him go, she shouted, "Have no fear, Paulo, I will perform a sacrifice to weaken the American's magic."

The mention of a sacrifice sent the remaining pirates into another wave of anxious muttering.

Studying their faces, the queen asked, "So, which one of you doesn't have syphilis?"

#

Faye stared up at the giant block letters spelling out HELL.

Micah felt her squeezing his hand and said, "Relax, honey."

Catalina asked, "I thought this area was uncharted?"

Micah said, "This is amazing. In the olden days, American petroleum companies bought up huge chunks of land along the Amazon to build rubber plantations. I never imagined any of them came out this far."

"Not a roaring success I take it?"

"It was a fiasco. This place must have been abandoned for seventy years." He pointed at the lettering on the tower. "That tower used to say SHELL."

Catalina said, "Well, they really built things to last back then. I mean this stuff should have rusted out decades ago."

"The metal's rustproof 'cause it's chock-full of lead."

"I guess they didn't know that lead would poison everybody."

"Oh, they knew, they just didn't give a shit about the people here."

Catalina laughed. "Capitalism at its finest."

Lightning flashed across the orange-hued sky. The rain gradually slackened from downpour to light drizzle.

Catalina said, "I don't know about you guys, but I'm soaked inside and out."

Faye eyed the ruins apprehensively then asked Catalina, "Do you—"

"Ever get scared? Yeah, it's normal, but we're going to get out of this."

"No, I was asking do you have to pee? I really need to go."

"Oh. Hey boss, Faye and I need to find a gas station." She pointed to a concrete foundation. "That might work."

Approaching the broken foundation, Micah said, "Let me take a look around first."

Catalina sat down on a low section of concrete, tapped the spot next to her and said, "Come here for a second."

Faye sat down next to her, leaning in close.

Catalina put her arm around her and asked, "You've seen a lot of really terrible things in the last few days, haven't you?"

Faye nodded.

"Trust me; I know how scary that can be."

Faye looked at her with an expression of disbelief and said, "Really?"

"Yeah, really. Can I tell you a little story?" Faye nodded. "I was born in a place called Equatorial Guinea. Ever heard of it?" Faye shook her head. "Don't feel bad, most people haven't. Anyway, it's in Africa. I lived there till I was seven. That country's run by a really evil guy, and one day he decided that people like me and my parents were undesirable."

"Why?"

"Because that's what people who are full of hate do. So, one night, soldiers came and burned our village, our home, everything. They killed a lot of people and we barely escaped. My parents and I spent months hiding during the day and traveling at night, trying to get away from the soldiers. We had barely any food or water and walked the whole way. And every day those soldiers killed more people."

"What happened?"

"Eventually we made it to a refugee camp, but along the way I saw things that still give me nightmares. But you know the one thing that kept me going?"

"Being brave?"

"Brave? Not by a long shot. I used to cry myself to sleep every night."

"Then what was it?"

Catalina pointed at Micah in the distance and said, "My father. He kept us alive, even when … well, even when we didn't want to go on anymore."

"Was he a tough guy like a cop or something?"

"Nope. He taught math at a school. But he never gave up and always protected us."

Faye gazed over at her own father.

Catalina added, "Your dad's never going to give up either. He's a smart, courageous guy who'll get us home somehow."

Faye smiled and said, "You're pretty smart too."

"Well, yeah, I'm totally awesome, but so are you."

Catalina gave her a hug and was relieved to hear the little girl laugh.

#

Micah picked through the broken foundations, cautiously tapping a stick against any likely hiding places. Peering around a concrete pillar, he came face-to-face with a four-foot coral snake. A twitching scorpion dangled from its mouth.

Micah waved the stick at it a few times, saying, "Shoo, you knucklehead, get lost. Go finish dinner someplace else."

The snake swallowed its prey and slithered off.

In a half whisper, Catalina asked, "All clear?"

After checking the ground for scorpions, Micah waved them over, saying, "Nothing here to worry about," without mentioning the snake. There was no point in adding to the day's cavalcade of terrors. He walked away, allowing them some privacy.

After finishing, Faye and Catalina rejoined him.

Pointing to the warehouse-sized building, Micah said, "I wanna take a look in there before we lose the light."

"Yell if you need me."

Peering into the dark building, Micah said, "Don't worry, I will."

The building's frame was three stories tall. Its bottom floor was still covered in leaded tin siding. In its heyday the upper levels must have had glass windows all around. The glass was long gone, but, thanks to the lead content, the structure survived. Micah cautiously stepped inside, his boots sinking into the mushy ground. He sniffed the air and froze. The building's upper levels were open to the elements, yet the air inside was acrid. His mind flashed back to the formic acid smell, but this was a distinctly different, ammonia tinged odor. After a few sniffs he recognized it. Urine—a lot of urine. He heard a chorus of soft, semi-melodic squeals emanating from above—like hundreds of tiny voices. After piecing together the clues, he backed out slowly.

Once outside, he said, "Don't go in there under any circumstances."

Drawing the Glock, Catalina asked, "Is it dangerous?"

"Only if you go inside. And please don't fire that gun, you won't like what happens."

Faye literally hopped up and down with excitement, declaring, "I know, I know; it's bats, right?"

Mussing her hair, Micah said, "The little lady wins a prize."

"What kind?"

"Of prize? I don't know."

"No silly, what kind of bats?"

"I think they're bulldog bats. Like a gazilion of 'em."

"Cool." Faye turned to Catalina and, beaming with pride, said, "Bulldog bats are ground feeders. They can find anything on the ground and even catch fish right out of the water. A group like this is called a cauldron."

Catalina said, "That's an appropriately spooky name."

Faye said, "They're not spooky," while trying to poke her head into the building. "Bats are awesome! They have sonar and can track anything."

Micah gently led her away from the building, adding, "They also have rabies, SARS and lice."

"Still cool though."

"Well, the sun'll be down in a few minutes, so you'll be seeing plenty of 'em."

Catalina muttered, "Can't hardly wait."

#

Paulo came to a break in the trees and crawled out of the stream, physically spent from walking against the current. Then he spotted a large Queen Victoria lily wedged in the reeds up ahead. It looked very out of place.

Once on the riverbank he hacked open a vine, greedily sucking down the sweet water inside. The relentless downpour had slackened to a drizzle. He took a moment to try to get his bearings, but a mix of hundred-foot kapoks and shaggy rubber trees blocked the sun, leaving him in near darkness.

Wiping down his rifle, he muttered, "Why's it always midnight and raining out here?" Then he saw water-filled footprints on the bank—three sets, leading into the rainforest.

"Got ya!"

After tying a marker rag around a tree trunk, he switched on his flashlight and followed the prints. The viscous mud sucked at his boots, making every step laborious.

"If I'm the executive officer, how come I'm stuck wandering around out here in the rain?"

After thirty minutes of hiking he came to some broken slabs of cement and more footprints.

A dead toad covered in ants lay next to one of the footprints.

Unzipping his pants, he said, "Drink up, assholes," and urinated on the scrambling insects. He was humming to himself when a distant sound caught his attention. After fumbling with his zipper, he hunkered down, listening intently. He heard it again—it was a child laughing.

He crept through the brush until he spotted them about a hundred yards out. The three Americans were sitting in front of an old plantation building. It looked like they were having a picnic.

"The bastards ain't even trying to hide."

\#

Micah leaned back against a chunk of cement and said, "You know, one thing doesn't make sense to me."

Catalina said, "Really? 'Cause I've been hunting for one thing that *does* make sense to me. So far, zippo."

"Very funny, but hear me out. The first thing that attacked us was the ants back at the fuel depot. Then the snake attacked the boats. But the second time a snake appeared it wasn't interested in the boats at all. It seemed obsessed with you. I had to throw a grenade just to get its attention."

"Well, I did blow away its twin brother with a machine gun. Maybe it was a Sicilian Boa."

Faye looked at her quizzically, asking, "A what?"

"A Sicilian Boa. They're super into vendettas."

Faye rolled her eyes theatrically.

Growing frustrated, Micah said, "Please guys, I'm being serious here. The next thing was the centipedes, and they were clearly gunning for us. If these things are trying to protect the Anomaly, why didn't they go after Batista?"

Catalina shrugged. "Maybe they did. For all you know Batista's being digested by some big-ass monster right now."

Faye was unwrapping the last of the salvaged nutrition bars when something clicked in her mind. She asked, "Dad, if I did something kinda bad, would you get freaked out about it?"

"What am I gonna do, ground you? What's eating you?"

Catalina said, "Poor choice of words."

Faye dug into her pants pocket, saying, "I kind of stole something from the boat, but I honestly forgot all about it till we got here."

As she spoke, Faye felt the fragment in her pocket start to vibrate.

And lightning flashed across the dark sky.

\#

Paulo put the AK-47 to his shoulder and squinted down the sights. Then he remembered that the queen wanted most of them alive. He crawled forward, careful to remain silent.

A bolt of lightning struck a treetop above him, followed by a sharp crack of thunder. Smoking branches fell to the ground a few feet away.

Paulo yelled, "Fuck!" then covered his mouth. Looking out he saw them still sitting there, totally oblivious. He started crawling again. Only a few more yards and he'd have the drop on them. Then he felt the ground beneath him shudder in short rolling tremors. To his left, tiny blue and violet lights danced across the sodden ground like fireflies.

He thought, *Ghost lights?* He'd heard about them but never actually seen any.

The dancing lights receded into the soil and the tremors ceased. A patch of ground in front of him puckered, as if something was clawing its way out. Worried it might be a burrowing coral snake, he wriggled back a few feet. More of the weird dimples appeared in the ground to his left and right.

"What the fu—"

A searing pain shot through his arm. Raising it up, he found a six-inch writhing insect dangling from his forearm. He felt a stabbing pain in his ankle and rolled onto his side. Another insect was clamped to his boot, its mandibles biting clean through the leather. Dozens of the red insects crawled to the surface around him. He grabbed the one on his forearm and yanked, feeling his flesh ripping away. He jumped up, swatting at the creatures, but they held on. His legs were now covered in vicious, biting monsters. The ground around him pulsed then burst open, alive with hundreds of the things.

He ran, screaming, tearing at the huge insects, a crimson wave of ants right on his tail.

CHAPTER TWENTY-TWO

A piercing scream echoed through the rainforest. Faye threw her arms around Micah. Lightning flashed across the sky, illuminating a man charging towards them, his body a squirming red mass.

Catalina jumped to her feet, aiming the Glock. There was another flash of lightning.

Micah yelled, "It's the ants!"

Catalina saw a writhing mass of red insects moving across the ground, heading straight for them. "Didn't we burn those fucks?"

Micah looked around. "We can't outrun 'em."

Catalina said, "What about climbing the tower?"

"Remember the depot? They'll be up there in minutes and we won't have any place to run."

Faye tugged at Micah's shirt, asking, "What about the bats?"

"They'll be fine, honey."

Faye yanked harder, shouting, "No, I mean… What about the bulldog bats?"

That's when Micah caught his daughter's drift. Pointing to the decrepit structure, he yelled, "Everybody, inside the building!"

Catalina asked, "But you said—"

Micah scooped up Faye, shouting, "Just do it!"

He ran in, with Catalina right behind. Four steps in she slipped, splashing down in the thick, urine-reeking muck. "What is this shit?"

"Exactly … but keep moving to the center."

Micah banged his flashlight against a steel girder. The chorus of squeals grew louder, but nothing happened.

Micah yelled, "Wake up, you lazy bastards!"

The trilling increased, but nothing moved. He panned his light to the entrance. The first wave of ants was already coming through the door.

Micah shouted, "Remember when I said don't fire the gun?"

"Yeah."

"Fire it now!"

"At what?"

"In the air!"

Without questioning him, Catalina raised the Glock and loosed two shots into the air. The pistol's roar was instantly drowned out by a shrill tone Catalina felt in her back teeth.

A second later, the air above them transformed into swirling black anarchy. A thousand bulldog bats, each with a three-foot wingspan, swarmed around them. A cluster of bats dive-bombed the trio, coming so close Catalina could make out their pug snouts and fangs.

Losing interest in the human intruders, the bats veered off—their echolocation having located more edible prey.

Catalina watched in amazement as the first wave of bats soared upward then descended in a barrel roll move, scooping up ants in their talons. A cacophony of ear-piercing trills rang out, signaling the rest of the cauldron.

Micah whispered, "That was the dinner bell."

With a grace borne from millions of years of evolution, hundreds of bats swooped down from the darkness, snapping up their insect prey then ascending without losing speed. The ants' vicious mandibles were useless against the bats, who routinely hunted scorpions without injury.

Micah lay on his back, watching as a second cloud of bats flew out the windows.

He yelled, "They're going for the ones outside!"

Faye put her hand over his mouth, whispering, "Don't yell, it'll confuse their sonar."

Micah spat, wiping away the bat guano her palm left.

Having no retreat instinct, the ants continued their attack, only to be plucked from the ground like grapes. Their thick exoskeleton offered no protection against the bats' talons, which were strong enough to crush shellfish.

One swooping bat missed its target, becoming entangled in Catalina's hair. She swatted at its three-foot wings until Micah wrenched it loose, releasing it. The bat soared aloft, performing an airshow worthy loop, then dove down to pluck an ant off Catalina's boot.

A second wave of ants crawled through the doorway, but their oversized bodies became bogged down in the slushy guano. Others marched over their sinking brethren, making themselves easy prey for the bats. Within minutes the doorway was ant-free.

Faye leaned close to Catalina and whispered, "I told you they were awesome."

Micah tapped Catalina and pointed towards the now cleared doorway. "Let's move."

They crawled to the doorway, mindful of the bats swooping around them.

Once outside they made a beeline for the old radio tower, running as fast as Faye's short legs allowed.

Somehow sensing their escape attempt, the surviving pockets of ants formed up into pursuing regiments.

Catalina glanced back and said, "A whole whack of 'em are still coming!"

Without looking back, Micah said, "Good, it'll be like a buffet table for the bats."

He boosted Faye up so she could grab a vine. Wedging his body behind her to support her weight they climbed together.

Looking up at the swirling cloud of bats, Catalina asked, "What if they get full?"

Faye chimed in, "Bulldogs have cheek sacks to hold extra food."

Micah added, "She's right, they'll chow down like a fat guy on Thanksgiving and still come back for more, and there must be a thousand of 'em."

The pursuing ants began climbing the tower. Bats broke rank from the cauldron, diving for the vulnerable prey. With each strike a bat snatched an ant in its talons, crushed it and stuffed the meat into its cheek pouches without losing speed. They dive bombed again and again in a gluttonous feeding frenzy.

Micah set Faye on a high platform then reached down to give Catalina a boost.

Once she was on the platform, Catalina said, "Pretty slick thinking for a TV hack."

"You should be thanking Faye; my only plan was run like hell."

By now the sun had set. The flashing lightning illuminated the swirling cloud of bats—a sight both hellish and beautiful.

Catalina said, "It's like sitting inside a tornado. They never even touch each other."

Faye waved to their airborne saviors, shouting, "Thank you!" Then she dug into her pocket. "Remember when I said I did something bad?" Micah nodded. "Well, I remembered that when we were on the boat you were really excited about this thing." She opened her hand. Resting in her palm was Batista's precious meteorite fragment. "I forgot about it till you started wondering why the monsters were following us." Handing it to Micah, she said, "I'm sorry. Maybe if I hadn't stolen it all those bad things wouldn't have happened."

Micah stared at the fragment for a moment then smiled at Faye. "Not your fault, princess, there was no way you could've known."

Slipping an arm around Faye, Catalina said, "Your dad's right. He has more degrees than a thermometer and even he didn't figure it out."

Faye added, "It sings you know," and she explained how the fragment vibrated and hummed before the monster attacks.

Micah studied the fragment more closely and said, "So it's like a LoJac on a car. That's how the Anomaly knows where to send its protectors. Too bad we can't hand it back to Batista. He deserves it."

Catalina said, "I'd like to feed it to him." Then she turned her attention to Faye. "You know, kid, that's a lot of bat poop on your face, mind if I clean some off?" Using her T-shirt she started wiping the worst of it away.

Micah bounced the fragment in his hand. This tiny specimen, the size of his finger, could prove every one of his theories, reopening the doors to those hallowed halls of legitimate science. A game changer—a life changer.

And with all his might he hurled it into the darkness, feeling like a giant weight had been lifted off his shoulders. He scanned the ground below, relieved to see the remaining pockets of ants shrinking by the minute.

Lightning flashed across the sky, and Micah stiffened—the old man was back.

The wizened ancient stood in the midst of the ants, bats swirling around him, completely unmolested. He stared back at Micah then held up his hand, as if showing him something.

The lightning passed, plunging the area back into darkness.

Micah grabbed Catalina's shoulder, pointing down. "Look, do you see him? Down there!"

"Who?"

"Wait for the lightning, you'll see him."

There was another flash of lightning, but all they saw was dying ants.

Micah sat back, muttering, "Never mind," but he knew what he'd seen.

#

Within an hour the rain stopped, and the rainforest came alive. Faye drifted off to sleep with her head in Micah's lap. He and Catalina sat quietly, listening to the symphony of insects, birds and unidentifiable animal calls drifting through the night air. From their high vantage point, they could make out the full moon through the surrounding trees. Most of the bats had returned to the roost, their bellies and cheeks stuffed with ants. A few still swirled around, occasionally zipping to the ground to snap up a survivor.

Micah said, "Those are some fat and happy bats."

Gazing up at the moon, Catalina said, "This place is so surreal."

"True. Maybe someday God will get around to finishing it."

"What do you mean?"

"The local tribes have a saying, 'God never finished the Amazon,' and maybe they're right."

"That doesn't sound like the agnostic 'science can explain everything' guy I know."

"I guess there's still a shred of poetry left in my soul. It's just that the rainforest has such extremes of beauty and terror."

Catalina said, "But you seem right at home out here."

"Well, my folks taught me enough to get by."

Catalina eyed him for a moment before asking, "So what's your real story? And I don't mean the one the TV people cooked up."

"They didn't have to cook up too much. My dad was a geologist and my mom was an ethnobotanist, so I spent my childhood traveling with them. Africa, South America, wherever their research took 'em."

"Sounds like every little boy's dream."

"Yeah, playing in the jungle all day, getting home schooled in tents at night. Of course that meant no real school, no friends and no senior prom. I barely even saw a television until I went to college."

"And graduated with honors if my dossier was correct."

"Yup," he said, sounding wistful. "Your intel was good."

"Then how'd you wind up on television being a—"

"A joke to the scientific community? Well, let me tell ya, it took some doing. On one of my research trips in Peru I found a unique meteorite sample, like the one Batista recovered. It led me to form a theory about intelligent alien origins. I published a paper on it, and let's just say my peer review was … unkind. It cost me my grant money, my academic standing and ultimately my marriage. To add insult to injury, some museum threw away my sample, claiming it had no value."

"Ouch!"

"I was flat broke when some publisher paid me to turn it all into a paperback book full of woo-woo speculation and hearsay. That got me on some talk shows and pretty soon the TV people were knocking on my door waving a checkbook."

"So that's how you became TV's science stud?"

"Yup, one minute I'm doing legitimate research and the next some TV executive's got focus groups rating how my ass looks in safari shorts."

Caught off guard, Catalina burst out laughing.

Micah said, "I hated it, but it was the only way I could self-finance my research."

"Well, if it's any consolation, your butt was tailor-made for safari shorts." Catalina saw that her compliment caught Micah off guard. "What? I'm a trained observer."

After a brief silence, he asked, "So, is Catalina your real name or just your spy alias?"

"Come on, what lunatic would pick Catalina as an alias? Using your real first name means one less lie to remember."

"From what I've seen you must be a Jason Bourne type, out kicking ass and toppling dictators."

"Believe it or not, I'm usually assigned to intelligence monitoring since I speak Portuguese, Spanish, French, Arabic and some preschooler Hindi."

"How'd you pick up all that?"

"Mostly by hanging around the house. My dad's Brazilian and my mom's from Equatorial Guinea. That alone adds up to about five languages."

"So where'd you grow up?"

"I was in Guinea until I was seven. Then President Nguema decided to do a little … ethnic cleansing. After months of hiding we made it to a refugee camp. My folks couldn't decide between staying in Africa or going to South America, so they compromised."

"To where?"

"Lincoln, Nebraska."

"Nebraska!" Micah couldn't help laughing.

"Hey, don't knock us cornhuskers. Like most immigrant parents they had my life all mapped out. Finish college, become a high school teacher then marry a nice man and have kids."

"And?"

"I started out fine. You know, mathlete, good grades, state finals in gymnastics, plus all those languages."

"I'm guessing something went haywire."

"I rebelled and joined the army. My folks didn't look too fondly on the military, which makes sense considering their life experiences. Since I spoke all those languages the army shipped me to the Defense Language Institute, out in Monterey, where I also picked up a black belt in Combatives."

"You're a fast learner."

"I was a mixed race, immigrant kid, living in snow white Nebraska. Trust me; you learn to fight."

"So how'd the spy thing happen?"

"One night, I entered a base fighting tournament, where some woman I'd never seen before kept whipping my ass. But I kept getting back up. Turns out she was a CIA recruiter, testing my determination. Next thing you know I'm out of the army and training at Langley."

"That's pretty impressive for someone who's only, what, twenty-five?"

"I wish. I'm thirty-four. Even half black don't crack."

Micah grinned at the newfound knowledge that Catalina was age appropriate; a ridiculous notion, given their slim chance of survival.

Catalina said, "This is only my second field assignment, but I never imagined anything this bat shit crazy."

"That's appropriate, since we're covered in actual bat shit. Don't worry; they'll be treating you like 007 when you get back. I mean, look at all the stuff you uncovered. A free energy source, criminals inside the rare elements trade, plus Batista's practically a Bond villain."

Catalina asked, "Speaking of villains, who's this latest bunch of killer clowns?"

Micah gave her a quick rundown of his pirate adventures, including his emerald mine ruse, while tactfully omitting his sexual liaison.

Catalina chuckled. "I leave you alone for a couple of days and you're off playing pirates."

Faye squirmed for a few seconds, whimpering in her sleep. Micah stroked her hair, whispering, "It's okay, honey, go back to sleep," until she drifted off. "Catalina, thanks for looking after my little girl. If it hadn't been for you—"

"No sweat. Faye's pretty sharp, probably gets it from her old man."

"Trust me, the brains all come from her mom's side. Crazy thing is that I only get her two months a year, but I've managed to pack in a lifetime's worth of emotional trauma."

"Don't dwell on it. Better to focus on getting our sorry asses home. Is there a plan?"

"At first light we get moving. Grab some fruit or anything else we can eat as we go. Then maybe we can slap together a raft, though how we can go back to civilization against the current is beyond me."

Catalina said, "If we can reach anyplace with a phone, I can call my people. They'll come get us, but you'll probably be interrogated for a while."

"I'll take life in Guantanamo Bay if it gets Faye home safely. All we have to do now is avoid the pirates, the Red Death and Batista. But we won't get anywhere without some sleep."

Gazing up at the brilliant moon hovering above the endless rainforest, Catalina said, "Totally surreal."

"Yup, Dorothy, you're not in Kansas anymore."

"It was Nebraska, smart ass. Don't make me throw your 'looks good in safari shorts' ass off the tower."

CHAPTER TWENTY-THREE

Micah bolted awake at sunrise, confused and uncertain of where he was—a natural side effect of exhaustion, hunger and waking up atop a vine-covered tower. Despite his exhaustion he recalled a vivid dream, where the old man had been sitting next to him holding the meteorite fragment. He looked down at Faye, her head nestled in his lap, snoring peacefully.

A moment later, Catalina awakened, stretching like a cat across the steel platform. "Is it morning already?"

"Just about. I'm gonna climb down and scout the area."

"Want me to tag along?"

"Nope, I know what I'm looking for." He stroked Faye's hair. "Can you keep an eye on her?"

"Goes without saying. Hey, at least the rain stopped—" She fell silent, awestruck by the sheer majesty of the rainforest stretching out before them.

The red sun had barely risen above the endless rainforest. Low-hanging fog lay across the trees. A symphony of bird calls and howling monkeys filled the damp air.

Seeing the look on her face, Micah said, "A sight to behold, ain't it?"

"Just unbelievable."

"Not to dampen the mood, but how many bullets have you got left?"

Catalina ejected the Glock's magazine. "I used the last two waking up those bats."

"That's a drag, but you can't argue with the results." Micah stood, stretching his back, groaning, feeling more like sixty-seven than thirty-seven.

Watching him, Catalina said, "If you say you're getting too old for this shit, I'll throw you off the tower."

Micah laughed and said, "Back in a few."

Once on the ground he did a fast recon, seeing no signs of ants, pirates or native tribes. He walked a hundred yards out, where he spotted some wide leafy plants and sipped the cool dew collected in the leaves.

Feeling refreshed, he moved on, until he came to a narrow path dotted with the hoof prints of Brazilian tapirs. The bashful wild pigs weren't a threat, but further on he spotted human footprints—all barefoot.

He thought, *Hunting parties.*

Along the edge of the path were yellow-flowered plants resembling blackthorn bushes. Sniffing the leaves, he caught the smell of tea.

Okay, hunting parties that like to party.

The bushes were Amazonian coca plants, planted by the natives, who chewed the leaves for energy. Such plants would be dispersed along the trail, indicating a regular route for the hunters.

Micah plucked a fistful of leaves, slipped one into his mouth and stuffed the rest in his pocket. After a few seconds of chewing he felt his energy level rise and his myriad of aches and pains slipping away. The leaves didn't have the narcotic effects of cocaine—it was more like three expressos followed by a Swedish massage. Feeling at least half alive, he hiked back to explore the route they'd come in on. The bats had scoured the area clean of any ants. All that remained of the man who'd run screaming from the jungle was bones. Micah was about to walk back to the tower when a detail caught his eye. The human skeleton was mostly intact, except the skull was gone. Then he saw the imprints of bare feet.

"Aw shit."

While they'd slept someone had come and taken the head. He jogged back toward the tower, scanning the tree line for any sign of life. Nothing.

Catalina saw him coming and climbed down, Faye in tow.

Once on the ground, she asked, "What's the verdict?"

"Moving inland to avoid the pirates was smart, but she's clearly on our trail. I say we get back to the river."

"Because?"

He told her about the footprints and the missing skull, adding, "Our best hope is passing boats. Even this far out there might still be river traffic. Or we might find somebody who'll sell us a canoe."

"What're we paying with?"

"That pistol you're carrying. It'll be a hot commodity out here."

"Ethically questionable, but who's counting."

"It'll be cool for a few more hours, so we'll walk till noon then take a break." He crouched down to eye level with Faye, and asked, "How're you doing, honey?"

She smiled, putting on a brave front. "I'm okay."

"That's my girl."

But the exhaustion in her eyes was plain to see, along with the bug bites, scratches and filth covering her body. His little girl needed decent food, sleep and a bath—none of which were on the horizon. He dug out one of the leaves and handed it to Catalina. "Chew on that, it'll help."

"What is it?"

"Let's just say you should avoid any mandatory drug testing for a while."

She chewed on it for a few seconds and said, "You're a very bad influence."

Faye asked, "Can I have one?"

Micah tussled her hair, saying, "No, honey, they're just for grown-ups. Now let's get moving."

They set out, but having a child with them kept their pace painfully slow.

#

The queen had no such encumbrances, quickly marching her pirates to the abandoned rubber plantation. The monkey perched on her shoulder showed no interest in joining the wild troops in the trees above.

She knelt down over the headless skeleton half buried in the mud. The body had been stripped of its skin, but she recognized its tattered shoes. She also noted the bare footprints around the body.

Turning to her men, she announced, "Benício, you are my new executive officer."

Benício stared down at his skeletal predecessor and gulped.

She walked on, waving for them to follow. After a brief search, she declared, "The American is already gone." Then she closed her eyes, lost in deep thought. After a few moments, she announced, "I know where he's going," and started walking.

Benício cautiously asked, "Where are we going?"

"Wherever I say."

The men fell in behind, their pace becoming sluggish, accompanied by muted bitching and moaning.

Sensing their reluctance, the queen declared, "What are you whining about? Have you forgotten our escape from Batista's emerald mine?"

Benício said, "Of course not, it was the day you led us to freedom."

Queen Caveira said, "We were only children, but we walked for days without food or water. Now you are men, so act like it!"

They pressed on, her harsh words shaming them into silent obedience.

The queen slipped her hand into her pocket, feeling the pool ball-sized emerald nestled there. No matter what happened she'd still have enough to start over—but only after Boiúna was avenged.

#

Micah pressed on, navigating by instinct and hoping to hell he was right. The noon heat had grown oppressive, and the air hung thick with humidity. The rising temperature evaporated the dew from the leaves, leaving them thirsty. Mosquitos and biting flies hovered around the trio, making regular attacks.

Micah dug out the last of the waterproof wooden matches he'd scavenged from the queen's dinghy and handed them out. "Suck on the end as we go." Faye put it in her mouth and grimaced. He said, "I know it tastes terrible, but the sulfur gets in your sweat and keeps the bugs off."

He mentally tallied their situation. Faye had grown lethargic from exhaustion and heat, forcing him to carry her for the last hour. The fruit they'd gathered wasn't going to be enough to sustain them. Their best hope was to reach the river and hopefully catch some fish—preferably not Megapiranha.

A break in the trees ahead led them to a steep muddy slope. Micah heard water flowing in the distance.

Catalina heard it too, asking, "Is that the river?"

Micah nodded and set Faye down. "We're close, honey, but I need you to walk down the slope. Can you do that for me?"

Faye nodded, too exhausted to feign enthusiasm.

Wiping the sweat off her brow, Catalina asked, "You got another one of those go-go leaves?" Micah handed one over. She chewed it, muttering, "I'm checking into Betty Ford after this."

Taking Faye's hand, Micah slowly worked his way down through the ankle-deep mud, the river growing louder with every step.

Halfway down he lost his foothold and shouted, "Grab her!"

Catalina latched on to Faye's arm just as Micah fell into the slick mud. He slid, gaining speed until he was rocketing like a luge down the embankment. After thirty seconds of mud-sledding he felt the ground beneath him disappear. While still airborne he managed one deep breath—a heartbeat later he was underwater.

Micah sank into a deep but remarkably clear pool. He was about to kick his way up when he saw something silhouetted against the sunlit surface. It was a fish, at least six feet long, with a tapered snout. Another equally large creature swam by, intentionally bumping him.

Micah thought, *Bull sharks,* while fighting the panic welling inside. Amazon River bull sharks were as vicious as great whites—genuine man-eaters.

He spun around, getting a clear look at the passing creature, and the panic slipped away. It was a boto—the elusive pink dolphins of the Amazon. Another swam by, eying him curiously before diving deeper. It used its long snout to poke at the riverbed in search of crayfish.

Micah swam to the surface and treaded water until he heard Catalina shouting his name.

He yelled, "I'm okay, and I found the river!" and dove under again, savoring the cool water against his skin.

He bobbed to the surface, looked up and gasped in amazement at the scene around them.

#

Faye charged down the slope, shouting, "Daddy," overjoyed to find her father not only safe but surrounded by pink river dolphins. She waded into the water and hugged him, yelling, "You found pink dolphins!"

One of the botos swam up, popping its head out of the water.

Micah said, "You think that's something? Take a look up there." He gently turned her head upward.

The little girl gasped.

Catalina saw it at the same time, muttering, "My God."

A brown clay cliff rose from the river, but its surface was hidden by an unbroken wall of brilliantly colored birds—hundreds of them. Flocks of green-headed parrots and rainbow-plumed macaws clung to the cliff face, pecking at the clay surface.

Catalina just stared at the endless carpet of birds, half whispering, "Incredible."

Jumping up and down in the water, Faye shouted, "Catalina, dive in! There's pink dolphins!"

"I noticed that." Catalina waded out into the water, asking Micah, "Why are all those birds eating dirt?"

"It's a clay lick. Birds come from all over to chew on the clay and get the salt. The rain must have exposed a new layer. There are clay licks all over the Amazon, but I've never seen one this size before. God, there must be a thousand birds on there."

Catalina floated on her back, gazing up at the cliff while dolphins swam past, saying, "I could pretty much drift here forever. It's beyond beautiful."

Micah was focused on Faye. The little girl reached out, touching a passing dolphin, and laughed, her face radiant. His record as a father had amounted to a cavalcade of well-intentioned mistakes and disappointments. But now he'd accidentally come through, delivering pink dolphins just when his daughter needed them the most.

"Yeah," Micah said, "beautiful is the word alright."

The fear in the pit of his stomach melted away, replaced by a glow of hope. They'd blundered into a tiny chunk of paradise, but he knew it didn't mean they were safe. He waded back to the shore and gazed up at the cliff, shielding his eyes from the sun.

Catalina asked, "What're you thinking, boss man?"

"I want to get to the top of that cliff for a bird's eye view of what's around us."

Cocking her head towards Faye, she asked, "Uh, do you really think we're in any condition to scale a cliff?"

"No, but I think I see an easier way."

At the far end of the cliff, Micah spotted a group of capybaras ambling down a well-worn slope. The hundred-pound gophers were likely coming down for a swim. Micah figured the slope would provide a fairly painless route to the top. Getting there meant crossing through a rainstorm of bird droppings, but it beat scaling a cliff.

Faye pleaded, "Can't we stay?"

Micah relented, saying, "Just a little longer, but we'll come back, I promise."

He allowed the ladies a few more minutes of swimming and splash fighting, while he took in their surroundings. The pond was fed by a stream connected to the wide tributary. Something odd caught his eye. Thick bushes with vibrantly colored violet thistles and red berries were growing all around the pond. They were unlike anything Micah had seen before. More grew along the edge of the tributary.

The tributary was the same one they'd been traveling down with Batista. Recalling the chart he'd memorized, Micah knew Batista's boats should have transferred to a series of narrow channels, meaning they weren't an imminent threat. But the pirates were still in the game, and the mad queen was clearly holding a grudge. Just the thought of her chilled him.

He said, "Ladies, we need to get moving."

#

Hans stood on the deck of Batista's yacht, his anticipation and relief growing with every mile. The channel they'd been navigating had widened into a vast, heavily wooded, floodplain—an area too open for the *Morte Tinto*'s cut and run attacks.

He said, "This is remarkable."

Santos leaned against the railing beside him, rifle slung over his shoulder, his face expressionless.

Batista emerged from his saloon carrying a glass of wine. Without offering libations to the others, he pointed to a stretch of downed trees. "Those mean we're coming up on the epicenter of the quake."

Hans said, "This floodplain doesn't look natural."

"You're right. I think it's caused by the dam my expedition built."

"Fascinating."

They traveled in silence for another twenty minutes.

Santos shouted, "There, look!" He pointed up ahead.

Barely visible through the mist was a boat similar to the *Valentina*. It lay on its side, half submerged. The upper decks were buckled, as if struck by a giant hammer.

Batista sighed and said, "Now we know what happened to the *Opala*," and took a sip of wine.

Hans said, "There's another one," pointing to the capsized hull of a tender boat. "What do you think happened?"

"The same thing that happened to the *Valentina*. Santos, once we get operations underway, we may need to siphon the remaining fuel from those wrecks."

Santos replied, "Understood." Then, without warning, he unslung and aimed his rifle in one fluid move.

Batista asked, "What do you see?"

"Fin in the water at ten o'clock."

Hans saw a dorsal fin slicing through the water.

Taking aim, Santos said, "It's a bull shark. Should I pop it?"

Batista put his hand on the rifle barrel, gently lowering it down. "Don't shoot. That shark's just conquering new territory, taking what it wants. I quite admire sharks."

Hans fumbled to light a cigarette. "But do you think there's another snake?"

"We'll find out soon enough. Ah, we're coming up on the dam. Get ready."

The yacht came alongside a crudely constructed dock jutting out from the crater's rim. Santos grabbed the bowline, jumped onto the dock and tied off. The gunboat pulled alongside it. Five armed men piled out. The heavily laden LST boat pulled up the rear.

Batista was off the yacht before it was even tied off, making straight for the dam.

Hans struggled to catch up, amazed at how fast the big man could move. "Shouldn't we wait for the guards to search the area?"

Batista waved his hand dismissively and pressed on.

Hans stopped for a moment to admire what lay ahead. The lake resembled a giant moon crater—a deep depression surrounded by a high rim of earth, covered in lush greenery. The rim formed a wall, obscuring any view of the water. It was fed by a single flow from the tributary. Batista's initial expedition had constructed a thirty-five-yard long dam of felled trees and mud, blocking its flow into the lake, creating the wide floodplain in the process. It must have been a huge project.

Without slowing, Batista trotted up the dirt incline running alongside the dam, saying, "It doesn't look like any boats survived. Do you think we'll be able to move it with the vessels we have?"

Hans trudged along behind him. "Impossible to say without actually seeing it. The largest meteorite ever recovered was the *Hoba* in Namibia, but it was only sixty tons. If that's the case here, we should have enough boats on hand to transport it in pieces."

"Sixty tons. Just imagine what we could accomplish with that."

Hans said, "It would be enough to power the entire world."

Batista muttered, "Or own it."

The prospect gave him chills. The man who controlled the world's energy wouldn't be an oil sheik, or even a king—more like a pharaoh, with the power of the gods at his fingertips.

He yelled to the armed men, "You five do a sweep. Be on the lookout for arrows or any other signs of Indians. If you see anything bigger than a mouse, kill it on the spot, Indians included."

One of the armed men asked, "Do you think we'll find any of our people alive?"

Without hesitation, Batista replied, "No."

The men fanned out. Batista reached the dam's crest. The high vantage point offered him a view of the two-mile-in-diameter crater lake below. He stood motionless, staring down.

Hans finally reached the crest, out of breath and wheezing. He gazed down at the lake, getting his first glimpse of the "Anomaly" and declared, "*Mutter Gottes!*"

With a Cheshire Cat grin, Batista said, "Looks like we're going to need more boats."

#

Micah led Faye and Catalina along the base of the cliff. For a moment he thought it was raining; then he realized the downpour was an unending shower of bird droppings.

Catalina wisely tore some wide leaves from nearby plants, creating improvised umbrellas. Pointing to the base of the cliff, she asked, "Hey, does Guinness have a world record for biggest pile of bird shit?"

What resembled a ten-foot-high snow bank ran along the length of the cliff face. In actuality, it was bird guano, interspersed with layers of thick green moss.

Micah glanced at it and said, "Once upon a time that mound would have been worth a fortune as fertilizer. Bird guano was so valuable that ships would risk sailing around Cape Horn jammed with it for Europe."

Catalina chuckled and said, "Have you ever noticed people avoiding you at parties?"

Faye laughed out loud. It was like music to Micah's ears. Her hollow gaze and physical exhaustion were gone, replaced by buoyant childhood wonder.

Micah thought, *And all it took were a thousand parrots and a couple of dolphins.*

Circumventing the mountain of bird droppings meant navigating over the jagged rocks along the river's edge. Nobody complained.

Thanks to generations of thirsty capybaras their ascent proved easier than he'd expected. The huge rodents had worn the upward slope into a smooth walking path. Another group of capybaras shuffled past them, oblivious to the human interlopers.

Faye ran alongside them shouting, "Dad, they look like humungous guinea pigs!"

Micah said, "I know, honey, but slow down, and please don't pet the giant rats."

Catalina asked, "You didn't slip her any go-go leaves, did you?"

"Nope, this is a nine-year-old's natural burst of energy. She'll probably drop like a stone once we get to the top."

"What about you?"

"I'm just hoping we spot something from up there, military, hell even smugglers would help."

"And if not?"

"Let's just say it's a long hike to Peru." As they walked, Micah noticed more of the odd bushes growing along the path. "Strange, I've never seen those before."

Shaking her head, Catalina said, "All the weird stuff we've seen and you're interested in flowers?"

"Mom was a botanist, so it runs in the family."

They continued on. Catalina warily eyed the passing capybaras.

Sensing tension, Micah asked, "Something bothering you?"

Catalina said, "I'm just amazed that the giant rats are the only thing not trying to murder us."

"Out here, giant rats are just a normal part of the scenery."

Catalina's tone grew more serious. "So, do you really think some intelligent force from outer space created those monsters just to kill us?"

"Maybe not us specifically, but they're definitely trying to stop anyone from reaching the Anomaly."

"And you're sure that's the only rational explanation?"

Micah pondered that for a moment. "Well, on the flip side you've got the pirate queen's version."

"Which was?"

"She was convinced the snake god and his dark minions had risen up to protect its home."

"And why does that sound any crazier?"

Micah thought, *She's right. Are the queen's spiritual beliefs really any more farfetched than my allegedly scientific explanation?*

Catalina asked, "But why aren't we seeing any monsters now? Not that I'm complaining."

"I think it's 'cause we got rid of the fragment."

"Or maybe you just passed the test."

Micah gave her a puzzled look.

Catalina said, "You keep saying some weird old man is guiding you. Well, what if he was testing you, to see if you had the right stuff?"

"Are you saying he was intentionally putting us in harm's way?"

"It's just a theory."

"That would be a dick move, but I guess it's possible. Or maybe the act of creation is exhausting and the intelligence is worn out. Didn't God have to rest on the seventh day?"

"You mean the day he should have been finishing the Amazon?"

"Something like that." He shouted to Faye, "Slow down and stick with us."

They reached the summit. Feeling winded, Micah stopped to take a few deep breaths while gazing out at the panorama of fog-shrouded rainforest and flowing river.

Catalina took Faye's hand and stood next to him, whispering, "I think God's done alright."

All three looked out, swept away by the sheer majesty of what lay before them. Micah was hypnotized by the grandeur, until a terrifyingly familiar voice snapped him back to reality.

"Hello, Lucky Man. Did you miss me?"

Followed by the sound of a pistol being cocked.

CHAPTER TWENTY-FOUR

Micah spun around to find himself face-to-face with Queen Caveira. The skull makeup was gone, but her eyes still radiated madness. Ironically, she was holding the very revolver he'd been carrying when they met. The monkey sat perched on her shoulder, baring its canines at him. Two men stood on either side of her, AK-47s held at the ready. Another three pirates emerged from the brush, weapons pressed to their shoulders.

Queen Caveira said, "When I saw the *Morte Tinto's* footprints, I knew you'd panic and head back to the river, but I got here faster. So, why did you betray me after I gave you so much?"

"I didn't, I just had to find my daughter."

The queen gazed down at the terrified little girl. "So did I."

Pulling Faye close, Micah said, "Look, just get out the chart, I'll show you exactly where Batista's mine is."

Queen Caveira looked insulted. "Do you think this is about money? You took something more valuable than emeralds, and now you must pay for destroying Boiúna." Shifting her eyes to Catalina, the queen asked, "So is this the scrawny bitch you've chosen over me?"

Catalina said, "What?" her eyes darting between Micah and the queen.

Micah thought, *Oh God, is the queen actually jealous?*

Glaring at Catalina, the queen said, "So you didn't tell your woman about our love? Yes, Lucky Man spent many hours worshipping his queen."

Locking eyes with her, Catalina said, "Oh yeah, he told me all about it. But he said I shouldn't be jealous, 'cause you were just a cheap *puta*." Seeing the rage burning in the queen's eyes, she added, "All he'll need to get over you is a shot of penicillin. But after that we'll laugh at you, while getting down to some hot, nasty—"

The queen lunged at Catalina, grabbing her by the hair. Catalina twisted sideways, latching on to her other arm. In a practiced move, she twisted the queen's arm behind her back and dropped down, jamming her knee into the queen's lower back.

The queen's men charged at her, fingers on their triggers.

Catalina drew the empty Glock, jamming it against the queen's head. "Anybody moves and I blow your queen's crown off!" She looked to Faye and Micah. "Run!"

Micah said, "But—"

Pleading with her eyes, Catalina said, "Go now… Please!"

Micah grabbed Faye's hand, shouting, "Run, baby, run for the trees!" And they both raced off.

The queen lay on the ground, offering no struggle. In a serene voice she began mumbling the same phrase over and over.

Pressing the pistol to her temple, Catalina whispered, "That tune's getting old fast."

Micah ran behind Faye. "Keep going, baby, don't slow down till we hit the trees!" He fought the urge to look back, unable to bear seeing Catalina.

Faye made it to the trees first, scrambling through the thick brush. Micah was only a few feet behind when he saw a ribbon of color in the weeds. It lashed out with lightning speed. Faye screamed, collapsing to the ground, clutching her leg.

Micah froze, staring down at the coiled, five-foot *jararaca*—a viper more commonly known as *fer-de-lance*.

Faye rolled on the ground screaming in agony. The hissing snake reared up, readying for a second strike. Micah lunged at it with adrenaline-fueled speed, grabbing it midway down its body. The snake writhed, furiously trying to bite him. Micah swung hard, slamming its head against a tree over and over until it went limp. Tossing it aside, he knelt down over Faye.

She whispered, "Daddy, it hurts," tears streaming down her cheeks.

Micah held her tight, telling her, "I know, baby, but it'll be alright."

But he knew it wouldn't be. The *fer-de-lance* was sometimes called a five step—meaning that's as far as the victim got before succumbing. Without antivenom, Faye would be dead within hours—every moment of it being sheer agony. Micah stroked his daughter's hair, knowing he was powerless to save her.

#

Faye's scream distracted Catalina for an instant—it was long enough. The queen jerked upward like a bucking bronco while rolling sideways. Catalina hit the ground, still keeping the pistol against the queen's temple. Then she felt a blade pressed to her throat.

The queen put her lips to Catalina's ear, whispering, "Go on, pull the trigger! Pull it now or I'll slit your throat."

One of the pirates ran forward, yanking the pistol from Catalina's hand. He popped out the empty magazine and held it up for all to see. The pirates laughed.

One of them grabbed Catalina, hauling her up onto her feet, while a second zip-tied her hands behind her back.

The queen brushed the knife blade along Catalina's cheek without cutting her. "I like this one."

In one blindingly fast move the queen swung her other arm around, delivering a left cross to Catalina's jaw. The pirate holding Catalina up let her sink to the ground.

The queen strode to the trees where Micah knelt, rocking his sobbing daughter in his arms.

Holding up the dead snake for the pirates to see, Queen Caveira proclaimed, "When he ran, I called upon Boiúna, who sent this mortal underling to take revenge. Everything is as I foretold."

Her pirates hovered around, amazed that her prayers had been answered.

Reeling with grief, Micah thought, *Christ, she almost makes sense.* But instead, he shouted, "If it's all as you foretold, then why'd Batista kick the living shit out of you?" He fully expected her to beat him.

But instead, her tone softened, becoming sympathetic. "Is there any sound sadder than the bellowing of a faithless man? Why are you clutching your dying child and shouting insults at me when you should be begging your own god for mercy? Boiúna tested my faith by leaving me with nothing. But I came from nothing, and therefore I will rise again. Now, with your aid, Boiúna's physical form will also rise again. All because you will make a genuine sacrifice. The life of your child."

"Why her? I'm the one you hate, so just kill me!"

"Lucky Man, your stupidity amazes me. If I kill you first you will die faithless. Sacrificing your daughter allows you to witness Boiúna's resurrection. Then you can pray for his forgiveness and redeem your soul before I kill you. You know, you really should be thanking me."

The queen's pretzel-twisted logic left Micah speechless. Faye let out a shriek, the caustic venom tearing through her like fire. Micah held her tightly, unable to hold back his tears.

Tossing the dead snake aside, the queen said, "Dying from the venom means hours of unbearable agony. Lucky for you, I don't have that kind of time." Gesturing to her men, she ordered, "Grab him."

Two men wrestled Micah away from Faye, zip-tying his hands behind his back.

The queen said, "Bring the child to the cliff so the river spirits can witness our sacrifice."

Two men lifted Faye up and carried her to the cliff's edge.

Catalina watched them, shouting, "What are you doing?" She tried to stand, but a kick in the chest sent her back to the ground.

The pirates hauled Micah to the cliff's edge. Benício, the queen's executive officer, grabbed him in a chokehold, forcing him to watch.

The queen knelt down over Faye, chanting under her breath. Then she raised the knife, saying, "Lucky Man, you are about to witness a miracle."

And she was right.

Benício suddenly gasped, his grip on Micah slackening. Benício toppled forward, pinning Micah under him. Micah twisted his body, struggling to free himself. That's when he saw the arrows jutting from the pirate's back.

A fusillade of arrows shot through the air. Two more of the queen's pirates dropped, multiple arrows in their backs. The three others spun around, blindly firing into the trees.

Micah struggled to push the dead man off him. Another salvo of arrows zipped over his head, cutting the remaining pirates down. They lay writhing on the ground, poison dart frog venom burning through their veins.

From the ground, Catalina saw a group of tall, loincloth-clad men emerging from the brush, bows held at the ready. They were *Morte Tinto* warriors.

The Red Death had come.

The queen stood, facing the warriors, declaring, "You have interrupted an important ritual!"

The Red Death warriors stopped and looked to each other, puzzled by the defiant woman.

Micah managed to shove the dead man aside and get back on his feet, his hands still cuffed behind his back.

Queen Caveira held the knife up high, hellbent on completing the sacrifice, and screamed, "Boiúna!"

Micah shouted, "No!" and charged, head down, slamming into her chest. The impact sent them reeling backwards.

And they both went over the cliff.

CHAPTER TWENTY-FIVE

Micah plummeted, enveloped in a cloud of birds, with the queen's hand locked around his throat. In that surreally slow instant, one of his father's survival lessons flashed through his mind.

Bouncing is better than falling.

Micah kicked out while twisting in midair. The maneuver broke the queen's grip while keeping his body close to the cliff face. He crashed through a clay outcropping, the impact breaking his fall slightly, along with some ribs. A colorful blizzard of parrots swirled around his tumbling body as he bounced off another outcropping.

Closing his eyes, he muttered, "I love you, Faye," and hit the ground, anticipating an instantaneous death.

But instead of crashing hard, he sank, velocity slowing with each millisecond, until he struck solid ground. His forehead bounced against the earth, and the air was squeezed from his lungs. He lay there, dazed and blind, engulfed in some viscous black void. His hands were still cuffed, but his feet were touching solid ground. Wriggling and squirming like a worm, he bored headfirst through the mire.

He was a heartbeat from blacking out when his head burst out into blinding sunlight. He took a deep breath, but there was no air to breathe—just searing ammonia vapor. Lungs burning, he wriggled forward until his body was free and he tasted clean air. The ammonia vapors still burnt at his eyes, forcing him to rub his face in the mud. After a few seconds, the pain subsided and his vision cleared, revealing a glorious sight.

Queen Caveira's twisted body lay sprawled on the rocks a few feet in front of him. A patch of the strange berry bushes surrounded her like a floral arrangement. She looked almost … peaceful.

Micah muttered, "Now that's your Netflix finale."

Something slammed down onto the back of his head, jamming his face into the mud. A second later, it hopped off. Micah raised his head, spitting out mud and bird guano.

Upon seeing the attacker, he said, "You again?"

It was the queen's ubiquitous monkey. The capuchin came to rest at its mistress's side, poking at her shattered body, squeaking piteously.

After a few more delicious gulps of air, Micah craned his head around enough to see what had broken his fall.

"Well I'll be dipped in shit."

While the queen's outward trajectory had sent her onto the jagged rocks along the river's edge, Micah had stayed closer to the cliff, landing face down in the ten-foot-high mountain of bird guano. Its layers of excrement and thick moss slowed his descent from fatal to extremely painful. The ammonia vapor had been gases trapped in the layers of feces.

He wriggled his limbs, relieved to find that his legs were intact and functional. His chest felt like he'd been hit with a sledgehammer, and his right shoulder was, best case, dislocated. His eyes were swelling up, indicating a broken nose.

He tried to stand, but it wasn't happening. Between his cuffed hands and the injuries, every attempt just landed him facedown again. The best he could manage was rolling onto his back. He found himself staring up at a trio of Red Death warriors.

Micah muttered, "Hey, guys."

They stared down at him in bewilderment, puzzled by his survival. One pointed to the mound of bird guano and the tunnel he'd bored through it. The trio burst out laughing, as if it were the funniest thing they'd ever seen.

The sheer absurdity of it all snapped something inside Micah, and he began laughing uncontrollably, while thinking, *It's nice to be able to remember the precise moment you lost your mind.*

Once the laughter died down the warriors hauled him up onto his feet, herding him towards the incline leading up the cliff. They didn't kill him, but they didn't untie his hands either.

Another group of capybaras ambled by, snorting in annoyance at the humans trespassing on their walkway. The sight of the mothers escorting their young cleared his thoughts.

Faye, flashed through his mind, and he stumbled up the slope.

#

Micah reached the clifftop, his cracked ribs throbbing against his labored breath. The Red Death warriors were clustered around Faye. One of them held up the dead snake and mimed biting. The rest seemed more interested in the laces of her boots than helping her. Another warrior examined her clothes, particularly fascinated by the zippers on her pockets. The warriors chattered back and forth in a series of strange, birdlike whistles.

Catalina was up on her knees, hands still cuffed, imploring them to help in every language she knew. She saw Micah running towards them and shouted, "You're alive! But... The cliff?"

"My face broke the fall."

He struggled to get close to Faye, but the men kept pushing him away.

Once the novelty of Faye's zippered pocket wore off, the tribesman reached inside. He let out a long, high-pitched whistle and held up his discovery. The other warriors pressed closer, intent on touching whatever he'd found. Then, almost as one, they approached Micah.

Catalina muttered, "Aw shit."

One held out their new discovery for him to see. Micah stared at it, dumbfounded. They were holding up the meteorite fragment—the same one he'd thrown off the tower.

The warriors' attitudes spun a hundred and eighty degrees. The leader rolled up Faye's pant leg, while others plucked berries from the strange bushes. The leader shoved berries into his mouth, chewed them up, and spat the juice onto

Faye's snakebite. Once the wound was saturated, he wrapped leaves around it.

The youngest warrior stripped off his arrow quiver and sprinted into the brush at Olympian speed.

Catalina got to her feet and trotted over to Micah. "I think they're trying to help her."

Micah watched, grim faced. "It's no good. That was a *fer-de-lance*. Without antivenom, she'll die."

Catalina leaned closer and, in a near whisper, said, "I hate to quote Queen Psycho, but didn't she say there's nothing sadder than the words of a faithless man?"

"She said a lot of crazy stuff."

"But maybe there was truth in that. Micah, these people have lived here forever, so, just maybe, they know something our medicine doesn't. Please, just try to believe."

Micah closed his eyes, and, with every fiber of his being, tried to believe.

While the leader ministered to Faye, other warriors descended on the queen's fallen pirates. They rifled through the dead men's belongings, showing no interest in the guns. The dead men's knives, however, were considered quite a prize.

At the leader's behest, two men lifted Faye with a gentleness that surprised Micah. They carried her towards the trees.

An older warrior, with multiple battle scars and a permanently squinted eye, helped Catalina and Micah stand up. He pointed to Micah's swollen eyes then to his own permanent squint and whistled in what Catalina assumed was laughter.

She whispered, "I think Popeye likes you."

The warrior gestured for them to follow. Micah fell in behind the bearers. Glancing back, he saw a tiny figure skulking through the brush, shadowing them.

Once he got a clear look at the stalker, he muttered, "You gotta be kidding."

It was the late Queen Caveira's monkey, warily following them. Then Micah noticed something much more alarming. The remaining warriors were eagerly testing out their newfound blades—by decapitating the dead pirates. Each proudly held up a severed head then fell in behind the group toting their trophies.

Eyeing them, Catalina said, "I'm calling that a positive sign."

"Why?"

"'Cause they ain't cutting our heads off."

"They're not untying us either."

"Give 'em time. Remember, we're the invaders here. If they hadn't found that piece of meteorite our heads would probably be going on the trophy shelf. We're lucky you didn't throw it away."

Micah said, "But that's the crazy thing… I did."

#

After a long trek, Micah saw clusters of gardens being tended by tribal women. That and the distant smell of cooking fish meant the village was close.

Through the fog-shrouded rainforest, Catalina made out structures up ahead. "I think we're there."

The young track star must already have spread the news. A group of warriors were gathered outside the village, awaiting their arrival.

The village itself was a cluster of large *yanos*, or longhouses, encircling an open communal area. From their size, Micah guessed each yano could house at least fifty people, meaning a population of between three and four hundred. At least a hundred tribesmen stood at the outskirts of the communal area, while others shyly peered out from the longhouses.

The warriors carried Faye to the center of the village, gently setting her down on some animal skins. The little girl was barely conscious, occasionally contorting from waves of pain. An elderly woman holding a gourd knelt beside Faye and poured steaming liquid into her mouth. She coughed most of it up until the woman massaged her throat, allowing the concoction to flow more easily.

A young girl unwrapped the leaves around the snake bite and spat more of the berry juice onto it. Once the wound was coated in purple saliva, she began massaging Faye's leg.

Micah and Catalina were led to a spot about twenty feet away. The squinting warrior gestured for them to sit. Micah attempted to go to Faye's side, but the elderly woman unleashed a torrent of what he assumed were obscenities until he took his assigned place.

A cluster of young girls knelt beside Faye, singing a ritual chorus.

Micah asked, "Why won't they let me near her?"

"I think it's a ritual, and they don't want you to screw it up."

Catalina, who'd been exposed to a myriad of languages, listened in fascination. She whispered to Micah, "It doesn't sound like anything I've ever heard. They sing like birds, I mean literally like birds. It's beautiful."

The warriors maintained a respectful distance while proudly showing off their collection of heads to the other men. Any that ventured too close to Faye were warned off by the elderly woman.

Catalina muttered, "Yeah, bitches clearly rule around here."

Micah watched sullenly and said, "Batista claimed these people were cannibals."

"Well, A, Batista's a murderous asshole. And, B, maybe that's just what they want people to think. They might take heads just to scare away outsiders."

"It's workin'."

Catalina asked, "So, we know their language is unique, but what else have you seen?"

"Huh?"

"Come on, you're not some reality TV dildo anymore, you're a man of science and we're the first people to ever contact this tribe and live. So how about making some observations?"

He knew she was just trying to distract him by busying his mind but elected to play along.

"Okay, they're tall, way taller than most Indians, and their skin is darker, more like Africans. And their legs are really long, almost like the Nilotic tribes of the Sudan."

"What else?"

"Most, maybe all of them, have a red ring around their corneas. It might be a genetic deformity or nutritional deficiency."

Catalina said, "Wow, am I the only one that noticed their heads?"

She was correct. Every villager's head was elongated. It wasn't the microcephaly, or "pinhead syndrome" seen in old sideshows. It was more of a gracefully sloped "five-head" matched with an elegantly elongated skull. They resembled ancient Egyptian statues.

Micah said, "That's some kind of ritual head binding, like the Mangbetu of the Congo. They believe it imparts wisdom."

"Yeah, except—" Catalina cocked her head towards a nearby woman holding an infant "—that baby's like three weeks old."

The newborn's red-ringed eyes stared at them intently. Micah noticed its elongated head.

"Son of a bitch, it must be genetic."

He studied the other tribesmen. Fortunately, the tribe considered staring to be a compliment and happily returned the gesture. He sat, studying them for at least two hours, his nerves soothed by the young girls' heavenly chorus.

He asked Catalina, "So, CIA agent, what've you observed?"

"That, so far, nobody's tried to kill us, and I have to piss like a racehorse."

The chorus abruptly stopped, replaced by the most beautiful sound Micah had ever heard.

A soft voice whispered, "Daddy."

"Faye!"

Micah tried to get to his feet, only to land facedown. He fumbled in the dirt until the warrior Catalina had christened Popeye helped him up.

Micah ran to his daughter, shouting, "I'm here, baby." He dropped onto his knees, placing his head onto her chest, tearfully whispering, "Daddy's here."

Faye hugged him, and, in a weak voice, said, "My stomach hurts," before throwing up on his shoulder. "I'm sorry."

"That's okay, princess."

The old woman shoved Micah aside and brought another gourd of the concoction to Faye's lips.

The little girl shook her head, saying, "It's gross."

Struggling to get up, Micah said, "You have to drink it, princess, it'll help." And, for the first time in his adult life, Micah found himself thanking God and any saints he could remember from childhood.

Faye choked down the contents of the gourd, making a scrunched face.

Laughing out loud, Micah said, "Hey, that's your spinach face."

The old woman wiped the poultice away from the bite wound. The horrendous swelling and inflammation was gone. All that remained was a neat pair of Dracula-like punctures.

Micah muttered, "Impossible."

The old woman spat a fresh coat of purple gunk on the wound.

Catalina came up behind him and said, "That's incredible."

Micah muttered, "It's a miracle, a godda—a genuine miracle."

The old woman tore open Micah's already ragged shirt, spitting berry juice on his roadmap of cuts and bruises. He felt a cool sensation, and, within seconds, the pain he'd struggled to suppress began ebbing away.

The young girls clustered around Catalina, pawing at her clothes.

Micah reassuringly said, "Let 'em do their thing. This stuff's incredible."

The woman tore Catalina's shirt open, revealing her bra. The bare-breasted village women whistled with laughter at the sight then coated her array of cuts in berry juice. Another girl deftly plucked some leeches off her back.

Catalina said, "I didn't know I was so banged up."

Micah replied, "I have a feeling we'll be showroom quality again after this stuff."

The leader of the warrior party came over and prodded Micah while pointing to a central longhouse.

Micah said, "You know, they really like shoving people around here."

"Don't take it personally, I think they're still scared of you."

With another push, the man steered him toward the longhouse.

Micah shouted back to Catalina, "Stay with her!"

She yelled, "I ain't going anywhere," then smiled at the giggling young girls snapping at the elastic on her bra.

Micah was guided into a large, smoke filled longhouse, adorned with totems of carved wood and braided grass. He'd spent enough time around indigenous people to recognize a shaman's hut. In the center, a group of elderly women clustered around a reed mat. At the far end, a trio of young girls sang in hushed, impossibly melodic voices. Though he was a lifetime agnostic, Micah couldn't help being moved by the reverence on display. The warrior ushered him closer, this time without the shoving.

Upon seeing Micah, the elderly women stepped aside, revealing a man laid out on the mat. Micah looked down and his heart skipped a beat.

It was the old man he'd seen in the rainforest.

CHAPTER TWENTY-SIX

Micah knew the old man must be the tribal shaman, revered above all others. Up close he looked positively ancient. His face was a roadmap of deep wrinkles, with only wisps of gray hair on his head. Sweat glistened off his frail, almost emaciated body.

The warrior tugged at the flex cuffs binding Micah's wrists. After some frustrated attempts at untying them, he slashed the plastic apart with his newly acquired knife. Once Micah was freed, he gestured for him to kneel down next to the old man.

Micah saw the bullet wounds in the shaman's chest, each coated in the purple berry juice.

Micah muttered, "I bet those were a gift from Batista's first expedition."

The poultice must have kept him alive, but the combination of internal injuries and age were an unstoppable combination—the shaman was dying.

The warrior knelt down at the shaman's side, pressing the meteorite fragment into his hand. As soon as he did the old man's eyes opened. He looked up at Micah, and, despite the injuries, his red-rimmed eyes beamed with a childlike radiance.

This isn't possible, Micah thought, *this old geezer couldn't even walk out of this hut, never mind wander around the rainforest.* But there was no mistaking it. It was him, right down to the bullet wounds.

The old man smiled at Micah, though doing so seemed to take all his strength. The expression on his face said, *I've been waiting for you.*

Holding the shaman's wrist, the warrior raised up his hand while gesturing for Micah to extend his. He did, his mind reeling with a thousand questions. The shaman squeezed his hand, the meteorite fragment pressed between their palms. It felt like Micah had grabbed a live electrical wire.

And, in that instant, all his questions were answered.

#

Catalina tried to stand still as Popeye sawed away at the flex cuffs binding her wrists, painfully aware that the rumbling in her stomach was reaching a crescendo.

"Try to hurry that up, Popeye, or we're both gonna be in trouble."

Eventually they snapped free. Popeye toyed with the plastic cuffs, amazed at their strength. Catalina massaged her bruised wrists while recalling that movie *The Gods Must be Crazy*. She hoped they weren't contaminating the local culture.

Popeye watched Catalina massaging her wrists, looking concerned. Catalina smiled and gave him a reassuring thumbs up gesture. Popeye glanced into the air to see what she was pointing at. Catalina couldn't help laughing out loud. Popeye awkwardly returned the thumbs up gesture while whistling his version of laughter.

Though still weak, Faye was sitting up and receiving small gifts from the village children.

For the adults, the novelty of their arrival had worn off and it was back to business as usual. A cluster of warriors were sharpening arrows while chattering loudly. Catalina assumed that, like most men, they were exaggerating their hunting exploits. The village women stood next to them, roasting impaled poison dart frogs over a fire. The heated frogs secreted a sticky white mucus. Once that happened, the women handed them to the warriors, who scraped the white venom onto their arrow tips. Popeye walked over to the group and the younger warriors all made a point of holding up their sharpened arrows for his approval.

Catalina watched with amusement, thinking, *Wherever you go in this world, a sergeant is still a sergeant.*

Noting the mountainous stack of arrows, she muttered, "Okay, something big's going down."

A bout of dizziness forced her to sit. Her forehead was clammy and, despite the heat, she was shivering. In the course of their exploits, she'd swallowed a ton of river water and the local insects had been using her as a chew toy. She thought, *I think you're looking at malaria with a dysentery chaser.* Her stomach rumbled audibly and she muttered, "I wonder where these nice folks go to take a dump?"

The old woman heard the rumbling and shoved a gourd into Catalina's hands, miming for her to drink. She obligingly took a long swallow. The concoction was pungent to the point of nauseating.

With a giggle, Faye said, "I told you it was nasty."

The old woman forced her to take two more swallows before slipping into the Shaman's longhouse.

Within minutes, Catalina's fever died down and her rumbling bowels declared a truce.

"I've got to take some of that stuff for the road."

A sense of relief washed over her. It wasn't just the pain subsiding, it was the revelation that, somehow, they just might survive.

Faye pointed at the central longhouse, asking, "What's Dad doing in there?"

"I don't know, baby, but I don't think we should interrupt whatever it is."

And they waited ... for three hours.

#

Faye was fast asleep, her head in Catalina's lap, when Micah finally emerged from the shaman's longhouse. Instead of joining them, he just paced back and forth, mumbling to himself while clenching and unclenching his fists. Sensing his agitation, the villagers steered clear of him.

Catalina tried to get up without awakening Faye, but the moment she moved, Faye's eyes shot open and the little girl scampered over to her father. Micah hugged her, but his thoughts were clearly a million miles away.

Catalina asked, "Hey, when you went in there, didn't you have a dislocated shoulder, some broken ribs and two black eyes?"

Flexing his arm, Micah said, "Yeah. They slipped me some of the magic elixir. I'm feeling almost a hundred percent."

"Except you're bouncing around like a teenager who lost his Ritalin. So, how about tapping the brakes for a minute and telling us what happened in there?"

Micah took a few breaths. "Sorry, it was pretty intense. I met the shaman and went on a little trip."

"Seriously? After all that's happened you picked today to start doing ayahuasca?"

"No, no, it's not like that. Well, kind of like that, except without drugs. The shaman told me everything."

"He spoke to you?"

"He didn't have to, he showed it to me." Micah tapped his forehead. "In here. And get this, he's the same old man I saw in the rainforest!"

"Uh, okay, but remember, you've been conked on the head about nineteen times since this all started."

"True, but ask yourself if that's crazier than the stuff we've already seen."

"I'll admit, the definition of normal's gotten … rubbery."

Micah knelt down to Faye and said, "Honey, you stay out here for a minute. Nobody will hurt you."

The little girl smiled and said, "I know that," then scurried over to her new friends.

Micah grabbed Catalina's hand, saying, "Come with me. Maybe he'll show you too."

He pulled her into the hut but stopped in his tracks when he saw the old woman reverently sewing the shaman's body up in jaguar hides.

Micah muttered, "Oh shit, he's dead." He turned to Catalina. "But he was alive a few minutes ago, I swear."

His voice was louder than he'd intended, earning a harsh look from the old woman.

Catalina whispered, "Relax, I believe you, now let's give these nice folks some privacy, 'cause you're definitely gettin' on that old lady's tits."

Once they were outside, she said, "Now, how about giving me the Cliff Notes on your long strange trip?"

"Okay, short version. Batista was right about one thing. The Anomaly is old, I mean really old. But it isn't a meteorite."

"Then what is it?"

"It's a spacecraft, or a probe of some kind."

"If it's a spaceship, where're the aliens?"

Micah gestured towards the villagers. "You're looking at 'em."

#

Batista stood atop the dam's crest, watching his men's progress. Under his iron hand the crater lake had become a hive of activity. He'd started his expedition with donkeys, tractors and enough manpower to do all the heavy lifting. In their absence the back-breaking task of hauling the generator up and over the dam was being accomplished by a combination of block and tackle, downed tree trunks and pure muscle. It was the same method the pharaohs had employed building the pyramids. Even the white-jacketed valets from his yacht were forced into becoming beasts of burden.

Hans cringed as the twenty-man work gang lost their momentum, sending the generator sliding back ten feet. Fortunately, the block and tackle caught it. Even after being stripped to its basic components the generator still weighed in at over five thousand pounds.

Wiping his brow, he asked Batista, "Do you think they'll really be able to get it over the dam?"

"Of course. We can't let losing our pack animals slow us down. Why, back in fifteen fifty-nine, Lope de Aguirre traversed the entire Amazon with only a hundred and fifty men, enslaving most of the tribes along the way. Most of them died, but he achieved his goal and declared himself King of Peru."

"And why did he do that?"

"Because it was an era of true empire builders who didn't let trivial things like rivers or natives stand in their way. An age of giants."

Batista watched the line of men haul the generator another five feet until one of them collapsed under the strain. He lay there in the mud until Santos delivered a sharp kick in the ribs, inspiring him to get back to work.

Batista mused, "I should have packed a whip for Santos. Once the generator's across, we can start shuttling the more delicate components over to the Anomaly. We'll need work lights running by sunset, and I want the generator assembled and the laser torch functional by mid-morning tomorrow. No one sleeps until the work is done."

"Are you serious?"

"Time is critical. We've left a trail of bodies and wreckage that even the Brazilian Navy could follow. Pirates and natives may steal, but governments just take what they want. I've lost too many boats and too much money to be robbed by bureaucrats."

Hans added, "Along with fifty men."

"Yes, that's slowed us down a bit."

Hans just nodded, finding it increasingly difficult to ignore Batista's malignant narcissism.

Batista stared at the Anomaly protruding from the shallow water, and asked, "How long has it been buried?"

"It could have been under there for hundreds of thousands, maybe even millions of years. We're only seeing about half of the entire sphere, but that section alone could produce enough energy to power the world indefinitely."

Batista muttered, "Unlimited power."

Hans wondered, *Is he referring to the world or himself?*

Santos jogged over. "Sir?"

Snapping out of his reverie, Batista said, "What is it?"

"I've pulled the machine guns and mortar off the gunboat and established defensive positions along the rim of the lake. If the Indians come by land or water, we'll be able to direct our full firepower on them."

"The Indians aren't our only worry."

"Understood. I'll establish a rally point near the mortars. If any big animals come at us the men will immediately fall back with their weapons. Even those snakes couldn't withstand that much concentrated firepower."

"Let's hope so." Batista turned to Hans. "You've done excellent work. More than any other engineer could have accomplished."

"Thank you." Hans stared out at the Anomaly in silence then asked, "Have you given any thought to what I said?"

"Refresh my memory."

"What if there is an intelligence at work here? A living consciousness beyond our understanding?"

"Well, if such a thing exists, I have a simple and elegant solution."

"What's that?"

"Kill it."

#

Catalina struggled to mentally process Micah's revelation.

"So you're telling me all these folks are aliens?"

"Originally at least. I'm sure they bred with humans or human ancestors. All of us probably have a splash of alien in us."

She pondered the concept while eying the villagers. All were uniformly tall, with long limbs, elongated heads and dark skin that remained undamaged despite a lifetime under the Amazon sun. They were, hands down, the most beautiful people she'd ever seen.

"Well, I can see how the interbreeding could happen. But why are they so, to be blunt, primitive?"

"Over time their history and technology transformed into mythology. The shaman didn't understand the concept of space travel, he called the object that came from the sky and created all life 'the egg.' To him, the berries they make medicine from were a gift from the ancient ones."

"And what do you think?"

"If you were going to send explorers to a primitive world you'd probably create some kind of universal medicine to keep them alive. Ideally something organic and self-perpetuating. Lucky for us it still grows around these parts."

"This all sounds suspiciously like your TV show."

"Even a broken clock's right twice a day. But it also explains the monsters."

"How so?"

"This is going to get weird."

Catalina chuckled. "Get?"

"Fair enough. The object is some kind of artificial intelligence that seeded the earth, probably after one of the mass extinction events. When threatened, it uses that capability to manifest protectors … like attack dogs."

"But why defend itself with prehistoric monsters?"

"They're only prehistoric to us. The Anomaly jump-started evolution then slept through the rest. Maybe, as far as it knows, those critters are still the latest model."

"So what's going to happen when Batista tries to cut it apart?"

Micah thought for a moment and asked, "Have you ever heard of Shiva?"

"The Hindu god with lots of arms?"

"That's the one. To Hindus, Shiva is death, the destroyer of worlds, but is also the one who restarts the cycle of creation. According to these people's mythology, if the egg breaks open, the destroyer will be released to begin the cycle of creation again."

"Can you explain that again, without talking like Yoda?"

"The Anomaly will assume that another mass extinction has occurred and press restart, which will wipe the current world clean. Supposedly there's a monster that kicks things off. After that... Well, just picture every prehistoric nightmare coming back, all at once, and overrunning the earth."

"That sounds ... shitty."

"Apocalyptically shitty."

"So why'd the old man pick you as his *Matrix* movie chosen one? I don't think they get your TV show out here."

"I guess the original aliens were telepathic and he retained that, which is probably why he was the shaman. He must have sensed that I was a believer who could help put things right."

"And how're you planning to do that?"

Micah shrugged. "I'm open to suggestions."

Catalina thought about that and said, "How about our hosts give us a canoe ride to the nearest phone? I'll make a call and see if we can get the Brazilian Army or Delta Force to come in, guns blazing, and wipe Batista out."

"Once the military knows the Anomaly exists, they'll try to do the same thing as Batista, maybe worse."

"Sad but true."

Micah pointed behind Catalina and said, "It looks like we'll have to come up with a plan on the fly."

She turned and saw a dozen warriors coming toward them. Their faces were painted red and each carried bows and multiple quivers of arrows. Popeye gestured for Micah and Catalina to join them.

Catalina said, "Looks like Delta Force is already here," while giving Popeye the thumbs up.

The procession of warriors marched toward the rainforest.

Micah jogged over to Faye, who was playing with some children.

"Baby, I have to go."

Faye asked, "Can I come?"

"No, I want you to stay here where you'll be safe. But I'll be back soon."

"Promise?"

"I promise."

The lead warrior whistled impatiently.

Micah kissed Faye's forehead and said, "I gotta go, but I'll be back, I swear."

CHAPTER TWENTY-SEVEN

The warriors continued marching through the rainforest. At sunset they came to a wide stream where a young warrior waited with three canoes. Popeye gestured for Micah and Catalina to climb into the middle one.

Catalina started to get in then let out a startled, "Oh shit!"

The canoe's prows were decorated with the decapitated heads of Queen Caveira's pirates.

Giving one head a closer look, Micah said, "I think I knew that guy."

Catalina took her seat. "Let's hope they're not there as snacks."

"Nah, these guys know they're going up against a superior force, so they're doing everything they can to frighten the enemy. Kind of like when pilots paint flying tigers on their fighter planes."

"Except the fighter planes don't usually have maggots crawling on them."

Micah settled down on the canoe's crude bench. "Hey, don't knock maggots. You know they can eat the infections out of open wounds and if you're ever lost in the jungle, they can be an excellent source of protein."

"You don't get invited to many dinner parties, do you?"

"Not more than once."

The canoes cast off, the warriors paddling with smooth, expert strokes.

Micah said, "I'm glad Faye didn't have to see those heads. She's already had enough nightmares for three lifetimes."

Catalina squeezed his hand. "Relax, I'm sure she's perfectly safe back there with the alien headhunters."

Micah's expression turned grim.

Catalina laughed. "I'm kidding, they won't hurt her. With all this weirdness, the village is really the safest place, at least until we stop Batista."

"And if we don't, there won't be any safe place on Earth."

Night fell, reducing the visibility to virtually zero. One of the warriors began pounding out a varied rhythm on a drum.

Micah said, "That's amazing. The drummer has the route memorized. He's warning them about rocks and turns."

The warriors guided their canoes through a winding maze of pitch-black channels without slowing down.

Catalina leaned back. "Well, they seem to know where they're going."

Micah felt himself sweating more than usual. He dipped his finger into the water then pulled it away and said, "The water's hot, like steaming cup of tea hot."

"Why?"

"There are thermal streams all around the Amazon, nobody really knows why."

Popeye turned to Catalina, half whistling something she couldn't understand.

In frustration, he grabbed one of the vines lashed to the inside of the canoe.

Micah asked, "What's he trying to tell us?"

Catalina followed his lead, saying, "I'm guessing it's hang on."

The canoes turned into another tributary, and shot forward, the drummer beating a tempo worthy of a Ramones song. With his guidance, the warriors expertly steered the canoes through the steaming rapids.

Micah yelled over the deafening current, "I think we just hit the jet stream!"

Catalina shouted, "I went white water rafting once, but it's got nothing on this," and clung on to the strap with a white-knuckle grip.

"Don't be nervous, we're just going down boiling hot rapids, at night, with no lights, in a bark canoe held together with vines!"

"Thanks, before you said that I was getting worried!"

Eventually Catalina grew confident of the warriors' skills. Leaning closer to Micah, she said, "It must feel good, knowing that all your crazy theories were right after all."

"I guess. I just keep wondering where they originally came from."

Catalina said, "Well, you have fun thinking about that," and lay back.

"You're going to sleep in this current?"

"Army training. Never stand up when you can sit, never sit when you can lie down and never be awake when you can be asleep." And with that she curled up at the end of the canoe.

Micah tried to sleep, but the day's revelations kept racing through his head. Catalina, on the other hand, snored away peacefully; a feat Micah chalked up to physical exhaustion. The sweltering heat and rhythmic swaying eventually lulled him to sleep.

The warriors continued shooting the boiling rapids for seven hours without rest.

#

Something jostled Micah awake. He sat up, amazed to discover it was dawn, wondering, *How long did I nod off for?*

The canoes had slipped out of the rapids, into a slower, unheated tributary. Between the warriors' efforts and the fast, boiling current, Micah estimated they'd traversed at least fifty miles.

Over the next hour the narrow tributary swelled into a marshy floodplain, blanketed in a thick layer of fog. The canoes paddled past black-bellied ducks drifting peacefully, while parrots in the partially submerged trees called out warnings to other birds.

A smaller, two-man canoe rendezvoused with the group. They excitedly shared their findings while showing off a pair of oars they'd stolen from an inflatable dinghy.

Micah thought, *It looks like they had guys out doing reconnaissance.*

The sound of shrieking laughter echoed across the marsh, followed by a second, even more maniacal round.

Catalina bolted awake, and whispered, "Is there a maniac loose out here?"

Micah said, "Relax, that's just a laughing falcon up in the trees. It'll go on like that for around five min—" He abruptly went silent.

A huge shape, obscured by fog, loomed in the water up ahead. The warriors saw it too, slowing down until they were barely drifting forward. Micah strained to make out the object.

He whispered, "Whatever it is, it's not moving."

Catalina asked, "Do giant snakes sleep on the water?"

They drew closer until Micah could finally make it out. "It's a boat. A big one."

A two-hundred-foot double-decker cargo barge lay half submerged in the water. Its upper deck was partially collapsed, and the flat, front deck had been torn apart. The wreck was wedged among some trees.

Micah said, "It looks exactly like the *Valentina*."

"And in almost as bad a shape. Think there's anybody aboard?"

The warriors steered their canoes alongside it, some reaching out to tap the metal hull.

A loud thud emanated from below deck, as if answering their knocks. Three warriors shot to their feet, bows held at the ready.

A massive yellow-headed bird hopped up onto the deck rails. Two identical ones flew up from the lower deck, roosting next to it. The warriors lowered their bows.

Micah said, "Those are yellow-headed vultures, a sure sign that nobody's aboard. At least nobody alive."

Catalina fished a sodden life preserver out of the tree branches. The name *Opala* was stenciled across it.

She said, "It was Batista's boat alright," and tossed it back in the water. "I bet his maritime insurance is gonna go through the roof."

Micah just shook his head.

"Hey, I'm just trying to lighten the mood."

The falcon let out another Bedlam-worthy round of laughter.

Catalina muttered, "At least somebody's got a sense of humor."

Micah said, "I think we're getting close." He gestured to the warriors, who had resumed paddling.

Catalina swatted at the black flies swarming around the severed heads on the bow. "Good, 'cause these pirates are gettin' pretty ripe."

#

Hans gazed out at the Anomaly gleaming like a jewel in the morning sun. Despite being physically exhausted, his mind was racing. He reminded himself that, first and foremost, he was an engineer and couldn't allow enthusiasm to overwhelm his discipline.

Starting at the generator on shore, he and Batista retraced the network of cables running along the causeway out to the Anomaly, double-checking every link in the technical chain. It offered Hans another opportunity to bask in the complexity of what he'd constructed; few engineers had the vision and expertise to conceive such an intricate plan, and a mere handful could have executed it in this godforsaken jungle.

Kneeling down to check an electrical connection, he said, "Sir, I'm convinced there's some form of intelligence connected to this Anomaly. What's hidden inside could be history's greatest discovery. Slicing it up like scrap metal would be a sin."

Batista replied, "A very profitable sin."

They continued their final checks, coming to the wide log hewn working platform abutting the Anomaly. Batista eyed the array of electronic equipment jammed onto the platform, mentally calculating his expenses.

He asked, "You're sure all these electronics aren't going to set the Anomaly off? Don't they emit some kind of fields?"

"That's why I've kept the generator at a safe distance. It's feeding these two super capacitors, both housed in Faraday cages to dampen any fields emitted." Hans opened up a fiberglass case with "Fragile" stenciled across it in large letters. Inside, nestled in protective eggshell foam, was a four-foot chrome tube with attached pistol grips.

"This 6kilowatt laser torch will slice through anything in seconds, even this."

Batista looked skeptical. "Won't the laser's heat cause it to … react?"

"I've taken measures to prevent that." Hans gestured to a pair of steaming, four-hundred-liter cryogenic Dewar flasks. "I'll continuously bathe the cutting area with liquid helium. At a temperature of minus four hundred and fifty degrees, it approximates the environment of deep space while negating the heat produced during cutting."

Batista held his hand close to the frigid steam hovering around the Dewar flask and said, "Kind of a local anesthetic?"

"Precisely. It should, theoretically, allow me to create a breach without tripping its defenses."

"And if, theoretically, you're wrong?"

"Then don't stand too close." Hans stood up, looking at Batista with pleading eyes. "If we just cut out a small piece, we'll be able to see what's inside. If I'm wrong, and it's merely a hollow shell, we can start slicing it up like a Christmas ham with no loss in time or money."

"And you're absolutely certain there's more to this thing than meets the eye?"

"More certain than I've ever been about anything."

Batista stared silently at the Anomaly for a solid minute before saying, "Fine. I'll let you cut a hole first and make your observations. But I want it large enough for a man to crawl inside."

Hans's face lit up. "Sir, may I be the first to—"

Batista was already walking back toward the shore, shouting, "I doubt anyone else will be volunteering. Now get on with it!"

Hans yelled, "You won't regret this, sir!"

Then, with trembling hands, he began donning his silver firefighting suit, thinking, *The greatest discovery in the history of science, and I'll be the first inside.* After steadying himself, he inserted a set of ear buds and scanned through his music library. Beethoven was his personal favorite but inappropriate for something this monumental. He considered Tchaikovsky then settled on something else. Only Wagner had the majesty for such an event. He selected *Parsifal* and pressed play, letting the operatic quest for the Holy Grail fill his senses.

Batista reached the end of the causeway, suppressing a smile. In truth, he had no interest in exploration or discovery.

Keying his walkie talkie, he radioed, "Santos, bring me that case full of Semtex."

"On the way, sir."

Hans seemed convinced there was some intelligence inside the Anomaly, one that had endured for millions of years.

Batista muttered, "Well, all good things must end."

#

The warriors paddled on. The thickly wooded marsh gave way to a floodplain dotted with broken trees.

The warriors rested their paddles, letting the canoes drift forward. Popeye pointed into the distance. Micah strained to see what had caught his eye until the warrior handed him a set of binoculars that had once belonged to Queen Caveira.

Batista's yacht was moored to a crude boat slip about a hundred yards ahead. The last remaining gunboat, now stripped of its weapons, was tied off next to it. Just beyond the boats was the earthen rim of the crater lake.

Micah looked beyond the moored boats and muttered, "Damn."

Catalina whispered, "What do you see?"

"Like I said, a dam."

Micah studied the thirty-five-year earthen dam and said, "That's a helluva piece of engineering."

Catalina replied, "Come on, even beavers can build a dam."

"Technically they build impoundments."

She snatched away the binoculars. "Try to stay focused." She trained them on the yacht. "I only see two guys, both armed."

One man with an AK-47 stood guard on the yacht's deck, looking far too casual for his own good. A second man was lugging a wooden crate from down below.

The canoes gradually drifted closer, until they were barely twenty yards out. Neither of Batista's men noticed their silent approach.

Micah whispered, "We need to move carefully and see what—"

The warriors all stood in unison, raising their bows, letting arrows fly. Four struck the man holding the crate squarely in the back, dropping him. Three arrows pierced the guard's chest, sending him spiraling off the deck. He slammed down onto the log boat slip, his body wracked by spasms.

Popeye grinned down at Catalina and offered her a thumbs up.

Slapping Micah on the back, Catalina said, "Or we could just charge in blind."

The warriors paddled furiously, bringing their canoes to the far side of the yacht, shielding them from the ridge. Catalina hopped out, sprinting for the yacht, a cluster of warriors right behind her.

Micah headed for the dam.

Catalina paused to grab the fallen guard's AK-47. The dying man stared up at her with tear-filled eyes, his foaming mouth struggling to form words. She hadn't realized how agonizing death by dart frog venom was and felt torn between moving on and trying to help. Popeye slashed his knife across the dying man's throat, solving her moral dilemma.

Probably for the best, she thought while unhooking the dead man's chest rig. It held six twenty-round magazines. She hoped it would be enough.

Catalina boarded the yacht. After grabbing two more magazines from the other dying man, she made for the pilothouse. The warriors stayed on the deck, running their hands over the yacht's smooth surfaces, whistling anxiously.

After rooting around, Catalina located two fiberglass cases labeled Semtex. The first was empty, and the second was barely half full but contained a generous run of detonator cord and blasting caps.

She muttered, "It'll have to do."

She found another case containing a hard wire detonator and hauled the load up onto the deck.

Micah was already scrambling up the grade to the crest of the dam. Catalina followed, whistling to the fascinated warriors and gesturing for them to come along. Two followed her, while the rest slipped off into the rainforest.

Catalina muttered, "Where're ya going?" then decided they must know what they were doing and kept climbing to the dam's crest.

She crouched down next to Micah, studying the lake below. It was less than two miles in diameter. The dam had reduced its depth to barely six feet. Batista's tender boat was zipping across the lake, laden with equipment.

She said, "Batista's been a busy little beaver."

A causeway constructed from felled trees extended from the shoreline, connecting to a wide working platform jammed with electronic equipment.

Micah stared at the Anomaly in amazement, muttering, "Look at that."

The Anomaly resembled a geodesic dome rising from the lake bed, gleaming brilliantly in the morning sun.

Catalina wasn't as impressed. "That's it? You're telling me that God's a big dirty Christmas ornament?"

Sounding defensive, Micah said, "Well, we're only seeing the top portion."

"And you're absolutely, positively sure it's not just a plain old meteorite?"

"A meteorite that big would've retained some of its cosmic velocity, hitting the earth at around one point five miles a second with the impact of four kilotons of TNT. If that happened the crater would be at least five times larger."

"You could've just said it's not a meteorite."

Undeterred, Micah went on. "From the crater size, I'm guessing it hit at maybe two hundred miles an hour. Not exactly a cushy landing, but it definitely had something slowing it down. That impact speed was fast enough to bury it underground, probably by design. It sat down there until the earthquake hit.

Sometimes, when a quake's violent enough, it causes liquefaction, where the vibration turns loose ground into soup—"

Catalina put her hand over his mouth. "Look, you're cute when you go all *Bill Nye, Science Guy*, but can we stay on point here?"

"Okay, but this part's important. It came up, meaning it's hollow. The outer shell that looks like a diamond is for protection. I'm guessing that when it's struck by heat or energy it reacts with exponentially greater energy, like a force field. That's why the fragment generated power."

"So, if that's the crunchy candy shell, what's in the chewy center?"

"Something we couldn't even comprehend."

"Can you be any more vague?"

Micah studied the causeway for a moment and muttered, "Shit."

"What's wrong?"

Handing her the binoculars, he said, "They're already starting."

Catalina saw a man wearing a head-to-toe silver firefighting suit hooking up some kind of gun and said, "That's got to be Hans, he's the only one left alive who can tie his own shoes."

Micah said, "And that thing he's holding must be some kind of cutting torch."

Catalina said, "It's a ten kilowatt ytterbium fiber laser-cutting torch with a parallel refracting beam."

Micah stared at her.

She said, "What? You think you're the only brainiac around here? But here's the thing; Hans has the morals of a garbage fly, but he's not stupid. So why's he doing it?"

"He must think he can outsmart it."

Catalina shook her head. "That thing can conjure up monsters, and he still thinks he's the smartest guy in the room. You've almost got to admire the arrogance." She panned the binoculars over to shore. "They've planted machine guns and mortars on the high ground, so a frontal assault will only get us killed." She lowered the binoculars and noticed the two remaining warriors had slipped away. "Hey, where'd Popeye and his pal go?"

"They must have gone off to join their pals, doing God knows what." Micah pondered their situation. Unable to come up with a solution, he said, "It's too bad we can't open up the dam and submerge the Anomaly. That would force them to stop, buying us some time."

Catalina tossed the binoculars back to him. "That's kind of what I thought you'd say. I think we can do just that."

"How?"

She started scrabbling down the incline. "You'll see." Then she added, "And just for the record, I still think it looks like a big dirty Christmas ornament."

CHAPTER TWENTY-EIGHT

Catalina climbed onto the yacht's deck, telling Micah, "Move one of the canoes over here!"

Micah paddled one of them alongside and waited to begin loading.

He was so focused on the yacht that he failed to notice the dorsal fin slicing through the water a few feet behind him. The bull shark silently glided past Micah, heading towards the dam.

Catalina tossed down the case of Semtex, followed by the hardwired detonator, saying, "That case used to be full, so Batista must have taken the rest with him."

Micah asked, "Is it enough?"

"I think we'll need some extra kaboom!"

"Is that a technical term?"

Catalina slipped below deck. She returned lugging a *Port-a-Torch* welding kit, comprised of two tanks wedged in a plastic carrying frame. Each tank held twenty cubic feet of gas. She handed it down to Micah, saying, "Batista was ready for anything. The lower hold is like a mini Home Depot."

Micah set the rig down in the canoe, saying, "Wow, oxygen and acetylene."

"Like I said, extra kaboom." She tossed down a small oxygen bottle pulled from a first aid kit, a hammer and a waterproof flashlight, then climbed down into the canoe.

They paddled the heavily laden canoe towards the dam.

Micah asked, "Where do you think our boys went?"

"Probably getting into mischief. I just hope they wait for us before starting the war."

Micah paddled on, his frustration growing with every stroke. "This is taking too long!"

"Don't worry; it'll all be over before you know it." After a moment's thought, she added, "That came out wrong."

Micah guided the canoe to the far edge of the dam. As soon as he bumped shore, Catalina was out, jogging along the dam's crest with an armful of gear. Micah followed, lugging the welding kit.

Midway along the dam, Catalina said, "This spot will work," and put her gear down.

As soon as Micah set down the welding rig, Catalina started wedging the clay-like Semtex between its tanks.

Micah asked, "You've done this before?"

"Nope."

"No?"

Jamming some blasting caps into the Semtex, she said, "That's what nope usually means. But I did take a seminar in defusing explosives at Langley, so I'm just gonna do it all backwards." Then she wrapped detonator cord around the whole affair.

Micah muttered, "Uh, okay… Cool."

Finishing the work, she grinned at him, saying, "Like the mad queen said, have a little faith. How deep do you think the water on this side of the dam is?"

"Maybe twenty feet."

She dropped the explosive rig into the water, playing out the detonator cord as it sank.

Micah asked, "So, are we good?"

"Nope, the charge has to be wedged in tight or else we're just making a bunch of noise." She turned on the medical oxygen bottle, taking two breaths through the mask.

Micah asked, "Does that thing work underwater?"

"Ask me if I come back up." And she dove into the water. She bobbed back to the surface, adding, "Maybe you shouldn't stand up there with a bullseye on your back," and went back under.

Realizing how clear a target he was, Micah scuttled back to the canoe, unspooling the detonator cord as he went.

#

Catalina kicked hard until she hit the bottom, where the welding rig lay waiting. She panned the flashlight along the base of the dam, looking for some way to jam the whole affair in snugly. Something caught her eye. The engineer had sunk water-filled fifty-five-gallon fuel drums as a foundation. A row of them rested lengthwise along the base, half buried in the muddy lakebed.

She thought, *That'll work.*

Using the hammer, she pried at the locking clamp around a drum's rim until the top came loose. After taking a long drag on the oxygen bottle, Catalina wrestled the drum's lid off.

She was too preoccupied to notice what was approaching from behind.

#

Micah jogged along the dam's crest, unspooling the detonator cord, until he reached the canoe. He popped open the detonator case and studied the connections. It looked simple enough, but he wasn't hooking up anything without Catalina. All he could do now was wait.

He hunkered down low, watching the water where she was working, thinking, *Every time I think we've done the most insane thing imaginable we manage to top it.*

He saw something out of the corner of his eye, and his heart skipped a beat. Knifing through the water was the dorsal fin of a bull shark—the Amazon's apex water predator. It was headed for Catalina.

Micah froze for an instant then scrambled for the rifle.

The dorsal fin slipped beneath the water, meaning the rifle was useless. Firing the rifle underwater wouldn't work either. Even at close range, the water density would render bullets too feeble to pierce the shark's thick hide.

"Come on, stupid, do something."

174

Then he glanced down into the canoe and saw a ray of hope.

#

Catalina hauled the welding rig out of the mud and slid it inside the open barrel. Detonating the rig outside the dam would have dispersed the blast pressure, making it ineffective. But being jammed underneath the dam's main structure would direct the force where they needed it—and some shrapnel wouldn't hurt either. She pushed the rig all the way into the drum and was ready to surface.

Something rammed into her, shoving her against the dam. Catalina spun around in a panic, shining her flashlight out into the muddy water. Through the murk she saw the distinctive caudal fin of a shark swimming away from her.

Fresh water sharks? But after fighting giant ants and snakes she'd stopped asking questions. Freezing in place, she thought, *Come on, just keep swimming away, shit head.*

In one graceful maneuver, the shark reversed course while gaining speed. The eight-foot bull shark jetted through the water at 20 MPH, heading straight for her.

Catalina grabbed the only defense available—the fifty-five-gallon drum's steel lid—holding it out like a gladiator's shield. The shark's snout struck it like a battering ram, slamming Catalina against the dam, forcing the air out of her lungs. The shark's tail swung side to side, propelling it forward, crushing her against the dam. With a twist of its head, the shark latched on to the edge of the steel disc, tearing through the metal. Catalina wrestled to keep the shark at bay, but her lungs were empty.

If the shark didn't kill her, drowning would.

#

Hans tightened his air mask and switched his air pack over to positive pressure. The continuous flow of air would keep him from inhaling the frigid helium mist. Wagner's *Parsifal* boomed in his ears, drowning out his labored breathing as he adjusted the oxygen and nitrogen tanks feeding the laser torch. Satisfied, he raised the four-foot torch, holding its pistol grips. The fact that he was wearing a silver fire suit, an air tank and holding a laser rifle made him chuckle.

A literal ray gun, he thought, though he'd never had time for frivolous space operas.

The cloud of helium mist chilled him through the insulated fire suit. For the past ten minutes he'd directed a constant stream of the frigid gas onto the cutting area, reducing the Anomaly's surface temperature to that of deep space.

Holding the torch two inches from the Anomaly, he squeezed the trigger. There was no Hollywood style light beam, just a shower of sparks flying off the Anomaly's diamond-hard surface and a sharp, red-hot line. The continuous jet of helium mist instantly cooled the surgically precise incision. The laser continued cutting flawlessly.

One thing confirmed his theory had been correct—he wasn't dead.

Batista paced at the end of the causeway while watching Hans work, muttering, "What's taking so goddamn long?"

A dozen of his crewmen, all filthy and exhausted, were sprawled on the ground nearby, their rifles within easy reach. The men had also been issued plexiglass riot shields. Such shields had proven invaluable during one of Batista's previous land rights 'negotiations' with an indigenous tribe, rendering their arrows useless … and them extinct.

Initially, he'd discounted Hans's theory about the Anomaly being alive, but the Austrian seemed so convinced he'd devised a plan to deal with it. Batista slipped a hand into his pocket and felt the wireless detonator inside. That detonator, and the plastic case resting at his feet, would ensure his place in history. He knelt down, popping open the suitcase-sized case, reexamining its contents. The top layer was a sheet of epoxy resin embedded with hundreds of ball bearings. Beneath it was forty pounds of Semtex plastic explosive, wired up and ready to explode. That much Semtex, combined with the ball bearings, equaled the killing power of thirty claymore mines. All he needed to do was toss it into the hole Hans was cutting. Detonating it in that confined space would destroy any intelligence, living or artificial, without damaging the priceless outer shell. With the press of a button, the extraterrestrial intelligence would, like all those inconvenient tribes, become extinct.

Closing up the case, he thought, *It's the way of the conquistadors.*

A booming voice shattered his concentration.

"Sir?"

Batista felt himself jump and shouted, "What?"

It was the yacht valet, his pristine white tunic now caked with mud. The man held out a plastic bottle, asking, "Would you like some water?" His demeanor was pleasant, considering he'd been forced into service as a human pack mule.

Batista nearly snapped at him then thought better of it. "Thank you."

"Sorry it's not cold—"

The valet let out a piercing scream and collapsed to the ground, an arrow jutting from his back.

Yanking the walkie talkie from his belt, Batista shouted, "It's an attack!"

His men scrambled up the rise, rifles and riot shields at the ready. Another barrage of arrows rained down, bouncing harmlessly off the shields.

Machine guns chattered as men poured gunfire into the trees surrounding the crater lake.

Batista yelled, "That'll teach you goddamn primates!" Then he ducked behind the rumbling generator. From that safe haven he glanced back at the causeway.

Hans was still working away, oblivious to the chaos around him. Batista considered warning him but saw no advantage in slowing down the process.

#

Catalina gripped the drum lid with all her might, knowing it was the only thing standing between her and a mouthful of razor-sharp teeth. The shark kept pushing forward, its jaws finally wrenching the lid from her hands.

She thought, *And now you're dead.*

Micah splashed down into the water next to the shark. He twisted his arm around its dorsal fin while wrapping his legs around its body. His attack sent the shark into a frenzy, releasing the pressure on Catalina.

The enraged shark thrashed, its body one gigantic coiled muscle. Micah hung on while using his free hand to stab at the shark's gills. The shark rolled in the water, snapping its tail like a whip, wrenching Micah loose. He sank to the bottom, the last bit of air in his lungs gone.

Catalina scooped the oxygen bottle off the bottom, took two quick breaths then pressed it to Micah's face.

The shark swam out thirty feet before reversing course for its second attack.

Catalina watched helpless as it jetted through the water, gaining speed every second.

But the shark's progress inexplicably slowed until it drifted to a halt only five feet from her. It rolled onto its side then sank to the bottom in its final death throes.

Catalina saw the feathered ends of three arrows protruding from its gill slits. The poison dart frog-tipped arrows had proven effective on sharks too.

Grabbing Micah's arm, Catalina kicked hard. Halfway up he started swimming along with her.

Micah broke the surface, taking a giant breath, unable to count how many drownings he'd survived.

After some hyperventilating, Catalina said, "Nice work."

"Do we need to go back down?"

"Nope, we're all set."

Bursts of machine gun fire echoed in the distance.

Micah asked, "What's going on?"

Catalina scrambled up the dam to its crest. "Sounds like our boys got bored and decided to attack."

Micah took a final drag on the oxygen bottle and said, "Well, let's blow this popsicle stand."

CHAPTER TWENTY-NINE

Santos crouched in the tender boat, radioing his men. "Form a firing line and stay together. Make sure somebody's manning those mortars. Use those riot shields, arrows can't punch through them. And somebody with half a brain find Batista and stick close to him, like you're dancing."

He clipped the radio back on his belt, satisfied that the front line was covered. Just as importantly, his boat was safely in the middle of the lake, beyond the range of any arrows. Using binoculars, he scanned the surrounding crater rim, muttering, "I bet you bastards are going to try an end run." He spied movement on top of the dam. "Got you!"

A man and woman ran along the dam's crest—and they weren't natives. The woman looked all too familiar.

"You bitch!" Santos shouted to the tender captain, "Go for the dam, those two are up to something," and grabbed the AK-47 at his feet.

#

Micah crouched behind the crater's earthen rim, bullets tearing through the brush around him.

He said, "I'm pretty sure he spotted us!"

From a few yards away, Catalina shouted, "Gee, ya think?" and went back to connecting the end of the detonation cord to a roll of electrical cable. She jogged back over to the detonator, spooling out the electrical cable as she went, then dropped down just as another burst tore through the brush above them.

Micah said, "He's a really good shot."

Catalina connected the AC cable to the detonator then grabbed the AK-47. She rose up onto her knees, firing twice without aiming, then dropped back down. Santos returned fire with another long burst. Catalina fired again—this time into the air.

Micah asked, "What're you doing?"

"I want him to think he's got us outgunned."

"He does!"

The gunfire abruptly stopped.

Micah whispered, "Listen."

They heard the sound of an outboard motor approaching. Catalina stuck her head up and saw Santos's tender boat running along the face of the dam towards them.

She said, "Perfect timing," while reaching for the detonator switch.

Micah grabbed her wrist. "Stop!"

"What's wrong?"

Peering through the binoculars, he said, "Hans is still working on the platform."

"So?"

"If something goes wrong with that laser it could be disastrous."

Catalina listened to the approaching boat for a moment and said, "Fine."

She flicked the AK-47 to full auto and stood, this time taking careful aim. The boat was thirty yards out, coming straight for them. Catalina opened fire. In under two seconds she emptied the magazine into the oncoming boat. It slewed wildly, its engine exploding in a ball of fire and black smoke.

As Catalina released the trigger, something flashed through her mind.

There was only one guy in the boat.

#

Santos swam along the face of the dam until he reached the midway point. He climbed up onto the dam's crest, about twenty yards from where the Americans were hunkered down, thinking, *Come on, take the bait.*

The woman popped up right on schedule, emptying her rifle into the oncoming tender boat. His ruse had worked. Batista would raise hell about losing the boat, but seeing her standing there, out in the open with an empty rifle, made it all worthwhile.

Santos raised his AK-47, finger tightening around the trigger. Something struck the rifle's forestock a fraction of an inch from his hand. The impact jerked his three-round burst wide of the mark.

An instant later, the woman was gone, and there was an arrow embedded in his rifle's forestock. Santos pivoted, dropping into a kneeling position just as a second arrow zipped over his head. He spotted one of the warriors standing on the distant boat slip, reloading his bow. Santos let off a series of short bursts, pumping at least three bullets into the warrior's chest.

He pivoted back towards the woman's position, hearing shots as he moved. A searing pain tore through his ribs and he collapsed to the ground.

Gritting his teeth, he thought, *The bitch got the drop on me.*

Past experience told him he'd been hit at least twice, but his gift for tuning out physical pain saved him. He instinctively slapped a fresh magazine into his rifle, loosing short bursts. The fire wasn't accurate but still forced the woman to take cover.

She stuck her rifle up, taking a few blind potshots.

Santos started crawling forward, eager to close the gap. As he inched along, his hand came to rest on something—a black plastic cord running along the dam's crest. Glancing behind him he saw that it ran halfway across the dam and down into the water.

He thought, *Detonating cord. They're blowing the dam.*

He grabbed the detonating cord and yanked, but the plastic cable remained intact. He groped around his belt and realized he'd lost his knife.

"*Merde!*"

In lieu of a blade he opted for the next best option—biting through the damn thing.

#

Hans kept cutting, the laser burning through the final inch of his circle. In a few moments the Anomaly's secrets would be revealed. Slinging the laser cutter over his shoulder he grabbed a crowbar. His hands were trembling so hard that he had to shut his eyes and take a few deep breaths while focusing his mind on Wagner's *Parsifal*. Once his hands steadied, he started prying at the cut. After a few seconds a neat, manhole cover-sized chunk fell away.

Hans stood there, awaiting some reaction. There was no destructive pulse of energy, no rampaging monsters... Nothing.

He thought, *What if I was wrong? What if it's just a dead rock?*

Then he saw a soft, pulsing glow emanating from within. Leaning closer, he stuck his head into the hole.

His body stiffened, and it felt like an electrical shock was coursing through his skull. Memories flashed through his mind, so vivid it was like reliving them. Dead natives being tossed into the river, the slave laborers in Batista's emerald mines—a cavalcade of his past sins. The last item wasn't a memory but a premonition of Batista's plan to cut the Anomaly up.

The Anomaly knew what was coming.

The electrical charge ceased, and in a soft whisper, Hans said, "*Mein Gott,*" while staring, wide-eyed, into ... infinity.

#

Catalina slapped another magazine into the AK-47, shouting, "Pretty sure I wounded him, but we can't wait much longer."

Raising the binoculars, Micah said, "I'll take another look."

She grabbed his shoulder before he could stand. "Santos ain't dead. If you stick your head up there, he'll blow it off!"

Then something caught her eye. The electrical cord connected to the detonator moved, just a hair, then it shook. Santos was tugging on the detonating cord. If he broke the cord, it was game over.

Catalina shouted, "It's now or never! Cover your ears!" She dove for the detonator, jamming her thumb down on the trigger.

#

Santos bit down hard, gnawing at the outer layer of plastic.

He muttered, "Come on," chewing at the cord.

He felt a split second surge of electricity and thought, *Oh fuc—*

A millisecond later, the entire thirty-yard run of detonating cord exploded—including the section in his mouth. The blast decapitated Santos at the jawline, sending most of his head rocketing skyward.

A millisecond later, the explosives detonated with a deafening roar, sending tree trunks and debris flying in every direction. The center of the dam vanished in the initial blast. Within seconds the water pressure tore away more, creating a ten-yard-long gap. Water cascaded through the gap, its sheer force tearing away swaths of the dam.

#

The sight that lay before Hans was hypnotic, beyond human experience. The sheer majesty of it overrode his lifetime of scientific discipline. *Parsifal* reached its peak—the triumphant moment when Wagner's "pure fool" reunited the spear of destiny with the Holy Grail. The chorus of *Redemption of the Redeemer* rang in his ears, and he thought, *For once in your life, be the pure fool.*

Hans had to go inside—his entire life, every fiber of his being had led him to this moment. If entering the Anomaly ended that life, so be it. That brief instant of enlightenment would eclipse a hundred men's achievements. He leaned forward, feeling like Neil Armstrong, only to be jerked back roughly. He realized the laser torch slung across his shoulder was still tethered to the oxygen and nitrogen tanks, preventing him from going inside.

He muttered, "*Verdammt!*" while struggling with the chrome nozzle. His efforts were hindered by the combination of heavy gloves, fire suit and bulky air pack. After some fumbling, he managed to slip it off his shoulder. Holding the laser torch carefully he walked towards its fiberglass case.

A thundering roar drowned out the music. The log platform beneath him shuddered violently, sending him reeling. He spun around, saw a huge section of the dam explode, then fell down onto his knees. His finger involuntarily tightened around the laser torch's trigger, firing a 3600 degree Fahrenheit burst straight into the liquid helium tank.

The laser seared through the cryogenic flask like tissue, rupturing the high pressure tank. A torrent of liquid helium, cold as outer space itself, drenched his left side. The sleeve of his silver fire suit crumbled away like dry leaves, exposing bare, blackened flesh.

Hans screamed, searing pain shooting through his right arm and leg. An instant later, those limbs were ice.

The laser was still firing. He tried to release the trigger, but his hand, now solid as marble, wouldn't respond.

Got to get up.

He tried to stand. With a sharp crack, his right leg snapped off at the knee.

Hans rolled onto his back, wobbling on the cylindrical air pack like an overturned tortoise. He watched in horror as the laser fired short bursts across the surface of the Anomaly. He managed to raise his left arm, pounding at the frozen one until it shattered and fell away. The laser torch fired one final burst—straight into the hole he'd just cut.

Staring up, he watched the dim, pulsing light bloom into a blindingly intense flash.

All the "pure fool" managed to say was, "Oh *scheisse!*"

#

Batista hunkered down behind the eight-foot-tall generator, certain that no arrow could pierce it.

One of his crewmen scrambled down from the crater's rim, shouting, "Batista!"

Batista stuck his head out for a moment, waving his arm before going back into hiding.

The crewman made a beeline for him, arrows striking the ground at his feet. He ducked behind the generator, panting like a dog.

Between panicked breaths, he said, "Santos told me to stick with you."

"Good man."

"Christ, those fucking cavemen can really shoot! But those shields you brought are doing the trick."

Batista said, "Good. Our best bet is to stay right here an—"

A massive explosion rocked the generator on its tires.

Off in the distance, the dam disintegrated in a ball of fire and smoke. Debris rained down across the lake.

The stunned crewman shouted, "Do those fuckers have bombs?"

"No, but they've got help." Batista glanced out at the platform just in time to see Hans stumble. A moment later, the platform and the Anomaly were enveloped in a white cloud. "What's that idiot done now?" He pointed down at the plastic case, shouting, "Grab that and follow me!" Then he ran for the causeway.

The crewman grabbed the case, shocked to discover it weighed over eighty pounds. Lugging the burden he followed Batista, just as another barrage of arrows arced across the sky. He'd barely made it ten feet when an arrow struck him between the shoulder blades. With a piercing scream, he collapsed to the ground. The poison coursing through his system reduced that scream to a bile-drenched gasp. He lay sprawled over the case, dying.

Batista sprinted down the causeway until the bilious white cloud forced him to slow down. The frigid air told him the helium tank had been ruptured. A lone bright light shone through the haze, and he made his way towards it, careful not to step off the narrow causeway. The cryogenic steam dissipated just enough for him to make out Hans lying on the platform. After a few more steps he saw the gaping hole in the Anomaly and a brilliant, flickering light glowing from within.

He knelt down over Hans, pulling the silver fire hood off his head. The Austrian's face was peeling away, as if acid had been poured on it, but he was alive.

Shaking him, Batista yelled, "What happened?"

In a rasping whisper, Hans said, "I was right. It's intelligent, but..." He drifted off mid-sentence.

"But what?" Batista bellowed, shaking him hard.

Lightning flashed across the clear blue sky, touching down on the water.

Hans managed to whisper, "Something is coming."

#

Splintered logs and debris showered down on Micah and Catalina. Miraculously, they weren't crushed.

Micah lay back in the grass, his ears ringing like the bells of Notre Dame, yelling, "That was a lot of kaboom!"

Catalina stood watching the water roaring through the breeched dam. "That oughta slow 'em down for now, at least till we come up with a plan." Then she saw the dead warrior lying on the boat slip and shouted, "Oh no!"

She ran along the water's edge towards the fallen warrior.

Micah yelled, "Where are you going?" Getting no response, he raced after her.

CHAPTER THIRTY

Micah stumbled along the water's edge, trying to catch up with Catalina. The breeched dam had transformed the floodplain into a fast-moving river. The current ripped the LST boat from its moorings. The landing craft careened off the bank, almost hitting Micah before being swept through the breech, into the lake.

He saw Catalina up ahead, kneeling down on the boat slip. The gunboat bobbed in the water a few feet from her, its mooring line straining against the rushing current.

Micah reached the boat slip, asking, "What are—" Then he fell silent.

The warrior that Catalina had nicknamed Popeye was cradled in her arms. Despite having two gunshot wounds in his chest, he still smiled up at Catalina with bloodstained teeth.

Catalina whispered, "You done good, Popeye."

Using his last ounce of strength, Popeye raised his right arm, giving Catalina a thumbs up. She returned the gesture before he died in her arms.

Micah said, "I'm so sorry."

Catalina gently laid the dead warrior down. "Popeye was looking out for us, right up to the end."

Micah asked, "So, what do we do now?"

She turned to Micah. "We return the favor."

"How?"

"We're going to attack and get our boys out before they're all slaughtered."

"You want to run straight into machine guns and mortars?"

Slapping her palm against the gunboat, Catalina said, "Nope, we're driving."

She climbed up onto the gunboat's deck, saying, "Too bad they stripped all the guns off."

Micah said, "You can't have everything," and climbed aboard.

Catalina entered the pilothouse, relieved to discover the boat didn't require keys to start. The bad news was that the controls looked foreign to her. Then she remembered that Riverine Patrol Boats, or PBRs, used water jets instead of props.

She muttered, "Guess I'm winging it again."

Micah leaned in, asking, "How can I help?"

Catalina kicked over a toolbox. "Look in there, find a knife and standby to cut the hawser. But don't do it till I gun the engines. If we start drifting with the current we'll turn sideways."

Micah dug a knife out of the overturned box and made his way to the bow.

Catalina twisted the ignition switch, firing up the twin 180 horse power diesel engines.

After allowing them a few seconds to level out, she muttered, "Here goes nothing," and engaged the water jets.

The boat lurched forward, straining against the taut mooring line. Micah crouched down, sawing at the rope, but the log dock gave way first. The gunboat launched forward, dragging half the boat slip behind it. Micah nearly went overboard before latching on to the boat cleat. He slashed the rope, releasing the boat slip.

Catalina took a minute to experiment with the water jets, sending the gunboat in erratic circles, thrilled by its maneuverability.

Micah hung on for dear life as the boat swerved and spun like a drunken sailor.

Feeling confident, Catalina turned the boat against the rushing water. Micah staggered into the pilothouse.

Catalina shouted, "I gotta get me one of these!" Then, by alternating the water jets, she pivoted the boat, steering it back toward the demolished dam.

Micah asked, "What's the plan?"

"We're going through the dam, straight for the Christmas ball. We'll hold that position and just keep shooting. That oughta draw Batista's fire away from the boys long enough to escape."

"But Batista's men will shoot at the Anomaly, maybe even with mortars. That's probably bad!"

"That lunatic came all the way here to get that thing, so I doubt he'll let his men drop bombs on it." She tossed him the AK-47. "If somebody comes at us, shoot 'em!"

Looking down at the rifle, Micah said, "After this I'm going to be a professor at some podunk community college where I can walk to work every day!"

"Bullshit, you'll be wrestling sharks and banging lady pirates till you're ninety. Face it, handsome, you're Indiana-fucking-Jones!" Gunning the water jets, she yelled, "Hang on!"

Seeing what was up ahead, Micah grabbed the handrail.

Moving at twenty-five knots, the gunboat shot through the breached dam, knocking aside any floating debris. The boat went momentarily airborne before slamming down into the lake. Catalina cut right hard, swerving around the drifting LST.

Micah slid in next to her, raising the binoculars to get a good look at the Anomaly.

He wished he hadn't.

The Anomaly and the causeway leading to it were enveloped in a white cloud. Lightning bolts flashed across the otherwise clear sky.

Catalina said, "I've seen that before."

"Me too, and it ain't good."

Bolts of lightning shot down into the churning water, sending explosive geysers into the air. The water at the opposite end of the lake was boiling like a witch's cauldron. The lake's surface burst upward, forming a giant waterspout.

Then something rose up from beneath, surrounded by the swirling sixty-foot waterspout.

Micah stared at what had just emerged, his fingers tightening around the binoculars. He'd been correct—this time it wasn't a snake or piranhas.

In a near whisper, he said, "I am become death, the destroyer of worlds."

Catalina saw this latest manifestation and yelled, "You gotta be shitting me!"

#

Micah stared at an unholy hybrid of every imaginable primordial horror.

It towered sixty feet over the water, balanced on a pair of powerful T-Rex-like legs. Its mottled skin was grayish green—the color of decay. Its gnarled arms reached below its knees, ending with four-fingered taloned hands.

A thick layer of mucus dripped off its body, accompanied by the stench of rotting fish.

The head was huge and bulbous, as if a giant squid had been set down on the creature's shoulders. If there was a mouth, it was hidden by a layer of writhing tentacles dangling down to its chest. The spherical skull was covered in a gleaming, ridged exoskeleton. The squirming tentacles groped upward, wiping away a layer of mucus from the face, revealing a pair of milky pink eyes.

The chest was covered in a layer of rippling tendrils, but in its center was a vertical gash lined with canine teeth. The vertical mouth had scorpion-like articulated mandibles on either side.

Catalina pivoted the boat sideways, yelling, "What the hell is that?"

Micah gazed up at it, his mind reeling back to a HP Lovecraft story he'd read in his teens— something about demonic elder gods.

He said, "It's everything bad, all rolled into one. The Destroyer."

The creature's pink eyes locked on to the boat and it strode in their direction.

Batista's men saw the monster too, opening fire with half a dozen machine guns. Bullets tore at the creature, serving only to get its attention. It changed course, making for land at a speed that belied its enormous size. A mortar round detonated at its feet as it stepped onto the shore. More explosive rounds followed. The creature staggered for a moment.

Micah saw black sludge that he assumed was blood pouring from its legs.

Catalina said, "It looks hurt. You think they nailed it?"

Within seconds, the bleeding ceased, as it if had healed itself. The creature went back on the attack. A fusillade of arrows arced through the air but bounced harmlessly off the creature.

Catalina yelled, "I hope our boys are smart enough to run!"

The beast leaned forward, its long arms whipping at the ground. It stood up straight, clutching a man in each hand. The mandibles on its chest grabbed the screaming men, guiding them into its vertical maw.

#

Batista stood on the causeway, staring up at the creature, the helium fog offering him a degree of camouflage. It was like glimpsing into a child's worst nightmare.

But he didn't have time for nightmares. He'd learned long ago that paralyzing fear could be an ally. The ideal time to strike was when others were too consumed by terror to act.

His true enemy was the Anomaly resting only a few feet away. Its protective shell had been breached—meaning it was vulnerable.

Batista yelled, "Where the hell is that case?"

Getting no response, he ran down the causeway until he cleared the frigid haze enough to see the shore. The dead crewman lay there, sprawled on top of his precious case.

#

Micah shifted his binoculars to the Anomaly and saw Batista emerging from the helium cloud. He was running toward shore.

Micah leaned close to Catalina, saying, "I need to get to the Anomaly."

She glared at him in disbelief. "Are you nuts? That thing'll have you for lunch!"

"I just saw Batista on the platform and I think he's up to something."

"What makes you think that?"

"'Cause he's running towards that monster, and he wouldn't do that without a reason."

Catalina shook her head. "No way. I say we scoop up our boys and make tracks then come up with a new plan."

"We can't leave this thing running loose."

"Maybe it'll just stay here, protecting the egg thing."

Micah pointed to the beast standing atop the crater rim. "It's not staying here. Look at its back."

The creature momentarily ceased its attack, arching its back, contorting and twisting as if in pain. The sound of ripping flesh echoed across the lake, accompanied by a putrid stench. A pair of boney appendages burst out from between its shoulders, dripping mucus as they unfurled.

Catalina asked, "What's coming out of its back?"

Micah said, "It's sprouting wings. Once it has those it'll go on the hunt, attacking the village and anything else it can find."

The appendages stretched out into a pair of enormous bat-like wings. The creature went back on the hunt.

Micah said, "Drop me off then go grab the warriors. Once you've got them, come back for me, if you can. If not, run like hell."

Catalina said, "I ain't leaving you behind and breaking the news to Faye. Plus, if you die I'd never get to hear your sexy pirate story." She gunned the water jets, steering the gunboat toward the platform.

#

Batista sprinted along the causeway towards shore. An unearthly howl echoed across the lake. Looking up he saw a huge tree trunk spiraling through the air, heading straight for him. He ducked down just as it splashed into the lake, mere feet from him.

The creature was about fifty yards away, standing atop the crater's rim, tearing the forest apart. It hurled more trees until its taloned hands snapped up a screaming man. It stuffed him into its vertical maw.

There was a soft thud, followed by a puff of smoke. A mortar round struck the creature squarely in the chest. Chunks of squirming tendril shot through the air. The creature staggered, letting out a banshee wail, viscous black mucus spurting from its wounded chest.

Batista yelled, "Yes, perfect shot."

But within seconds the layer of tendrils covering the creature's abdomen grew back. It quickly spotted the mortar's smoke and went on the attack.

Batista pressed on. Once he reached the lakeshore he dashed for the explosives. Shoving the dead crewman aside he popped the case open, relieved to find the Semtex and ball bearings inside undamaged. He took a moment to assess his situation. The machine gun fire had grown sporadic, and the mortars had fallen silent, indicating that most of his men were dead.

He thought, *I've got explosives, a cutting laser and the yacht. I can still kill this thing and leave with enough pieces to bring the world crawling to my doorstep.*

A gruff voice shouted, "There he is!"

Batista spotted eight of his men staggering down the crater's rim. They were ragged and bloody but still had their weapons.

A wild-eyed man advanced on Batista, screaming, "You bastard, you got us all killed!"

The desperate men surrounded Batista, rifles at the ready.

He calmly held up the wireless detonator, declaring, "There's forty pounds of Semtex wired in that case. Shoot me and you'll all die."

Recognizing the detonator, the men took a few steps back.

Seizing the moment, Batista pointed up at the creature. "You see that thing up there? Well, I know how to kill it."

The creature was standing atop the crater, arching its back, exercising its newly formed wings. It sniffed the air, searching for new prey.

The crewman said, "It can't be killed."

"You're right, it can't. But that thing out in the lake controls it." Batista tapped the case. "And I've got enough explosives in here to destroy the Anomaly. But to do it, I need you men to fall back toward the yacht while giving me cover fire. Draw that monster off me for two minutes and I'll blast the Anomaly to bits."

"But what about that monster?"

Batista said, "Destroy one and the other dies." He didn't know if that was true, but men with a ray of hope were more easily manipulated.

"How do you know it'll work?"

"Do you have a better plan?"

The men looked to each other, muttering.

Batista said, "Then just do it!"

The lead man said, "Alright, but don't try screwing us over," while holding up his rifle to punctuate his threat.

The eight men raced along the water's edge, firing up at the creature as they went. The moment the first bullet hit, the creature went on the attack.

Batista ducked behind the generator, allowing them enough time to draw it off. He knew the bastards intended to steal the yacht and abandon him, but that didn't matter. They'd all be dead long before reaching the boat.

He grabbed the case and made for the causeway. At eighty pounds it was like hauling an anvil. He trudged along, thinking, *Maybe I should've used two cases.*

#

Catalina pulled the gunboat alongside the platform, barely slowing down.

She said, "Get out fast, I don't want to draw it over here."

Micah scrambled onto the mist-shrouded platform. Catalina pulled away the moment he was off. The frigid air against his wet clothes chilled him to the bone. Through the haze he could make out a ruptured cryogenic tank, emblazoned with the chemical symbol for helium.

He muttered, "Son of a bitch, you froze it," momentarily impressed by the complex rig. Then he saw the neatly cut hole and the pulsing light emanating from within. "Oh no."

Hans lay a few feet in front of the Anomaly, his silver fire suit in peeling tatters. Micah knelt down over him, amazed to discover he was alive—barely. The Austrian gazed up at him, his face a mass of cryogenic burns.

Micah cut to the chase. "Did it react when you cut into it?"

Through scarred lips, Hans whispered, "No. My theory was correct."

"Yeah you were right." *Along with reckless and arrogant.* "What went wrong?"

"Accidental discharge."

Micah saw the line of laser torch burns leading directly to the hole. The torch must have fired into the breach. It might as well have been a declaration of war.

Hans said, "I saw inside. It's not a closed space... It's infinite." He tried to say more but it proved too painful. He closed his eyes, drifting off.

Micah took a moment to process what he'd just learned. *Hans's subzero trick successfully skirted the Anomaly's outer defenses but still led to disaster.* Something clicked in Micah's head. *The outer shell and the internal intelligence must work independently.*

It made sense. The Anomaly's outer defenses would function constantly, protecting the Anomaly during its long journey and while on Earth. But the intelligence within, be it artificial or organic, would only awaken to seed life or defend itself at a long distance.

One thing was clear—Pandora's box was open and it needed to be shut.

#

The gunboat roared across the lake. Catalina saw a cluster of Batista's men in the distance, firing erratically while dashing towards the demolished dam—some becoming monster chow in the process. She gave them a wide berth, keeping plenty of distance between her and the creature.

She thought, *My boys are brave, but even they wouldn't move closer to that thing.*

After maneuvering the boat a few feet from shore, she killed the water jets, banking on the assumption that the warriors would have retreated in the opposite direction.

She muttered, "Come on, where are you knuckleheads?"

Her answer came in the form of a hail of arrows pinging off the pilothouse windows.

"Shit, you think I'm the bad guys." But she couldn't step out on deck to show herself without becoming a pin cushion.

She switched on the boat's PA system and grabbed the microphone then remembered she didn't know their weird birdsong language. In lieu of that, she whistled her imitation of a meadowlark. Her childhood rendition of Nebraska's state bird had won third prize at a state fair. The humiliation of only being in third place had branded the song in her mind.

The distorted bird song echoed from the bullhorn speaker. A few seconds later, the arrows stopped.

There we go. Third prize my ass.

One of the warriors charged down the crater rim and onto the shore, his bow at the ready. Catalina stepped onto the deck, holding her hands over her head. The warrior grinned then let out a series of loud singsong whistles. More warriors slipped out of the thick brush. Catalina counted eight out of the original fourteen. Sad, but still a better survival rate than Batista's lunchmeat brigade.

She frantically waved for them to board. After some hesitation, they filed onto the deck, gathering up any arrows they'd shot at the boat.

The moment they were aboard, Catalina fired up the water jets. The startled warriors jammed themselves into the pilothouse with her. Catalina mimed grabbing the rail then kicked in the jets. The warriors scrambled to grab the rails as the boat roared off.

#

Micah surveyed the tools at his disposal. Two charged super capacitors, a high-voltage AC power line and one non-ruptured canister of liquid helium. It wasn't much. He pondered applying an AC charge directly to the Anomaly then decided it might not be enough to get the reaction he needed. It had to be something bigger.

Machine gun fire chattered in the distance. He watched the last of Batista's men scrambling to reach the boats while battling the creature. It was turning into a bloodbath.

Through the frigid haze he saw someone lumbering down the causeway towards him. It was Batista, lugging a heavy case.

Micah shouted, "What're you doing?"

Seeing Micah alive stopped Batista in his tracks. "You! Get out of my way!"

Micah recognized the case he was lugging—the same type Catalina had found the explosives in. And from the way he was struggling, it was a heavy load. He scooped up the crowbar lying beside Hans and pointed it at Batista, shouting, "Tell me what you're planning!"

Batista marched forward, saying, "I'm going to stuff this down that thing's throat and kill it. Now move!"

Micah remembered what the shaman had shown him about the global consequences of "breaking the egg" and Hans saying the interior was infinite. Batista's plan wouldn't kill anything, but it would guarantee a global reset.

Micah implored him, "It won't work; it'll just make it worse! You've got to trust me."

Batista stopped and set the case down. Micah lowered the crowbar, relieved that he was listening to reason. Then the big man drew a pistol from his belt, aimed, and fired once.

Searing pain tore through Micah's side. He collapsed onto the log platform, clutching at the wound. His hand came back bloody.

Batista slipped the pistol back in his belt, picked up the case, and strode on.

Micah begged him, "Please, don't do it. It'll destroy everything. Literally everything!"

Batista yelled, "Shut up," kicking Micah in the side as he passed.

Micah kept crawling towards Batista, the low-hanging helium fog stinging his eyes.

Batista stopped a few feet from the Anomaly and studied the hole, muttering, "Hmm, that outer shell might interfere with the wireless signal. Better do this the old-fashioned way."

He snapped open the case, switching on the wireless receiver. Satisfied it was working, he lugged the case closer to the Anomaly.

Batista turned back to Micah, proudly displaying the wireless detonator. "I'm setting the timer for two minutes. I can jog to shore in that time. Can you? Looks like you'll have a front row seat, so enjoy the show."

He pressed the button, initiating the countdown. He was preparing to hoist the eighty-pound bomb into the hole when something latched on to his leg.

Batista shouted, "Goddammit!"

Hans's intact arm was locked around Batista's ankle. In a barely audible voice, the Austrian pleaded, "Don't, please."

Batista slammed the case down on Hans's head then grabbed the Austrian by the throat and heaved him over the side of the platform. The wounded man sank like a stone.

Micah kept crawling, groping through the ground fog for something to stop Batista. His hand came to rest on what felt like a pistol grip. Pulling it closer he realized it was the laser torch. The LED light on its side was flashing green—fully charged.

Batista hoisted the heavy case up, preparing to lob it into the hole.

Raising the laser torch, Micah squeezed the trigger. With a hiss of gas, the tip lit up a brilliant red.

A pencil-thin line of flame zipped across Batista's waistline. The big man froze in place, every muscle tensed. The case slammed down onto the platform. Batista tried to bend down and pick it up, but his upper torso snapped off at the waist, toppling into the water. His severed lower half stood there, teetering in place until the knees buckled. It flopped down onto the platform, legs still twitching. There was no blood from the cauterized wound, just the stench of burnt flesh.

Micah realized the wireless detonator's control had gone over the side with Batista's upper half. He staggered toward the case of explosives, blood jetting from his gunshot wound with each step. For an instant he considered tossing it into the lake.

No, that still might send the Anomaly into overdrive.

Micah popped the case open, but all he saw inside were sheets of epoxy embedded with ball bearings. He yanked out the sheet, uncovering blocks of plastic explosive and a cigarette pack-sized electronic box. The box was wired to a baby-sized stick of dynamite—the blasting cap.

Muttering, "Screw it," he yanked the electronic box and blasting cap free, hurling them into the water. A second later, it exploded with a muffled thud, followed by a three-foot geyser.

Micah peered out over the platform. Batista's upper half was still alive, thrashing in the water. He thought, *Sliced in half and thrown into the Amazon, just like Aguirre.*

Something shot up from beneath the surface, latching on to Batista's arm. With two savage bites it tore the limb off. More of the four-foot brown fish attacked, dragging him under the water.

Micah muttered, "Megapiranha." Then he had the terrifying realization, *It's still manifesting protectors, and it's not going to stop.*

He limped closer to the leaking helium tank, letting it blow across his bullet wound. The frigid mist staunched the bleeding while numbing the pain. He heard the roar of the gunboat's water jets in the distance and wracked his brain to come up with a plan. Everything he'd learned about the Anomaly raced through his mind, until something Hans had said finally stuck.

It reacts to energy by producing a counter burst of energy orders of magnitude greater.

He studied the equipment at hand, thinking, *It might work.*

Moments later, Catalina pulled alongside. Micah positioned himself near the ruptured tank, using the helium mist to conceal his gunshot wound.

Catalina asked, "Jesus, what happened? Did you find Batista?"

Micah said, "Yeah, but he had to split," and forced himself to smile at his subpar 007 witticism.

Catalina wasn't amused. "Get in the boat."

"Uh-uh. New plan. I need you to draw that thing over here."

"Are you nuts?"

The tribal warriors peered over her shoulder, pointing at the severed legs kicking on the platform.

Micah said, "Probably."

"Get in the fucking boat or we'll drag you—"

"No! I need to shut it down. It's creating more protectors and it may never stop. We don't have time to argue."

Seeing no point in debating, Catalina asked, "Alright, what do you need?"

"Just draw that thing to me, and as soon as it's here, run. You'll need to get to the other side of the crater rim, like fast."

"What about you?"

"Don't worry; I'll be fine. Just do it, please!"

"Alright, but if you blow yourself up, I'll come back and kick your ass." And she gunned the water jets.

Micah watched the boat tearing across the water then looked at the components at his disposal. His plan was feasible, with the exception of one colossal flaw.

It was suicide.

CHAPTER THIRTY-ONE

The gunboat zipped across the water, heading straight for the creature. Catalina saw five of Batista's men firing at it while falling back towards the demolished dam. The creature snapped one up in its claws, jamming him into its vertical mouth.

The lead warrior grabbed Catalina's shoulder and pointed at the creature while whistling a mile a minute.

Catalina said, "Yeah, I get it, we're goin' in the wrong direction." Though she had no love for Batista's men, she couldn't just stand by and watch them be slaughtered. She switched on the PA system, shouting, "Hey, you ugly mother, over here!"

But the creature just continued its rampage. One of Batista's men threw down his rifle, making a mad dash for the dam. The creature took three giant strides, crushing him beneath its foot. The surviving men threw down their empty rifles, scrambling in opposite directions. The creature snapped one of them up in its claws.

Catalina brought the boat around, running parallel to the shore. Holding the AK-47 with one hand she let off a three-round burst. They all missed.

She muttered, "I can't drive and shoot."

Sensing her dilemma, the warriors raised their bows, loosing eight arrows. Despite firing from a moving boat, they were a hundred percent accurate. Most struck the creature's chest, but one arrow lodged itself in its eye. It bellowed in pain and rage, turning its attention to the boat.

Catalina yelled, "That sure pissed him off!" Then she keyed the boat's PA and, remembering her state fair experience, began singing, "Beautiful Nebraska, peaceful prairie land, laced with many rivers, and the hills of sand," while spinning the boat around to hold its attention.

The enraged creature waded into the lake, lumbering towards them. Fortunately, the water level had risen to almost ten feet, slowing its stride.

Catalina cranked up the water jets, but even at fifteen knots the creature was right on their tail. She glanced over at the platform. The breeze was blowing the helium mist away from them.

Turning to the lead warrior, she said, "What say we go once around the lake then come in on the downwind side? That might give him a little smoke screen... And you don't understand a word I'm saying."

He stared at her like she was insane.

Catalina hit the PA again, belting out, "Beautiful Nebraska, as you look around, you will find a rainbow, reaching to the ground."

#

Micah scrambled to put his plan into action, starting with the electrical feed,

194

from the shore. Donning a pair of insulated gloves, he opened the distribution box and killed the bull switch. A pair of thick cables ran from that distribution box into a smaller switch box. He disconnected the pair of black and red copper "suicide pins" running out of it and kicked the useless switch box into the lake. Next, he set down the crowbar, laying the suicide pin cables at either end. The laser torch's LED was flashing red but still had enough juice to spot weld the positive and negative cables to either end of the bar.

The water rushing in from the dam had raised the lake's level. The far end of the causeway was already underwater, and water was lapping at the platform's edge. It would be underwater soon, shorting out the generator lines.

A Megapiranha leapt onto the platform. It came at Micah, moving much faster than a fish out of water should. He jabbed it with the tip of the laser torch, using its last charge to fry its skull. The dying fish rolled onto its back, fins thrashing. Micah saw that its pectoral fins had reshaped themselves into small, mudskipper style limbs.

"They're evolving."

Three more of these evolved Megapiranhas had leapt onto the causeway and were waddling towards him.

He saw the boat about three quarters of a mile away, coming in fast, the creature only twenty feet behind. Its long arms lashed out, coming just short of the boat.

Micah looked around for something to get the creature's attention. He saw the pistol still tucked into Batista's belt and dug it out.

The boat's PA system crackled, and Catalina's distorted voice boomed, "I'm coming in fast and cutting right. Hope you're ready!"

#

Catalina glanced back. The creature was right behind them. Slowing down, even for a second, would make them easy meat. But just zipping past the target might inspire it to follow her, rather than staying at the platform.

Grabbing the PA microphone, she shouted, "Micah, if you're gonna get its attention, now would be a good time!"

She came straight at the platform doing fifteen knots, her hands gripping the water jet controls. She started counting down, "Five, four, three—"

The warriors stared at the oncoming platform, whistling like a flock of deranged birds.

Catalina yanked one water jet control back and the other forward without slowing down.

The gunboat pivoted one hundred and eighty degrees. For an instant it hung stationary in the water. The creature stood directly overhead, staring down at them.

Catalina jammed both water jet controls, rocketing the boat forward, zipping right between its legs. The sudden acceleration threw the warriors down onto the deck.

#

Micah raised the pistol in one hand while yanking the front of the super capacitor's Faraday cage loose with the other. He fired five shots at the creature, most hitting the target.

The creature turned away, still focused on the boat zipping between its legs.

Micah fired two more shots, finally getting its attention. It took a few giant steps towards him—coming way too fast. It would be on him in a minute, and he desperately needed two.

#

Catalina glanced back and saw the creature as it moved in on the platform. "You better know what you're doing!"

The warriors were sprawled across the pilothouse floor. She wondered how much more of this insanity they'd take without mutinying.

Micah had been adamant about them being on the other side of the crater rim. With the jets going full bore she steered toward the far end of the lake with no idea how much time they had to escape.

#

Micah felt something brush his foot and jumped back. The lead Megapiranha waddled forward, gnashing at the air. Without thinking, he lowered the pistol and fired into the top of its skull, narrowly missing his own foot.

The creature was still advancing, only seconds away from the platform.

Micah yelled, "Think, stupid, think!" Then he dashed to the edge of the platform, kicking the intact helium tank over the side. It bobbed in the churning water. Micah aimed the pistol, fired once and missed. His second shot hit the tank. The rupture released a cloud of frigid white mist, billowing toward the oncoming creature. More helium sprayed across the water, vaporizing on contact. The arctic cloud forced the creature to pause.

Micah had just bought himself a few seconds—the downside was that he couldn't see a damn thing in the fog. After wasting precious seconds groping, he found the crowbar and jammed it against the super capacitor. Next, he grabbed the Faraday cage's metal grid door and laid it on the platform, trying to bridge the super capacitor to the probe. It fell three feet short.

He needed something conductive. Anything. Glancing around he saw something that would work.

"Water, salt and chloride … everything I need."

He grabbed Batista's severed lower half by the feet and slipped. The helium cloud had turned the wet platform into a hockey rink. On the plus side the ice had slowed down the waddling Megapiranhas.

He dragged Batista's lower half over to the Anomaly, yanked its shoes off and laid the bare feet on the cage. Using the laser torch like a spear he jammed it into Batista's cauterized torso and propped it against the Anomaly. The body would likely incinerate within seconds, but the Anomaly's defenses should activate by that point.

"You're getting a Viking funeral."

A claw shot down through the haze, its taloned fingers groping blindly.

Micah pumped a bullet into its fingertip at point-blank range. The claw retreated for a moment then came back down, sweeping across the platform. Micah tried to fire again, but the pistol clicked empty.

The groping talon inched closer. An attacking Megapiranha mistook it for Micah, locking its jaws around it. The talon retreated with the fish latched on.

Micah crawled over to the power distribution box and realized that when he turned on the high-voltage power, the box's breaker would trip, defeating the purpose. He grabbed the breaker unit and yanked hard. The solid component came out, leaving an empty void he needed to fill. Thinking fast, he popped the clip out of the empty pistol, wedging it into the gap. It was like jamming a penny in a fuse box, only a thousand times more dangerous.

The claw shot down, tearing away a chunk of the causeway behind him. Thankfully the high-voltage AC line running from shore remained intact.

Micah crouched, gripping the distribution box's bull switch, muttering, "Now or never."

He'd just built the mother of all Tesla coils, capable of producing a combination of high-voltage, electromagnetic pulse and X-ray radiation.

The reaction will be orders of magnitude greater.

Staying on the platform would reduce him to ashes, but jumping into the about to be electrified piranha-infested lake was also suicide.

He looked up through the thinning layer of fog and saw the creature rear up, arching its back. Its huge bat-like wings unfurled. With one mighty flap it blew away the last of the fog.

Micah whispered, "I love you, Faye," and threw the bull switch.

At that same moment the creature's talon swept across the platform, catapulting him back. The impact sent him skidding across the icy surface like a hockey puck, flailing for anything to grab. He latched on to something a heartbeat before going over. It was the edge of the hole in the Anomaly. His insulated glove stuck to the helium cooled cut like Velcro.

The AC charged crowbar lit up like a bolt of lightning, sending high-voltage alternating current surging through the fully charged DC super capacitor—a clash of electrical titans.

Micah's insulated gloves and rubber-soled boots protected him from the initial surge. But things were about to get a hundred times worse.

He pulled himself up, thinking, *Screw it*, and dove headfirst into the hole. His feet were still outside when a blinding flash transformed the platform into a lightning farm. The rubber soles on his boots melted, but he made it through the hole.

And into the void.

#

Catalina saw the initial flash behind them, followed by giant tendrils of lightning leaping into the air.

It's happening.

She was only seconds from reaching the shore but elected not to slow down. An old James Bond movie flashed through her mind—the one where speed boats jumped over embankments and cars. The crater's upward slope was like a ramp—sort of. The gunboat hurtled forward, skimming across the water at thirty knots.

"Hang on!"

The boat hit the shore and shot out of the water, sheer inertia propelling it up the sloping crater rim.

At that moment the Anomaly's protective shell reacted to Micah's Tesla coil.

The platform and causeway vanished in a bloom of white light, brighter than the sun.

The gunboat cleared the grade, going airborne. It spun in midair, the bow tipping straight down, plummeting toward the ground forty feet below.

Staring down into her impending death, Catalina thought, *Movies are so full of shit.*

But the ground stopped coming closer—or, rather, the boat ceased falling. Catalina held on to the controls with a white-knuckle grip as her feet rose from the floor.

Through the window she watched downed branches and logs float upward, bouncing against the hull. The warriors were swept into the air, becoming plastered against the overhead, wide-eyed with terror.

Catalina thought, *Micah just broke the laws of gravity.*

And then, in the duration of one long breath, the gravity ramped up again from zero, to lunar, to normal.

The gunboat slammed down onto the muddy ground, the sloping gravity reducing its impact velocity by half. Catalina was thrown against the bulkhead. The warriors all dropped onto the deck. With gravity restored, branches and logs rained down on the hull.

Catalina tasted blood in her mouth and spat it out, along with her two front teeth. She stood up, feeling bruised but not broken. The boat lay on its side, forcing her to crawl across the moaning warriors to get out.

A torrential downpour of water and ash rained down from the sky, coating her in filth. She scrambled up the crater's rim and gazed out. The inner rim of the crater lake was now scorched charcoal black and a phosphorescent haze hung over the water.

She thought, *If we'd been on this side of the rim we would have been toast.*

A dead Megapiranha slapped to the ground next to her, bursting like a water balloon on impact. More dropped from the sky, sounding like drumbeats as they slapped to the ground.

Catalina strained to see through the haze and ash. The Christmas ornament was still there but was now glowing a soft blue. The creature, the platform and the causeway were gone—vaporized.

She whispered, "Micah."

The warriors clustered around her, gazing out in silence. The leader looked at her, solemnly acknowledging her loss.

Catalina shook her head, shouting, "No! I ain't buying it," and bounded down the rim toward the water.

She'd only made it halfway when the ground beneath her feet began to shake, knocking her down. The lake water churned violently, generating ocean-worthy waves.

And the Anomaly that had been stationary for millions of years began to rotate.

#

Micah was floating inside the sphere. But he wasn't adrift in a confined space; it was as if all of infinity stretched out before him. Phosphorescent strands swam by, connecting with each other to form new, brilliantly colored light sculptures. Vaporous shapes of extinct creatures drifted around him, like ghosts from millennia past. Micah couldn't tell if they were near or a hundred miles away. In the distance, thousands of those glowing strands intertwined, forming some huge pulsing celestial ball. The only sound was an endless, oscillating wind rushing past.

Micah realized he was looking at firing brain synapses. *I'm not just inside the Anomaly, I'm inside the intelligence. A mind functioning outside of space and time.*

Looking back, he could see the hole in the sphere—but it seemed so far away. The hole momentarily lit up in a brilliant flash of light. Micah tried to turn towards it, but he was being propelled forward, towards the pulsing celestial ball.

One of the phosphorescent strands veered off its course, coming straight at him until it touched his head. A low electrical shock coursed through Micah's skull, accompanied by a deafening burst of static. The initial jolt was agonizing; then the electricity and sound diminished as if tuning to a comfortable volume.

Other glowing synapses coalesced into floating images. But this time they weren't forming the ghosts of extinct creatures. It was Micah's life.

Images of an infant Faye rippled in front of him, followed by more recent memories. Pulling her away from the snake. Holding her out so Catalina could save her. Embracing her on the dinghy as Megapiranhas leapt around them. Finally, her serene, smiling face as she stroked the pink dolphin.

Micah looked at the image floating in the air and whispered, "Faye," then closed his eyes, certain that would be his last word before he was dragged into some alternate reality. The electrical charge in his skull ceased, and something squeezed his hand. He felt himself being drawn backwards, towards the entryway.

Opening his eyes, he found himself face-to-face with the ancient shaman. Somehow, the old man was walking, despite not having a floor, or anything, beneath him—an amazing feat, considering that he was dead.

Nothing to be freaked out about. You're floating in a celestial black hole with a dead man dragging you along. Totally normal.

The old man gazed at Micah with a smile so beatific that it melted away the panic welling inside him. The shaman released his grip, and Micah was sent rocketing through the void towards the exit.

A heartbeat later, he was fired through the hole like a human cannonball. He hurtled through the air, bracing himself to land on the hard wooden platform. But instead, he splashed down into violently churning water and sank.

CHAPTER THIRTY-TWO

Micah sank straight to the bottom of the lake. Once his feet touched the bottom his survival instincts sprang into action, driving him to kick hard until he broke the surface, coughing up water. But something seemed determined to drag him back under.

It was a whirlpool.

He tried grabbing the Anomaly for support, only to discover it was spinning. Its rotation was creating a water vortex he couldn't escape.

A voice, barely audible over the churning waves, shouted, "Grab it!"

Micah went under again, sucked straight to the muddy bottom. Using his legs, he pushed off the lakebed, kicking like a madman. The action propelled him to the surface, where he managed one deep breath before feeling himself being dragged under again.

He heard that voice again, shouting, "Grab the ring, dummy!"

Something bounced off Micah's forehead; then he caught a flash of red and white bobbing in front of him. He latched on to it before going under again. Someone wrapped their arms around his waist, pushing him back to the surface.

Catalina popped up from beneath the water, slipping the red-and-white life preserver under his arms. Despite wearing two life jackets she'd salvaged from the gunboat, she could barely stay afloat. Once the life preserver was secure, she frantically yanked on a rope running back to shore.

Grabbing on to the edge of the life preserver, she shouted, "Now kick!" and started swimming.

They both swam furiously, fighting for every inch of forward motion. The rope on the life preserver snapped taught, and their speed increased. Someone on the other end was pulling them toward land, while the water vortex was hellbent on hauling them under.

Micah was able to make out the distant shore, where a line of warriors stood, the rope slung over their shoulders. They marched forward in unison, pulling them a few feet, before reining in the slack and repeating the ordeal.

The water grew shallower until Micah's feet finally touched ground. His legs trembled from the seismic activity below.

He shouted, "What's happening?"

"Whatever you did triggered an earthquake."

"Oh."

After a few more steps, Micah was clear of the water. He crawled a few feet before flopping down on his back, chest heaving. The ground beneath him still shook, but he was too exhausted to care.

Catalina plopped down next to him, looking just as spent. She looked at him, smiled and asked, "So, did the Earth move for you too?" Her words whistled through the gap where her front teeth should have been.

Despite the pain in his … everyplace … Micah managed to laugh. With her help he sat up, watching the top of the Anomaly slip beneath the surface in a giant whirlpool. Moments later, the lake's water was sucked down into the earth, like a giant bathtub drain, reducing the water level to mere inches. There was no sign of the Anomaly.

Micah said, "The quake must have caused soil liquefaction, the same thing that made the Anomaly rise in the first place."

Catalina chuckled and said, "Only you could make Armageddon sound boring."

"Hopefully that's what we stopped. Now it's back underground where it's supposed to be."

"Along with your pants."

Micah realized that he'd been stripped naked by the whirlpool but couldn't summon the energy to be embarrassed.

He said, "I think it's going to sleep again."

The warriors lined up along what had been the water's edge and dropped to their knees, their ethereal voices ringing out in unison.

Catalina saw the wound on Micah's side. "Christ, you're shot!"

"Yeah. I also have second-degree burns on my feet and frostbite. I think being inside sort of helped me heal up."

"Inside what?"

Micah said, "The Anomaly. I went inside."

Catalina stared at him in amazement. "Wow… What was that like?"

Cocking his head toward the chanting warriors, he replied, "Well, if I wasn't so beat up, I'd be right there singing hymns with 'em."

Catalina asked, "So why didn't it, you know, reset the world? I mean it was clearly under attack."

"I think it saw something that changed its mind."

"What was that?"

"Faye."

Catalina gave him a puzzled look.

Micah said, "I guess the intelligence decided that, despite the attack, there was hope for the world after all." He lay back, staring up into the sky. Brilliantly charged particles rose from the lake into the sky, dancing like a daytime aurora borealis. He said, "Pretty, ain't it?"

Catalina gazed up at the dancing lights and sang, "Beautiful Nebraska, as you look around, you will find a rainbow reaching to the ground."

"You know, most people would have just sung 'Over the Rainbow'."

Catalina curled up closer, placing her head on his chest and whispered, "That's Kansas, dummy."

Micah started laughing until, overwhelmed by his injuries and the sheer absurdity of it all, he passed out.

CHAPTER THIRTY-THREE

Micah slowly opened his eyes, uncertain of his surroundings. The room was dim, but he could smell incense, herbs and cooking food—a homey mélange that made him feel safe. He let out a long grunt, attracting the attention of an elderly tribal woman. She hovered over him for a few seconds then slipped away.

Moments later, a familiar voice chimed in with, "Well, look who's finally awake." Catalina looked down at him, offering a gap-toothed smile.

Micah asked, "Are we at the village?"

"Yup. You've been out cold for three days. Mostly with young native girls massaging and bathing you."

"Kinda sorry I slept through that." Micah tried to sit up, but a throbbing headache made him reconsider. "At least I'm not waking up on a boat, 'cause that never ends well. So, how am I?"

"Intact and remarkably well. That bullet just went through the meaty part of your side, and the burns on your feet are healing up. You also cracked some ribs, bruised a kidney and probably had a concussion. You were just a hot, steaming mess, but their herbal medicines work miracles. I'm getting the impression some of these folks are going on two hundred years old. You'll probably be up and hobbling around soon, and once that happens, they'll help us get back to civilization."

"Can't we just take Batista's yacht? Trust me; he's not using it."

Catalina shook her head. "Not happening. Your little stunt created an EMP that fried everything for miles. That yacht's just a million-dollar rowboat now."

"It had too many bad memories anyway." Micah looked around. The hut was jammed with fruit, arrows and clay statuettes. Resting among them was the fragment of the Anomaly he'd returned to the tribe. "What's all this stuff?"

"Gifts. You're quite the celebrity around these parts. I guess some folks think restoring balance to the universe is a big deal."

Faye charged in, letting out an excited squeal that echoed in Micah's throbbing skull.

She shrieked, "You're awake!"

The little girl threw her arms around her father, squeezing his cracked ribs. He didn't even wince. Seeing her safe was more restorative than any herbal medicine.

Micah said, "Hey, honey bunny, did you miss me?" Faye just laughed, squeezing him even harder. He asked, "So have you gone native?"

Faye was dressed in a loincloth, her hair adorned with decorative feathers.

She replied, "My other clothes were ruined," then launched into a rapid-fire account of her new friends, the games they played, animals she'd seen and every other conceivable detail. She bookended it with, "Here's my other new friend."

Queen Caveira's monkey slunk into the hut, still wearing the tattered remnants of its sailor suit. Upon seeing Micah, it took refuge behind Faye, clearly remembering their previous encounters.

Micah said, "Is that little bum still hanging around? I kinda hoped somebody would've eaten him by now."

Faye petted her simian friend, insisting, "No, he's a good monkey. I named him Bandit 'cause he always brings me stuff."

"Other people's stuff no doubt. You know, the tribe was wasting their miracle medicine 'cause your mother's just gonna kill me anyway."

Sensing the tension, the monkey scurried into the far corner of the hut and began furiously digging at the dirt floor.

With a groan, Micah said, "Oh, please tell me it's not gonna take a dump in here."

After a few seconds of digging, the monkey came back over, carrying something. It cautiously approached Micah, placing the object next to his head, then ducked for cover behind Faye.

Micah picked it up, gaping at it. "Well, I'll be damned."

Catalina asked, "Is that what I think it is?"

It was the emerald that had traveled from Batista to Micah to Queen Caveira before winding its way back to him.

Locking eyes with the monkey, Micah said, "The queen taught you well. I'm officially declaring a truce." He turned to Faye. "Honey, can you go play with your thieving pal outside for a minute, so Catalina and I can talk?"

Without hiding her disappointment, Faye said, "Okay. But don't take forever," and left with her monkey pal in tow.

Catalina studied the emerald, saying, "Ain't that something? It goes all the way around the jungle and then plops right back into your lap."

"Your point?"

"I'm just saying, maybe there's a little woo-woo magical stuff going on here. Things science and logic can't explain."

"I get it. Relax, I'm one hundred percent sold on the whole, 'more things in heaven and earth' deal. Now, how about helping me up?"

"You sure?"

"No, but let's give it a shot."

With a little work, and a lot of groaning, Catalina helped Micah out of the hut. The cool night air felt revitalizing. Members of the tribe eyed him bashfully then went about their business.

With a mischievous grin, Catalina said, "See, they're acting all shy 'cause you're the big man on campus. So, what're you gonna do?"

Micah leaned back against a post, asking, "What do you mean?"

"You just proved all your whacky theories and discovered an alien artifact to boot. You can pretty much write your own ticket now. So ... whatcha gonna do?"

"Absolutely nothing."

"Really? 'Cause the clean energy from that thing could save the earth."

"Humanity's not the earth, we're just one of its tenants. One who's only been around for the blink of an eye in geologic time. The Anomaly seeded the planet, helped life emerge and take hold."

"But using it as a clean energy source might save humanity."

"Think about it. Even if we reversed climate change, we still have the potential for nuclear war or a global pandemic or AI running amok. And let's not forget how people will react when we tell them that God's ... what did you call it?"

"A big dirty Christmas ornament." She took a moment to ponder that. "Yeah, that news might cause some social unrest."

"More like World War Three. But here's the thing; even if humanity puts a gun to its head, and kills everything else in the process, Mother Earth will still have her insurance policy. The Anomaly can reset the clock and give life a second chance. Then, who knows, maybe in three or four billion years humanity'll get another turn at bat. But if we share this discovery, governments will descend on this place like locusts; hell there'd probably be a war just to see who gets their grubby mitts on it."

"So what happens to humanity?"

Micah said, "Humanity has to put on its big boy pants and save itself." He watched Faye innocently playing with the village children and his tone grew wistful. "You know, I think that, just maybe, we have a decent shot at that."

"What if somebody else finds it?"

"It's hidden again, and everyone who knew about it is dead, except for our pointy-headed friends, and they ain't talking. Let's just leave it be and let these folks keep their simple life."

Catalina grinned.

Micah asked, "What, no argument?"

"Nope, Faye and I figured that's what you'd say."

He gazed up into the night sky, where a ribbon of blue light rippled among the countless stars.

Catalina said, "It's been like that since the big hoedown. Our own little aurora borealis. It's getting a little dimmer every night."

Tossing the emerald up and down in the palm of his hand, Micah said, "Well, my show's probably cancelled, which means I'm broke and out of work. So, what say we sell this off and split the take?"

"I can't accept any money."

"Why?"

"Because I'm a government employee who's on the clock."

"So nothing? Not even a used Honda or some cosmetic dentistry?"

Catalina laughed. "Oh please, even with missing teeth I'm still way out of your league. But how about I let you buy me dinner? And I'm not talking piranha and dragon fruit either. I want someplace back in the world where they have plates and silverware and shoes."

"I think I'd like that."

"Oh, believe me, you will. Now rest up and get your strength back. If you play your cards right, you'll need it."

Micah gazed out at the children playing, pondering all the madness they'd been thrust into and how destiny or some higher force had intervened to save the world.

But what about them? he thought. *These ancient people, and perhaps the Anomaly, are still vulnerable to outsiders.* He couldn't stay here because he had a life back home and a daughter to raise.

Maybe, he thought, *somebody else will come along to protect them.*

EPILOGUE

With the dam destroyed, the crater lake gradually swelled to its original level. Batista's yacht floated across the remnants of the dam to drift in the lake's now peaceful waters.

It floated there, abandoned, until the woman arrived.

Queen Caveira smiled, secure in the knowledge that Boiúna had once again provided. Gazing out at the water she offered thanks while reflecting on the mystical journey that had led her here.

For at least a day she'd lain on the rocks, barely conscious, her body a mass of shattered bones. Her pirates were dead, her boats destroyed, and that ungrateful monkey had even run off with her emerald. Despair and pain were her only companions as she waited for the carrion feeders to feast on her.

Then, in her darkest moment, he had appeared.

She'd awakened to find an old man staring down at her with the red-rimmed eyes of the *Morte Tinto.* She tried to shout, *Finish me, you bastard, and choke on my meat,* but only managed a pathetic groan.

The old man didn't kill her. Instead, he kissed her, his lips delivering a mouthful of bitter-tasting berries. Almost immediately she felt a dim spark of life coursing through her fractured body. The old man repeated the process over and over, disappearing for hours only to return with another kiss of life. She lay there, feeling stronger but still as helpless as an overturned tortoise.

One morning, at sunrise, a ten-foot caiman crawled out of the river, advancing on her.

She thought, *Death has arrived.*

But life also came, in the form of a twenty-five-foot anaconda. Her protector slithered out of the water, battling the caiman until its coils finally crushed the life out of it. Once the caiman was dead the anaconda took up a silent vigil. As it lay sunning itself, the queen stared into its black eyes, certain it was Boiúna's messenger.

The old man returned, feeding her more berries and rubbing a poultice on her broken limbs, all under the watchful eyes of the anaconda. Within days she grew strong enough to pick her own berries, gorging herself on the fruit, feeling her bones knitting together. Eventually, she was able to hobble a few feet without collapsing.

The old man silently observed her progress then slipped away into the forest. As soon as he was gone, her serpent guardian slithered into the river, its sacred mission complete.

At nightfall, another unlikely savior wandered out of the brush. It was a donkey. The animal was filthy, with ticks feeding on its hide, but its leather bridle indicated it had once been decently cared for.

The queen stroked its filthy coat, noting a row of partially healed claw marks on its back.

"It looks like you tussled with a jaguar. You've traveled a hard road to find me, little one."

The burro raised its ears in response. A sign of trust.

After a few agonizing attempts she managed to mount the donkey, who accepted the burden without protest.

Queen Caveira gazed up at the stars to get her bearings, whispering, "So, little one, where shall we go?"

Her answer was written in the sky. Dancing among the brilliant stars was a serpentine ribbon of blue light. The queen stirred the donkey forward, following the sign.

Days later, she arrived at the crater lake, where Batista's yacht waited.

Upon boarding, she discovered that the electronics were damaged beyond repair. She tore them out and did some rewiring. After hours of toil, the engines rumbled to life. The bilge pumps went to work, pumping out excess water. She navigated the yacht to shore, tying it off to a tree stump, and began to explore.

Below deck she discovered a case containing four brand-new AK-47 rifles— a significant improvement over her old arsenal.

The main saloon was a luxurious wreck. Paintings in broken frames lay across the floor. A row of glass display cases had been reduced to splinters. A conquistador's helmet lay among the shards of glass.

She said, "My new ship even comes with a crown," while admiring her reflection in the shattered glass.

Picking through the wrecked galley she uncovered tins of gourmet anchovies and white tuna belly, washing it all down with a bottle of warm Dom Perignon. Satiated, she sat back, pondering how she'd come to possess Batista's yacht, when something occurred to her.

After some frenzied rooting through cabinets and hatches she finally uncovered a hidden steel box. It was packed with gold coins, American dollars and Brazilian *reais*—it had been the pig's escape package. Feeling content, she slung an AK-47 over her shoulder, popped another bottle of champagne and retired to the main deck.

Two haggard, nearly naked men staggered out of the jungle, cautiously approaching the yacht. Both froze at the sight of a woman wearing a conquistador's helmet and brandishing an assault rifle.

Looking them up and down, Queen Caveira said, "You two look like a couple of drowned rats."

"We've been hiding in the jungle for days; the *Morte Tinto* are everywhere."

Raising the rifle, she said, "The *Morte Tinto* resurrected me from the dead, so if you harm them, you'll answer to me." She cocked the rifle to punctuate her point. "Is that clear?"

They both nodded mutely.

"Are you sailors?"

"Yes."

"Done any pirating?"

With a broad grin, one replied, "Sure, before we signed on with that bastard

Batista, may he rot in hell."

Queen Caveira said, "Oh, he will." Then she tossed each man a gold coin, proclaiming, "You may join my crew. Grab some food in the galley, then get all the broken glass cleaned up. After that, one of you pluck the ticks off my donkey."

"Yes, ma'am!"

"Address me as queen!"

After a bit of nervous hesitation, one asked, "But, Queen, where are we going?"

With infinite calm, Her Highness replied, "Nowhere. This is my new domain. You're welcome to rob and kill any intruders, but the *Morte Tinto* and this lake are under my protection. Now get to work!"

The half-starved men slipped below deck. The queen relaxed, gazing up at the sliver of blue light dancing across the starry sky. After all her hardships, Boiúna, sacred god of the river, had led her here, providing a ship, guns, money and men. In return she swore to protect its domain. And if she got to rob and murder too ... well, that was just a bonus.

A sixty-foot-long serpentine shape rippled across the peaceful waters of the lake, crossing in front of the yacht before slipping beneath the surface.

Queen Caveira held up the bottle of champagne, declaring, "Life is good."

God save the queen.

* * *

ACKNOWLEDGEMENTS

I always wanted to write a novel about a contemporary Odyssey with new dangers and monsters lurking around every bend in the river. This was inspired by my early love of films like *Jason and the Argonauts* and the *Seventh Voyage of Sinbad*, and my later appreciation of literary works like *Heart of Darkness*. My sincere thanks to Severed Press for having the faith to join me on this voyage downriver.

Creating that fictional journey required a great deal of research, as well as input from experts. I want to especially thank Alican Kilinc, Naval architect and marine engineer for his nautical expertise. I owe my knowledge of pirate go-fast boats, cargo ships and Multi Cat barges to him.

I'm also grateful to Ken Darrow, MA for making it look like I paid more attention in English class. I can't thank him enough for his diligent proofreading and editing work.

I invite you to visit my website williamburkeauthor.com where I'll be posting articles about Amazon River pirates (who are nothing like my fictional ones), prehistoric Amazon monsters, terrifying modern rainforest wildlife, and other entertaining stuff.

I want to thank all the people who read my previous novel *Scorpius Rex*. Your great reviews and high customer ratings led to this book being published. I promise that *Scorpius Rex's* heroes Dave Brank, Goon and Emily will all be returning in an upcoming adventure.

On a final note, please DO NOT attempt to make a giant Tesla Coil using the instructions in this book! You'll die, while causing a citywide blackout in the process.

AUTHOR BIO:

Primeval Waters is William Burke's third novel, following a long career in film and television. He was the creator and director of the Destination America paranormal series *Hauntings and Horrors* and the OLN series *Creepy Canada*, as well as producing the HBO productions *Forbidden Science*, *Lingerie* and *Sin City Diaries*. His work has garnered high praise from network executives and insomniacs watching Cinemax at 3 a.m.

During the 1990's Burke was a staff producer for the Playboy Entertainment Group, producing eighteen feature films and multiple television series. He's acted as Line Producer and Assistant Director on dozens of feature films—some great, some bad and some truly terrible.

Aside from novels Burke has written for Fangoria Magazine, Videoscope Magazine and is a regular contributor to Horrornews.net

He can be found at williamburkeauthor.com
His YouTube Channel is http://www.youtube.com/c/BillBurke
His Facebook page is https://www.facebook.com/pg/williamburkeauthor/

CHECK OUT OTHER GREAT DEEP SEA THRILLERS

THE BREACH
by Edward J. McFadden III

A Category 4 hurricane punched a quarter mile hole in Fire Island, exposing the Great South Bay to the ferocity of the Atlantic Ocean, and the current pulled something terrible through the new breach. A monstrosity of the past mixed with the present has been disturbed and it's found its way into the sheltered waters of Long Island's southern sea.

Nate Tanner lives in Stones Throw, Long Island. A disgraced SCPD detective lieutenant put out to pasture in the marine division because of his Navy background and experience with aquatic crime scenes, Tanner is assigned to hunt the creeper in the bay. But he and his team soon discover they're the ones being hunted.

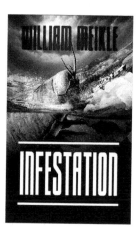

INFESTATION
by William Meikle

It was supposed to be a simple mission. A suspected Russian spy boat is in trouble in Canadian waters. Investigate and report are the orders.

But when Captain John Banks and his squad arrive, it is to find an empty vessel, and a scene of bloody mayhem.

Soon they are in a fight for their lives, for there are things in the icy seas off Baffin Island, scuttling, hungry things with a taste for human flesh.

They are swarming. And they are growing.

"Scotland's best Horror writer" - Ginger Nuts of Horror

"The premier storyteller of our time." - Famous Monsters of Filmland

CHECK OUT OTHER GREAT
DEEP SEA THRILLERS

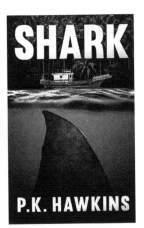

SHARK: INFESTED WATERS
by P.K. Hawkins

For Simon, the trip was supposed to be a once in a lifetime gift: a journey to the Amazon River Basin, the land that he had dreamed about visiting since he was a child. His enthusiasm for the trip may be tempered by the poor conditions of the boat and their captain leading the tour, but most of the tourists think they can look the other way on it. Except things go wrong quickly. After a horrific accident, Simon and the other tourists find themselves trapped on a tiny island in the middle of the river. It's the rainy season, and the river is rising. The island is surrounded by hungry bull sharks that won't let them swim away. And worst of all, the sharks might not be the only blood-thirsty killers among them. It was supposed to be the trip of a lifetime. Instead, they'll be lucky if they make it out with their lives at all.

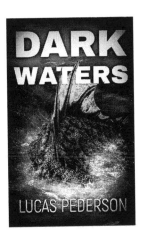

DARK WATERS
by Lucas Pederson

Jörmungandr is an ancient Norse sea monster. Thought to be purely a myth until a battleship is torn a part by one.

With his brother on that ship, former Navy Seal and deep-sea diver, Miles Raine, sets out on a personal vendetta against the creature and hopefully save his brother. Bringing with him his old Seal team, the Dagger Points, they embark on a mission that might very well be their last.

But what happens when the hunters become the hunted and the dark waters reveal more than a monster?

CHECK OUT OTHER GREAT
DEEP SEA THRILLERS

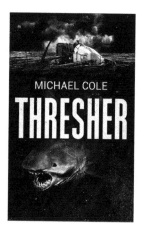

THRESHER
by Michael Cole

In the aftermath of a hurricane, a series of strange events plague the coastal waters off Florida. People go into the water and never return. Corpses of killer whales drift ashore, ravaged from enormous bite marks. A fishing trawler is found adrift, with a mysterious gash in its hull.

Transferred to the coastal town of Merit, police officer Leonard Riker uncovers the horrible reality of an enormous Thresher shark lurking off the coast. Forty feet in length, it has taken a territorial claim to the waters near the town harbor. Armed with three-inch teeth, a scythe-like caudal fin, and unmatched aggression, the beast seeks to kill anything sharing the waters.

THE GUILLOTINE
by Lucas Pederson

1,000 feet under the surface, Prehistoric Anthropologist, Ash Barrington, and his team are in the midst of a great archeological dig at the bottom of Lake Superior where they find a treasure trove of bones. Bones of dinosaurs that aren't supposed to be in this particular region. In their underwater facility, Infinity Moon, Ash and his team soon discover a series of underground tunnels. Upon exploring, they accidentally open an ice pocket, thawing the prehistoric creature trapped inside. Soon they are being attacked, the facility falling apart around them, by what Ash knows is a dunkleosteus and all those bones were from its prey. Now...Ash and his team are the prey and the creature will stop at nothing to get to them.